T0337771

ALEX SHAW has lived and worked in Ukraine, the former USSR, the Middle East, and Africa. He is the author of the number one international Kindle bestselling Aidan Snow SAS thrillers. His writing has also been published in several thriller anthologies alongside international bestselling authors Stephen Leather and Matt Hilton. Alex, his wife and their two sons divide their time between Ukraine, England and the Middle East.

🐦 @alexshawhetman
📘 /alex.shaw.982292
www.alexwshaw.co.uk

Also by Alex Shaw

The Aidan Snow Series
Cold Blood
Cold Black
Cold East

The Jack Tate Series
Total Blackout
Total Fallout

The Sophie Racine Series
Traitors

Total Control

ALEX SHAW

ONE PLACE. MANY STORIES

HQ
An imprint of HarperCollins*Publishers* Ltd
1 London Bridge Street
London SE1 9GF

www.harpercollins.co.uk

HarperCollins*Publishers*
1st Floor, Watermarque Building, Ringsend Road
Dublin 4, Ireland

This paperback edition 2022

2
First published in Great Britain by
HQ, an imprint of HarperCollins*Publishers* Ltd 2022

Copyright © Alex Shaw 2022

Alex Shaw asserts the moral right to be
identified as the author of this work.
A catalogue record for this book is
available from the British Library.

ISBN: 9780008441777

*For my wife Galia, my sons Alexander and Jonathan,
and our family in England and Ukraine.*

Prologue

No one spoke. That suited him. He didn't like to talk. People talked too much and said too little. He had always taken issue with it. Roe Kwang stared out of his passenger window into the black abyss of night. It was 3 a.m., and the ballistic-plated Chevrolet Tahoe was heading east on the I-94.

It was the middle of nowhere. That was the point. The GPS coordinates of their destination had been received just two hours prior. It was a classified facility, a new 'black site' on US soil. One of an unspecified number of places built after eagle-eyed plane spotters and the world's media had rendered rendition flights somewhat less than clandestine. In short, it was a place that officially did not exist, just like the prisoner by his side.

Roe glanced at his charge. The man was Chinese, but, having been raised in the UK, his English was fluent. He hadn't uttered a single word, which Roe appreciated, since they'd left the old facility. The prisoner wasn't physically strong, the shackles he wore were overkill, but they were part of the 'protocol' which Roe's deniable unit of 'babysitters' had to abide by. Nevertheless, the prisoner was dangerous. He had masterminded cyber terror

1

attacks on the assets of several sovereign states, culminating in his last strike at the US, which had caused a staggering amount of financial and infrastructural damage. Roe knew the man sitting shackled beside him was the world's best hacker. To Roe, and without internet access, the man was nothing. He had been in US custody for almost two years and in Roe's opinion the US should have saved the money it had already spent on his protection, transportation, and the building of a new facility by simply putting a bullet in his brain. That, however, had not been his decision to make, and he had orders to prevent anyone else from doing just that.

Roe's gaze returned to the window. He scanned the dark, flat lands. Out there it looked as quiet as it was inside the Tahoe, but Roe understood this was all an illusion.

'Exit. One minute out.' Roe's earpiece crackled as the driver of the lead vehicle updated the two others. The only words spoken by any of the team for over a hundred miles garnered one-word acknowledgements from the drivers of the second and third vehicle.

Tahoe 2, Roe's Tahoe, started to slow as it negotiated the off-ramp. They left the highway and headed north, creeping through a miniscule place with a sign naming it as 'Windsor', whose only commercial building was a bar with a red and white Budweiser sign. The three full-sized SUVs crossed over a railway line, leaving the slumbering settlement they passed through a crossroads and took a still smaller country road dissecting the vast, flat plains.

Roe had the sensation he was no longer in an SUV, but in a plane cruising thousands of feet above a sleeping earth. The absolute lack of light from the world around him gave the impression that the stars above were burning in the clear, cold, cloudless sky. Between two constellations he saw a shooting star, or perhaps it was a comet or maybe it was something else entirely. It grew larger. It seemed to be heading directly towards him … it streaked past him …

2

Instinctively Roe screwed his eyes shut as an explosion momentarily turned night to day. The heavy Tahoe came to a squealing halt as its tyres bit into the rutted, rural tarmac.

Sudden chatter on their comms network stated the obvious. They were under attack.

Ahead, white reverse lights replaced red taillights and the lead vehicle jerked backwards, tyres smoking. Sitting directly in front of Roe, and riding shotgun, his teammate unclipped his assault rifle from its secure position on the dashboard. As Roe reached for his own, their driver, following the lead vehicle's actions, slammed their Tahoe into reverse. He jerked forward, his seatbelt tightening. Beside him, the prisoner shrieked.

A second explosion from behind made the convoy stop again. Roe turned to see Tahoe 3 on fire. But it continued to move backwards, to pick up speed as it attempted to evade the attack. Roe's own Tahoe was barrelling backwards. It jerked to one side, as the driver performed a 'J-Turn' and brought it nose to nose with the vehicle behind. Which had stopped moving, and which was now being hit by heavy 0.50 cal rounds. The thunderous thud … thud … thud … registered in Roe's ears like the heavy punches of a prize-fighter. Flames flared from firing positions in the fields on both sides. The front of Tahoe 3 dropped as the fusillade from numerous rifles ripped away the run-flat tyres, wheels and all.

Roe had been taught never to leave the vehicle, to stay inside the impregnable ballistic skin, but now as what had to be armour-piercing rounds shattered the windows and ripped through the bodywork of the stricken Tahoe, he could see there was no cover at all. The driver and then the man next to him convulsed as they were hit.

The driver of his own vehicle let out a yell as he floored the accelerator and they tore forward, clipping the other SUV before powering back the way they had originally come.

Next to him, the prisoner had become hysterical; he was now shouting in Chinese and shaking and pulling at his restraints. Roe

3

had no time for this, so punched him in the head. The man's head jerked, then fell forward and his noise ceased.

'Comms are down!' the voice of the team member in front of him shouted.

The driver, like Roe, said nothing as they left the burning hulk of Tahoe 3, Tahoe 1 following on their tail. It was time for action, not talk. They reached the crossroads as explosions on both their left and right forced them to continue straight on. Funnelled back towards Windsor, the incoming fire followed them. The rear windscreen of Roe's SUV shattered as rounds pierced the ballistic glass and chewed up the empty backseats. A new noise now sounded above the whipping wind and roaring engine – the whine of rotor blades.

A helo buzzed them, then jinked and arched into the sky before it bore back down on them. In the darkness Roe couldn't tell who it was, or what it was. But then this made no difference as flames erupted from either side of its bulbous body as more heavy lead hurtled towards them.

Every instinct told Roe to run. Instead, he turned sideways and fell on top of his prisoner, shielding him with his body. The glass around him exploded and the Tahoe shook but continued on.

He pushed himself back up and grabbed his weapon. Turning again, he now saw Tahoe 1 had become a rolling ball of flames. He knew his Tahoe was the target, and the attackers wanted to take the man next to him alive.

'I'm hit …' The driver's voice was husky, weak.

Roe pulled himself forward; his teammate in the passenger seat was slumped sideways, a shard of ballistic glass glinting from where it had embedded itself in his neck. Roe looked at the driver as the man's hands slipped from the steering wheel and the bulky SUV lurched to one side. Roe braced himself against the seat back as the Tahoe continued and slammed into the wall of the nearest building. Airbags deployed around the two dead men as the front of the vehicle crumpled. Roe's chest was slammed against the seat and his lungs were punched shut. He slid off the seat and landed on top of his already unconscious prisoner.

There was a sudden silence, made even more eerie by the bright-white lights now flooding the interior of his SUV. Roe turned his head, but a spotlight directed at his eyes blinded him. A gruff voice barked in a language that wasn't English but was one that Roe recognised and then he felt needles of pain and heard a crackle as a blast of electricity short-circuited his entire body. Unable to resist and unable to move, it was just Roe's eyes which told him he was being dragged from the Tahoe. Through the ghosting caused by the spotlight, he caught glimpses of his teammates, slain, slumped in their seats and then the bright stars filled his vision as he was dropped, face up, on the unforgiving tarmac. Roe tried to fight his paralysis as two masked men hurried his prisoner from the shattered SUV, but his body would not comply with his orders. A figure loomed above him, face hidden and dressed in black coveralls. The man's right leg stamped down, and a boot connected with the side of Roe's head. A starburst flashed in his vision before everything went black.

Undisclosed Location

Fang Bao was a British national, the son of a Hong Kong Chinese couple who had emigrated to the UK. He was also one of the world's most-wanted cyber terrorists. His talent had been prized by all those he had worked for, and it was this which afforded him some comfort. He doubted whoever it was who had gone to such lengths to take him from the Americans would want him dead. However, this did not stop Fang from worrying.

Early morning light seeped into the room from around the externally mounted boards that obscured his view. His room was larger and much more comfortable than anything the Americans had kept him in and whoever his new jailor was, they certainly feared for his safety enough to have two guards posted on the other side of the door.

Unable to sleep because of the stress of the situation and the discomfort he still felt from the burns on his left arm, he had watched the sun come up; as much of it as entered his room, that was. The quality of light leaching in from the shutters had changed as the new day banished the night and its shadows. But the shadows had always been his friend, it had only been once he had been pushed into the light of publicity that he had been caught. Yet that had also led further to his notoriety, which he imagined was the reason he had been snatched.

He finally rolled out of bed as what he imagined was full dawn warmed the other side of his shuttered window. His cell was a room which rivalled the luxury residences he had been put up in by his paying clients, and the air was just as he liked it; sharply filtered fresh. In fact, it was only the lack of a view or any way to communicate to the outside world which reminded him he was a prisoner.

He took a step towards the bathroom and almost instantly there was a sound outside, the result he knew of hidden cameras recording his every moment. There was the sound of a bolt being drawn back, and then the grating on the key and, finally, a click. The door opened and a man entered. It was the guard who had brought his food for the two days since he had been incarcerated. Stepping into the room, his feet sank into the thick pile of carpet.

'Yes?' Fang's hands were folded and his head was held high, even though his voice trembled.

'Uncle wishes to see you. Get dressed.'

'Uncle?'

Fang wanted to know exactly who 'Uncle' was and why he had rescued him from his American captors. The guard retreated without reply and Fang continued his way to the shower, pulling off his pyjamas and leaving them in a heap on the floor. He washed and then, ten minutes later, after applying a new dressing to his arm, stood dressed by his bed in the simple clothes and plimsoles he had been provided with. The door opened and the guard beckoned him out. He had been brought to this place cuffed and hooded, and only now saw the space outside his room. The hallway too resembled a luxury hotel. There was a faint whiff of paint, as though the place had recently been decorated and the carpet felt springy and newly laid. Standing by the elevator was the second guard; he, like the first, was Asian probably Chinese, possibly Korean, but Fang couldn't tell from their harshly accented English and he hadn't wanted to anger them by asking them either in English or Chinese. The second guard was haloed by the diffused light emanating from the floor-to-ceiling obscured-glass windows at the far end of the hall. He pressed a button and the elevator doors opened. Without being told to, Fang stepped inside. Both guards followed and then the last one in pressed a button for the top floor, just a floor above. The pair both had 9mm Berettas on their right legs. He imagined these were for show because attempting to draw them, in such a confined space, would take far too long.

The elevator opened at the top floor. Again, the light from the windows was diffused by obscured glass. With one guard in front and the other behind him, they proceeded along the corridor. Passing a window, Fang noticed the glass had been obscured by a film, which he thought incongruous with the rest of the decorations, fixtures, and fittings.

They stopped at the far end of the corridor. A pair of giant, arched double doors gave the impression that beyond lay a Viking longhouse. The doors simultaneously opened inwards, Fang was pushed into the room and they immediately closed behind him. Directly in front of the doors, a huge floor-to-ceiling window, which he imagined showcased an impressive one-hundred-and-eighty-degree panorama, were again hidden by film. An Asian man with a shock of white hair sat behind a large dark-wood desk. He stood, faster than Fang had believed a man of his age could.

'Mr Fang, how delighted I am to finally be acquainted with you. Please take a seat.'

Unlike his own Essex-tinged English, the man's words were said with a crisp, clear Home Counties accent.

'Thank you.' Fang sat.

'How is your arm? Not troubling you too much?'

'It's fine.'

The white-haired man returned to his desk chair. He sat back, interlaced his fingers, and then he smiled at him. 'I am Gu Joon. I am the one responsible for ending your captivity with the Central Intelligence Agency.' Gu raised his right palm. 'I do not expect you to thank me. How do you like your room? It's one of the best, currently.'

'It's OK.'

'OK?' Gu smiled.

Fang studied the man. His face gave off the impression of a friendly uncle, perhaps that was what had earnt him the nickname? Sitting as he was now, he looked almost harmless, but Fang had seen the speed at which he moved and knew that he was more than he seemed.

Gu continued. 'I have followed your career, Mr Fang. You have been quite successful.'

'Quite?' Fang felt his eyes twitch at the slight; he was the best there was. 'Thanks.'

'But then of course you chose the wrong partners, and everything went wrong.'

Fang frowned. 'Did you bring me here to tell me you are the partner I should have chosen?'

'No. Not at all. What I am offering you is the chance to right a wrong, to get back at those who were responsible for selling you out to the Americans – your former partners – the Ah Kong triad.'

Fang's forehead furrowed. 'I knew it!'

'Why, of course. Who else could it have been? You were like a needle hiding in a field of haystacks, if you'll pardon my clumsy wordplay. It was your partners – the Ah Kong triads – who told the Americans specifically where to look. And one can merely imagine what the Americans have put you through these past two years.'

Fang felt his face burn with anger. He'd had his suspicions, but this made complete sense. 'I want to make them pay.'

'That's the spirit, and I of course want to help you, but for me to do this you must help me.'

Fang knew it had been a pitch, but he had no option not to hear it. 'What do you want from me?'

'All I require from you is one solitary ingot of information.'

'If I give you that, what? You'll help me get back at the Ah Kong?'

'Exactly. They are no friends of mine either. I already have a plan. Only you can carry it out. You shall have your revenge.'

Fang's breath caught at the sudden realisation that to go against any of the triad groups was a death sentence. Who was this man, and could he really take down the triads? And, more importantly, could he protect him from them? 'And then?'

'An astute question. I can see the concern on your face, and I know what you are thinking. I can offer you sanctuary. Somewhere the Ah Kong and the Western intelligence agencies can not touch you.'

'They can find me anywhere.'

'That is not true. Places exist in the world, where those who would lay claim to you have no reach. I am not speaking of a Third World country without an extradition treaty, I am talking of a powerful nation which neither the blackest of black US operations nor the most vicious of criminal gangs can enter.'

Fang now understood. 'You're working for North Korea.'

'Mr Fang, I am North Korea.' Fang frowned, not quite understanding, but Gu continued, 'I will grant you safe passage into the only nation on this earth the United States will not enter if you give me this one piece of information.'

'And if I refuse?'

Gu's eyelids fluttered. 'Why would you? There is nowhere to go.'

'And then, I'd be what, working for Pyongyang?'

'Mr Fang, we have a unit of six thousand patriotic cyber-warriors. Imagine what you could achieve if you oversaw them, if you were their boss?'

Fang's eyes widened. He already knew he was the best, but numbers meant power; he'd be invincible. But something was niggling him. 'How do I know I can trust you? How do I know you are who you say you are?'

'I can promise you asylum in The Democratic People's Republic of Korea.' Gu pointed with his index finger. 'It is I who will take the risk on you – what if you lie to me? This is the nature of trust, Fang. It is like building a bridge across a fast-flowing river; the first brick must be solid, for if it is not the rest will fall into the muddy waters.'

'Yeah, trust is essential.' Fang sighed. He really had no option but to assist the man who sat across the desk from him. 'OK. What would you like to know?'

'I would like to know the identity of a man you know. You worked together when you were employed by an organisation named "Blackline".'

Fang felt his jaw drop. Not even the Americans knew he'd undertaken work for Blackline, the organisation which had several years before carried out the first tactical EMP attack on the US, causing a nationwide total blackout, innumerable deaths and damage to the US infrastructure and economy. 'How did you …'

Gu smiled again. 'I have my ways, Mr Fang, and of course my means. Now, I would like to know the identity of the man who created one of Blackline's many projects.'

Fang managed to stop himself from speaking for a moment as he thought the situation through. How did he know that Gu wasn't really the CIA, and this wasn't all a fake operation to get him to talk?

'Again, I understand what you are thinking, Mr Fang, perhaps

Gu Joon is a CIA asset? You saw the Americans around you ripped to pieces by the rounds my men released. The bullets, the flames and their unfortunate yet necessary deaths were real.'

Fang nodded. Just like the burns on his left arm and the bruises, it had been real, and this had to be too – didn't it? 'OK.'

'So, Mr Fang, what is the name of the man who created "Project White Suit"?'

Fang let the words roll around inside his head for a moment. He knew little of 'White Suit', but he did know its creator. 'I have a question. Why do you want to know?'

'I want to know, Mr Fang, because I intend to use Project White Suit to rebuild North Korea.'

Chapter 1

Two Months later
Hamburg, Germany

Jack Tate studied the cargo ships on the river. Grubby with the rigours of their voyage from the Far East, they waited to be unloaded. Returning his focus to the enhanced images from the high-powered scope, he watched the target vessel as containers were hauled high into the sky, then placed delicately on dry land like giant Lego bricks arranged by a conscientious child. Each, he imagined, was full to capacity with goods made on the cheap to be sold at ridiculously inflated prices to German consumers. There was a creaking sound as a container slipped, then shouts from men on the ship and the dock. The rusty-red-coloured monolith swung back and forth before coming under control once more and being stacked next to its siblings. Tate idly wondered how much a container weighed. Of course, he understood that all depended on the cargo within, but there had to be a maximum and a minimum.

Tate wasn't in Germany to track dodgy goods; he was there to track, intercept and apprehend a highly sophisticated and dangerous cyber terrorist – Fang Bao. The British national had established links with several international crime syndicates, including – most worryingly for the UK government – one whose major cyber-attacks on both the London Stock Exchange and NHS mainframes had narrowly been avoided. Fang was an electronic gun for hire and allegedly protected by powerful people in China, but he had abruptly vanished two years before under the noses of an SIS, less formally referred to as MI6, surveillance operation. He had become something of an internet celebrity, his occasional videos and hacking notoriety garnering him the name, by his band of followers as 'the non-anonymous', which Tate didn't think was actually a word in the English language. Yet now he had been 'pinged', like a blip on the UK government's threat radar. He had broken cover, been identified, and British Intelligence had no idea why.

Tate continued to watch the containers. These were tangible, physical items produced on one side of the world and shipped to another, not the computer algorithms, viruses, and programs that Fang Bao employed. Tate's brow wrinkled as a thought struck: 'Does data weigh anything?'

In the corner of the dingy room behind, the man who sat tapping away at a computer looked up. 'Weigh?'

'Does it have a physical weight?'

Neil Plato, the MI6 computer whizz assigned to Tate's team, stood and walked to the window. 'A stored byte of data weighs approximately one attogram.'

'Attogram?'

'It's one-quintillionth of a gram.'

'And that's?' Tate said, blankly.

'That's a zero then a decimal point followed by seventeen zeros and finally a one. I suppose if you placed two mass storage devices with large enough capacities side by side and picked them up, one at a time, it would be, in theory possible to feel which one was full of data.'

'How big would this device have to be?'

'Big.'

Tate jutted his chin towards the docks below, 'The size of a container, maybe?'

'Jack, a bit smaller. I doubt you could fit one of those in the palm of my hand.'

Tate smirked. 'What's the latest?'

Plato blew out his cheeks. 'More noise in the chat rooms from Fang's fans, but nothing new. However, the increased chatter does imply that something big is about to happen.'

'And we don't have a clue what,' Tate stated flatly.

'Nope.' Plato shrugged. 'Let's hope Fang is polite enough to tell you when you ask him.'

Tate smirked and returned his focus to the view of the vast docks outside. The Port of Hamburg was the third busiest in Europe and the fifteenth largest in the world, facts he'd learned before arriving several days ago with his team. The vessel Tate was observing had sailed from the Port of Shanghai, the planet's largest container port, and intel confirmed their target, using genuine government-issued documents, had joined its crew as a deckhand named 'Chi Kong Pang'. Whilst Tate kept his eyes on the ship and surrounding dock, the feed from a high-powered scope was being analysed by Plato's facial and gait-recognition software, as was all live feed from the CCTV systems of the port and local area. If Fang appeared on deck, he'd be spotted. If he stepped off the container ship he'd be digitally followed, and if he attempted to leave the port, he'd be physically tailed by the two other members of Tate's E Squadron team – Paul Page and Chris Salter.

Finally, the last of the containers was unloaded and then, minutes later, a pair of officials wearing white shirts and black slacks with hi-vis vests and matching yellow hard hats entered the vessel via the gangplank. It was another forty minutes before they left, and then minutes more before, in dribs and drabs, crew members left too.

'Hello …' Plato said, 'I think we've got him!'

Tate nodded. He saw it too – a solitary sailor heading down the gangplank.

'Yep,' Plato continued, 'that's an 89 per cent on the face and pretty high on the gait.'

'Let's see what happens,' Tate said as he studied the livestream.

Two further sailors followed the man Tate and Plato believed to be Fang Bao. The trio headed towards the cargo containers that had been offloaded. Tate moved the scope, to keep the image centred. As he watched, he saw Fang nod at the men and then slip away into a narrow gap created by two layers of towering containers.

'I've lost visual. Can you pick him up on the dock's CCTV?'

'I already have,' Plato confirmed.

Tate crossed the room to Plato's large monitor to see Fang appear from the other end of container alley and head directly towards the exit of the complex.

Tate pressed a button on his ear mic. 'Be advised target is confirmed and mobile. Do you have visual?'

'Wait one,' Page replied, the tone of his voice distorted by both his mic and the motorcycle helmet that covered his face, 'I have eyeball.'

Plato tapped a key on his laptop and video feed from Page's helmet cam popped up. The image was shaky, as though Page was moving his head. Fang could be seen standing at the exit to the dockyard, next to the window of a security cabin. He handed the guard inside what appeared to be a pass of some sort. There was a pause and a conversation between him and the guard before it was given back to him and then he walked past the barrier and out of the facility. Without breaking his stride, Fang carried on along the street, heading north.

'Stand by,' Tate said to Page, not wanting the seconded SAS man to move before he had to.

'Have that.'

A silver VW Touran appeared from around a bend and not too subtly came to a halt next to Fang. Both the front and rear passenger doors opened and two Asian men in jeans and black leather jackets clambered out. Fang was trapped between them, words were exchanged and he was physically hauled into the back seat. The men got back in, and the vehicle pulled away.

Tate felt a sudden sense of panic. Had his target been snatched? Were these the people he was meeting or a third party? 'Go.'

Page followed the VW as it navigated away from the docks and headed south. The footage from his helmet cam and that of the Hamburg's CCTV system had made up two panels on Plato's monitor, but now dropped to one as they left the city. A new panel appeared with two mugshots.

Tate said to Plato, 'These are the heavies who have our target?'

'Yep, the two we saw.' Plato tapped his keyboard and details of the men appeared under their faces. 'Chinese. Former military, but that's as much as I've got.'

'It doesn't make sense,' Tate said, as he peered at the screen, 'Why would he risk leaving China to meet a Chinese group in Germany?'

Plato tapped at his keyboard. 'The vehicle is owned by SIXT.'

'Find out where it was rented from and who hired it.'

'On it.'

Tate continued to watch the footage from Page's helmet camera and made no comment as Salter spoke over the net to confirm he was taking over the follow. The footage now switched to the feed from the dashcam of Salter's Audi.

Tate needed not tell either operative to hang back, they had been selected for this E Squadron mission because of their capabilities. For the next hour Tate and Plato watched the VW continue south-west with the occasional comment from Page and Salter about road conditions and possible destinations. Both vehicles had full tanks of fuel but, even so, they had started to wonder just how far from Hamburg Fang was being taken.

Tate didn't want the distance between his team to be stretched further. 'We're going mobile.'

Tate moved away from the screen. It was time they packed up and left – in his opinion they were already too far away from the target. It would take minutes to store their gear, but longer to sanitise the space they had been using.

Plato pushed the live feed to the screen of a tablet as he packed away the rest of his equipment. Ten minutes later, Tate cast a final glance out of the grubby windows at the dock below before they both left the room.

Their transport, a Ford Galaxy, was parked on the road outside. Whilst Plato continued to monitor the footage from the front passenger seat, Tate started the Ford and updated the other two. 'We're "complete". Going mobile.'

Using the sat nav, Tate took the same route the VW had just over an hour before. The pair remained silent as Plato, using a mobile connection, continued to monitor both the footage and the online chat rooms.

Tate took in the passing landscape. He didn't know why, but he liked Germany. He supposed it was because it felt to him like a much cleaner version of the UK where everything was efficient. Things just worked in Germany. The fact that he was also a fan of their beer, sausage, and cars probably helped too.

Plato pointed at the screen. 'OK, the VW was rented two days ago from Hamburg airport. It's due back the day after tomorrow. It could mean whoever's taken Fang isn't based here either?'

'Perhaps, or perhaps they don't want to use their own cars. Find out if the two goons flew in on the same day the car was taken?'

'It'll take a while; I'll need to interrogate the German immigration database, which of course is an illegal act.'

'So's our mission,' Tate stated, 'in the eyes of the German authorities.'

An hour and a half passed with more minor updates from Page and Salter.

'They're approaching Munster,' Plato noted. 'What's in Munster?'

'The Munsters,' Tate replied, deadpan. 'Oh, and a Panzer Museum.'

'Let's hope they're not trying to steal a tank,' Plato replied, bringing up a detailed map of the area.

The footage from Salter's car now showed the VW take a turning off the main road. Salter continued on and now Page took over the eyeball once more. The road was bordered by lush green fields and hedgerows. Ahead, the footage showed the car make a turn into a smaller road. Page drew level and turned his head to provide an image of what lay ahead. It was a driveway leading to what looked like a modernised farmhouse.

'Neill, can you find out who owns that place?'

'Already checking.'

On screen the car grew smaller as it neared the house and Page remained static.

'Mobile 2, remain where you are. Mobile 1, park up where you can.'

There were a pair of clicks as both Page and Salter acknowledged their instructions.

'The house is owned by a Munich-based investment group,' Plato said. 'They specialise in rental properties for short-term lets.'

'How short is this one?'

'That information I do not have. Yet. Hello.'

'What?'

'Still nothing concrete from the chat rooms, but one of Fang's loyal fans seems to think he's developed some type of worm. Before you say anything funny, Jack, it's a digital super key.'

'So why would he need to travel to deliver something that's digital?'

'Perhaps the instructions are too complicated for anyone but him? Or perhaps it's in a piece of standalone hardware that he's developed to deliver the key?'

'How good is Fang?'

'He's world class.'

Tate wet his lips as they overtook an ancient Mercedes. 'Better than George?'

'Better than me, different to George – it's not the same discipline.'

Tate nodded. Plato and George Eastman – who was back in London – were both experts at what they did, he just hoped Plato was being modest in his underassessment of his own abilities.

'OK, I've managed to access the computer system of Bernt AG – they're the people who own the farmhouse. It was booked for a week by a company based in the Bahamas.'

'A shell company.'

'I don't think they sell shells.'

Tate chuckled. 'And?'

'Their rental ends in two days' time.'

'Like the car. So whatever Fang is up to will happen in the next two days?'

'Or it could just mean that they will only be there for two more days. I can't think of anything that would take Fang that long to set, sell or explain.'

'Find the schematics of the place, Neill, I need to know how we're going in.'

Tate slowed the large people carrier as they entered the outskirts of Munster. He brought it to a halt on the same side of the road as Salter's Audi, but not near enough to hint that the vehicles were part of a team. He pressed a button on his earpiece. 'Mobile 1, update?'

'No exterior movement. I can see shapes moving insider. Ground and first floor.'

'OK. Have that.'

Tate looked at the sat nav display. They had to move back far enough from the farmhouse to discuss their extraction plan for Fang. Of the four-man team, Plato was desk-based whilst the other three were experienced operators. Tate and Page were both SAS, whilst Salter had been seconded from the SBS – the Special

Boat Service, the Royal Navy's tier one Special Forces unit. He requested each man as they'd worked well together before. They'd discussed the various options for taking Fang, depending upon where he ended up and making entry to a secluded farmhouse with an unknown number of hostiles inside was something they knew how to do, but like everything else about their mission it would be an illegal act in the eyes of the German authorities. Such was the clandestine nature of E Squadron and the missions it was tasked to undertake.

*

Whilst remote cameras, planted by Page, kept an eyeball on the target building, the team sat in the Ford, which Tate had now parked in the large car park of the local supermarket. They took the time to eat and hydrate as Tate went through the plan and they discussed what they knew, limited as it was.

'We have an unknown number of x-rays inside, which includes the two who collected Fang and their driver. Their VW is the only vehicle at the property, but it's a Touran so there could be perhaps six?'

'Or more if they have another car that's somewhere else,' Page said.

'True, but we have to deal with the known unknowns. So that's three x-rays minimum, plus Fang. OK, Neill stays with the Ford to provide us with a digital overwatch. We three approach through the field, then find a point to make entry. We know for a fact that the place has fixed surveillance cameras covering the approach from the drive and the field behind in addition to both side accesses. We come from the east side, and we move quickly. There is no way we can deactivate any motion sensors from here but hopefully if we do trip them, it will be put down to a stray wildlife. Questions? Thoughts?'

Salter looked at Plato. 'Can you turn the cameras off?'

Plato shook his head. 'It is a local system that sends live feed to a monitoring station, and we don't know if they are even on whilst the place is occupied. I think there is some federal German law about privacy or something that forbids it, but I'll check. They're probably off.'

'That's reassuring,' Page said.

Tate checked his watch. 'We've seen the plans; four bedrooms and two reception rooms, a large kitchen and a long hall and first-floor landing. Unless movement dictates otherwise, we'll go in at 3 a.m. We don't know who these guys are, and we have not been told, but we keep it quiet. If it does "go noisy", we subdue, but if fired upon we engage. We're in and out with Fang and any technology we find. Are we good?'

The other three men nodded.

'Er, Jack, something seems to be happening here,' Plato said, tapping his screen. 'The same online user in the chat room now says there's going to be an announcement at midnight Beijing time.'

Tate checked his watch. 'Beijing is six hours ahead of us here, that's means we've got an hour.'

'It could mean nothing,' Salter stated. 'I mean, who even are these armchair anarchists?'

Tate saw movement outside; he beckoned for silence, checked the mirrors and confirmed it was German shoppers.

'Her screen name is YanYan19,' Plato continued. 'She's a vocal user of the chat room, and by the number of points next to her fat cat emoji, she's well respected. I don't know who she really is, or where she is. If I had time, I could run a trace.'

'Fang's not a real terrorist,' Page said, 'not in the "bang-bang" way.'

'So, sod it, let's go in.' Salter had a twinkle in his eye. 'I'm sure they won't be expecting us.'

Tate continued to watch the shoppers toing and froing. It was his decision to make; did they go in before a potential deadline set by an unconfirmed source, or did they strike as planned in the middle of the night when the vigilance of those inside would be at its lowest ebb? 'OK. We go now. There's no way to hide in daylight once we're clear of the fields. We wear Bundespolizei caps and body armour and make entry via the east side and try the backdoor. We still need this to stay quiet for as long as we can. But if it goes noisy then we make it noisier still – flashbangs, the lot.'

*

Plato drove the Ford to the edge of the turning and stopped. The assault team got out. To a casual observer they would look like a German police team, and that was the impression Tate wanted them to give off when they encountered the opposition. Tate's German was worse than even his French, but he knew enough to tell whoever he met to 'drop their weapon and lie on the floor', and their official uniforms would buy them a couple of seconds.

They had forty minutes to the time of the announcement. Tate knew what they were doing was risky, but they were trained to deal with risk. Each had been drilled over and over on how to clear a room and how to extract a hostage. Tate had switched to game mode now, which meant his senses were alert, he had tunnel vision on the target, on the objective, yet all the while he was highly aware of his environment.

They left the Ford and crossed into the field. Thankfully those at the sides were grass not crops or barren earth, which could grab at their feet like glue and hinder their progress. Tate took the lead of the three-man stick, with Page followed by Salter. They were not expecting any opposition until they attempted to make entry to the building. Sentries had not been posted which struck Tate as a sign that whoever was inside with Fang was not expecting to be interrupted.

Tate heard a noise, an odd whirring of a low-powered engine.

'You have a vehicle heading in the direction of the target,' Plato stated. 'It's a lime-green Fiat 500. One occupant.'

'Have that,' Tate replied, holding up his fist for the others to stop. They hunkered down in the cover of the hedgerow and peered through the foliage to the other side, watching the vehicle approach. The car had red and yellow decals on the side – flames and a dragon, and the name of a restaurant.

'They've ordered in,' Page whispered dryly. 'I hope there's enough for us.'

The Fiat passed them and pulled up directly outside the front door, with its rear to Tate and the team. The driver got out. He was wearing jeans, a baggy, black satin-look bomber jacket and a black baseball cap. From the restricted, fleeting view Tate had of the driver's profile, he'd say he was Asian and in his thirties. The driver walked around the car and opened the front passenger seat. Tate now noticed he was wearing black gloves. He collected two large white plastic carrier bags which tugged heavily at the handles and then took the steps up to the front door and rang the doorbell.

'Neill, are you getting this?'

'Yes. All on cameras, but I've not got a clear shot of his face to ID him.'

The front door was opened by one of the heavies Tate had seen earlier. He nodded at the driver, exchanged a few words and then beckoned him in. Tate frowned, wondering why he'd gone inside. A little over two minutes later there was a sudden sound, the unmistakable man-made barking of a handgun. Two rounds fired, a few seconds apart.

'Jack! I heard gunshots!' There was a note of concern in Plato's voice.

'Yes.' Something was happening, and it wasn't anything good. 'What do you see?'

'Nothing ... wait! Movement, upper-floor window. I think it's the delivery driver.'

'Moving,' Tate commanded.

They bounded forward and reached the edge of the hedgerow. There was a break which meant they would be exposed as they crossed the hardstanding to the wall of the building. Tate remained where he was, in cover, scanning the windows with his HK, looking for targets but finding none. The two others leapfrogged past him and reached the building. They were in place. Tate darted towards them as something zipped past his head. It was another round, but this one was supressed; this one was from a second weapon, and this one had been aimed at him.

Tate dived forwards and pressed his back against the rough bricks of the farmhouse wall. Silence from inside the house and the distant rumble of tyres on tarmac carried on the light breeze, the only external sound reaching their ears.

Tate had a decision to make; his team had been compromised. Inside there was a minimum of three hostiles, plus Fang, and the delivery driver. But two weapons had been fired, and only the second had been at him. Memories of the innumerable hours spent at the SAS 'Killing House' practising house clearing and hostage rescue techniques swam before his eyes. House clearing was second nature to him and the others. His team were the best in the world at this, but they no longer had the element of surprise, and, unlike a real hostage scenario, there would be no time to back off, or to negotiate. He really had no choice if he was going to continue his mission and grab Fang, he had to go in now.

They moved along the east wall to the edge of the building, paused, listened once more, and spun around the corner, fire selector switched to burst on his supressed HK G36K. The back-door was ajar. They moved towards it, ducking under the level of the windowsill. Tate held up his fist, a sign to stop, to listen before they engaged. A new sound made its way on the air through the gap in the door; men's voices speaking in angry-sounding German. Tate cursed the fact he didn't speak enough of the language – he was a Russian specialist – and gently pushed the door open knowing that at any moment he could be met with a blast of lead. He whirled into the kitchen, dissecting the space into arcs with the end of his HK, knowing that his two team members behind him would be doing the same.

The kitchen was large, modern and had an island in the middle. On the island lay the two bags of takeaway Chinese food and sprawled forward over the island between these was the heavy who had opened the door. Tate recognised him by the colour of his shirt, and not his face which had imploded.

And that was when Tate knew this was a hit.

Tate bypassed the island, eyes and HK trained as one at the door beyond, which he knew from the floor plans opened onto the hall. The German conversation drifting from the next room had grown louder. A female voice spoke, and music suddenly played. It was a television, and it had been left on to hinder his approach.

Taking point once again, Tate moved from the kitchen into the hall. It was empty and led to the two reception rooms, the stairs, and the front door. Ahead he could hear German television adverts coming from the room on the right, the room with an open door. The room on the left, whose door was exactly opposite, was closed.

He advanced, slower now and more aware of the feel of the sole of his boots on the wooden flooring. His tunnel vision drew in, his entire focus, his entire world was now the space in front of his eyes; the two-metre-wide hallway, the two doors and the wider space beyond. He knew there were two elite shooters behind him, he knew his six was secure which made him even more aware that any danger would lie ahead.

Tate paused and craned his neck, to listen, and then he entered the room with the blaring television, at speed. To his left along the wall a long, luxurious grey leather settee sat, past this a large bay window gave way onto the small lawn at the front of the house, directly ahead of him, an expensive-looking wall-mounted television took pride of place and to his right another matching but shorter settee faced the window. It wasn't what was on the television however that took Tate's attention, it was what was on the second settee. The other heavy lay sideways half on, half off the piece of furniture, as though he had tried to get up but failed. The driver was flat on his back. Both men had been executed in the same manner, one round in the chest and one in the head. There was no need to check if either was dead; the splatter of bone and brain matter on the leather gave him a definitive answer. A Glock G19 lay where it had fallen on the floor, just out of reach of the dead driver's hand. The stench of gunpowder hanging in the room and the holes Tate now noticed on the wall around the door indicated that he'd got two shots off, which in Tate's mind indicated some level of competence.

Unless there were more minders already in the house, and this was something they did not know, that now left just Fang and the delivery driver, whom Tate now had no doubt was an assassin.

Tate met the eyes of his men, nodded, and pointed with the fingers of his left hand. The pair nodded, understanding. They now moved to the closed door of the room opposite. Standing a step back to the left with their HKs pointing down the hall, Page and Salter were ready to bomb-burst inside or take on any target that appeared from upstairs. Page reached forward, grabbed the handle, and pulled the door open as Tate went low and rushed into the room. He immediately moved right, and, three steps later, was once again dissecting the space with the barrel of his HK. The room was identical to the television room in size, but this had a large dining table and six chairs placed in the centre. This room also did not have any corpses.

Tate pointed to his chest then to the open door, he then moved his fingers in a walking gesture to show his intention to move back into the hall then take the stairs up to the first floor. Page and Salter nodded.

HK sniffing out potential threats, Tate advanced along the hall, the sound of the TV retreating behind him and his ears straining to hear anything new, anything ahead. Light now came through the dappled glass panel in the front door, throwing a shadow from a coat stand to his left and reflecting from a vast mirror on the facing wall. Still no movement or new sound. Tate swung his HK to the right and up to cover the stairs and pushed himself against the opposite wall. He waited, he listened and then Page and Salter silently darted past him and into the hall, their HKs aimed up the stairs and into the void beyond. Tate waited. If the stairs were not clear he'd soon know it. There was a sudden movement ahead, the front door clicked opened. All three men prepared for contact, but nothing happened and then it swung a little more open and then back on itself as the wind took it.

Tate wanted to ask Plato if there was anyone outside, but knew that if there had been he'd have warned him.

Page beckoned Tate forward. It was Tate's turn to leapfrog the pair's position and get to the stairs. This was the time of maximum exposure; he was a slow-moving target and anyone above him would obviously have the higher ground. So far, they had encountered no opposition and three of the known four occupants of the building were dead, two more upstairs – in theory – and one of those was a killer. As the noise of the television faded into the background, Tate's own breathing become the loudest sound in his ears. He was aware of it. Slow, controlled, rhythmic. Thus far they had relied on stealth, but that was all about to change. Tate removed a percussion grenade – a flash-bang from his vest pocket, pulled the pin and tossed it up the stairs onto the landing.

It bounced and rolled along the wooden flooring and then exploded with a deafening clap of thunder and light so white it would temporarily disorientate anyone within its immediate range. Even though Tate and his team had been expecting it and had their hands clamped firmly over their ears, backs turned and eyes screwed shut, it was loud enough to rattle their teeth and bright enough to ghost their vision.

Tate rushed up the stairs, reached the top and without pausing immediately sought out targets. The landing was long, mirroring the hall below and led off to four rooms, and each of the doors were open. Not good odds. Tate burst into the nearest room, with Page and Salter on his heels to repeat the room clearing procedure.

It was a bedroom overlooking the fields, at the rear of the property. To his left was a large bed but, on his right, where a vanity unit should have been, was a long, sleek desk. On the desk were three large, curved computer monitors and in front of these was a laptop and a keyboard. A fallen chair rested on its side and a figure lay next to this. Blood had seeped from wounds in its head and chest, staining the thick, cream carpet.

With a sickening realisation, Tate realised his mission had failed. Fang Bao.

Tate gestured the others should clear the remaining rooms as he checked Fang, but knew he was dead.

'Clear!' Page's voice was loud from the landing.

'Tate,' Salter said via his earpiece, 'the window in the next room is open. We've got a runner.'

Tate stood and through the window in front of him his eyes latched onto a shape halfway across the vast field behind them, a figure, a dark-haired man moving with difficulty through the tall crops.

'Salter, stay here, secure the site, get Plato in to secure the tech. Page, grab your bike. I need you to get to whatever is on the other side of that field.'

Tate started to turn, to leave the room when a sudden bleeping from the computer made him stop. He turned his head and saw that all three screens were suddenly showing the same thing, a clock counting down from ten.

'Bomb!' Tate yelled and stormed towards the door.

Half running, half falling, the three men hurtled down the stairs, banging against the walls and the bannisters and each other before they all but knocked the front door from its hinges as they shot out onto the drive.

Tate heard Plato in his earpiece but ignored the panicked voice asking him what was happening as he sprinted away from the house. He lost track of time, had no idea if the countdown had finished, all he knew now as he stood panting, his hands on his knees alongside his team, was that nothing had exploded.

'Bike,' Page managed to say, and jogged away in the direction of the road.

'Go back inside, be careful,' Tate ordered Salter. 'I'm going after the runner.'

Tate sprinted back towards the house.

'Jack, what's happening?' Plato again, in his ear.

Tate pressed his earpiece to respond. 'Fang is dead, the Chinese are dead. I'm going after the shooter. Drive up to the house and meet Salter inside.'

'Right.'

Tate soon reached the field and found the path pushed into it by the fleeing man. Tate moved as quickly as he could, his boots continuously being tugged at by stalks, stones, and uneven earth.

Tate picked up his pace, moving as fast as he could whilst holding his HK now by its grab handle. He had to reach the assassin; he had to know who had stopped his mission. Tate arrived at the edge of the field and vaulted a wooden fence to find himself facing a country road. He stood, paused and listened. Left, right or straight on into the next field? On the bike, Page had the advantage on the road, unless the man had been picked up – collected by a colleague. Tate crossed the road, climbed over another fence, and continued. The edge of the field was grass, and there was nothing to show any trace but then further ahead, in the tall crops he saw several birds suddenly scatter, disturbed by something. That something, Tate realised, had to be the assassin.

'Mobile 1. I've entered the next field. Check the roads.'

'Have that,' Page confirmed.

Tate's legs started to feel heavy, but he knew it was nothing. He could run for miles if he had to.

He saw a path, crushed crops. It had to be his man, who else would be mad enough to run through a field? Tate carried on, upping his pace, pushing himself faster to try to close the gap. Tate felt his legs become suddenly light as he unknowingly had crested a rise. His legs moved faster, and he now used his arms for balance as the field started to drop away, undulating far more than he would have expected for a piece of commercial agricultural land.

And then he saw a head.

A head of black hair bobbing fifty yards or so ahead and below him. Tate couldn't see his face, but he recognised the clothes, the jeans, the baggy black satin-look bomber jacket and baseball cap of the delivery driver. Hollywood clichés flashed through Tate's mind of chases where the authorities call out to the suspect 'Stop, police' or 'Stop, thief'. Tate gave no warning as he continued to hurtle downhill towards the assassin.

Tate was gaining on him now, each step taking him nearer to grabbing the man he had been sent to extradite. Perhaps it was the sound of his feet or some other sixth sense, but the assassin abruptly turned.

In the fraction of a second it took Tate to realise what was happening, the man had raised his handgun and two, supressed rounds were hurtling towards him.

Tate skidded left but was too slow as both rounds slammed into his chest with the force of a sledgehammer. Tate was punched sideways. Crashing into the ground, his back smashed into the earth, the air was abruptly forced out of his lungs and the HK tumbled away from his grip. As his vision started to grey out, Tate's fingers frantically felt for the quick release strap holding his Glock securely within its leg holster. Pushing with his left arm he managed to sit up, eyes narrow with pain, and one-handed aimed the sidearm back down the narrow path in the crops. The assassin's head turned away as, with his own sidearm held in a two-handed grip, he scanned the ground for Tate. Shakily, Tate pulled the trigger and sent a round back at the man. It went wide as the man seemed to sense Tate's shot and dropped to his knees to return fire before Tate's round had the chance to reach him.

Tate rolled into the crop as the incoming supressed rounds kicked up clods of earth where, a moment before, he'd been lying. Tate's rational mind wanted to know who this man was who had been sent to kill Fang Bao, but he ignored this. He had to defeat the man who was trying to kill him, he would only worry about who he was later.

Tate rose to his knees, wincing at the pain in his chest, and crawled parallel to the path through the wheat. He could see his HK lying on the other side of the path, but there was no way he could get to it without presenting himself as an easy target. He started to take deep breaths to expand his bruised chest. It hurt, but the pain was a welcome sign as it meant that he was still alive. His vest had saved his life.

A noise reached Tate's ears. A voice just audible over the throaty sound of an engine, a motorbike. Before Tate could reply, there was more gunfire. It reached him from both his earpiece and the world outside. It was the assassin's supressed 9mm coughing again at what Tate realised could only be his fellow SAS man, Paul Page.

Tate heard the sickening sound of metal striking metal. Ignoring his burning chest, Tate pushed up to his feet, Glock extended in front of him … but he had no target. The running man, the assassin had gone.

Silence fell over the field, broken only by the idling of a motorbike engine. Tate turned and retraced his route as each step sent a sword of pain through his chest. He found Page lying on his side, pinned by his bike. His visor was up, and his face was pained.

'The bastard got me in the leg!'

'The bastard got away,' Tate said, flatly.

There was a crackle in Tate's ear; his earpiece was loose. He pushed it in. 'Neill?'

'Jack, you need to get back here.' Plato's voice was panicked.

'What's happened?'

'Fang has declared war!'

*

Tate and Salter had manhandled Page into their VW where they had cleaned and bandaged his wound. Each of the three men were trained in battlefield medicine and knew that although the injury was a through and through, and not life threatening, it still needed immediate professional treatment. Salter dropped Tate off at the farmhouse before leaving with Page for a medical facility, the details of which they had been given in their mission briefing.

Tate entered the farmhouse, having popped a couple of pain-killers, and made his way upstairs to the bedroom containing the computer equipment. He saw Fang's body had been moved away from his terminal to one side. Plato was standing over the computer set-up, wearing a pair of black latex gloves and tapping at the keyboard.

Tate ignored the dead man. 'What have we got then?'

Plato turned, only now realising Tate had entered the room. He looked concerned. 'Jack, are you OK?'

'I'm peachy, but my vest isn't.'

Plato gestured at the body on the floor, his voice now a little shaky. 'Before Fang went dark, he was employed by the Chinese triads.'

Tate knew this. 'Yes, and?'

'From what I can understand, it was the triads Fang was meeting and trying to sell to.'

'The super-worm he'd apparently developed?'

'Yes.'

'But someone decided he should be shot instead?'

Plato nodded. 'That's still not the worse part. Fang has somehow managed to break into the triads' banking system. He's emptied every single one of their accounts!'

'So, this is a robbery?'

'I think it's more than that.' Plato pressed a button on the keyboard. 'Look at this.'

'This is the chat room you were monitoring?'

'Yes. Fang managed to release his announcement early. Look what it says!'

Tate read what had been posted. 'Sheesh …'

'Exactly,' Plato said. 'Fang claimed he'd stolen two billion US dollars from the Ah Kong triads for his new masters.'

'New masters?' Tate shook his head in disbelief. 'Who?'

'I don't know, no one does. It says an announcement will be made at sunrise.'

'Sunrise when? Here or Beijing time?'

'I don't know, but dawn in Beijing is only five hours away.'

Tate moved to the window to gather his thoughts. The man he had chased, the man who had shot him, was a professional operator, and his reflexes had been outstanding. Tate had caught just a partial glimpse of the man's profile, but something was telling him they'd met before. Tate closed his eyes as his chest throbbed. Did he know the assassin, would he recognise him again? The assassin was out there, and every minute they wasted was another potential kilometre further away he was from them. He wanted to track the man down, and to find out who he was working for but that wasn't his mission. They had to leave; they couldn't risk staying at the farmhouse any longer, especially with three corpses to explain away. Tate clenched his fists as his anger rose. If he had just himself taken Fang off the street and bundled him into a van, he'd have both the man and anything he was selling. Also, he thought bitterly, three men would still be alive, and Page wouldn't have a hole in his leg. Yet his orders had been to follow, observe and then intercept. Tate let out a large sigh.

Fang was dead and his killer was in the wind. 'Neill, we need to be out of here now. Unplug everything and we'll bag it up.'

Plato's gaze fell upon the dead hacker. 'I chatted to him once, a few years ago, when he was new on the scene. He seemed like a nice kid.'

'Nice kids don't work for the triads.' Tate stopped, realising he'd made another mistake. 'That's your first dead body?'

Plato nodded, said nothing.

'Come on, we need to hustle. Once we're mobile we'll update Newman.'

'I know.' Plato's face had lost its colour.

Chapter 2

Oxnard, California, USA

Cal Conners stumbled out of the ocean, panting for breath, removed his goggles and collapsed on the sand. He lay on his back, staring at the sky, with the waves gently lapping at his feet as he brought his breathing under control. Battling the cold ocean water was the best cure for a hangover he knew, and the night before he'd drunk a silly amount.

Oxnard Shores, the community Conners now called his own, was miles away from his landlocked hometown of Barnsley in the UK. As a kid the nearest thing he'd had to the sea was Worsbrough Reservoir, which although now developed into a picturesque country park was in his opinion an overgrown concrete puddle. A wry smile crossed his face; those were fighting words in Barnsley. As was saying he didn't miss the place, with its overweight men and women in ill-fitting catalogue clothes. Conners' smile grew larger. He was being unfair, he told himself, and mentally apologised to his fellow Yorkshiremen. A moment of melancholy engulfed him as he continued to remember his old home, and his former life.

Conners could never go back.

Conners was dead.

He sat up and faced the water. He could watch it for hours, moving, sparkling and beckoning him to come back in. He enjoyed the warmth on his face. The sun had not yet started to blast the sand with its full ferocity, but it would. It was a given, it was predictable, as was Conners himself now that he had a routine.

He glanced at his G-Shock diver's watch. It wasn't a flashy item, but then nor was he, anymore. He had more than enough cash to live on and over the past three years he'd been happy to lead a simple existence, his mornings filled with long swims and home workouts, and his evenings spent eating, bar hopping or 'Netflix and chilling' with his neighbour cum girlfriend Darcie. So far it had been a casual affair, but something inside him said that she was special. The question was, could he allow himself to lead her on, to let their relationship develop into something more substantial as sooner or later he would have to tell her who he was. And that would put her in danger, if she decided she wanted to stay with him, which he mused she probably wouldn't. Hell, he realised she was already in danger now. For the moment he was hiding, playing the burnt-out beach bum, with his long hair and had even changed the way he spoke. California was a magnet for misfits from all over the US. No one remembered someone with an out-of-state accent, but everyone remembered the guy who sounded to locals like Sean Bean's brother. He'd given up his old accent when he gave up his old life and become Cal Conners from Jersey, New Jersey that was, because he enjoyed *The Sopranos*, and it was the only accent he could convincingly pull off.

Conners sauntered back into the surf, submerged himself to wash away the sand from his shorts and matching O'Neill rash-vest, then collected his camo-coloured Crocs and wrap-around Oakleys from where he had left them higher up the beach, in the gap between two oceanfront houses.

He blew on the lenses, donned his shades and popped his Crocs on to cross Mandalay Beach Road. He entered Driftwood

Street. His rented flat, or apartment as he had learned to call it, was in a complex of five buildings further up on the right. At this time of day, before 10 a.m., the street was devoid of traffic; those who worked real day jobs had gone, leaving behind only those who pretended to. He saw the same cars every morning parked outside the same buildings and, in his head, he'd worked out a storyline for each and its owner. The first vehicle he passed was the white Chevrolet Silverado owned by the guy he'd pinned as a retired small town insurance salesman. He'd seen him getting into his truck, and he really put the 'small' into small town – he was barely five foot in his socks, which had been stunningly white and pulled halfway up his legs almost meeting his professionally pressed chino shorts and matching khaki polo shirt. Conners chuckled.

Next, he walked by an old cherry-red Ford Explorer, it had several bumper stickers on the back for political candidates and was parked outside the only house in the street to fly a US flag. It was driven by a large middle-aged woman who each time Conners had seen her had a scowl on her face and a large purse in her hand. She'd nodded at him but never spoken a word. He thought she may perhaps have once been in law enforcement or work for the IRS, either way now she didn't keep regular hours.

Then, on the other side of the road was a jet-black Mini. This car made him miss England, even though this model was twice the size of the original and made by BMW. Now this owner he'd never met, but he'd seen her, and she was gorgeous, and always wore black, in the Californian heat, and that intrigued him.

A pair of motorbikes were up next. Parked, as always outside number 5511, the property painted a dark grey. He had no clue what model they were, and he didn't care – if it didn't have four wheels and seats, he wasn't interested. There was a rocking chair on the balcony, and, as usual, it was occupied.

'Been swimming?' a gruff voice called out, as it did each time he passed.

Conners never knew if it was a question aimed at him or a statement needing no answer. He played it safe and nodded back.

The street outside his apartment complex at this time of day was usually empty, usually clear of cars or trucks of any kind apart from his battered ten-year-old Toyota. Today it was not. The space was taken up by a huge black SUV.

Conners stopped in his tracks, the water still trickling down his face from his long hair. It was not the type of vehicle he expected to see in his relaxed and down-at-heel neighbourhood; it looked official, it looked mean, it didn't belong. Subconsciously he raised his left hand and stroked his damp beard in concentration, an old tic that he had not managed to leave behind.

He was probably being paranoid. This was probably nothing to do with him. Probably.

A sixth sense, a fear, some sort of threat radar however told him that the SUV, and whoever it had transported to this sleepy street, were there for him. Conners knew if he ran now – wet, and dressed for the ocean without ID or cash, he'd get nowhere. He had a bug-out bag but, like a fool, it was safely stashed under his bed. He had no choice; if he was forced to run, he needed that bag. Head facing front, but eyes darting about, Conners moved towards the complex.

The SUV he now identified as a Tahoe, one of the preferred models used by various branches of the US government whose long names were famously shortened to a handful of letters. The driver's side window was open, and a thick, hairy forearm hung outside with a cigarette trailing smoke from its fingers. As Conners drew nearer, the driver leaned out of the window a few inches to take another drag, keen perhaps to keep the smoke outside. But then why stay in the vehicle? Conners was puzzled, but he was also now aware that a huge bloke with a military-style haircut was waiting outside his adopted home.

There was a playful bark and a little dog scampered down the path at the side of the complex and made for the sidewalk, its owner pulled behind it on a taut lead. Conners wasn't a dog fan and didn't know breeds, but he knew this dog; he was called Snowflake and he belonged to Darcie.

Snowflake saw him, wagged his fluffy white tail, and strained even more against his leash. Darcie waved.

Conners was a few feet behind his Prius. He took a step to his left and into the road, seemingly to give Darcie and Snowflake space to pass but, in reality, to make himself harder to spot from the Tahoe.

Snowflake danced up at him. Conners slowly bent down to stroke his head as he asked Darcie, using his Jersey accent, 'Who's the guy in the Tahoe?'

'I dunno,' Darcie replied with her usual cheery grin. 'There was another one inside talking to the super and blocking my way.'

'They don't look like the sanitation department.'

'Probably a team of killers come to blow us all away.'

Conners straightened. 'You're kidding?'

'Hey, Cal.' Darcie used his name, but not his real name – rather the name he was known by, as an American. 'What's eating you? Course I'm kidding. A group of guys appears here in a flashy SUV and sharp suits, it's gotta be business, right? Real estate investors or developers, right?'

Conners nodded. 'Right.'

'So, you wanna come by tonight? I've got the good wine.'

'Netflix and chill?' An idea struck Conners. 'I need to talk to the super myself, I got an issue with my shower. Look, Darcie, can I use your bathroom, I mean shower?'

Darcie's lips pursed and the ends turned up into a small smile. Her hand disappeared into her jeans pocket and retrieved a key. 'Here. You know where everything is.'

'Thanks.'

'No problem and, hey, stay for a coffee – I won't be long. We can do some Netflix.' She winked and moved away as Snowflake, now bored, tugged at the lead again as the beach called to him.

Conners started to walk. Outside the apartment complex the Tahoe driver opened his door. Without thinking, Conners wheeled to his right and cut down the same narrow space between his apartment complex and the next building that Darcie had used. In the UK they called them 'desire paths', routes created by the footfall of the lazy, he had no idea what Americans called them. Using this path, however, meant that he'd avoid the reception area and could also get to Darcie's apartment without passing by his own.

Conners made sure he was hidden in the shadows before he snuck a look back at the street. The driver was standing outside talking on his phone, his tone was hushed but the words '… not seen him …' wafted towards him.

Conners felt his body stiffen and his breath came in short, sharp bursts. He managed to walk further along the path, negotiating the weeds and litter, both his breaths and his strides thankfully lengthening. He reached the next street and the backdoor to the complex. There was no one out of place on the street outside. He took a deep breath and pushed his way through the door. Turning immediately to his left, he entered the courtyard. The main entrance was behind him now and in front were two sets of stairs, one for each wing, leading to the first floor. His and Darcie's flats were the opposite end of the left-hand block to each other, with two flats in between. He took the steps up with a gait as casual as he could muster, his heart in his throat. Feeling exposed, he started to walk along the landing, mere metres away from Darcie's door. Then another opened, his immediate neighbour. Key in hand, Conners fumbled with the lock and managed to scoot inside Darcie's place just as footfall and voices sounded further along the walkway.

Conners leaned, suddenly panting, with his back against the door, trying to listen. Inside his chest, his heart pounded and outside he registered another pounding; that of fists on the next door along. He heard the elderly owner open the door and then a gravelly voice announcing to her that he was 'an FBI agent'.

Conners doubled up, as though he'd taken a gut punch from a giant fist. He could feel blood rushing in his ears. He knew they'd come for him, eventually, but he just hoped that it would be when he was old and grey and had done something to, in a small way, make amends for his mistakes and the deadly chaos it had caused. This was too soon, far too soon. He'd had what, three years of living as Cal Conners and before that just five hiding as himself? He took a deep breath. He was going to escape; he had to because all other options were far too unsavoury to comprehend.

He listened, ear pressed against the door, to the FBI agent asking questions and the resident next door offering her replies. Their voices were muffled, yet he could hear the agent's tone becoming terse. He heard the words 'Thank you', and then footsteps. Conners moved away from the door, in case the agent could see his shadow underneath it.

Darcie's bell was broken, so the agent banged his fist against the wood, making the flimsy door shake.

'This is the FBI. Please open up,' the same voice barked through the thin wood.

Back against the wall, next to the door, Conners was frozen. His two options were run or hide, and, unless he could squeeze into Darcie's wardrobe, there was no realistic place to hide. Taking slow, considered steps he started to move towards the back of the apartment, cursing as his Crocs made miniscule squeaks on the tiles.

The banging continued. 'This is the FBI, please open the—'

'Can I help you?' Darcie's voice too was loud and unmistakable. 'Stop beating on my door! You break it you replace it.'

Conners relaxed slightly. Darcie was formidable, and he was lucky that she had chosen to like him.

'Are you Darcie?'

'Who wants to know?'

'I'm an agent with the FBI.'

'And?'

'Is this your apartment, mam?' The FBI agent asked.

'Why are you asking me, you should know, you're the FBI.'

Conners frowned. That was a point. Surely the FBI knew who lived in the complex; they had access to records and databases of all sorts. Why was the agent going from door to door if he was looking for him? Why ask if she was Darcie, he'd surely have used her full name – Darcie Molloy – unless he didn't know her full name, unless he had just been given her name by the woman next door. If that was the case, was he really FBI at all?

'I'm going to need to search your apartment.'

Darcie bristled. 'Do you have a warrant?'

'Do you have something to hide?'

'No.'

'Just open up.' The voice had gone from authoritative to angry.

'No.'

'I said—'

'I think I need to call the cops and ask them to confirm your identity.'

'There's no need.'

Snowflake started to bark, then whined as though he was hurt.

'You kicked my dog!'

'Give me the damn key!' The agent's voice had now lost all trace of civility.

Conners clenched his fists, his fears becoming suddenly real. With the FBI he stood a chance; they had protocols, his life wouldn't be in danger, it would be merely his freedom they would take away. However, it wasn't the FBI who had come for him, it was 'them'. Against them there was nothing he could do.

There was a thud, as though something had been thrown at the door and it shuddered on its hinges. Conners panicked and scooted behind the breakfast bar. There was another, louder thud and this time the wood around the lock splintered and the door flew open. Conners heard the agent charge into the apartment.

The agent roared, 'Show yourself, Cal – I've got your lady!'

Conners was shaking, but even through his fear he realised that the fake agent was using his fake name – 'Cal'.

'I know you're here! We saw you entering the complex. Look, I'm a reasonable guy, I'll let the lovely Darcie go. On the count of three. One … two … three …'

Conners didn't move, there was no way he was going to give himself up, no way. Perhaps he could make it to the window and throw himself out. Sure, he'd get injured and break a bone or two, but it was still better than doing nothing.

'Cal, you're running out of time. You see, Darcie can't really breathe on account of my hand crushing her throat. If I keep squeezing, she dies. Or perhaps I'll just shoot her. If you want to stop that, you come out now.'

Frantically Conners' eyes searched the space for something he could use as a weapon. The handle of a heavy wok protruded from the door next to him.

'This is your last chance, Cal.'

Conners' hand reached for the wok.

'OK, so the dog gets it first!'

Conners stood, wok in hand below the level of the counter. He saw a huge man, in a black suit. His left hand was clamped around the back of Darcie's neck. His right held a handgun fitted with a suppressor. Conners said, 'I don't know who you think I am, but there's been some kind of mistake.'

'The mistake was yours for not cooperating and opening the goddamn door.' A smile appeared on the agent's face as he sized Conners up. Snowflake growled and the man's eyes flicked to the floor. 'You can shut it too!'

Conners saw the end of the gun traverse towards Snowflake, and an unexpected anger and outrage flared behind his eyes. His right arm started to move and then, before he knew it, he had acted. The wok sailed through the air at the man who claimed to be from the FBI. It hit him squarely in the chest, making him stumble and grunt. Darcie broke away, but the handgun fired.

A cocktail of sounds mixed as one in Conners' ears. The retort, sounding like a heavy book dropped on a tiled floor, was immediately followed by the sound of the 9mm round slamming into the floor, shattering ceramic, the yelp of the dog, Darcie screaming and, of course, the rushing of blood in his own ears.

Conners felt himself moving. His feet slammed into the floor as he closed the gap between himself and the man with the gun, the man who had threatened Darcie.

'Run!'

But Darcie didn't run. She swung a fist at the large man in the suit. He batted away her arm and shot her at point-blank range in the stomach. Darcie was propelled backwards, crumpling and skidding across the tiled floor.

'Ya bastard!' Conners yelled, pure guttural Yorkshire, the anger in his voice breaking through the phony accent. He crashed into the larger, suited, armed man, shoulder first like a rugby player and both men crashed to the floor. Both were winded, but the gunman's head also hit the tiles. There was a crack and Conners hoped it was the bloke's skull.

There was a momentary stillness, broken only by the whining of Snowflake.

Conners' eyes darted to Darcie. She'd come to a stop against the wall. Her left hand was clamped to her stomach. Her light-yellow top was now decorated with a blossoming red flower. Her right hand was reaching for her dog.

The man below him moved.

Conners didn't know how to fight, he'd never had to learn. But he knew how to shoot, in theory. He saw the man's gun had come loose from his hands. He pushed himself away from the large man and lunged for it. Hands were clamped around his right leg, but his own hand reached the gun. Conners managed to roll and point the pistol. The man looked up, Conners looked down and his hand shook as he pulled the trigger.

The man's head exploded. He instantly became limp.

'Cal …' Darcie's voice was raspy.

Shaking, Conners met her eyes and noticed that the red flower now covered all of her lower half.

Her eyes suddenly became wide, her right hand pointed at the door. 'Cal!'

There was a noise, which made Conners turn and as he did so another supressed round slammed into Darcie. Without hesitation, Conners pulled the trigger again and this time he shot the new gunman who had appeared behind him in the doorway. The man staggered and his gun arm started to drop. Conners got to his feet and now held the gun in a two-handed grip, as he'd seen on television, and fired again and again. The gunman fell backwards over the railings and to the unforgiving concrete a floor below.

Conners turned back, gun still raised, and saw that Darcie was still. The gun fell from his hand and he staggered towards her. Falling to his knees, numb, he cupped her face. He opened his mouth to speak, to say her name, but the words would not come. Grief had rendered him mute.

Snowflake started to lick Darcie's hand.

Had she been the one? Conners didn't know, but she had been someone and now she was nothing. Darcie was a memory, like him she was a ghost.

His hand felt glued to her face, he felt rooted to the spot. It took him every ounce of willpower to stand and turn away. He left her apartment, and when he reached his own, he saw that the door had been broken down. He rushed inside – a sense of urgency now taking over from shock – and, to his relief, found his grab bag was still beneath a pile of dirty shirts, under his bed.

Conners grabbed the bag and ran. With tunnel vision he sprinted along the walkway, down the steps and past the crowd of neighbours who were now gawking at the dead man on the ground. He again slipped out of the side exit and made for the alley. He looked right and saw the black SUV was still there, but the driver wasn't. Conners stopped. Surely, he couldn't risk running to his car. Someone would see him, wouldn't they? The driver had obviously heard the gunshots and then there would be the other residents and random gawkers. No. There was no way he could get into his car. He turned around, retraced his steps, and burst onto Breakers Way.

A sense of panic had now set in. What had he done? What had he caused? He understood his actions in his past life had led to the deaths of many, perhaps thousands, but now someone had died trying to save him, and she had died without knowing who he was, and what he had done. He started to shake, and his chest felt tight. Darcie was dead, and so was her killer. He concentrated on putting one foot in front of the other and made for the beach. Logic told him that he was dressed for the ocean, and that the sight of him carrying a black holdall would not look that out of place to a casual observer. Perhaps it contained scuba gear, or some other items he'd need for the water, and, most importantly, the man in the black SUV would not be able to follow him. He crossed Mandalay Beach Road once again, and cut between the beachfront houses; his only plan to leave the area. Then, in a blinding flash of clarity, he knew what he had to do. Hidden from the road, he paused in the shadow of the nearest house and retrieved a burner phone from his bag. He switched it on and from memory retrieved an email address and logged into a web-based email account he kept active. He tapped out a message, an SOS to someone he trusted, someone he knew would help him if he could.

Chapter 3

Düsseldorf, Germany

To distance themselves from the actions at the farmhouse, Tate and Plato darted south-west to Düsseldorf. The seventh-largest city in Germany was a good place to hide. Using Irish passports and credit cards, they booked into an anonymous business chain hotel on the city's newer, commercial west side. Their rooms were interconnected. Plato immediately set up his equipment and tried to find the assassin.

He opened a new command window on his laptop and accessed a database. He tapped in the parameters. 'Right, this is not exhaustive, but it's a list of all known Asian hitmen with suspected links to various triad and Tong factions, who have been active in the past two decades. I'm sending it to you.'

Tate picked up the tablet and tapped the screen as the list appeared. 'Thanks.'

As Tate wandered back through the door into his own room, Plato turned back to his computer and assessed the two screens. He was using the local Munster CCTV systems to attempt to back trace the Fiat and in doing so get a clearer image of the deadly delivery driver. Plato was stretching and thinking about making himself a cup of tea – wishing he'd not run out of Earl Grey – when a pop-up message appeared on his left screen. He clicked it. The alert was from the internet chat room he'd been monitoring. Another counter ticked down from ten.

'Jack, get back in here. Fang's making an announcement!'

'Posthumously?' Tate said as he came back into the room. He stared over Plato's shoulder as the counter hit two. Two seconds later, a new statement appeared, and Plato's eyes went wide as he read it aloud:

This is an official announcement from the non-anonymous – Fang Bao. I have confiscated the funds of the Ah Kong triad on behalf of The Democratic People's Republic of Korea. They will no longer tolerate the illegal and immoral activities of the Ah Kong, which serve to undermine this great nation. It is an affront to our dear Respected Leader. The Ah Kong are the first to be punished, they shall not be the last.

'Christ …' Tate muttered.

'I don't understand,' Plato said. 'What's the link between the triads and North Korea? And why has an Anglo–Chinese hacker agreed to work for Pyongyang?'

'I wonder what Fang's cut was?'

Plato slowly shook his head. 'Jack, would you steal from the Triads and publicly admit it?'

'No. Not unless I knew they definitely couldn't get to me.'

'But they did.'

'Someone did,' Tate replied.

'Who?'

'My money's on North Korea.'

'Loose ends.' Plato nodded. 'So our assassin may be North Korean?'

'Maybe, but unlikely. If he's caught, he leaves a trail. No, they'll have contracted in.'

'Either way, the Hak dynasty in Pyongyang has a two-billion-dollar windfall.'

'That'll make the UN happy,' Tate said flatly.

Plato shrugged. 'I'm not an expert on North Korea, but I know they're prohibited from conducting general trade and importing luxury goods.'

'Hence needing the triads' cash.'

'Exactly.' Plato saw from Tate's body language that he was deflated. They'd failed.

'I want to know who that was who tried to kill me,' Tate said.

*

The video link to London was secure, and the image on the monitor screen of Tate's controller at SIS aka MI6 – Pamela Newman – was sharp. She listened to Tate and Plato as they provided her with a brief after-action report on the failed mission to extract Fang Bao.

Newman took a sip of tea before she started to talk. 'Well, this hasn't gone to plan, has it?'

Tate didn't reply, there was no need.

Newman continued. 'Prior to this attack we had no inclination that Fang was aligned to Pyongyang. Either he wasn't, and something made him change his allegiance, or he was, and we didn't know about it.' Newman finished her tea and on the video screen she pushed her cup and saucer to one side. 'Neill, there is something about this which I don't understand.'

'Yes?' Plato said.

'Why would such a skilled individual, such as Fang, have to travel to meet the triads to drain their accounts, why couldn't he have done it remotely from elsewhere?'

'I've been thinking about that too.' Plato nodded, sagely. 'Some of his followers thought he'd developed a digital super key, and the only conclusion I can come to is that it had to be manually inserted into whoever's network it was designed to break.'

'So, it was carried on a USB?'

'Not necessarily, it may have been carried in his head.'

'What do you mean, Neill?'

'He may have memorised the code for it and was able to simply type it into the computer we found at the farmhouse.'

'Is that feasible?'

'For someone with Fang's ability, yes.'

'Can this act be repeated?'

'I have no idea.' Plato shrugged. 'We don't even know if this super key ever existed or if Fang simply hacked their systems.'

'Well, I sincerely hope the key was merely a code in his head.' Newman wet her lips. 'We don't know how or when Fang started to work for the North Koreans, and now we never will. If the North Koreans have access to this technology or whatever it was Fang may have created, there is nothing to prevent Pyongyang from bankrupting their enemies, including those who placed sanctions on them.'

Tate felt a chill as the full impact of Newman's words registered. 'That's not good.'

'Not good at all, Jack.' Newman picked up her reading glasses and slipped them on. 'I have a file on the Ah Kong triads. Have either of you heard of them?'

'No,' Tate and Plato both replied.

Newman lifted a sheet of A4 from her desk. 'The Ah Kong, which translates into English as The Company, ran the heroin trade in Europe from the seventies to nineties. Its founder members were from Singapore and had bases in Amsterdam and Bangkok. The 14K triads took over their operations as Ah Kong leaders were gradually assassinated, imprisoned or died of old age.'

'So, this triad group doesn't exist?' Tate said, with confusion in his voice.

Newman looked up at the screen. 'That is the interesting part, and forgive me if I sound rather vague, but this additional intel is very new to me too. There was a core group of young and ambitious Ah Kong members who vowed to restart their operations. They were led by the sons of several of the founding individuals. This new unit was then, however, targeted by several European intelligence operations before they simply walked away from the business and vanished. Then, five years ago, more than two decades later, they reappeared in the Chinese city of Shenyang.'

'I'm going to ask the obvious question,' Tate said. 'Where had they been for twenty years?'

'North Korea.'

'I see.'

'It's a dark secret that from the late seventies up until the mid-noughties, North Korea sought to lessen the financial impact of UN sanctions against them by propping itself up with income derived allegedly from sales of its locally produced poppy crop. Farmers were ordered to plant poppies, which state-controlled factories then processed. Allegedly, the Ah Kong grew the trade for the North Koreans and then persuaded the leadership to switch to the production of methamphetamine. For a while China and the Far East was awash with high-quality crystal meth, but then production abruptly tailed off.'

'The triads fell out with Pyongyang and moved to China?'

Newman removed her glasses. 'That is what we now believe. Hak Jong Un, the current ruler of the North, decided to distance himself from past initiatives, especially when he was both courted by the US president to be more open and under pressure from Beijing to stop the flow of drugs. I believe Fang Bao was ordered to target the Ah Kong to cripple their operations.'

Tate remained silent, not quite knowing what to say.

'Our mission failed, and there was nothing either of you could have done to change that outcome. Return to London.'

Newman ended the video call, Tate exhaled deeply and got to his feet. 'She's right, you know.'

'About what?'

'If Pyongyang has whatever it was Fang's developed. But why on earth would Fang steal so much money just to give it to the North Koreans?'

'You do know he was highly anti-capitalist.'

'Even for two billion US dollars?'

'It's ideological then; you know he did it for the motherland.'

'He's ethnic Chinese.'

'Perhaps he wanted to kickstart North Korea to effect change?'

'With their existing leader?'

'No idea.'

Tate shrugged. 'Me neither, I grew out of politics.'

San Francisco, California

The room was dark and the furnishings sparse and sharp, as though they had been selected for their aesthetic appearance rather than comfort. A blackout blind obscured the large window which otherwise would have framed a stunning panorama of the city below. It was the first time he had been in the room, but the second time in a decade he had met his uncle. As Roe waited for the older man to enter, his mind wandered back to the events of two months before, when he had been activated. A sleeper no more, a US agent no more, he had finally become a weapon of change.

The man, dressed in black with stark white hair, sat with his hands in his lap. 'You are perhaps wondering why I have summoned you here?' the man said, his voice stronger than his aged appearance would have suggested. The old man's lips momentarily formed a thin smile. 'I understand it was not an easy matter for you to give your former life up based upon the promise of a man you had not seen in ten years.'

'It was my duty, and it is an honour.'

'Quite. It is now time to commence the operation. This has been a long time in the planning, but, like you, it is ready. That was the reason I contacted you. It is why you are here. Do you have any questions before I continue?'

'Yes, Uncle.'

'Go ahead.'

'Am I the only survivor?'

'You and every other man in your convoy died when your prisoner was taken by an unknown force. You all will, one imagines, be mourned for an hour or so by fat men in ill-fitting suits at your employer's office in Langley. A suitably doctored cadaver was left in your place. It was convincing enough. It was burnt in the fire which engulfed the convoy. Its teeth were altered to match your dental records. So, you are dead, but not yet alive.'

'Because I don't have an identity?'

'Correct. A situation we shall now remedy.' Gu Joon inclined his head, and briskly clapped his hands twice, the sound surprisingly loud. 'You may come in.'

The door behind Roe opened and he heard footsteps. Roe fought both his natural instincts and his training; he did not turn to face the newcomer, to do so would be an insult to his uncle's hospitality. The man drew level with Roe's chair but remained standing in front of Gu. Roe noted the man was the same height and build as himself. What abruptly struck Roe, however, was the resemblance to him did not stop with his stature. The man had his face.

'Have you brought all the documents I requested?'

'I have, Uncle,' the man replied.

'Place them on the table for me.'

'Yes, Uncle.'

Roe shifted slightly in his seat. He studied his doppelgänger putting a pile of documents on the table. He could see it included a passport and a driver's licence.

'Thank you.' Gu stood. Roe's doppelgänger started to bow, but didn't complete the action as a pair of silenced rounds tore through his chest and head, fired from a Beretta Gu held in his right hand.

Roe had no time to react or to hide his horror as the dead doppelgänger dropped.

Gu sat once more, placed his gun on the desk and pushed it aside, as though it had become distasteful. His eyes came to rest on Roe. 'There were two men, both dedicated to the cause. This one, now deceased, and the other, who will on my command on board a flight from Seoul. This one, Dan Tae, was a US citizen of first-generation Korean descent, as you are. He was an only child from Fairfax County, Virginia. His parents were the victims of an appalling robbery/homicide two years ago. He is dead so you may live. These men were chosen, Roe, because of their uncanny resemblance to you, which I instructed be made even more so by cosmetic surgery. You now have a new identity which will hold up to all but DNA testing.'

'Thank you, Uncle.' Roe had regained his composure. He was impressed by the man's ruthlessness, cunning and commitment.

'Kwang,' – Gu used Roe's first name, it was the only time he had ever done so – 'this other man may have called me Uncle, but that was purely an honorific. He meant nothing to me. You are my sister's son. You are my blood, my only blood. This quest of ours is because of our spilt blood, never forget that. The blood that was spilt by the rulers of North Korea. It is because of blood we will succeed.'

The sound of the door opening behind him brought Roe back to the present. He stood and nodded as his uncle, Gu Joon, entered the room – his gait straight-backed and military. Roe waited until the older man was seated on an uncomfortable-looking armchair before he sat too.

'In the United States, the men I have contracted have failed me. What I require is their involvement cleaned away permanently and for you to complete their original instructions.'

'Which were?'

'You will locate and capture a British citizen by the name of Colin Jericho. He is currently using the alias Cal Conners. You will commence this immediately. On the table in the corner, you will see a large envelope that contains your briefing pack and further instructions. Do you have any questions?'

'No, Uncle.'

The old man nodded. 'Excellent, that is what I suspected.'

Chapter 4

Fresno, California

The office was corporate, and any visitor would be hard pushed to understand the true nature of the organisation that rented it. Behind the logos and customer endorsements for their alarm and CCTV systems, ES Security was the front for a far more hazardous and lucrative business. Tony Carter, CEO and founder, had welcomed Roe with a crushing handshake and bid him to take a seat in his plush office.

'Listen,' Carter said, his incomer's inner-city, East Coast accent scratching Roe's ears. 'Firstly I've gotta apologise for our operation so far. I personally selected the men for this assignment, and I just don't understand how we lost two of them.'

Roe didn't respond. His briefing pack had stated that Carter was a 'talker'. Roe had met his type before, vets who exaggerated and embellished their military careers for financial gain. In Carter's case it was to attract contracts and the men to undertake them, but those he attracted were more in the category of military-trained, hired muscle than 'operators'.

Carter continued, 'Look, Mr Ho, what I'm saying to you is that we need more time to catch this clown.'

Roe nodded. If Conners was a clown, then that made Carter's operation a circus, which he thought was apt. 'How many staff have you got working for you?'

'On the home security side?'

'Let's start there.'

Carter smiled, proud no doubt to run his mouth off to impress the man sent by his mysterious client. 'I've got a fleet of nine vans, with a trained technician in each. One guy is one of your people.'

'My people?'

'From the local Hmong Chinese community.'

'Good.'

Carter continued talking, unaware of Roe's sarcasm. 'Then there's an installations manager, office manager and an accountant. I try to keep staffing to the essentials, mean and lean. I take care of hiring – the personnel stuff – myself; I mean who needs an HR department – am I right?'

'Is this business separate from the business we hired you to undertake?'

'Absolutely.' Carter bobbed his head. 'The home and commercial security operation is completely legitimate. Heck, I've got a reputation for it. ES Security is the leading local business in its field, and, as Fresno is the most populous inland city in California, that makes us a pretty big deal. Look, any guy I contract to work for me on the "black side" is under strict orders not to say anything to anyone, or else.'

'Or else?'

'I'm sure you know what I mean, Mr Ho. The trick is whilst ES Security is a modern, digitally up-to-date operation, fully accountable and audited, etc., the other is analogue. It's in my head or on paper and can't be traced, hell there's barely enough paper to start a campfire. I could be raided by the FBI or Homeland or whoever today and they'd find nothing here at all.'

'What about other locations?'

'Such as?'

'Where are you storing details of our operation?'

'As I say, I have the odd piece of paper, just enough to act as insurance, if you know what I mean, at home. And again, it's so close to my goddamn fire that even if the FBI or the cops come ringing the bell, I can have it burning before they're breaking down the door. But once the operation is over, and I get paid in full, I burn it all. No record, no trace, no comeback and everyone is happy.'

'My employer, Mr Carter, is not at all happy. In fact, he is extremely unhappy with the progress so far. He has started to wonder if you have become a liability to his own operation.'

Carter held up his palms in a placatory manner. 'Look, I know how things have gone. I understand the optics, but this isn't an easy operation. Your boss insisted this was a simple task. A straightforward snatch and deliver on our part of some untrained average Joe. Then look what happens; the mark goes and slots two of my guys in Oxnard.'

'Then vanishes,' Roe added.

'Decisions were made upon instructions received. Instructions received from your boss, I don't need to add. I kept him informed and he agreed to each and every action my men took. Hell, it's easy to be a helicopter here, to hover over the action and criticise. Your boss just has to wire the cash, it's me who has to take the heat and console the relatives.'

'You lost two men. How many were on the team?'

'Three.'

'Where is your third man?' This was a loose end.

'South of the border. He's former Mexican military. He won't talk.'

'I understand.' There was no point chasing, it would take too long.

'Now, Mr Ho, if your boss wants me to continue the operation I will, but, given the amount of heat this guy is now drawing, it's gonna cost more.'

'How much more?'

'An extra fifty per cent, on top of what we agreed. That'll put my best men on it.'

'I thought we had your best men already working on it?'

Carter's face reddened. 'Look, what can I say? Your boss told me it was an easy op. To be frank, Mr Ho, I'm the injured party here. It's my men and my reputation that's suffered. I've gotta consider my position on the circuit as a provider of quality assignments. The men I contracted were for an abduction, now it's something else. Now we've gotta locate the guy, abduct him and avoid the cops.'

Roe ignored the outburst. 'When could these men get here?'

'I've already spoken to my go-to guy, and he's in.'

'Go-to guy?' This was a complication.

'Yep.' Carter turned a photograph that was on his desk around so his visitor could see it. 'Big piece of meat on the left of me, Jamie Mason. He'll not fail you. He's what you call a specialist in these matters. He's like a dog with a bone, never gives up until he's got his man. He'll handpick his team once I've briefed him in person.'

'Mason served with you?'

'Sure did, in the Screaming Eagles. Give me the go-ahead and I'll meet with him today.'

'Who else knows about your agreement with my employer?'

'Just me, Mason and my cash drawer.'

Roe reached down and swung his pilot case onto his lap. From this he withdrew a thick envelope. He lay it on Carter's desk. 'We'll pay thirty per cent extra. Here is half the extra money you want. You'll get the rest once the operation is a success. Now call your man.'

'Agreed.' Carter took the envelope and his eyes widened as he inspected the contents, 'It's like you've got a sixth sense, Mr Ho. I'm a fan of the way you do business.'

Roe stood his pilot case back on the floor and remained silent as he watched the man quickly check the notes.

'OK, I'm not gonna count it all. I trust you, and your employer.'

'Call your man. This is urgent.' Roe crossed his arms, an action which together with his facial expression told Carter he was waiting.

'Yep.' Carter squirreled away the envelope into the jacket hanging on his seat back, then opened a desk drawer and removed a small metal box. From this he withdrew a phone. 'It's a burner, but you can never be too careful, know what I mean?'

'I do.'

Carter powered up the handset and tapped in a number. Roe could hear the line connect and ring twice before it was answered by a gruff voice.

'Hey, Mase, I got that client with me, the one I told you about. That's right, the important one.' Carter looked at Roe and smiled. 'Listen, he needs to move on this ASAP. Can you be at my place for eleven? OK? Yep, see you then.'

Roe waited until Carter powered down the phone before he said, 'Your place?'

'Yep. Mase is an old friend of mine, it won't raise any eyebrows if he's seen at my place. Anyway, I turn off the cameras so it's all on the down-low.'

'I see.' Roe knew Carter lived alone on East Saginaw Way; it had been in his briefing pack.

Carter glanced at his wristwatch, a gaudy metallic lump that was meant to impress. 'Listen, Mr Ho, I need to be leaving if I'm gonna make that meeting. So, if you'll excuse me?'

'I will.' Roe stood and held out his hand. Carter swiftly stepped around the desk and held out his own. Roe let Carter grip his hand and start the shake. It was as crushing as before, and Roe tried not to smirk.

Roe left the office and noted the receptionist's empty desk as he passed. He was glad they hadn't met, because collateral damage was never pleasant. He stepped out of the building and crossed the parking lot to the one used by the company next door. He

61

had not wanted Carter or anyone from the company to see his car, even though it was rented using false papers given to him by Gu. It was parked nose in, which went against his usual operating procedure but, in this instance, it was essential if he was to maintain a visual on the front door he had just exited through.

The car's interior was warm, but he had endured far worse on operations and sat with the AC off, and the windows open a crack. The temperature of LA was nothing compared to the humid jungles of South America and Asia or the blistering deserts of the Middle East. Roe's mind drifted back whilst he waited to his time in the US Army. At each stage there had been racism, both overt and implied. The further he ascended, from his original unit to passing selection for Delta before finally being 'asked' as a tier one operative to be part of the CIA's 'Activity' division, the less overt the racism became, yet still it remained. The most recent nickname his 'brothers' had called him was Hak Jong-Thin, often shortened to 'Hak' – the family name of the corpulent ruler of North Korea. They thought it was highly amusing, they also thought that he had taken it as they had expected it to be received – as a joke. Roe had not. The fact that, even at the pinnacle of the Special Forces community, he was defined not by his ability and intelligence, but by his race disgusted him. It was not that he was ashamed of his heritage; on the contrary, he was furious that these men, these soldiers, these operators, these brothers would use his race as though it were some type of insult. That was something that he could not and would not ever forgive or forget. So, when, as a sleeper agent, he finally received the order to 'activate', he felt nothing when the men around him were slaughtered when the team hired by his uncle extracted both him and his Chinese prisoner.

At that moment the old Roe had died to be reborn as a man who was a weapon for his true country, an implement of death and a force of revenge.

Movement behind the front door of Carter's office brought

Roe's focus fully back to the present. He had been waiting for exactly nine minutes when he saw the office door of the security company open, and Carter step out. He was wearing the suit jacket that had been on the back of his chair and he patted the chest pocket for reassurance as he made for his car, a red Porsche 911 drop top which was parked in the 'reserved for MD' space. Roe knew where Carter lived, but didn't know if he was actually going there. In an ideal world Roe would have affixed a tracker to the Porsche and then followed the digital trail from a distance, but he did not want to leave any trace behind of his involvement, so would rely on his training to maintain his tail. Fresno was not a city he knew well at all, but a red 911 was a hard car to miss in downtown traffic.

Roe waited until Carter had started his engine and dropped the power hood. With a refined purr, the Porsche reversed out of its space and headed for the street. Roe waited to see which way it turned before he followed, in his much more mundane Malibu.

The red Porsche drew some glances as it growled along the streets of Fresno. This part of the city was a huge grid system and again Roe wished he'd used a tracker so that he could have followed Carter via a parallel street, but that would have meant him affixing it to the sports car and potentially being seen doing so.

The Porsche joined East Dakota Avenue, which they followed for a while before it turned north onto North Palm Avenue and then took a turning to East Saginaw Way. Before following onto East Saginaw Way, Roe looked down the street. It was much narrower than the others they had used and was tree-lined with a variety of sprawling evergreens, giving it an almost country feel. Roe slowed as much as he dared and let the Porsche move further away. Now he realised that the street was just wide enough for two vehicles to pass and had no sidewalk on either side. The road was bordered immediately by the gardens of the properties, which were in many cases half-hidden by trees. In some parts the branches met with their neighbours opposite, creating a high, green canopy. Through what gaps there were in the foliage Roe noted that the properties were long and low, some 'cabin style' and others 'ranch style', but each different from the next. He carried on along the road and saw the Porsche make a left turn into the driveway of Carter's house. Roe carried on past the house and cast a quick glance at the target address. Like its neighbours it was a single-storey construction in what the local real estate agents would call 'cabin style'. The greenery around the property was unkempt, but the drive itself was spotless concrete and the walls of the house looked to be freshly painted in a dark cream. The lack of high fences on either side of the street meant that neighbours on opposite sides of the street overlooked each other and was, he imagined why the shrubbery and green stuff was left to grow. Carter's neighbour, however, had a clear view of sight from his own front door, down his drive and into the street. And that was a concern for Roe, but there was nothing that could be done about that now.

He drove on, the houses now getting larger and taking up bigger plots of land. Carter may well have the aspirational sportscar, but he lived at the cheap end of the street. But these things would soon be meaningless, Roe mused. He reached an intersection and went across. The trees now became more spaced out, the properties were larger and the road itself became wider.

Roe realised that there was nowhere that he could park up and observe Carter's house from and there was also nowhere he could leave the car to go in on foot. So the only course of action left open to him was to blindly wait out of location until the time of the meeting and then drive on to the property, blocking in both Carter's Porsche and whatever Mason was driving. Roe checked his watch, a functional Casio. There was still a little over quarter of an hour to go. Roe took the first right he could, then drove south for ten minutes before heading west and then north. As far as cities went it seemed fine, but he had no illusions; after his mission was completed, he'd not be able to live in the US. Canada at a push, but much more likely he'd end up in the land of his ancestors, Korea. There was nothing wrong with that, he thought as pride burned his chest.

He finished his loop and was once again on Carter's street. It was twelve minutes past the allotted meeting time, and he wondered if Mason was professional enough to be punctual. He needn't have worried because as he drew close to Carter's cabin, he saw a second vehicle on the drive; it was a custom gun-metal grey Ford F150 Raptor.

Roe slowed his Malibu and pulled onto the drive. He slipped on a pair of black rubber gloves, then stepped out of the car with his pilot case in his left hand, and his right inside his jacket, looking like an insurance salesman adjusting his wallet. He passed first the F150, then the Porsche and rang the bell. He waited, hearing voices inside. A shadow appeared behind the frosted full-length glass pane of the front door and grew larger until it opened.

Carter's expression was curious. 'Mr Ho?'

Roe's hand was out of his jacket; it was holding a handgun and that was pointed at Carter's face. Roe's Ruger Mark IV .22 semi-automatic had an integral suppressor which, in the right conditions, was no louder than a book dropped on a wooden floor. Before Carter could comprehend what was happening, Roe fired twice. Both rounds entered Carter's brain and he fell to the floor with a thud.

Roe stepped over the corpse, entered the house and shut the door. He left his pilot case in the hall before taking the ninety-degree turn which led him immediately into a cavernous, open-plan living area with a wooden floor, wooden-panelled walls, and a matching ceiling with architectural wooden beams. Two arches at the far end gave way to what appeared to be a kitchen and a bedroom. It looked like a mini 'hipster barn' except the man who had been sitting in one of a pair of burgundy leather La-Z-Boys facing the brick fireplace was not a hipster. He did have a thick beard and an impressive amount of hair, but his bulky frame was covered in acid wash double denim – jeans and a short-sleeved shirt. More importantly, he was already on his feet and had snapped off a shot with a serious-looking chrome handgun.

Roe instantly recognised the weapon as a Desert Eagle and threw himself forward and further into the room as a thunderous retort reverberated from the floor and wall and a heavy magnum round tore a hole through the wall he'd just passed. Roe landed on the polished wooden floor and half turned, half rolled, bringing his Ruger up and acquiring Mason. However, his opponent was fast for his size and the Desert Eagle had started to move towards Roe. Both men fired at once. Roe's round struck Mason in the chest, and he stumbled backwards towards the La-Z-Boys. Mason's own round missed Roe's head by less than a foot and smashed into the fireplace. Roe fired again and again struck Mason in the chest, who now fell backwards over the nearest reclining chair. His gun dropped from his hand and clattered away under the coffee table.

Roe got to his feet. He'd had to use the bell, he couldn't risk breaking or sneaking in, being spotted and raising louder alarm bells. What was unfortunate, however, was that he had clearly misjudged Mason. The man may well have been pushing fifty, but he was fast, and unafraid to open fire. Roe knew he had minutes before the police arrived – there was no way the neighbours would ignore the retort of a 0.50 cal round, but he knew what he was looking for was in the room, close to the fireplace.

Mason was lying on his side, raggedly panting with his arms extended in front of him. Roe slowly walked over to the large, denim-clad mercenary. He was happy; he'd fired twice and hit the man twice in the torso. Roe's ears were ringing and he worked his jaw to restore his hearing, knowing that Mason's own hearing would be far worse. Roe said, casually, 'Hello, Mason.'

'Who … the hell … are you?' Mason spat, as pain and anger punctuated his words.

'It's need to know, and you don't.'

Roe raised his Ruger; there was no need for Mason to live any longer.

Mason kicked out with his long left leg and the tip of his work boot struck Roe's right ankle. Roe fired a millisecond later, just as his balance had started to alter, just as he started to fall sideways. His round missed its target and buried itself in the nearest chair. Roe slammed into the ground, the air bursting out of his lungs. Mason was now scrambling towards him. Roe tried to push himself to his feet, but a giant fist slammed into the side of his head. His vision momentarily greyed out and he fell back. He managed to roll away, grabbing the stone fireplace for support, and pulled himself upright. Mason was directly in front of him, eyes narrow with fury and fists up. Roe realised that the man must have been wearing Kevlar or perhaps the small calibre rounds of the Ruger had not been enough to put him down, or perhaps both.

'Come on, boy!' Mason's words were rage tinged as they flew from his mouth.

Roe took a step back, Mason took the invite and stepped forward. He launched a left hook, which Roe ducked and then followed up with a quick, straight right. But Roe was faster and sprang forward into the punch before Mason had enough space to plant it. As Roe did this, his right knee drove up into Mason's exposed groin. Before Mason could understand what was happening, he was doubling up. Roe darted around the larger man now, grabbed his head and drove it into the unforgiving stone fireplace. He backed away as Mason rested, his face pressing against the rough ornamental rock. Roe collected his Ruger from the floor and shot Mason in the back of the head. The dead man dropped into the hearth.

Roe tactically advanced to the kitchen; it was clear, but if it hadn't been he mused it would have been too late. He then inspected the bedroom – empty too. He walked back to Mason's body, gave it a casual glance then collected his pilot case from the hall and put his Ruger inside. He stepped past the dead man to the glass-topped coffee table, separating his chair from the second. The table was covered in a series of handwritten sheets and several 10×8 photographs. Roe studied the prints. They were of his target, Cal Conners. He left the papers and prints where they were for the moment whilst he conducted a 360° visual scan of the space. Apart from the twin chairs in this room, a king-sized bed in the bedroom and a functional dining table set in the kitchen, the cabin was unfurnished, as though Carter had either just moved into the property from somewhere far smaller or he was in the process of moving out and his belongings had just been packed, or perhaps he just didn't care for furniture and decorations. Whatever the reason, the only difference it made to Roe was it meant the place was easier to search.

He found what he was looking for almost immediately. Directly in front of him, part of the hearth seemed a fraction out of line, dislodged it seemed by Mason's dead weight. Roe rolled Mason to one side, then scrutinised it by running his finger along the join between the bricks. He could tell there was a void below. He took hold of a brick and gently lifted it. It came up and he had to use both hands as it pulled with it two more bricks by its side. He placed the brick cover on the floor and looked at the square hole. It was roughly ten inches deep, lined with smooth concrete and just wide enough to accommodate a pile of letter-sized paper. Roe pulled out the papers and found that underneath these were six bound bundles of $100 bills. Spoils of war, an added bonus he'd not pass up. He put the cash in his pilot case, next to his Ruger. Then he added the papers to the pile on the table, which he butted together into an inch-thick ream. Removing a set of his own documents from his case, Roe laid these on the table next to Carter's. He inspected the two piles. The writing was a match. his employer's forger had done a commendable job. Roe placed Carter's papers into his case, then took the fake documents and slotted them into Carter's hidey-hole. He hefted the brick cover back into place, but was careful to leave a few millimetres of paper protruding from underneath.

Case in hand, Roe left the lounge and went back into the hall. He searched Carter's body and retrieved the envelope of cash he had handed him earlier. Roe slipped this back into his own pocket, then opened the front door and stepped out onto the drive. He closed the door, pilot case in hand like an insurance salesman, started his rental car and drove away along East Saginaw Way as the sound of approaching sirens reached his ears.

Chapter 5

London

Plato was tired. He knew he had no right to be, but nevertheless he felt wiped out, burnt out, even though it wasn't him that had done the hard lifting on the mission. It certainly wasn't him who'd been shot at. Plato stirred his Earl Grey, slowly blew across the surface of the liquid, and then took a moment to breathe in the aroma. It was still too hot to drink, so he bit on a Fig Roll as he gazed out of his kitchen window at the dark, wet London sky. He'd missed his tea and biscuits and had underestimated how many he'd needed to take to Germany, well that was something he wouldn't do again when he was in the field. If he was ever in the field again, he reminded himself. He'd never wanted to be a field agent, but had to admit to himself that when he wasn't feeling scared to death it was actually quite exciting and although he was doing exactly the same work for MI6 as he had been at his office in Vauxhall Cross, he felt that being with E Squadron overseas made him feel as though he was contributing in a measurable manner.

Something caught his eye in the garden below – the garden he shared with the three other flats which made up the large

Victorian house he lived in. A cold fear engulfed him. What if they had found him? What if the Ah Kong triads had traced him to London and were after him? He knew he should do something, he had to move away from the light, from the window, but he was rendered immobile like a block of granite. He saw the move-ment again, a flash of auburn and then the security light rigged up by the chap in flat 1, who always wore shorts even in winter, blinked on. A pair of foxes were illuminated as they calmly trotted across the lawn.

Plato laughed out loud, then realised that his window was open a crack and he must have sounded to his neighbours like a cackling lunatic. He continued to chuckle, although quieter now as his mind wandered back to when he was a child, living in Brighton. His house then had been Victorian too, but, unlike his current London pad, had been split into two. His mother and he had the top floor and Mr Farley had the bottom. His neighbour didn't believe in curtains and Plato had vivid memories of seeing the man plugged into to an electric violin and spiritedly playing whilst he whirled around his lounge looking to all passers-by like a gyrating madman. He remembered telling his mum that he thought Mr Farley was 'mad'. Her reply was: 'Who isn't, dear?'

Plato sipped his tea and moved into his own lounge. He pulled his personal iPhone out of a drawer and switched it on. Just like Jack and the others, he had not taken any item with him that could be traced back to his true identity. He readied himself for the numerous texts and answerphone messages from his mum, who didn't understand that when he told her he was 'away on business' he couldn't be contacted, unless it was an emergency, and she rang his office. The number she had was for a trained MI6 operator who would intercept the call pretending to be some non-descript government department. There were twelve text messages, which he read in turn – each one becoming longer but all of them explaining that she felt he was neglecting her and why hadn't he called her? They also detailed who she'd seen in

Sainsbury's and what the doctor had said. Plato sighed. He loved his mum but sometimes felt she played up her own loneliness and ailments and acted like a pensioner although she was barely into her sixties. He then listened to the five voicemails she had left. They were of a similar vein. He checked the time. It was after nine and he knew from experience that it was too late to call her. That and he was too tired to have a rational conversation as her 'uncaring son'. He'd call her in the morning. Plato checked his email. The usual junk and spam clogged up his inbox, which he deleted but then he saw a message which made him stop, and blink and think. Was what he reading possible? He read it again.

Plato read the email for a third time, and still could not believe both what it said and its implications. Spoof emails were commonplace, but this account was unknown to anyone but a select few. It was an account which he rarely used because he didn't trust unencrypted email. In fact, he'd contemplated abandoning the address altogether, but he hadn't, which was lucky, because it was the email address family and old friends had. Here was an email, sent two days before, purporting to be from such an old friend. Indeed, if the sender of the message was who he said he was, this was an extremely serious matter.

Plato sat back and finished his tepid tea. He collected his laptop from his bedroom and now opened the email on that. He started to run a trace on the message, to see if the server and IP address it was sent from had been altered or hidden. It hadn't. As far as he could tell, the email had been sent from a mobile device in Los Angeles, California. Miles away from the UK, and miles away specifically from where its sender had drowned a decade before.

Plato's fatigue had vanished. He sprang to his feet, made another pot of tea and grabbed a packet of Fig Rolls. He had to reply, there was no way he could not. He had to know if what he had read was as real as the emotions it had stirred. Plato decided his reply had to be a short, inquisitive sentence that would require knowledge of a specific event and a shared memory in order for the receiver to craft a reply of his own.

Plato tapped out his sentence, pressed Send and gazed at his screen, willing a reply to arrive, and knowing that if it did it wouldn't be instant.

After half an hour of sitting and staring, he left the room and went to run a bath. He wanted to talk to someone and to explain what he'd received, but he couldn't do that until his dead friend replied, could he? Plato was wide awake; it was just ten in the evening – still early for some. He dialled Tate's personal number; a number he had in his head and not recorded anywhere, but, even so, he used WhatsApp.

'What gives?' Tate answered on the third ring. In the background, Plato could hear noise. It sounded like he was watching wrestling on the television. 'Are you missing me already?'

'Hi, Jack. Look, I know this is odd, but if it's real I have to take action.'

'Have you been drinking?'

'I've been drinking Earl Grey. Listen.'

'Yes. What is it?'

'I've received an email from a dead man.'

'Was he a Nigerian prince?' Tate chuckled on the other end of the line.

'No. Have you ever heard of Colin Jericho?'

'Brother of Chris?'

Plato was confused. 'Chris Jericho?'

'The first WWE Universal Champion.'

'No, Jack.' Plato sighed. 'Colin Jericho was a brilliant chemical engineer. A genius. We were at uni together. I joined the Secret Intelligence Service, and he went into some hush-hush government weapons research programme.'

'And he's dead?'

'He was flying his Cessna from Shoreham. It ditched a few miles out to sea; his body wasn't recovered. Colin was officially declared dead.'

'And now he's not dead?'

'I don't know. Look, I needed to tell someone about this, and if he is alive, well, it's got to be classified or something, hasn't it?'

'Has it?'

'Yes, it has to be because it means he faked his own death.'

'Or he was abducted by aliens.'

Plato ignored Tate's comment. 'He always wanted to do something special, to change the world. He was bloody single-minded. There was a film he obsessed about, an Ealing comedy starring Alec Guinness – *The Man in the White Suit*. Do you know it?'

'I may have seen it on TV as a kid.'

'It's about a chemist who invents an indestructible fabric, only to be hounded out of town by all the mill owners.'

'And this email you got mentioned the film?'

'Yes. It was signed as Sidney Stratton. That's the role Guinness played, and that's the character Colin identified with.'

'Who else knew he liked this film?'

Plato shrugged. 'We're talking over fifteen years ago now, when we were studying. A few friends, maybe, but no one knew Colin was saved in my Nokia at the time as Sidney.'

'It's pretty hard to fake a plane crash; it's not as though he walked into the sea like Reggie Perrin.'

'Reggie Perrin?'

'It was something my dad watched. So why, if it is him, has he decided to come back from the dead now?'

'He wants my help, Jack. He says he's being chased by people who want what he knows.'

'What does he know?'

'I guess all the designs for the projects he worked on at the Ministry of Defence. He wants to come home.'

Tate's voice now sounded serious. 'Neill, you know more about spoofs than me, but you still need to report it to Newman. Even if it's not him, it's someone who knows of your link to him, and they could be trying to compromise you.'

'That's what I thought. I'll email Pamela and ask to see her first thing in the morning.'

'Goodnight then.'

'Yeah, goodnight.'

The call ended and Plato wandered back into his kitchen. He could now hear the foxes barking.

Santa Monica

It was hard to hide if everyone knew your face and was looking for you, which was why Conners had shaved and resorted to using his British accent. He'd managed to get a room in a motel on Ocean Park Boulevard by giving the old guy on the night-desk a sob story about losing his passport and an extra hundred dollars. If the guy was dubious, he didn't show it.

Conners knew that he couldn't stay at the place very long, in fact he wondered whether he had time for a shower, but knew that he had to. He removed his clothes and took the cheap motel cosmetics set and shaved, making a better job of it than he had in the McDonald's rest room with a pair of scissors. He once again saw his face and realised for the first time just how old he had started to become. He was mid-thirties, but the stress of the situation had made his eyes sink and dark circles form under them. He rinsed his face in the sink and decided against trimming his hair – he'd fit in more with the beach-bum crowd if he kept it longer.

Conners stepped into the shower with Darcie's ghost. He remembered the first time they had met, their first kiss, and how – as the hot trickle of water hit his dirty body for the first time – they had shared a shower. He felt faint and fell back against the wall as his tears mixed with the water. He started to shake with remorse. A clichéd saying came to mind, which he now knew to be true: 'You don't know what you've got until its gone'. He now knew that he really had loved her, and he was the sole reason she was no longer alive. She had died trying to warn him, to save him, but she had never really known who he was, what he was, because if she had she would have thrown him out. He vomited into the shower pan, his last meal washing away with any hopes he once had.

He slid down the wall until he was sitting on the floor, the water cascading around him. What was the point of going on? What was the point of continuing to live? The life he had created over these past five years had been torn away; Cal Conners was a wanted man, yet so was Colin Jericho.

He stopped shaking and started to think as a cold, hard resolve spread through his body. What he held inside his head, the knowledge he had and the breakthroughs he knew could stop wars and save thousands, millions if put into the right hands. This was why he had to escape, this was why he had to go on, this was why he had to live. It was his purpose to deliver his knowledge to those who would use it wisely and he finally understood that had to be the country he grew up in. Nowhere and no one was perfect, but they were better than most, and certainly more moral than many. If he were to be captured by those who would use his discoveries for the dark side, well then, he would just have to end his life himself.

Conners pushed up to his feet, finished his shower, then, covered in two threadbare motel towels, sat on the sagging bed. Paranoid about being traced, he'd ditched his old burner phone and bought a new one at a small electronics shop. He took the packet containing the new phone from his bag.

He removed the burner from its hard plastic wrapping, cursing as it cut into his skin, inserted the sim and attached the battery. The salesman had told him how many minutes it had, but Conners was only interested in the fact that it could connect to the internet.

Pausing, now feeling paranoid, Conners rose from the bed and put the room's sole chair in front of the door to block the entry. He moved to the window and, standing to the side, glanced out.

He looked left and then right to ensure that no one was either watching him or about to grab him. Reassured, he slumped back onto the bed and switched on the phone. He accessed the internet and typed in the details of his web-based email, the one he had used to contact Neill Plato and checked his messages.

In addition to messages attempting to sell him Bitcoin, life insurance and eager Russian wives, there was one from Plato. A smile formed on his face and even before he read the reply, he felt a sense of relief hit him like the breaking surf.

He studied the message, which was addressed to Sidney. It asked him for more information in order to confirm that he was indeed Sidney Stratton. Conners smiled. Plato was being cautious in not mentioning his real name, and it was annoying if not unexpected that he would want more information before he believed the email was from a dead man who actually was no longer dead. The email asked Sidney to describe the place they used to go to have lunch every Friday. Conners shook his head slowly as the memory of the greasy-looking fish & chips shop appeared before him. He tapped out a reply: 'Mick's Fish. You usually ordered huss, chips and a pickled egg. I was a fat bugger back then and always had huss, chips and a battered sausage on the side.'

It abruptly occurred to Conners he could actually prove to Plato he was alive by using the same bloody evidence that was damning him in the first place. So, he added: 'I'm in California using the name Cal Conners. Check the LA TV news. There is a report on me, I'm being framed for homicide. You know I could never do this, but they are showing two photos of me. Run them through that fancy facial-recognition software I know you must have at work, and you'll see it is me! Now please, I need your help. You're the only person left I can trust, please come and get me. It has to be you. I'm a scientist, get me out of here!'

Conners clicked Send and prayed Plato would reply quickly, and also that he would want to help him. He knew his message sounded desperate – especially demanding that Plato himself be the one to bring him in, but he was desperate. He also knew he was running out of time.

San Jose, California

The one-bed apartment was on a tree-lined street which bordered the city's historic Hensley and Japantown districts. It didn't have a gym, clubhouse or pool, which was good for Roe as it meant less chance of interaction with potential nosey neighbours. It did, however, have quick access to several freeways, which made it an adequate, anonymous base.

Roe sat on the bed, reading through the notes taken from Carter's cabin in Fresno. Although handwritten, the hand was highly legible. First he read what Carter had on Cal Conners and the mission to find him, and then he moved on to the rest of the notes. These were a mixture of concise after-action report-style paragraphs detailing operations stretching back for the last five years. They were mostly low-level stuff with a couple of 'extractions'. All highly illegal. The notes would have made interesting reading to a prosecutor or the FBI, but Roe was neither and Carter was no more. Roe came to a sheet which made him pause.

He put the paper down and leaned back against the leather headboard. He studied the bedroom, taking in every remaining trace of the man whose life he'd assimilated. The bare white walls were broken up by three Impressionist paintings. They were posters, the type students bought and stuck on the walls of their university dorm rooms, but these had been framed in an attempt to make them look more believable as paintings, as works of art. Roe had Googled the prints, to learn what they were.

At the foot of the bed, across the room, was a print of the *San Giorgio Maggiore at Dusk*. Roe imagined Dan Tae had found the colours of the Venetian monastery island calming as they watched over his bed. On his left and immediately next to the window was *Impression, Sunrise*, one of Monet's earliest works. Roe knew it was far more inspiring than the actual sunrise from the window. The last print, on his right and next to the door leading to the lounge, was of the Rue Montorgueil. This one Roe liked the most. It depicted the festival of 'peace and work' held in France in 1878, but it reminded Roe of the tickertape parade in New York to commemorate the end of WWII. To him it meant peace from war, and perhaps that was something his country would achieve.

Roe knew his doppelgänger's mother had been a lover of art and the curator at a small gallery, and he imagined that the Monet prints adorning her dead son's apartment were a direct result of this. The prints were facsimiles, copies, fakes; good likenesses, but not perfect. As was he, a copy of the man whose face had been made to look more like his.

Roe picked the paper back up. Just like the others Roe had read, it was an after-action report on a job Carter's company had undertaken. Unlike the others, he recognised three names in this report – Mason, the guy who had presumably carried it out and the name of the targets: Dan Du-Ho and Dan Sun-Jung. A middle-aged married couple. Mr and Mrs Dan. The parents of the man whose apartment he was in, the man whose life he had taken over. The paper detailed the operation that killed Dan Tae's family.

His uncle, Gu Joon, had ordered the death of these people so he could take their son's place. So that he, Roe, could continue with the mission. Roe had never kept a tally of how many targets he'd eliminated during his military missions and CIA operations, but he hadn't specifically targeted non-combatants. Yet some had died. It was inevitable, they had been in the way. As had been the Dan family. He was all in with his uncle, and his organisation. The operation wasn't about money; it had never been about money. It was about blood and putting right a wrong that had been enacted upon his family. Roe fully understood that sacrifices had to be made, and collateral damage was a reality. To specifically target civilians was another step towards the darkness, but it was only by walking through the darkness that they would reach the light on the other side. Roe reasoned he had avenged Dan Tae's parents by killing the man who had ended their lives, and that was all he could do, that was all anyone could ever do for them now. He hoped the family had been reunited in the afterlife.

He put the paper with the others and then pulled over his laptop. This was where the true identity of Cal Conners was stored, and this was where illegal programs had been installed by his uncle's technical wizards to aid him in finding the man. He was conversant with the use of electronic intelligence, but had never pretended to understand exactly how it worked, and he'd not had to. Even now it was his job not to gather the intel but to act upon it. He was a weapon, still the tip of the spear, and he didn't mind this at all.

He watched the footage of Conners, the same video footage released to the TV networks and then the raw footage taken from various surveillance cameras his uncle's technicians had gained access to. Conners was a klutz, but a damn lucky one. How he'd managed to escape both Carter's men and the police was beyond him. Carter had been specifically chosen by Gu Joon because he wasn't the best, because he was dispensable, but even so, he and the goons he contracted should have been enough to stop a total burnout like Cal Conners.

Roe rose from the bed and moved to the window. It was now mid-afternoon, and he was hungry. He decided he'd take a shower then head out and get lost in the bustle of Japantown and find somewhere to eat in public for the first time in a month. The sound of an alert reached his ears. He collected the laptop from the bed and looked at the screen. It was a report of a potential sighting of Conners. Roe perched on the bed and tapped on the link. It was an audio recording of a call to the Santa Monica Police Department. Roe listened.

The call had been placed by the night porter of a hotel in Santa Monica some six hours earlier when the guy had finished his shift. In the call the night porter stated that a guest had checked in who he thought looked familiar, and it wasn't until he'd gotten home, he'd realised it was Cal Conners. The dispatcher had asked the porter to describe the man, and he had done so but said the guest claimed to be a British tourist. At this point Roe detected the dispatcher's tone change, the result of mental processing which concluded that the sighting had a lower probability of being Conners and a higher one of mistaken identity. The night porter explained that the guest had lost his passport and was contacting the British Embassy in the morning for an 'emergency travel document'. This seemed to pique the interest of the dispatcher again, however. The call ended with the dispatcher reconfirming both the hotel and the porter's details before saying he would send a patrol over to investigate.

Roe mentally calculated the distance to the hotel. It was about a five-and-a-bit hour drive from his apartment. He knew he needed to go.

Vauxhall Cross, London

Plato stood outside Newman's office. It was unusual for him to have to wait; he studied his emails on his tablet, still attempting to catch up on his workload. He wasn't the only specialist in his field that MI6 had, but on occasion he felt like he was, which was flattering but also tiring.

Newman opened her door; her reading glasses were in her hand. 'Neill.'

'Pamela,' Plato said.

'Well come in then.'

She returned to her desk, leaving him to close the door behind him. He now saw Tate was already in the room. Tate looked tired.

'Hi, Neill.' Unseen by Newman, Tate winked at him.

'This is the first time I've had you both together following our failure in Germany.'

81

'It is,' Plato said. They'd only arrived late afternoon the day before and he had yet to complete his written after-action report.

She addressed them both. 'Our mission was frustrated by a third party. A party we suspect to be the Hak regime of North Korea. It was highly unfortunate that it happened, but I understand that there was nothing that could be done.'

Plato nodded although 'unfortunate' wasn't the word he would have chosen to describe the events of the last few days. The face of the dead computer hacker, slain by the unknown assassin, swam before his vision. He blinked.

Newman seemed to read his mind. 'Neill, I am aware this has been a difficult operation for you to be an active, on the ground part of. Let me apologise for that.'

'No need.' Plato didn't feel he was owed an apology because the mission objectives had not been met.

'Now.' Newman clapped her hands together. 'You'd like to discuss Colin Jericho?'

'Yes.'

'I've been skimming your most recent email again.' Newman gestured to her computer with her reading glasses. 'I've looked into your Colin Jericho – it wasn't a name I knew. The MoD is being cagey with me on what exactly it was he was working on before his apparent death, which is even more reason for me to be interested.'

'Pamela, I've analysed the photographs the US authorities have published and there is a high percentage chance that Cal Conners is Colin Jericho, and then of course there's the content of his message to me.'

'Yes, you mentioned that. In short, Neill, if he is alive, we most definitely want him back. However, given his predicament, that is not going to be easy or, more importantly, legal.'

'What's new?' Tate said.

'Quite.' Pamela looked at him for a moment before she continued. 'He wants you to be the one to bring him in?'

'He said it in his message, but, Pamela, I'm not a field agent.'

'Which is why it should be you who does meet him. He knows you and, more importantly, you know him and will better than anyone be able to initially provide a positive ID and, secondly, assess his state of mind and the truth in his claims with regards to him being sought by a third party. As this is a fastball, I have no other option but to send you, Neill, immediately over there and have Jack accompany you.'

'I see,' Plato said. 'I'm sorry, Jack.'

'Don't be, I love collecting Air Miles.'

'Well yes, quite. You'll both be flying with a commercial carrier – Business as it's an overnight flight. I'll get your new passports and tickets to you within the hour. Jack and I have already discussed the logistics.' Pamela now looked at both Plato and Tate in turn. 'It is imperative that this stays absolutely under the radar. If Cal Conners is Colin Jericho, the Americans must not find out. You are going to the United States to ID this individual and if he passes that, you are to get him out of the country ASAP.'

Chapter 6

Santa Monica, California

Roe had studied the motel from the air, with the help of Google Earth. It was on Ocean Park Boulevard, was a blocky single-storey rectangular structure – three times as long as it was wide and had a slim, central courtyard. The exterior walls were painted a gaudy yellow, whilst the interior walls facing the courtyard were a powder blue. It looked economy and gave him the impression that it was one of those places where the staff 'didn't ask' questions. Yet this night-desk guy had. Roe parked his new rental – an official-looking, dark-blue Ford sedan, on the motel lot before he walked inside the reception area. It was half-past six in the evening and Roe expected the same night porter to be on duty, and he was. A bearded, middle-aged guy sat behind the desk reading a paperback. His nameplate displayed the same name the caller had given to the police dispatcher: Peter Bartnicki.

'Evening, can I help you?'

'I'm here to follow up on the earlier police visit.' Roe flashed a police ID wallet at the man.

Behind his tortoise-shell-framed glasses, the motel guy's eyes blinked, as though he was trying to understand the request. 'I see. Well, what more can I say? I don't know how much extra there is I can actually tell you?'

'I'm from Forensics. I was instructed to come and see if I can find any prints, etc. You know, to check if your guest was our perp.' Roe held up a small black plastic case, the implication being it held his kit.

'I see.'

'Look, you know how it goes, right? Someone gives you an order and you've gotta follow it.'

'Yeah, tell me about it.' Bartnicki smiled through his wiry salt and pepper beard. 'Procedures.'

'Exactly.' Roe pointed. 'Procedures. Were you told I was coming over?'

'No.'

'Now that's just typical Nealen.' Roe shook his head. 'It was Nealen and Harris they sent over, right?'

Bartnicki's brow furrowed, and he looked down at a Post-it note. 'No. It was Crawford and Summer.'

'Ah, I see.' Roe memorised the names, just in case. 'Now that's the issue.'

Bartnicki nodded, accepting Roe's assessment of the officers he had met.

'Did they ask to see the footage from that?' Roe pointed up to the CCTV camera in the corner of the room.

'They did.'

'Can I see it?'

'No. Like I told them, the system has been busted for the two weeks. The owner is on vacation and, let me tell you, I'm not going to be the one to interrupt his Caribbean cruise!'

'Ah, I see.' The CCTV footage would have been a double-edged sword, confirming Jericho's identity – if the guest had been him – but also recording Roe's face. 'How about the room this guy stayed in, is it unoccupied?'

'Of course. I was told to keep it that way, untouched, until the patrol came over. Housekeeping won't get to it until the morning.'

'But no mention of Forensics coming over?' Roe made a show of shaking his head. 'Anyhow, if you can show me to the room I'll get started and then I'll be gone.'

'Sure, Officer?'

'Sauer, Sam Sauer. Now, where's that room?'

Roe followed Bartnicki along the hall of the low-slung, squat motel. He waited while the guy used a key-card on a door with number 5 printed on it and stood aside so Roe could enter.

'Let me know when you're done, and as I say to all the guests – don't steal the towels!'

'Good one.' Roe smiled back as he shut the door.

Once alone, Roe surveyed the unmade, cramped room, looking for anything that had been abandoned, or forgotten. The double bed took up most of the space with hardly enough room for the bathroom door to open. He saw nothing in the bedroom area apart from a couple of hairs on the bed, which if he really had been who he said he was, he would have bagged and tagged. The bathroom, however, was another matter. A disposable razor, still covered in shaving foam, lay in the trash as did the outer hard plastic packaging of a burner cell phone. Whoever had stayed there obviously had either no idea how to or didn't care about covering his tracks. Roe fished out the cell phone packaging and inspected it. It was too generic to give him anything, apart from where it was manufactured and the sticky price tag which displayed the price but was bereft of any store logo or name. He left it where it was. Roe assessed the situation. He had a feeling this was Jericho, aka Conners. The British accent was the fact that made him sure of that, but why had the guy stopped in Santa Monica and not vanished into the US interior? More still, why had he bought a burner phone? He was making contact with someone, someone who could help get him out of the area and perhaps the country. Roe thought back to the briefing packs he had on both Conners and Jericho. Conners was a beach bum with no known circle of friends apart from the girlfriend he was accused of killing. Jericho had been dead for a decade, whilst secretly working for Blackline. So who would he call, someone new who had not shown up to the men Gu Joon had paid to investigate him or someone from the past?

Roe let all this marinate in his mind whilst he set about acting the part of Forensics guy. In his case he had a choice of two types of powder to use. The first was a white, talcum-based powder for dusting on dark surfaces, the second a dark graphite-based powder for light or coloured surfaces. He hadn't bothered with the third type of powder, which was fluorescent and glowed under a black light. He then took a brush from the case, chose the correct powder for the surface, and dabbed the bathroom mirror and taps. Ghostly fingerprints appeared. He knew it wasn't the correct method, but he'd been told that if the print was clear enough, he could, so Roe retrieved his iPhone and carefully photographed each powder-covered print before sending the images to his tech support team. He then wiped the area clean before applying powder again, just to make it look as though he hadn't sanitised the area. Satisfied he'd obliterated any prints that may have belonged to Jericho, he moved back into the bedroom. There he carried out the same procedure with the bedside table, lamp and, finally, the TV remote. There were far fewer prints here and they were less distinguishable, but he sent them off anyway.

Roe examined the room once more to ensure he'd got rid of immediate, ready evidence that would point at the true identity of the guest. He doubted that Jericho's DNA was on file with a US database, so he'd ignored the errant hairs. Of course the fingerprints were a different matter, and he reasoned it was best they didn't discover that Cal Conners was Colin Jericho risen from the dead. Something in his gut told him that the guest who had stayed in the room had been Colin Jericho, and he expected his uncle's tech team to confirm this once they'd examined the prints.

Roe shut the door behind himself and walked back to the reception area. He found Bartnicki reading again. On seeing Roe, the man put his book to one side. Roe saw the cover. It had a 1950s-style cover of a man in a suit holding a gun whilst a voluptuous blonde woman hung on to his leg, smoking a cigarette.

'That any good?'

'Yeah, I love detective noir. It's what made me want to be a cop.'

Roe nodded, internally reassessing the man. 'You served?'

'Nope. Never applied, stuff got in the way and then, well, I woke up here. Life, eh?'

Roe nodded, although he didn't understand how someone could end up in a dead-end job.

'So,' Bartnicki asked. 'Did you find anything?'

'I took some prints, and, as you asked, I left the towels.'

'Thanks.'

'The maid can go ahead and clean it now.'

'Thanks.'

'Just one question, this guy paid you for one night, right?'

'Yeah, one night but he said he might stay longer.'

'But he checked out?'

'No, according to the day guy, he left around ten this morning, said he'd be back but he's still not appeared.'

'Thanks for reporting this.'

'It's my civic duty. Do you know if it was Conners?'

Roe shrugged. 'I can't say until I examine the prints back at the lab. You have a great night.'

'Ha ha, in here? Sure, every night is great.'

Roe stepped out of the motel and looked around in the fading evening light. Now he had an estimate of when Jericho had left, all he needed to do was guess where he was heading and try to see if he'd been pinged on any surveillance cameras. The motel was only a few blocks from the airport, could Jericho have jumped on a jet? No. It was impossible. So why had he been in the city less than twelve hours before and why had he stayed there after escaping from both the police and Carter's men in neighbouring LA? He walked to the front of the hotel. The only CCTV cameras he could see were the enforcement traffic cameras overseeing lights on the junction with Cloverfield Boulevard. Those he knew would not take in all of the sidewalk. He walked around the side of the motel, past his rental car and looked at the street behind. It was an access road, spotted with dumpsters, bordering the backs of the houses and apartments which faced the next street. There was no immediate way through to the next street without going to the very end of the row. He walked this and saw not a single camera recording his path, however there were several floodlights linked to motion sensors. Either by design, or luck, Jericho had chosen one of the only places that had not captured him on film. But something had spooked him. No, that wasn't it. Something had made him leave the place after one night, or had he always intended to stay for just one night? Roe reached the parking lot and the rear of the hotel, then carried on past, looking at the rest of the buildings, eyes still scanning for cameras and mulling over his options. He saw another floodlight and then one that seemed to be linked to a camera. He stopped and stared, assessing the angle.

There was a noise on his right and the gate of the property opened. A middle-aged Hispanic woman with a large plastic refuse bag made for a trash can on the street, immediately in front of him. She deposited the bag and then, as she turned to go back inside, finally saw Roe. Dressed in a suit, he looked official. She became still and waited to be addressed.

'Excuse me, ma'am, do you live here?' Roe tried to both look and sound like a police detective.

The woman's face became lined with what Roe took to be either worry or incomprehension. He tried a different approach and switched to Spanish, 'Do you live here?'

There was a slight relaxing of the woman's face, but still she looked guarded. 'Yes. Why? Who are you?'

Roe allowed himself to smile, 'Please don't be alarmed, you've got nothing to worry about. I'm Detective Sauer. I'm looking for a suspect who was staying at the motel last night.'

'I see.'

'That camera on your wall, does it work?'

The woman looked up, then looked back at Roe, as though checking that the camera was indeed on the wall. 'Yes. We had problems with people setting fire to the dumpsters and breaking windows, so my daughter put it up.'

'Is the footage recorded anywhere?'

'On my computer. It is motion-activated. In daylight it is good, but at night the picture is no good.'

'Can I see the footage from last night and today?'

'Why?'

'I'm investigating the possible sighting of a suspect in the area.'

'Who?'

Roe saw no reason to not tell the truth. In fact, if the woman believed it to be a serious matter, she'd be more likely to help. 'A man named Cal Conners.'

The woman's eyes widened. 'The killer of that poor girl? I saw him on the television news! Come inside.'

Roe followed her through the gate and onto the property. Like the back of the house, the side and front were wooden clad and painted a pastel green. Looking past the woman to the street beyond, Roe saw that it was tree-lined and suddenly suburban.

The woman opened the door. 'You can sit at the kitchen table.'

Roe entered the kitchen. It was dominated by the table and a set of chairs covered with a white, plasticised lace-effect tablecloth. The woman vanished deeper into the house and returned with a laptop and a pair of glasses in her hand. She sat opposite Roe, opened the computer, put her glasses on and then tapped at the keyboard. 'What footage do you need to see?'

'Yesterday's and today. If I may.'

'You may.' She made a couple of clicks and tapped the keys

again, then turned the laptop around to face him. 'These are the files. Do you know how to work the program? It is simple, my daughter set it up for me. She's thirty-two.'

'Yes, I do. Thank you.' Roe looked at the screen. It was a standard program he had seen before. Each video had a thumbnail of the image that had triggered the recording and the recordings were all sixty seconds in length. A couple of videos seemed to have been filmed immediately after each other. There were forty-five recordings.

'Are you going to watch them all?'

'I think I need to.' Roe looked at the controls. 'But I will watch them on a faster frame speed.'

'Good.' The woman stood. 'I need to start cooking for my daughter. You know she has an extremely good job, and she is unmarried. Can I get you a coffee?'

'A coffee, thank you,' Roe said and looked back at the screen. He used the mousepad to open each video in turn and to fast forward through them. It was the not unexpected collection of passing cars, passing pedestrians, trash cans being opened and closed and a man who seemed to be a chain smoker appearing from the rear door of the motel. Up until ten in the evening Roe drew a blank, but then he paused the footage he was watching, rewound it, and watched it on normal speed. It was black and white and not as sharp as the daylight images having been captured using infrared.

'Like I said, not good at night.' The woman placed a coffee cup by his side. It was black, she didn't offer him any milk. 'Is that him?'

Roe paused the footage. He was looking at what he thought might be Jericho. 'No, I don't think so.'

The woman left the room and returned a minute or two later, whereby she busied herself taking ingredients out of the cupboards and mixing them.

Roe watched the footage again. The figure appeared on the left of the frame for several fleeting seconds before disappearing.

Roe drank the coffee. She had also added sugar. It was far too sweet for him, but he finished it nonetheless. He watched the rest of the videos for the same day and found nothing more. He then started on the footage taken after midnight. A few images of what appeared to be drunks, a cat and then nothing until the smoke appeared at 7 a.m. and then a procession of cars passing, perhaps locals starting their commute. He found Jericho at ten twenty. He appeared again on the left of the screen and this time walked directly past the camera. Roe froze the image and studied the man. He was clean-shaven, and he had changed his clothes, but Roe knew the shape of his face, the length of his hair and his build. Roe played the footage again and noted the gait and assigned that also to memory. And then he deleted the file. He stood.

And then a doorbell rang.

The woman left the kitchen and went to answer it.

Roe heard the woman exchange a few excited phrases in Spanish with another, younger woman. Roe had his hand on the backdoor when the younger woman spoke to him.

'Hello. My mother tells me you are a detective?'

Roe cursed inwardly. He'd had enough of pretending to be polite for one day. He turned to face her. 'Yes I am.'

The younger woman nodded. 'What is your name?'

'I'm Detective Sauer.'

'Sauer?' the younger woman said. 'That does not sound Asian.'

'I was adopted.'

'I'm sorry.'

'It's not an issue.' Roe nodded at both women. 'I have to go. Thank you for your time and your help.'

'Wait,' said the younger woman. 'What is your first name?'

Roe felt his left eye twitch. 'Sam.'

'I am Rosa García. Detective García. We do not have a Detective Sauer in the Santa Monica PD.'

Roe spun on his heels as he saw García start to draw her

service-issue Glock 19. He shot out a kick, slamming her hard in the stomach and sending her falling backwards into the wall. She cried out in pain as the back of her head hit.

'Stay away from my daughter!' The outrage in her mother's voice was unmistakable.

Using his right hand, Roe struck the older woman in the neck with a knife-edge strike. She collapsed, her hands scrabbling at her throat. Roe calmly bent down and removed Detective García's Glock. Without considering any other option, Roe fired twice, calmly placing a bullet in each woman's head.

Ears ringing, he collected the laptop, dropped his coffee cup into his jacket pocket, then left. There was now another loose end he had to fix. He exited the house, went through the gate and headed back towards the motel. He heard voices in the houses around him, but no one had ventured out; no one wanted to get shot. He reached the motel lot, passed his rented Ford and walked back into the motel reception.

As the door opened, Bartnicki got to his feet behind his desk. 'I heard shooting!'

'It's all over now.' Roe shot him twice, once in the head and once in the chest with the woman's gun.

Pushing the body of the desk guy out of the way, Roe took the motel's petty cash box, exited and made for his car. He could hear sirens now and undoubtedly there would be watchers behind windows, but he could do nothing about that. He drove away north and within minutes was lost in the traffic.

Chapter 7

Santa Monica, California

Roe had driven out to East LA, where he'd dumped and sanitised the rented Ford. Now wearing jeans and a hoody, he was riding a bus back into Santa Monica. He was annoyed with himself at allowing the mother and daughter almost get the better of him and derail the operation. Their deaths, and that of the hotel guy, had been necessary to keep his involvement with Conners away from the authorities. They could not discover that Conners was Jericho. Roe's support team had got back to him on the finger-prints, saying that two of them were a high probability match to the MoD records of Colin Jericho. In turn, Roe had given them the location of his sighting of Jericho and ordered a search of possible CCTV footage. Now, as the sun started to rise, he was seeing the results. He had ordered anything with a 50 per cent or above match rate to be sent to his encrypted iPhone. Headphones in, pretending to listen to music, or whatever it was civilians did, Roe assessed each potential sighting. He knew Jericho was still out there somewhere, and he had a hunch that he was waiting to meet someone. Who or what that person was he did not know, but it was up to him to grab Jericho first.

He examined the still image on his screen. It was from the forecourt of a gas station and showed a figure mid-stride, passing a pump. The image received a 56 per cent match. The next still was taken inside the station. This from a camera over a till. The image was of a figure, head down, paying for a can of Coke and a bag of chips. This got a slightly higher rating of 62 per cent. Roe enlarged the image to study it. Was it Jericho? The clothes were different, but perhaps. He just didn't know. He moved on to the next hit and dismissed it instantly. The guy was too fat, yet the clothes and hair matched. And then the next hit was curious. It was taken from a security camera monitoring the entrance to a shopping mall in Santa Monica. Whilst it only rated an even 50 per cent, it was a series of shots showing a figure entering and then exiting thirty minutes later with shopping bags for a formal menswear outfitters. Roe closed his eyes to chase away his fatigue. He was getting nowhere.

He stepped off the bus in downtown Santa Monica and headed for the beach. The sand was mainly deserted except for a few eager surfers and early morning swimmers. Swimming wasn't Roe's thing, although it wasn't something he disliked. He stood and watched the waves, and the gulls. He'd been an American since the age of two yet soon he'd be giving all of this up. Would he miss it? Would he care? Roe thought the answer to both was no. He turned and looked at the Santa Monica pier in the distance before he headed away from the water and back to the street. He'd check into a hotel and monitor the situation from there. He felt Jericho was near, very near.

Santa Monica Pier, Santa Monica

Conners waited in the surf. He was an hour early for his meeting with Neill Plato and hoped to god that his old friend had managed to make it. Contacting Plato had been a last resort, but it was his least worst option and the only one that guaranteed he wouldn't wind up dead.

He was wanted by the police for homicide, and he was hunted by others for what he knew. Despite the heat, he shuddered at the thought of his old employer. The company who had lured him away from his work with the UK Department of Defence by tripling his salary and giving him free rein to develop his ideas, and the same company who had used those ideas to create a new form of terror which had resulted in an attack on the US – Blackline. The company had been responsible for the world's first tactical electromagnetic pulse bomb (EMP) attack on a sovereign state. Such was the size and sophistication of the EMP that it had caused a total blackout across the continental United States, as in short anything and everything with a computer chip had been rendered inoperable. As Conners bobbed in the water he wondered whether it would just be simpler to let himself silently slip beneath the waves, to be dragged to the bottom under the authority of Neptune and become food for the sharks. In the past he'd tried to count, to estimate the sheer number of people who had died because of the attack he had been instrumental in creating. He was certainly a mass murderer, and probably ranked just below a couple of rogue states in terms of numbers. He had believed what he was helping to create was to be an advance in non-lethal weaponry, with defensive and law enforcement uses. He had believed that the UK government had not wanted to develop his work because it would mean the end to their multi-billion-dollar arms trade, and he had wanted to save lives and that was why he had joined Blackline. Too late, he realised he had been nothing more than a deluded idealist. Tears filled his eyes. He knew there was no use in crying, no point whatsoever, but the little boy who lived inside him, the one who had wanted to be a famous scientist and inventor, didn't know what else to do. Conners had failed his nation, he had failed his family and he had failed that little boy. He had failed himself.

A breaker crashed over him, filling his mouth with seawater and he let himself sink before his latent buoyancy brought him back to the surface. He coughed as the salt stung his throat, and continued now to watch the pier.

*

Tired from travel, Tate was dressed in a pair of cargo shorts, a loose-fitting shirt and trainers. His face was hidden behind a pair of impenetrably black Oakleys. Plato, walking by his side, was dressed in similar attire but favoured a pair of Crocs and matching green-framed Ray-Bans. In an ideal world, Tate would have wanted more feet on the ground – a team to watch and alert them of any threats – but such was the delicacy of operating on US soil that extra manpower had not been sanctioned. Even his request for 'local talent', former serving British soldiers and intelligence operatives who were based in the States and periodically contracted by MI6, was turned down. And, worst of all, in the land of the free, he was unarmed.

'A white suit,' Tate said, 'and you're sure of this?'

'Yes. He'll be wearing a pure white suit.'

Tate made no reply. He trusted Plato both as a colleague and now a friend. Plato believed that Colin Jericho was alive, and he was sincere in his belief. What concerned Tate, however, was that anyone could have, for whatever reason, pretended to be Jericho specifically to lure Plato to where he was now.

The duo continued along the pier, ambling past tourists, concession stands and those whose only purpose for using the place was to fish. Pelicans and other seabirds bobbed and weaved on the eddies and dived for fish, frustrating the fishermen.

They reached the end and leaned up against the railings to stare into the sea. Plato took a green baseball cap from his pocket and placed it squarely on his head, as per the stipulated instructions from 'Jericho'.

'Come on, Colin, where are you?'

Tate turned and looked back down the busy pier at the tourists, day-trippers and locals. He couldn't see any white suits; he saw the occasional white shirt and ill-fitting white shorts, but not paired together and certainly nothing that had any sartorial elegance.

They both waited.

'There!' Plato exclaimed, with more exuberance than Tate would have liked him to have had on a covert operation. 'On the beach.'

Tate turned and saw a figure on the beach below and to their right, struggling into a set of clothes. He was buttoning up a white shirt and as Tate watched he pulled a white jacket out of a beach bag. His outfit glowed as it reflected the harsh Californian sunlight. Tate finally had to agree that what he was seeing was a man in a white suit.

They watched the figure walk up the beach to the promenade, where he slipped on a pair of white Crocs.

Plato raised his sunglasses and squinted. 'That doesn't look like Colin, he used to be a fan of pies.'

'Death changes a man,' Tate said, dryly. 'OK, let's go. If it's not him nothing will happen, this is a public place. And, besides, you'll protect us.'

'Ha ha.' Plato laughed nervously.

*

Conners watched the two men meander away from their position on the pier. He instantly recognised the gait of his old friend, who, as promised, was wearing a green baseball cap. The other man he did not know, but pegged him as MI6. From behind a pair of dark sunglasses his eyes now flickered from face to passing face, all the while assessing and reassessing for threats or anyone who looked out of place. However, dressed like a bad Don Johnson tribute act, it was he himself who perhaps looked out of place, but he had wanted to do more than just reference their favourite film, so he had worn a white suit. It had been the only way to make Plato believe that it was really him: Colin Jericho, back from the dead and wanting to come in. It was time to come clean, to state exactly what he had given his former employer and give what he had held back to Her Majesty. He was resigned to spend the rest of his days in some type of facility in the UK. But that was far better than death, and although he would never be able to bring back any of those who were killed by the EMP, he might be able to stop further deaths with his inventions.

Conners stood up straighter, turned to his right and made for the pier and his friend, Neill Plato.

*

Tate was on alert. Outwardly he looked relaxed, casual, but his eyes were scanning the crowd, observing the passing vehicles, and looking at doorways and rooftops. He knew Jericho, or the person claiming to be Jericho, was wanted by the Los Angeles Police Department for homicide. Plato was certain that the man whose face he had run through his custom facial-recognition software was Colin Jericho, although how a man who had died when a light aircraft had crashed after take-off from Shoreham airport was both alive and living in the United States, he did not know. But that was the reason they were meeting with him, and that was the reason why they were taking him in.

Tate and Plato neared the beginning of the pier. A man in a white suit, with a clean-shaven face, appeared at the very start of the pier and started to walk towards them.

'It's Colin.' Plato's voice caught in his throat. 'It is really him.'

'You'll need to verify his identity and be absolutely sure before we can take any action,' Tate said.

The white suit drew a few looks, but it was far less conspicuous than it would have been elsewhere. The man wearing it had his hands by his sides, palms up and open and a half smile on his face.

The trio stopped, like gunfighters on the main street of some long-forgotten, dusty frontier town.

'Hello, Neill,' the man in the white suit said, as he removed his sunglasses, his South Yorkshire accent at odds with the Californian setting.

'Colin,' Plato replied. 'Why did you do it?'

'Being dead paid better than being alive.'

'Why now?' Tate said, 'Why come out of hiding now?'

Jericho's eyes slowly moved to fix on Tate. 'Who are you? I don't know you?'

Tate removed his own sunglasses and the two men locked eyes. 'I'm also a friend of Neill's.'

Jericho glanced back at Plato, then once again addressed Tate. 'Because Blackline have found me.'

Tate felt as though he'd been punched in the chest and there was a sudden roaring in his ears. Blackline, the same organisation who had attacked the US three years before, and the same entity who had murdered his parents in a London bombing. 'Blackline no longer exists.'

Jericho snorted. 'You tell that to the blokes that have been trying to grab me for the past week because of what I've got inside my head.'

'So, what do you want?'

'I want to come home.'

'To the country you betrayed?'

'To the country who will pass judgement on me. I didn't just disappear, I joined Blackline and I helped them create their EMP.'

Tate felt his eye twitch. Until that moment, Tate had believed Jericho had just worked for the MoD and was someone whose classified knowledge could be sold to the highest bidder or stolen. He'd never imagined he'd encounter any element of Blackline again, yet in front of him stood one of the architects of the largest-ever terror attack on US soil. Jericho had created the EMP, and this meant whoever controlled Jericho also controlled Blackline's back catalogue, and that potentially included the ability to develop more, and more effective, EMP weapons. Tate knew at that moment, without fail, he had to get Colin Jericho back to the UK. Tate glanced at Plato, who seemed just as shocked as he was. 'You faked your own death to work for a Russo–Chinese terror organisation?'

'I made a mistake.'

Tate's incredulity had turned to rage. He clenched his fists and breathed deeply, in an attempt to control himself. 'Did you know they were planning to use their EMP on the US?'

'Yes.'

Tate felt himself start to shake.

'And you did nothing to stop it?' Plato asked.

'No. It was too late to do anything. I ran.'

Tate flexed his fingers and let out a long breath. 'The woman on TV, the one the police say you killed?'

Jericho screwed up his eyes. 'They killed her, and I couldn't stop them.'

Tate had killed innumerable times for HM Government; some would label him as a cold, callous killer, and perhaps they'd be right, but indiscriminately targeting civilians was another matter. 'What if we say no? What if we say we aren't going to protect you?'

Jericho looked suddenly panicked. 'But you have to! You are the British government; my country's government and I need your protection.'

'Colin Jericho is dead,' Tate said, flatly.

'But if they get what I have inside here out—'

'Throw yourself in front of a bus for all I care, or, better still, I can throw you off a high roof.' It was a bluff; Tate couldn't walk away and let Jericho and his knowledge be taken by a third party.

Jericho looked at Plato. 'Neill, please! You're my friend! You have to help me!'

'The Colin Jericho I knew would never have been part of anything like that!'

Before Plato could reply, Tate saw figures in uniform behind Jericho and heading in their direction from the boardwalk onto the pier. 'I see police. We have to move. You two head towards the funfair. Go.'

The two old colleagues crossed the width of the pier and angled for the amusement park, which was not on the pier proper, but rather on the wide concession and parking area. Meanwhile, Tate walked towards the police officers; he'd block their path to Jericho if he had to by becoming the confused British tourist. As he neared the pair one broke stride, halted, and spoke into his radio. He said something to the other and then they turned on their heels and swiftly retraced their route back onto the boardwalk.

Tate continued on, reached the railings and rested against them as through admiring the view. He watched the retreating officers, and confirmed they had not gone to intercept Plato and Jericho. He started to breathe deeply, filling his lungs with the fresh, coastal air. The waves below were small, lapping gracefully against the shore whilst inside Tate a storm raged, and waves of anger engulfed him. He turned and walked towards the funfair. His mind was a mess. If elements of Blackline were still in operation, they posed a clear danger to the US and her allies. He had to get Jericho somewhere secure ASAP.

Tate reached the pair as they passed the Ferris wheel; both looked nervous, and it was then again that Tate had to remind himself Plato was not supposed to be out in the field. 'We're leaving, the three of us, and now.'

Chapter 8

Santa Monica

In the hotel room, as they awaited new travel documents to be delivered for Jericho, Tate stared at the pair of geniuses. One on the side of good and one who, in his opinion, was very much on the dark side. He remembered the chaos caused by the EMP attack three years earlier and the unfathomable cost it had created, human and otherwise. He'd been lucky to survive the events of that day but so many others had not, and here – just metres away from him – he had one of the architects of that attack sitting and smiling like nothing had happened at all. Tate decided the smile had to go.

'Tell me about the woman you killed.'

Jericho looked over at him, his smile instantly vanishing. 'She died because of me. If I could change that, I would.'

'I'm sure you would. What about all the others, eh? All those people who died when the EMP you helped Blackline develop cut the power and cut their lives short?'

Jericho looked down.

'No words? Is that it? Or are you just too ashamed to speak?'

'I am ashamed, you've no idea how ashamed I am. You can't comprehend the grief I've felt ever since.'

'Oh, I think I can. You see, what I can't understand is why you didn't try to stop it? You ran away from your old life, you ran away from Blackline and then what, you just sat back wringing your hands when they pulled the plug?'

'I didn't know they were going to launch it when they did. I didn't know they were going to attack the US like they did.'

'I can't believe you were that naive.'

'You have to believe me. If I had known exactly what they were doing, I would have stopped them.'

'I don't have to believe you, and I don't. You are complicit in the world's largest terrorist attack and yet you want us to save you from the bad guys?'

'Yes, I do. Look, if the bad guys get hold of what I know there will be other larger terrorist attacks. And those won't be stopped.'

Tate glared at the Yorkshireman. He hated him and he hated that what he was saying made sense. But he was bitter. 'You want to stop terrorists and rogue states from knowing what you do then be my guest, open the window and jump out. Or, better still, ask me nicely and I'll break your neck.'

'Jack!' The concern was clear in Plato's voice. 'We need him, and we have orders to return him to the UK.'

'Yeah, I know,' Tate said, tasting the bile in his throat. He turned away and looked out of the window. The panorama of the city wasn't the worst he'd ever seen, he just wished that for once he'd get to go places by choice and not necessity. He grabbed the bottle of water he'd placed on the table and drank angrily, wishing it was something else but knowing that he'd drink nothing stronger until he was safely in the air.

Behind him, Plato and Jericho started to talk again, Plato asking questions and Jericho giving answers. Tate tuned out as he didn't understand their highly scientific conversation; they may as well have been chatting in Welsh. On the street, floors below, Tate saw a black SUV pull into the car park. It was a Tahoe and although he knew he was being jumpy, a sudden chill struck him. Blackline had used Tahoes, but it was a common enough form of transport. Tate took a deep breath and let it out as he stared at the large SUV. Was it the team sent by Newman? Two men or they could be women, he reminded himself, either way they would be providing Jericho with a new passport which, in theory, would pass any inspection or facial-recognition program, especially with Plato able to run interference. As he watched, a suited driver opened the Tahoe's rear doors and a young couple jumped out. Tate relaxed a notch. His encrypted iPhone vibrated. He retrieved it from his pocket and read the message he'd received.

ETA twenty minutes.

Tate turned away from the window, leaned against the sill and folded his arms. He attempted to listen to the conversation again.

'I know I can make it work on a large scale. It's just a matter of creating the right conditions, sourcing the materials, and building the perfect facility.'

'The applications are astounding,' Plato replied.

Tate had to admit he was interested now. 'Now, explain to me, in terms a thicko can understand, what you're talking about.'

Jericho looked nervously at Plato. Tate rolled his eyes. 'I'm waiting.'

Jericho turned on his chair to fully face Tate. 'Imagine, and this is just for instance, imagine if you could make a bulletproof vest for an airframe.'

Tate frowned. 'Ballistic armour for a plane?'

'Yep.'

'It already exists.'

'Yes and no.'

'Explain.'

'Think historically about armour; blokes on horses with axes and shields.'

'Their armour was expensive, weighed too much and impeded their manoeuvrability.'

'Exactly.' The smile was back on Jericho's face. 'In a battle, if you knock little Lord Knobhead from his shire horse he slams into the ground and becomes an easy target.'

Tate nodded, remembering innumerable suits of armour he and his brother had gazed at in castles when they were kids. 'So, what have you invented? Lightweight armour?'

'Ah, it's more than that. If a commercial jet is downed by a missile, unless it's hit by a MPAD system like say a Stinger, the catastrophic damage occurs because the missile explodes close to the fuselage and sends its payload of shrapnel into the plane, ripping it apart.'

This was a simplification, but Tate said, 'Yes. And?'

'I'm sure you're aware, heavy armour plating aside, all existing airborne defence systems seek to either avoid the missile, by confusing it with chaff or flares or jamming its signal or by shooting it out of the sky. The Israelis used to have a doppler radar system fitted to their commercial airliners which fired invisible flares. Then they spent a decade updating and improving this and created something they call C-MUSIC or Sky Shield.'

To Tate it sounded like the name of his internet service provider. 'So?'

'What happens if these countermeasure systems fail?'

'The plane is hit.'

'The plane is hit.' Jericho nodded. 'The plane is hit and the plane dies. So does everyone on board. But what if that didn't happen? What if being hit by the payload of an anti-aircraft missile, or directly by a MPAD, was survivable for the airframe? Imagine this, a passenger plane is targeted – either intentionally or unintentionally – but it manages to take the hit and limp to the airport.'

'You can't limp in the sky.'

'Point taken. It performs an unscheduled landing at the nearest airport.'

'And you can do this? You can create this magic armour?'

'He thinks he can,' Plato said.

'I know I can. Now, it's not armour as such, it's a weave, and it can flex; it diverts the force of the impact, and it can be layered – like Kevlar, but a bloody lot stronger.'

'Weapons manufacturers will simply make their missile payloads larger.'

'They will, eventually, but this could buy at least five years. That's five years of safer flying, fifteen years or more before everyone has missiles that can defeat White Suit.'

'White Suit?'

Jericho nodded, his smile now wide. 'That's what it's called: White Suit.'

'Jack, this is just what could happen with aeroplanes. Imagine other vehicles.'

'Humans, too! It would be possible to create a level 4 or higher ballistic vest that is both lightweight and flexible – no more waddling with heavy plates. You could even use multiple layers. In theory it could be a sheet that you throw over a suspected IED.'

Tate realised just how large an advance this would be. No wonder Blackline wanted this. Tate realised then just how serious his mission had become.

'It would work on frying pans too,' Jericho added.

'Really?'

'No.' Jericho smirked.

Tate glowered at him. 'And this is what you took with you from the MoD to Blackline?'

'No, no, no. The Ministry of Defence wouldn't let me even look at it. They said it was a stupid idea and wouldn't work. They were all about developing lasers and, of course, EMPs.'

Tate felt sick. 'The Ministry of Defence were responsible for the creation of Blackline's EMP?'

'No. They were not. Then we couldn't get it to work.'

'But at Blackline you could.'

'Yes.'

Tate remembered back to the events of three years before and the

Russian scientist he'd met who had been part of Blackline. He too had been brilliant and, just like Jericho, he had continued to pursue science regardless of the outcome until, too late, he realised what was happening. Tate wondered if this was a flaw with all scientific geniuses. If Jericho was to be believed, he had never intended to kill civilians, but it was a moot point. Whatever Jericho's intention or convictions or motivations, a multitude had died. Tate hoped this was the last time he ever had to deal with the fallout from Blackline and their attack, but something niggled at him, telling him that there was more to Jericho's situation than he knew. Tate's phone vibrated for a second time as he received a second message.

We are here.

Tate tapped a reply, only now giving the sender of the message their room and floor number.

Tate addressed Plato, his voice calm but firm. 'Both of you get in the bathroom, it's the safest place.'

'For what?' Jericho asked.

'In case the people who messaged me aren't who they say they are and storm the room.'

'Colin, bathroom,' Plato said, rising from his chair.

Tate exited the hotel room, darted down the hallway and took up a position in the stairwell at the end. He had given the MI6 team the number of a room on the opposite side and several doors away from their own. He had no idea if it was empty or occupied, but wanted to see who exactly was coming for them. His iPhone may have been encrypted, but he still employed old-school tradecraft as a backup.

Tate listened and heard no footfall on the stairs below him, but he did hear the sound of the lift ascending. Tate scowled again at the fact he was unarmed and glanced at the fire axe in its glass box before discounting the idea. The lift stopped at his floor and a couple stepped out, a man and a woman. They had their backs to him as they walked along the landing to the wrong room, the one Tate had given them on the opposite side to the actual one they were using. Tate slowly shook his head and casually followed them. He was five paces away when the man turned. It was Tate's brother, Simon Hunter.

*

Whilst Plato fiddled with his laptop, Jericho was in the bathroom receiving a makeover from the MI6 make-up artist.

'Did she cut your hair too?' Tate asked his brother.

'Jenny works at the embassy, and yes she did. Why?'

Tate shrugged. 'No reason. What did she call it: "The Boris"?'

'Now that would be an honour. Anyway, the ladies love it.'

'She seems nice.'

'She is, Jack, and she's a colleague.'

Tate smirked. This was the first time in several months, since Hunter's official return to the British Embassy in Washington, that the brothers had been in the same continent. 'Speaking of which, are you seeing anyone?'

'No.' Hunter's expression became serious. 'Not since my head injury and not since ...'

'Sorry.' Tate also lost his smile. He didn't want to bring up the past, however distant or near, and the woman he'd lost.

'What's the matter?' Hunter's eyes narrowed. 'You not pleased to see me, Jack?'

Tate sighed. 'You know I am, Simon. I just don't think you should be in the field again.'

Hunter laughed out loud. 'Well thank you for the vote of confidence!'

'Don't be a silly sod, you know what I mean. How's your head, any pain after the flight down?'

Hunter touched his temple and felt the lump under his skin, which was all that was left of the entry wound of a 9mm bullet; an unwanted gift from a Russian mercenary the year before. 'I get the occasional headache, but that's probably just the wine.'

Tate stared at his brother. 'You're not lying to me?'

Hunter sighed. 'Yes, I got shot in the head, but look – I lived! Jack, I'm fine. If anything, I'm concerned about you.'

'Me?' Tate didn't understand. 'I'm fine and so's the boy wonder.'

'Oh, is that my new name?' Plato said, looking up from his emails.

'Speaking of names. Here.' Hunter handed Tate a worn-looking UK passport. 'That's for Chris.'

'Colin,' Plato said.

Hunter winked. 'I know.'

Tate inspected the name on the passport. 'Christopher Keith Irvine?'

Hunter shrugged. 'I didn't think Terry Bollea was subtle enough.'

'I don't get it?' Plato said. 'Oh, is it another wrestling reference?'

Tate nodded. Even now, during a serious operation, he couldn't ignore his brother's sense of humour. 'Where's the photograph from?'

'His file with the MoD.'

Undisclosed location

'I trust the men and equipment I have delivered to you are satisfactory, Kwang?'

'Yes, Uncle, they are,' Roe said back at the video screen.

'Very well. You are in charge of this, I need not give you any instructions or advice. My location is ready to receive them.'

Roe nodded and before he could say another word, his uncle ended the call. Roe closed the laptop and handed it back to one of the men who had been sent by Gu Joon. 'Tell the men we roll out in twenty minutes – two-oh minutes.'

'Yes, sir.' The man was Korean, by his accent from the South, but this made no difference to Roe. 'Your team is ready.'

'Are they aware we cannot afford for anyone to become compromised?'

'They are aware, and they will not allow themselves to be taken.'

'That is all.' Such words and resolve were all very well before a battle or operation, but when the rounds started to zip by the eyes, he'd seen men crumble and missions fail. The man walked away towards the rest of the men, who stood or leaned against their vehicles in the corner of the warehouse. Roe knew his own abilities, and he knew the men he had served with in both Delta and the CIA's 'Activity' group were equally as good, but he never took the word of anyone on the ability of someone he had not assessed himself. This time, however, he had no choice; he had no time to review and select his men, and this was not optimal.

Roe moved to a trestle table that had been set up and inspected his rifle. It was exactly as he had ordered, but again, he'd had no time to zero it, and there was no time and indeed no space nor place to do so now.

That was two strikes against the operation, yet he knew if there was a third, he could not walk away. If the mission failed it would be down to him to sanitise it, and if that meant he was to be the only man in the warehouse who was still breathing by nightfall, then so be it.

Chapter 9

Los Angeles

There were three of them in the SUV – Tate, Plato and Jericho. Tate imagined that Hunter and his friend from the embassy were already in the air and Washington-bound. Once this was all over, he was due some time off and would see if he could spend it with Simon. Perhaps he'd finally get him to go to Camden, Maine with him, which, after all, was much greener than his home of Camden, London.

Tate glanced at the sat nav, or, as the locals insisted on calling it, GPS. It was a short sprint north-west on the Interstate 405 San Diego Freeway to Van Nuys Airport where a jet, owned by a shell company and chartered by another shell company that was owned by MI6, awaited them. Tate hoped there was something to drink on the flight. He'd not touched a drop since landing in the US and although he wasn't addicted to booze, he liked the occasional 'bit of medicine' as his dad used to call it. One or two on a transatlantic flight would be fine.

In the rear-view mirror Tate saw that both Plato and Jericho seemed tense and tired. Each staring out of their own window lost in thought, or perhaps just gazing at the local flora, fauna and wildlife which, other than the passing traffic, was limited to views of the nearing hills and the concrete walls enclosing the freeway. However, Tate preferred it that the two were quiet rather than chatting about things he didn't understand. It wasn't that he thought he was particularly stupid, but they were just particularly brilliant. Their conversation, peppered with scientific terms, to him sounded like Klingon. Tate had left school as soon as he was legally able to and had joined the army; he'd never regretted his decision not to take A levels like his brother and then get a degree. Perhaps he would once he had to stop what he was doing now for a job. He'd never thought of a future without the army or the MI6 but knew that he had at most ten more years left of being able to operate at his physical peak. Less, he knew, if he kept getting shot by runaway assassins and sodding farmers. He increased the flow of the AC and lowered the temperature another notch as his back had started to sweat against the leather seat.

Ahead, the traffic started to slow. It was midday and not any rush hour he'd heard of.

'We're slowing. Why are we slowing?' Jericho's voice was panicked.

'So I don't crash into the car in front.'

'It says on my Waze app,' Plato said, 'that police have been reported ahead.'

'We need to take another route!' Jericho blurted.

'Look.' Tate was calm. 'You have a new, real UK passport which has been backstopped to show you entered the US a week ago. You're a rich tourist going to catch his flight. It all checks out.'

'My life is in your hands, Jack.'

Tate didn't reply. He despised the man, and if it had been up to him, it would have been Jericho's blood on his hands. So he said, 'Neill, I can't see any alternate route here and I'm not going to mess with this sat nav. What does your Waze say?'

'Hm, just a mo.'

Tate focused on the slowing line of traffic ahead now he could see that the lanes were filtering down to one. So perhaps it was an accident or, less likely, a roadblock.

'There's an exit just over a mile ahead – Exit 61 – which would lead us down a local road. Yep, we could take that and re-join the I-405 later or stay on the surface roads. Either way gets us to Van Nuys.'

'Thanks. I think we'll be past whatever this is by then,' Tate replied.

'I think we should take it anyhow,' Jericho stated. 'Smaller roads mean less traffic. Less chance of being stopped or seen.'

'By Blackline or the police?' Tate's tone was terse.

'Both.'

They reached the end of the line of cars and came to a complete stop. Tate sat up higher in his seat; in his SUV he could see over the several sedans ahead, but not his fellow SUVs and taller trucks. They slowly edged forward. Stop start, stop start for the next five minutes until Tate found himself four cars back from a roadblock. He peered back at Jericho, who looked pale and was sitting as though he was about to grab the door handle and make a run for it.

'Don't even think about it,' Tate warned him, making sure the doors were locked.

'But it's the cops, they've got to be looking for me!'

'Do you think you're the only wanted scumbag in the Greater Los Angeles area?'

'Jack's right, Colin. Besides, there's nowhere to go now.'

'Just stay cool, channel that surfer dude you were pretending to be, and it will all be fine.'

'What if that's not the police?'

'I think you've seen too many Hollywood movies,' Tate stated.

The car in front was waved through after a couple of questions and now it was Tate's turn. He powered down the window, letting in the warm, petrol-scented, dusty air. 'Good afternoon, officer.'

The officer nodded and quickly glanced at Tate and then at the others, one by one. 'You're British?'

The passport Tate was travelling on was Irish and he told the officer so.

'Do you mind telling me where you are heading?'

'Home. We've got a flight to catch.'

'Van Nuys?'

'Yes.'

'You must be celebrities.'

'Only in my own house,' Tate replied.

'OK. Enjoy your flight.' The officer stepped away from the car and gestured for them to drive on.

Tate closed the window and accelerated. 'Panic over.'

They continued in silence for no more than a minute before Tate noticed a jam ahead. 'What was the junction you said we could take?'

'Exit 61.'

'Take the turn.' Jericho still sounded ill at ease.

'Will do.'

'Look for a sign saying Sepuleda Boulevard,' Plato noted.

The flow of traffic slowed, but they managed to get into the correct lane and take the exit. Immediately after the off-ramp, Tate made a turn and joined Sepuleda Boulevard. Unlike the freeway that ran through a trench seemingly cut into the hills, this road followed the geographical contours until the road builders had given in to topography and created a tunnel through the hill directly ahead. Traffic was much lighter, and Tate noticed little coming his way but there were three other large SUVs behind him.

'That's odd,' Plato stated. 'I've suddenly lost my signal.'

'Probably the terrain,' Tate replied, although he was suddenly on alert. He looked again in his mirror and now saw that the three SUVs were Tahoes, and something told him they were not ferrying a celebrity and their entourage to the airport. He cursed under his breath; there was nowhere to go – no turning he could take. He decided he'd floor the gas once they were in the tunnel to double-check if he had a tail, and, if he did, to attempt to lose it.

They were seconds into the tunnel when a pair of explosions detonated behind them.

'Christ!' Jericho yelled.

Tate looked back. Two SUVs were blocking the road and black smoke was bellowing from them. Two figures, dressed in black fatigues and wearing balaclavas, were jogging towards the third SUV, which had seemingly stopped a safe distance away from the other two.

Ahead, at the other end of the tunnel, three more SUVs raced into view. Two slewed to a stop, blocking both lanes, whilst the third made directly for Tate, Plato and Jericho.

'Shit,' Tate muttered. Why was nothing ever easy?

Tate pushed the accelerator flat to the floor, making the V8 engine growl. They tore towards the oncoming SUV, which was an identical-looking Tahoe. The distance between the large, heavy vehicles grew less and less. 'Hold on, you two.'

Tate slowed his breathing and tried to relax. He really didn't want to cause a collision, but if that was his only option … The oncoming Tahoe grew larger and larger as it careered past other cars and trucks, caught in what Tate now had to believe was an ambush. The distance between the two vehicles was rapidly reducing and the closing speed increasing. In the fluorescent gloom of the tunnel Tate swore he could now see the eyes of the oncoming driver. Tate closed his own and let out a long breath.

There was a metallic screeching and screaming as the other Tahoe missed Tate's by an inch. Tate opened his eyes as they rocked in the wake of turbulent air. He started to breathe again and angled for the narrow gap at the mouth of the tunnel, the space between the two blockading SUVs.

But there was something on the bonnet of the SUV on the left. Tate realised it was a tripod-mounted rifle. A figure behind it moved, as though adjusting, getting ready to take a shot. At the distance Tate couldn't identify the rifle, but knew it was large and had to be capable of delivering a 0.50 cal round.

There was a flash, a flame, and a bark echoed in the tunnel. Instinctively, Tate ducked. The Tahoe shuddered and then started to shake. A violent grinding came from the bonnet and the immediately the car started to slow. Tate figured the round had hit the engine block, and it had to have been armour piercing.

'What's happening? What's happening?' Jericho's voice was shrill.

Plato too had started to panic. 'Jack! What do we do?'

Tate let the Tahoe trundle on past frightened motorists, cowering in their cars. The two Tahoes behind were following, ready, he imagined, to chase down any runners. There was no way past the improvised roadblock, and these weren't police; these were the people who wanted Jericho.

'There's nothing we can do. They've got us.'

There was a popping sound now from the engine and the shaking increased. Tate used the brakes, put the Tahoe into Park and turned off the engine. Immediately men exited the two SUVs behind, each of them was dressed alike in black fatigues, wore black balaclavas and had HK submachine guns aimed at Tate's vehicle. By the way they were moving, Tate thought they looked like a slick military unit.

'You can't let them take me!' Jericho said.

'Listen,' Tate's tone was terse, 'if they'd have wanted you dead, you would be. Be compliant, don't fight them and don't talk. Just let them take you. If I can get us out of this I will, but until then just do everything they say. Got that?'

Jericho made no reply whilst Plato furiously tried to get a signal.

The gunmen now appeared at each of the vehicle's four doors, weapons aimed at the occupants. Tate felt his heart start to race in his chest. Jericho was safe, they wanted him alive, but he and Plato they would either incapacitate, execute or abduct. At this point Tate had no idea which one was the most likely. He tried to relax his body; he took deep breaths. All he could do was wait. His life was now out of his control.

'Slowly raise your hands,' he commanded the other two. 'Show them you're unarmed.'

Tate pressed the Unlock button. Three of the doors were immediately yanked open.

'Out! Out! Out!' The instruction was clear, concise and barked with authority.

Tate started to move and immediately the barrel of a short-stock HK 416 was pressed into his chest, pinning him back into his seat. If the guy holding the other end squeezed the trigger, that would be it. Lights out. It would be instantaneous, and he wouldn't know a thing about it. In the row behind he felt and heard both Plato and Jericho being dragged from the stricken SUV. There was nothing he could do except wait.

A command was shouted in a language he didn't recognise, and the barrel moved away and the man holding it said, 'Out! Out!'

This time Tate was allowed to move. He stepped down from the SUV and saw that Plato and Jericho were being manhandled into the back of one of the Tahoes. Two more gunmen had their weapons trained on him, whilst the one who had prodded him in the chest now pushed him in the back towards another Tahoe. Tate clambered into the back. He thought it was odd that he hadn't been cuffed, but then from inside another man in black jabbed him with an autoinjector pen. A sensation, like stepping into a cold bath, instantly washed over him. Before he lost consciousness, he heard the squeal of the Tahoe's tyres as it sped out of the tunnel.

Undisclosed location

Gu Joon clasped his hands in front of his chest. 'Now that we have Colin Jericho, we can proceed with the next part of the plan.'

'When do we leave, Uncle?'

118

'We are going nowhere yet, Kwang. Not until I have proof that his invention works. And of course there is the added complication of the two members of MI6's fabled E Squadron we scooped up.'

'They were sent to return Jericho to the UK.'

'Evidently, yes. The very place Jericho worked against was ready to take him back because they want what he has stored inside his mind.'

'What will you do with these two men?'

'I have no need of a British soldier. The MI6 technical officer, however, is very much another matter. If he cannot be persuaded to work for me for conscientious or political reasons, then I am sure the fear of his mother being murdered will be just the carrot needed. Yes, Neill Plato will work for us in one way or another whilst Tate will be terminated.'

'He is a highly skilled operative. It was Jack Tate who ended Blackline.'

'Really?' Gu Joon's tone was sceptical. 'One man did that?'

Roe nodded. 'Blackline took his parents with the Camden bombing in London; he vowed revenge. And he got it.'

Gu frowned. 'How is it that you know all this and not I?'

'It's hard to keep a secret in the CIA. Word was the US president wanted to pin a medal on his chest.'

'You know his name from leaked reports and "office gossip"?'

'I know his name because I know Jack Tate. I worked with him on JSOC operations in Iraq.'

'When you were in Delta Force, and he was with the SAS?'

'Yes.' Serving side by side with Tate, Roe had come to respect him as an operator. His reactions were almost as fast as his own and his shooting just as sharp, yet his fatal flaw had been his loyalty to others. And on that day in Baghdad, fourteen years ago, it had been this loyalty which had risked Roe's life. That was the difference between them, and that was the reason Tate had tried to end Roe's military career and put him behind bars. That

119

Tate would dare attempt to take away his livelihood, his status and his life was something Roe could neither forgive nor forget. Each time he had heard Tate's name his hatred had returned and threatened to bubble to the surface, like the evidence of a submerged volcano. This was one grudge Roe had held, yet he had been unable to do anything about it until now. 'I would like to be the one who kills Jack Tate, Uncle.'

Gu Joon steepled his hands. 'Then this gentleman I should very much like to meet, before he dies. But you have not told me why you wish to be his executioner?'

'Because he is too dangerous to be alive. Jack Tate, like me, is a man who will never give up.'

Chapter 10

'How's the coffee, Colin? Is there enough cream?'

Having lived for over three years as Cal Conners, Colin Jericho now found the sound of his own name unusual, especially when it came from his captor's lips. 'Yes. Thank you.'

'That is good,' Gu stated. 'Many of my countrymen have expressed their love for tea, but for me coffee is the absolute pinnacle of taste. Although, one must admit, I prefer to take it black.'

'It's nice. Thank you.'

'Ah, the English use of the word "nice". Now that I have always found amusing. The weather can be nice, a woman can be nice, food can be nice, in fact anything can be nice and if it is an Englishman using the word one never knows if, in fact, he does like the object he is commenting upon, is being sarcastic or is just being "nice". Language is a wonderful invention.'

Jericho drank his coffee.

'You will have many questions and I shall endeavour to provide you with full, honest answers, Colin.'

'That's very good of you.'

'Good, yes. Nice also.'

Jericho sighed. 'Look, you abducted me, you drugged me and knocked me out for, I don't know how long …'

'For that I must apologise. No, actually, I will not. It was necessary.'

Jericho frowned. 'You know who I am and you've been trying to get me and, of course, that's because of what I know.'

'Of course. It is because of what you know. It is also because of what you have achieved and what you can continue to achieve. First, I must broach an unpleasant matter. I must apologise for contracting highly inappropriate partners when initially I attempted to find you and make you an offer.'

'Inappropriate?' Jericho felt his grief rush to the surface. He shuddered. 'They killed Darcie. She was an innocent woman and your partners shot her like she was nothing.'

'Yes, they did.' Gu Joon sighed. 'If there is any solace to be taken in this matter it is that the men involved in that operation, and their boss, are no longer with us. They have been permanently removed.'

Through his anger Jericho understood the implication, but made no comment. 'So, what is the offer you wanted to make me? Is it one I cannot refuse?'

'One can always refuse an offer, Colin. Whether one should or not is the real question.' The white-haired man paused to drink from his own cup. 'My name is Gu Joon. I am Korean. For many years I was an operative for the North Korean Intelligence Agency. I was extremely successful, until I made a mistake. I was assigned to assassinate the president of South Korea. I failed. I was reha- bilitated and that gave me the chance to became what I am today.'

'Which is what?' Jericho was confused.

'Just a man with a dream, but a man who has the financial means to make his dreams a reality. Wealth alone, however, will not create my reality. For that I need a team of brilliant minds. That, Colin, is why I need you.'

Jericho drank in the words. It was a pitch, but thus far it had not made any alarm bells ring. 'So why exactly are you so desperate to have me as part of your team?'

'I am aware of what you were working on, and I am aware of what both it and you can do.' Gu nodded, drank more coffee, and then explained.

Jericho sat, transfixed, and once Gu had finished, he said, 'You think White Suit can do that for your country?'

'I know it can, I am banking on it.'

*

Tate woke up and knew that something was not right. The first thing he noticed was that his feet were cold. Air conditioning blew viciously at him through a high vent. He sat up and felt a giddiness and an almost imperceptible throbbing in his head. Whatever he'd been jabbed with had knocked him out straightaway and how long he'd been under for he did not know. The room he was in was white and featureless. Light came in through a window to the left of him, but it was filtered through heavily obscured glass. There was no way for it to be opened and looking around the room, apart from his body there was nothing that could be used to break it.

Gingerly, Tate stood and had to shoot out his arms for balance as a wave of dizziness threatened to make him keel over. He took a deep lungful of the frigid air and let it out gently whilst he recovered. There was a door immediately ahead of him and another in the wall on the right. If he didn't know better, he'd believe that he'd woken up in a minimalist Scandinavian hotel. But this was a cell, albeit a comfortable one, and that fact in itself was comforting. He walked on wobbly legs to the door on his right and found it to be both open and a bathroom. The space was white, and so was everything in it. Tate looked at himself in the mirror and was confused. He'd shaved before they left for their flight, but staring back at him was a face with at least three days' growth of stubble. And the clothes he was wearing were not his own.

He turned on the tap and splashed water on his face as the dizziness and throbbing lessened. There was a bottle of water next to the sink. He opened it and drank greedily, knowing that if his captors had wanted to poison him they would have done so already. He wiped his lips on the back of his hand and now felt as though he'd just woken up from a good sleep and was surprised by how remarkably fresh he looked. The fatigue of the back-to-back missions had seemingly vanished from his face. Had he been out for three days? That was impossible, surely, he wouldn't feel as good as he did. He noticed bruising on his left arm and instantly knew that he'd been hooked up to an IV, but just what had been pumped into him? He pulled the polo shirt away from his chest and poked his nose inside. The mild, margarine odour told him to shower. Before he did this, however, Tate stepped out of the bathroom and tried the other door. It was locked, as he'd expected. There was a spyhole and looking through this he was surprised to see that it was unobscured and gave him a fish-eye view of the hallway outside. It appeared to be a landing, much like in a hotel. Confused, Tate moved back to the bathroom, stripped off and got into the shower. Two white bottles, one of shampoo and one of shower gel were standing on a shelf for him.

'What, no conditioner?' Tate muttered aloud to himself as he opened the shampoo. It was lemon scented.

As Tate showered, he contemplated his situation. He wasn't dead, which meant that whoever had grabbed him, wanted to know something from him. These people had to know that Cal Conners was Colin Jericho, which in turn meant that he and Plato were very obviously MI6. Plato … Tate knew what to expect from being interrogated and had been trained by the SAS to resist and to drip-feed information, but Plato had not. Tate was bitter and angry at Jericho for dragging Plato into this. Plato was, in Tate's opinion, a valuable asset for any opposing intelligence agency and, of course, that included criminal organisations too, such as Blackline. The thought of that organisation raising its head again made Tate shiver, despite the warmth of the shower. He knew that the greatest enemy of any captive was their own mind. It was the fear of what may, what could or what would happen that drove those held hostage to breaking point. If Tate dwelled on errors he had made, decisions he had made, then that too was a road to madness. So, Tate looked at the positives. He was alive. He had not been beaten and he was being held in what looked like a brand-new hotel room with both air conditioning and water. He wondered if there was a room service menu he had yet to find.

Minutes later, Tate stepped out of the shower and grabbed one of two towels that were folded and waiting for him. It was the softest towel he had ever felt, another thing to be thankful for. He dried himself, then slipped on a matching white bathrobe that was next to the towels and walked back into the bedroom area. He stopped. On his bed was a folded pile of clean clothes, and a bottle of 'conditioner'.

*

Plato put his ear against the windowpane and listened. Could he hear the distant sound of traffic from outside, or was that the wind he could hear? He hated not knowing. He flexed his fingers and drummed them against the glass. He was worried, he felt like he had when he'd been a kid and was summoned to the headmaster's office with no idea why. Then it had been because he'd been seen with a boy – Cliff Sim – who had thrown a stone at a window of the art room, this time it was because he had been with Colin Jericho. Sim had thrown the stone and Plato was in the clear because he had just been a witness. On this occasion, however, Plato had been trying to get Jericho to safety.

Sim. It was just a name that back then, in primary school, had not meant anything to Plato. It was only years later that he had heard the surname used as a noun. Plato sighed, wondering why this was coming back to him now. It was the stress of being locked up, he supposed, the fear of knowing that at any moment the door to his cell could be opened and a man with a gun could come for him. And then what? Take him outside and shoot him?

Plato tried to relax. There was a bottle of mineral water on the small shelf by the side of his bed. He moved to it and sipped. The headache he'd had when he first awoke had now gone and, to be honest, he felt fine, although if he let himself think, the hopelessness of his situation made his chest tighten and his stomach cramp. He'd never tried to think too much about his own worth as an asset. He enjoyed what he did, and he was proud that his work saved lives and safeguarded those who chose to live in the United Kingdom. Not once had the thought ever entered his head that he may one day be held captive because of his job. Yes, this was something that had been discussed during the recruitment process and there had been several training sessions on what to look out for and who to report it to if approached by a foreign intelligence agency. In fact, he had even been to a talk about 'resistance to interrogation' given by an old SAS friend, and although it had been interesting it was not something that he had retained or contended as a real threat. Yet here he was. In a room, like a hotel room but with a locked door and window. He was in a cell. Plato felt his chest tighten again and he tried to breathe deeply to reduce his anxiety. He had a shower, which he hadn't used for fear of being dragged out naked and wet by whoever had abducted him. Although he'd woken to find himself wearing clothes that were not his own. Someone had seen him naked and dressed him again! But when, and how? Plato could remember nothing. They were attacked in the tunnel; Tate had instructed them not to struggle and then … and then he'd felt a stab in his neck and, without realising, must have passed out.

But how long had he been, what, asleep? Drugged? He moved to the bathroom and splashed water on his face. Had his stubble grown longer? He only shaved every few days so couldn't notice much of a change. He moved back towards the bed and sat, but was immediately up again.

Plato paced the room. He needed to think rationally and for that he needed to drink tea and munch on a Fig Roll or three. He thought about his mum, all those miles away at home in Brighton. She knew he was away on business but, undoubtedly, she'd have been messaging him again, complaining that he hadn't called her and asking why he couldn't be more like her friend Susan's son who was a branch manager for HSBC. He always visited his mum on Sundays and took her out shopping in his very nice Mondeo. Plato sat on the bed and started to shake as he thought about his mum, on her own at home and in the dark. If she really knew what he did she would be proud, but if she knew where he was now, the worry would kill her.

He started to think about what exactly it was he knew, and what damage his information, if used, could cause to the service. He had never thought about dying, but that was where his mind was drifting to now. He knew he couldn't defend himself; that was not his skill set, that was why he was meant to be safely ensconced in an office fighting with his fingers and a keyboard, not out in the real world with guns and bullets. His oldest friend had put out a plea for help and Plato knew that he'd never be able to look himself in the mirror if he'd rejected that. It was, Plato thought, the last chance he had to bring Colin back home and have him atone for his sins.

There was a noise outside. Instantly, Plato felt his throat contract and become dry. He reached for the bottle and took a swig just as his door opened. He dropped the bottle and his hands shot up.

Chapter 11

Undisclosed location

Hands cuffed behind his back, Tate was marched along the corridor by two men. He was wearing his new clothes – a light training outfit and a pair of slip-on plimsoles that remined him of primary school PE. The walls of the place were completely bare and the large windows at both ends were obscured like his own.

The men pressed the button to open the lift doors and pushed Tate inside. He made no effort to face them, but studied them in the mirror. He was confused. Thus far every person he had seen was Asian; he hadn't heard them speak anything apart from English, but even if he had he wouldn't have had a clue what language it was they were using. So who were these people, who was the group who had both been powerful enough to snatch them from the street and had the technical ability to locate them in the first place? Could it be the Ah Kong triads? Was there a link between the events of Germany and his current mission? Or was it a group he didn't know, a foreign power, or, and this he feared the most, Blackline. Could it be that elements of the Chinese arm of Blackline had managed to stay under the radar? Tate slowed his breathing; what he was doing was not at all helpful. They would either tell him who they were, or they wouldn't and that was that.

The lift doors opened and the three of them – Tate and his two silent guards – headed for a pair of double doors at the far end of the hallway. The doors were opened from inside and they entered.

'Please take a seat, Mr Tate.' The voice came from a large chair, its back facing him. 'Do you like cityscapes or are you more one for the country?'

The accent was English, and certainly a lot posher than his own. Tate said, 'I like mountains.'

'Ah, yes, some like to climb mountains, but I prefer to fly over them.' The chair swivelled around to show its occupant. 'But forgive me. I am being rude. I am Gu Joon.'

The name meant nothing to Tate, so he said nothing.

'You are Jack Tate, a serving member of Her Majesties Special Air Service who has been seconded, on a semi-permanent basis, to a covert special operations group named E Squadron which is run by the Secret Intelligence Service – the SIS, or MI6 to use its popular name.'

Tate made no reply. The man knew exactly who he was, so there was nothing to be gained with either a denial or a confirmation. But how did he know everything?

'Tell me something, Mr Tate. Why did you not seek the assistance of your allies, the US, in locating and extracting Colin Jericho?'

'What difference does that make to you? You have him. You've won.'

'Yes, I have, but I am merely curious. Look, there is no need for you and me to be on opposing sides, Jack.'

'That's nice.'

'Ha, ha. Yes. Nice.'

'So, Gu, what are you? Blackline?'

Gu Joon's eyebrows shot skywards. 'Good heavens, no. However, I can understand why you would think so. I am merely the head of a private organisation who wishes to effect a permanent and positive change in the Korean peninsula.'

'You want a united Korea?'

'I want progressive Koreas; a united Korea would be "nice".'

'Good luck.'

'Thank you. Luck I do believe is on my side, especially now that I have the services of Colin Jericho. He has been most forthcoming.'

The double doors opened behind Tate and Plato was ushered into the room. He too was handcuffed, but unlike Tate he looked unwashed despite wearing clean clothes.

'Ah, Mr Plato! Welcome, and please take a seat next to your colleague.'

It was evident to Tate that Plato was petrified. 'Relax.'

'You look like you could do with a good wash,' Gu Joon said, with a grandfatherly tone.

Tate knew that it was important in any hostage or captivity situation for those in charge to see their captives as real people with real lives awaiting them. The fact that Gu Joon seemed concerned about Plato's appearance was encouraging.

'Thank you. I will.' Plato's voice was reedy, as though his throat was constricted.

'Now. Why are you both here? That is the question one imagines is on your lips? I shall tell you. What I am engaged in is the culmination of my life's work. I have been attempting to formulate a way in which I can unite my country, which has been divided for far too long. For this to work I must have the best team available. I have experts in various scientific and technical fields, and I have highly trained military operatives – you've seen them in action. Mr Plato, I believe your computing and technical abilities would be a boon to my organisation, and I am willing to make you an unbelievably rich young man if you would work for me.'

Tate looked at Plato. His mouth was opening and closing like a goldfish. 'I ... I ... ca ... can't,' he stammered.

'Oh, you can. You will. It is all about the price, Mr Plato.'

'Not everyone is for sale, Gu,' Tate said.

'I was not talking of a merely monetary price, Jack. Mr Plato, I am aware, has a doting mother who I believe lives in the British seaside resort of Brighton. Is that not the case, yes?'

'I ... I ...'

'So that's it, Gu? You pretend to be, what, a philanthropist but when it comes down to it you are a gangster?'

'No, Jack, I am not a gangster. I am like you. I am a patriot. I am doing this to unite my broken country, a task that the West and the East have failed to accomplish.'

'How will you achieve this where others have failed?'

'I simply will.' The older man's voice now displayed a telling note of irritation. 'Mr Plato, I have no wish to have you held here as a captive. I am aware what you are capable of, and that is why I want to be reasonable. If you work for me, your mother's safety will be guaranteed and once our mission is completed, you will be free to go. You can take her anywhere in the world, you could buy her a villa in Barbados.'

Tate knew the thoughts running through Plato's head. He also knew that Plato was the last person who would dream of betraying the service, but, unlike himself, Plato had a living parent. 'It's OK, Neill.'

'I'm sorry ... the answer is still no.'

Gu rose to his feet, faster than Tate would have expected. 'That is not an acceptable answer. Very well, Neill, I see I shall have to use the stick.'

Tate sensed movement behind. His two guards were back, and this time they were armed. Tate was unarmed and next to Plato; any move he tried would probably result in Plato being caught in the middle. Tate knew he had to do something but now was neither the time nor the place. He'd wait, but one thing was for sure: he was not going down without a fight.

Gu said something in his mother tongue. Two more guards

131

entered and each grabbed hold of one of Tate's arms and pulled him to his feet. Then, in a blur of movement, Gu lunged at Tate and drove his left fist into his gut. Tate winced and, in spite of the hold the guards had on him, doubled over. Gu now used his right fist and slammed it into the side of Tate's head. Tate felt his legs buckle, but the guards held his weight and he remained standing.

'You, Jack Tate, I believe to be the archetypal "fly in the ointment"; never to be underestimated. It is a great pity that we are on opposing sides of history. It will not give me an ounce of personal satisfaction when you are dead. You live now because I wanted to meet you, I wanted to look you in the eye and understand you. You are a dangerous man, and because of that I cannot have you anywhere near my operation. My apologies.'

'Thank you for your sincerity,' Tate managed to say through the fog of pain.

Gu Joon spoke again to his men, in what Tate took to be Korean, then two guards started to hustle him out of the room.

'Please wait, you can't!' Plato too was on his feet. 'Look, I'll work for you, I'll do anything you want me to do but please don't kill him! Keep him as your prisoner, but please let him live.'

'I admire your spirit, Neill, and, because I am a gentleman, I will consider your request. Perhaps he may be worth something?'

Tate managed to turn his head and meet Plato's eyes, and, unseen by the others with his left eye, Tate winked.

The men took Tate back the way he had come, out through the doors, into the lift, down five floors and then along the landing back to his own room. They opened the door and Tate turned and waggled his hands.

'Any chance you can cut me loose?'

Neither guard spoke as they ignored his request and shut the door.

Tate walked the length of his room and leaned against the windowsill. He had questions running through his head, but knew he had to focus on the most important aspect first, and that was escape. He had been taught that the best time to escape was as near to the time of capture as possible. This had not been the case here, especially when he had been drugged. However, he now had more understanding of where he was and what he was up against. He had no doubt that Gu's men would be ruthless, but the man had stayed his execution for the moment, so the question was: would the guards shoot to kill if he attempted to escape? It was a slim chance, but that was all he needed. Using his eyes, but keeping the rest of his body still, Tate scanned his room for any surveillance devices. He knew that someone had heard him bemoan the lack of conditioner and bring him a bottle, but were there cameras also? He focused on the corner of the room, high and to the left of the door where the two walls met the ceiling. Now a fish-eye lens there would capture the entire space; it was the most appropriate place to mount such a device. He compared the corner with the opposite corner. Yes, the one on the left seemed flattened slightly, as though something was buried beneath. He had to mark it as a camera. Tate felt the windowsill with his hands; as expected, it was smooth and useless in terms of sawing against his bonds. He knew he could break the handcuffs apart if he could weaken the links in the chain. There was a technique, but it was easier to do if his hands were front of his body. Whilst Tate tried them for any give or movement, he ambled to the bathroom. He faced the mirror, but again searched the space with his eyes. A camera in here would be more problematic to both hide because of the white tiles and operate because of the humidity and moisture. He got onto the floor and lay on his back. He saw a speaker under the sink which in a hotel would carry the sound of the TV or 'in room' sound system; here it could be a microphone or perhaps it was just a speaker? He had no idea if this place was an actual hotel or just a commercial property built specifically for Gu Joon. But he hoped it was the former because hotels were built in areas that expected trade, tourists, and as such he hoped that this place was somewhere large enough for him to escape into and to call for help. However, before he did any of that he needed to free his hands. Tate wriggled on the tiled floor, on his backside, until his head was touching the wall. He pushed himself up as bit so that his shoulders were flat against the wall.

Tate was now sitting on his hands. He pushed his upper back against the wall whilst arching his lower back and then he tried to raise his pelvis off the floor whilst at the same time pulling his arms lower. He rocked back and forth like a manic contortionist until finally his hands were lower than his buttocks. Bending forward he pushed his chest into his legs; the bruises from Germany still registering as did the gut punch from Gu as he dragged his hands lower until they reached his knees, then his ankles and finally under his feet so that his hands were in front of him. Tate lay flat again for a moment and listened before he sat up and again rested his back against the wall. The steel cuffs had dug into his wrists and caused his hands to feel a little numb; it would have been so much easier if they'd used cable ties, but such was life. He brought his hands together and started to turn them in opposite directions, twisting the chain until it all but locked. He then pressed the twisted chain at either end, and tried to use the torque of the twists as leverage to break the link nearest his left cuff. It was an old trick and some newer cuffs had been redesigned to prevent such breakages from happening, but it was his only hope. After minutes of repeated twisting, untwisting and pulls, he felt the chain start to give. And after that, the link snapped and his fists shot in opposite directions. Tate closed his eyes and inhaled deeply. Finally something was going his way. Tate stood and looked at himself in the mirror and winked.

He had a decision to make. He moved back into the bedroom, making sure to keep his hands behind his back, as though he was still restrained by the cuffs. He looked directly at the camera, or where he suspected the camera was, and started to shout. He shouted about needing to have his hands free to use the toilet and then, just for added effect and drama, he started to throw

134

himself at the door to the landing. He doubted the guards cared about his bodily functions, but hoped they couldn't ignore the ruckus he was making.

His actions didn't take long to get a reaction. The door opened and one guard burst in, followed by the other one. Neither held their weapons. Neither seemed to be at all concerned that Tate may have freed his arms, but they should have been.

The nearest guard had his hands up as though to grab Tate. Tate turned sideways, let the guard grab at him, then slammed a right hook into the man's unprotected jaw. The guard's own momentum made him take another step before his knees gave way and he fell onto the carpeted floor. Tate immediately shot out his right foot at the second guard's knee, knocking it sideways with a satisfying crunch. The man's mouth opened as a howl of pain was about to escape, but Tate foreshortened that by closing it with a right upper cut. The guard dropped next to his partner, who had now pushed himself up to his knees. Tate thought about leaving him conscious to question, but decided that a boot to the head was a better option. So, he kicked him. Both guards were now unconscious.

Tate knew it was a gamble, but it was one he had to take. He had only ever seen the two guards on this floor, and he hoped that meant that there no more stationed there. But who was watching the camera, and where were they? He had to move; he didn't have time to stick around to have his questions answered. Tate could see from a visual search that both men had a Glock 17 strapped to their right thigh, and a *Kbar* knife strapped to their left. To him it seemed like overkill, but whatever got them through the night was fine by him.

Tate took one of the Glocks and ejected and pocketed the magazine from the other. He also took both knives and stuffed them and their sheaths into his pocket. He started to search the nearest guard for keys or a key-card and breathed a sigh of relief when he found both. Willing the key to work, he inserted it into his left cuff and turned. The steel restraint fell onto the floor. A wide smile spread across Tate's face as he now unlocked the other cuff. He slipped the key into his pocket; he'd try it on Plato's cuffs when he found him.

Tate cautiously moved out of his room. He saw a door further along the corridor was open. Weapon up, he advanced towards it, his every sense on high alert. He spun into the room and saw that it was the same size as his own except that the window here was not obscured and there was a table and bank of CCTV monitors instead of a bed.

Tate crept to the window, momentarily mesmerised by the neon-tinged sunset. Tate shook his head in disbelief as he realised he was in Las Vegas. He looked at the monitors. There were four of them, and three of them were empty. However, in the one marked 'Room 1429', two figures could be seen arguing. The two figures were Plato and Jericho, and neither one was wearing a pair of handcuffs.

Tate checked to see what number room he had and figured out that if these were normal room numbers, then the room containing the two missing Brits was two floors below his own.

He looked around the room for anything else that may be a help to him. Unsurprisingly there was not a discarded mobile phone or even a land line, so much for simply 'calling the cavalry' but he did spot a roll of duct tape lying under the table next to a piece of carpet that was sticking up, perhaps a repair in progress. He collected the tape then studied the monitors again; he noted that there were several that were cycling through views of the lift, landing and the building's lobby. So far, the alarm had not been raised, so far there was no reason for Tate to believe that anyone except for the two unconscious men in his room knew of his escape bid. Tate took a moment to study the screens again; he saw no more men. He returned to his room, Glock up and ready to face either or both guards if they had come round. Neither had.

He tied both men up with their belts and tape then left them to their slumber. Tate used the guard's key-card to shut his door and made his way to the stairs. He carefully looked both up and down and listened before slowly descending a step at a time. The plimsoles he was wearing were far lighter than his own boots and had made less noise on the carpeted hallways, but he knew that they were much more likely to squeak and give away his position on the concrete steps. He reached the floor below and paused before he passed the door to the hallway. He had no idea who or what lay beyond that and had no intention of finding out. He reached the next floor too without any resistance before he came level with the door to the floor two below his own, the one that he hoped contained the room that Plato and Jericho had been in.

The door opened and another guard stepped out, looking left and not seeing Tate to his right. He had a lighter in one hand and a cigarette in the other. Tate noticed that the window on the stairwell was open and there was a pile of cigarette butts under it, ground into the floor. *That'll kill you*, Tate thought to himself.

As if sensing he was not alone, the guard looked up right, so Tate punched him full in the face. There was a crunch as Tate's fist flattened the man's nose and crushed his cartilage. But before the guard could register what had happened, Tate sent a kick into the man's groin. Doubled up, blood pouring from his destroyed nose, the guard dropped to the unforgiving concrete floor. The man was still but gurgling as the blood ran into his mouth. Tate had no time to be a nursemaid, so stepped over the incapacitated guard and through the door onto the landing. Placed next to the door and leaned up against the wall was a supressed HK short-barrel 416.

'And now I have a machine gun, ho, ho, ho,' Tate said quietly as he shouldered the weapon and tactically advanced along the landing.

Eyes scanning every inch ahead of him, and ears fully open to listen for any movement, any footfall, Tate picked up the sound of two British voices. He edged nearer; they were emanating from the room he had expected them to be coming from. Tate reached the door and lifted his left hand to knock, then realised the absurdity of it. They were locked in like he had been. He pulled the stolen key-card from his pocket and presented it to the lock. There was a two-tone electronic tone and the lock released.

Tate pushed his way into the room as a fist flew in his direction.

'Jack?' Plato said, but not before his right fist had connected with Tate's left ear.

'Whoa, Iron Mike! It's me!'

'You escaped!' Jericho said, stepping out from his hiding place behind the door.

'Not yet,' Tate replied. 'We need to move.'

'What's the plan?' Plato asked.

'We're in Las Vegas. We just need to get out of the front door of this place and then get lost in the crowds of tourists and gamblers.'

'Vegas?' Plato said. 'Wow.'

'Well never mind "wow", we need to move now.'

'I'm not going to come with you,' Jericho said.

'What?' Tate was incredulous.

'Look, they aren't Blackline. These people are trying to make a difference, to create real change.'

'Are you mental?'

'Jack, I've been trying to tell him, but he won't listen,' Plato said.

Tate looked Jericho square in the eyes. 'I have a gun, I'm a dangerous person. You are coming with us. End of discussion.'

'No.' Jericho folded his arms.

Tate backhanded Jericho across the face, sending him into the wall. 'Enough.'

There was a noise outside, and then, before Tate had time to assess the situation, the door opened. A guard stepped into the room and Tate shot a fist out, connecting with the man's chin and sending him stumbling sideways. However, he wasn't alone. Three more armed men were directly outside, they had seen Tate, and their weapons were rising.

Without time to warn the others to move or drop to the floor, Tate fired a burst of 9mm rounds into the wall of men. The nearest went down, his chest ripped open. The second fell too as his colleague's corpse pushed him to the floor whilst the third jinked away to the side of the door and out of Tate's field of fire.

Tate did the only thing he could do; he advanced, HK aimed at where the third gunman had disappeared to. It was point-blank range, it was stupid, but his only other move was to shut the door and that was what the gunman would have expected.

Tate threw himself out of the room. He sailed over the two men on the floor and landed on his right shoulder. The impact jarred his insides, but he didn't release his grip on the machine gun. Less than a metre away and caught completely by surprise, the last gunman standing had his back flat against the wall and was facing Tate. The man's face displayed no emotion as Tate eviscerated him at point-blank range.

The second gunman was frantically trying to draw his sidearm, but he was pinned. Tate fired a single round into his skull. Springing to his feet, Tate checked both up and down the hallway for any further targets. He moved back into the room, knowing that even though the rounds fired had been supressed, there was a good chance someone had heard.

Plato and Jericho had managed to turn the bed on its side and were hiding behind it. Tate decided not to tell them that it wouldn't have stopped a single round.

'We go and we go now.' Tate ducked his head back out of the room. The landing was still empty. 'Get into the landing then run to your right and take the stairs. Stop and don't make a sound or say a word when you reach the door, just open it and go through. Got it?'

Plato nodded, Jericho just glared. 'We're going to take the stairs down nice and slowly. I'm going to need you to follow me and do exactly what I say. OK?'

'OK,' Plato said.

Jericho nodded.

Tate checked the landing again. 'Go!'

Both men moved past him and jogged to the door. They opened it with a creak. Tate followed, keeping his HK trained back up the landing. He reached the door and closed it behind himself. So far so good. Tate realised both men were looking back at him with odd expressions on their faces. It was because he had just killed three men without a second thought. It was something, however, that Tate had been trained to do; he had a switch which he had to flick from 'standard behaviour' to 'maximum aggression'. Psychologists had forever been stating that soldiers were damaged, barely functioning psychopaths but without them what would the world do? Tate was a killer, but he knew he wasn't a murderer. He knew the distinction.

'You both follow me. If I raise my fist, you freeze. If I tell you to get down, you do just that. If anyone comes from behind, you duck, and I shoot. There are no friendlies in this place, everyone we see we neutralise. Got that?'

Two dumbstruck faces nodded at him. Tate nodded in return and edged forward. He held his fist up and was cheered to see that Plato and Jericho immediately stopped without question, or sound. Tate peered over the gap in the stairwell, to make out the ground floor, but the angle and size of the stairs prevented him from doing so. He could see the stairs for the floor below and no further.

Tate moved. One step at a time; it felt agonisingly slow, but it was steady and, most importantly of all, it was silent. Tate reached the door to the floor below; he held his fist up again and then pressed his ear to the fire door. Silence, nothing. They continued. He could now hear the erratic breaths of the two untrained men behind him, erratic because their fear was preventing them from breathing in the most economical and effective manner. They descended past two more floors before Tate made them halt. He could hear voices, and he could smell smoke. Tate peered over the edge of the stairwell and could see two heads below with wafts of smoke rising from them. He was glad smoking was such a popular pastime among Gu Joon's men. Their path was blocked, but it was a good sign. If their escape bid had been noticed, the two men below would not have been casually smoking. There was nothing for it but to wait. He didn't want to kill the men if they were going to move out of the way of their own accord.

They stood and waited. Tate hoped they would take no more than five minutes with their smokes. But he was wrong, it was two, because after two minutes of waiting there were excited-sounding yells in a foreign language from the floor below. Both smokers stubbed out their cigarettes and hurried back through their door.

Tate made a decision. 'We move faster, but we don't run.'

Tate started to move down again, this time at double the pace of before, which was still no more than a brisk walk. He managed to keep his footfall silent, but every few steps there were squeaks from behind. They cleared five more floors before Tate raised his fist again. The other two concertinaed into each other but didn't say a word. Tate cocked his head. He could hear footsteps and they were getting closer, their sound growing louder as, unseen, they climbed the stairs below. Tate motioned for the other two to stay put and advanced. He looked around the next flight of stairs and saw a train of men purposefully moving up, weapons tactically scanning each and every inch for a target. The lead man saw Tate and fired. The three-round burst kicked up chips of concrete around Tate's head as he half-fell backwards.

Tate had another decision to make. The gunmen had the advantage in numbers and firepower, but they were hemmed into a narrow angle of advance and attack. It was possible that Tate could hold them off or force them to retreat, but that would leave the rest of Gu's guards free to advance on Tate and come at them from above. Without firing a round, Tate bounded back up the stairs to the door of the floor they had just passed. He found Jericho and Plato cowering around the corner two steps up.

'Follow me and stay low!'

Tate burst through the door, weapon up, seeking anything that posed a threat. He was temporarily dazzled by the amount of neon glaring at him from outside because the entire space was one open glass box. The floor was made of glass with thick support columns clad in white marble and mirrors holding the floors above. Tate looked down, through the floor, he saw the level below was glass also. It was as though a child had built a Lego tower but had decided to use clear blocks for two levels. If Tate had had time to think he would have thought it was quite an architectural achievement, but he didn't. To Tate's relief, it was completely empty.

Perhaps it was going to be a function room, or a restaurant or a nightclub, he had no idea but whatever it was, apart from the support columns, it gave the three of them absolutely nowhere to hide. Tate ran through the room, knowing that they could be cut down at any moment, and pulled open a glass door to the terrace. He was instantly battered by a desert wind that he had not expected and with it came the cacophony of sounds from the busy city. It was not yet night, although the sun was setting fast. Tate looked over the edge. Two floors down, he could see a large flat roof that extended, housing it seemed another part of the hotel complex, and beyond this were foundations and the access road leading to the city's main drag. Tate had been to Vegas before, whilst training at the nearby Nevada Test and Training facility, so recognised their location.

Plato and Jericho arrived next to him.

'It's a pity we can't just base jump,' Jericho said.

'Be my guest,' Tate said, only half kidding. It was too low and both men knew it.

Tate moved off again and ran around the terrace towards the opposite stairwell. An idea was forming in his head. He reached the door to the hallway, held up his fist and then pointed to the thick support column. Plato and Jericho scurried behind it, the only piece of cover.

Tate took a deep breath, exhaled, then threw himself out of the door and into the landing. It was a crazy technique, the same one that he had used earlier, but the only one that would give him the element of surprise. Again, he landed on his shoulder, but again he had his firearm ready. The door to the stairwell was open and a gunman was positioned at the threshold. He was crouched, attempting to minimise his target profile.

Tate sent a burst of 9mm rounds into the doorway. The crouching gunman convulsed as he was hit and dropped his weapon.

Tate moved into the doorway. The man had been alone. He beckoned Plato and Jericho to join him. This was the stairwell at the other side of the building to the one they had been using, and he hoped it would remain clear. He held his fist up, telling the others to stop, then pulled open the door and started to go down. He was halfway to the next floor, the second level of glass, when he heard boots slamming on the concrete steps as men raced upwards towards them.

'Go through the door and move it! There's a second balcony, get on it and get low behind one of the corner columns!'

Plato and Jericho jerkily moved past him and through the door. Tate waited until the lead gunman rounded the corner before he shot him in the head, the retort of the supressed rounds echoing like a heavy pan dropped onto tiles in the confined space. The gunman fell backwards, landing on the man behind him and blocking the rest of his team's advance. Tate moved forward and put two more rounds into the next man, who fell and made the human barrier even larger.

Tate sprinted across the fishbowl-like room. Ahead he could see a door to the terrace was open and he surmised Jericho and Plato were hiding behind the column to its left. His feet squeaked and squawked on the floor, but the plimsoles gave him enough grip to power ahead. He was suddenly aware of shadows above him and over him. He looked up to make out the almost comical sight of gunmen on the floor above, pointing their weapons at him but unable to shoot through the layers of heat-strengthened laminated glass. Tate carried on towards the balcony as now shots rang out from behind him. Ahead, the glass crazed as rounds penetrated the top layer of laminated glass but did not pass through. He zigzagged around the two support columns that stood between him and the terrace before he managed to get to the open door. It too crazed as rounds barely missed him.

Out on the terrace he moved to his left and saw the others cowering. It was a surreal experience, as the sounds of Sin City were joined by the whizz and ping of silenced rounds impacting around them.

More rounds now slammed into the windows, but the glass held. Tate looked over the edge of the terrace and now knew what he had to do.

'The only way out is down. I need you to climb over the edge and drop.'

'W … what?' Plato was shaking and didn't look as if he knew where he was.

'Get to the edge. Look, the railings haven't been put in yet. Just shuffle over and off. There is a flat roof a floor below. If you drop it's only a few extra feet to fall.'

Jericho lumbered, as though his body was made of lead, to the edge and peered down. 'That's a ten-foot drop.'

'Get on your stomach, legs over first, hang onto the edge and drop. When your feet hit, just try to bend your knees and roll.'

More rounds slammed into the glass by the pillar and Plato put his hands over his head.

Jericho lay on his stomach and edged backwards into the darkening void. First his feet, then his lower legs and then everything below the waist was hanging over the edge. He hung onto two steel-support pins that were to be used to secure the missing glass panel.

Tate could see the gunmen rushing into the glass room on this level now, seeking him and the others out. He watched from behind the support column as they fanned out into two teams, each heading for a different door to the terrace; it was only a matter of time before his small group was encircled – and then they would be trapped.

Tate turned back to Jericho. Just his chest was now above the ledge, and, through the glass, Tate could see the rest of him dangling in the darkening night.

'Go!' Tate hissed.

Jericho nodded and slipped away. A full two seconds later, the sound of an impact on the flat roof and a pained cry reached Tate's ears.

There was movement to Tate's left; the gunmen were edging nearer. Tate gave them a three-round burst, hitting one and sending the rest back a space. Tate fired again, but felt the HK click on empty. Now all he had was the Glock.

'Neill! Time to go!'

Plato looked up; his eyes seemed far away. 'I can't – you go, save Colin. Leave me.'

'Get over that edge, or I'll bloody shoot you myself!'

'I can't!'

Movement again, from the same direction. Tate fired a single round from the Glock, it sent them back again, but the other side would be advancing and all they had to do was wait it out until they shot him or made him run out of ammo.

'Neill, do it.'

There was a low thudding as a line of supressed rounds tore into the pillar above Plato's head, raining broken tiles onto them like jagged pieces of ice. It prompted Plato into action, and he shuffled towards the edge, until he froze before finally moving again.

Tate went prone and sent another two rounds back around

145

the pillar and then, looking in the other direction, saw more men advancing on their position. He fired two further rounds at them, driving them back behind the next support pillar.

'Neill, it's now or never.'

'I just can't! I don't know how to!'

Tate tried not to curse; he took it for granted that in a moment of crisis he had the ability to seemingly slow time, to assess and to act accordingly. He turned so he was face down and his feet were pointing over the edge. 'Neill, get on top of me. Put your arms around my back and hold on.'

'Wh … what?'

'Get on! Hold on! Now!'

More rounds swirled over his head and he could hear the slapping of fast feet approaching. Plato shuffled on top of him, and Tate lifted his neck. He then shuffled backwards and felt his feet and legs dangle in the air.

'Hold on as tight as you can to me.' Tate took the weight, felt it in his chest as he slithered off the glass then in his shoulders and hands as he grabbed hold of the two pins. The metal dug into his palms; his shoulders screamed at him. Tate was strong, he had trained to be, but he couldn't hold their combined weight for much longer. Plato started to slip, but slipping slower than he would have done if he'd let go of the edge himself.

'Let yourself slip down me, then drop. Bend your knees and roll!'

'Urgh …' was all Plato managed to say as he continued to slide. His hands grabbed at Tate's shirt and then his jeans and then Tate felt a sudden lightness as Plato dropped. Tate chanced a glance down and saw Plato lying on his side and Jericho pulling him to his feet. They were both alive, which was all he could have hoped for. Tate let go of the poles, his hands slid over the glass, and he fell.

One second … two seconds … his feet hit flat, instantly he let his legs bend and then as they did so he rolled. He ended up on his back, staring up at the balcony. He'd made it, but his old freefall instructor wouldn't have been impressed.

Tate scurried over to Plato. He was limping and having to lean on Jericho. To their left and all but hidden in the shadow of the tower they had just left, Tate saw the tops of metal railings protruding. Grabbing Plato under the opposite arm to Jericho and not wasting a single second with words, he steered them towards it.

Jericho and Plato leaned against the wall of the taller building, directly under the terrace as shadows swarmed above. Night had fully fallen now, and the stark shadows cast by the 'on–off' pulsating neon helped obscure their position. Tate looked at the railings; it was an inspection ladder which ran from a concrete-slabbed path hidden behind large, lush palm trees to the roof. Probably some requirement of a fire code or something, but, if that was the case, Tate was for once glad of red tape.

'There's a ladder down, quick, move!'

In the darkness Plato and Jericho hobbled forward like a drunken three-legged beast. Tate looked up and saw a face looking down, directly at him. The gunman was upside down and suspended by his feet. Tate shot him in the head. The man went limp, and his HK fell. Tate grabbed for it and although the impact of the weapon bruised his tired arms, he managed to keep a hold of it. He aimed back up now, at the walkway above, as the dead man was dragged back by his colleagues.

Tate hurried for the ladder. Supressed rounds, too quiet to be heard among the noise of the party city, zinged into the roof around him. Tate grabbed the railings with his right hand, and, holding the HK in his left, slid down the side of the ladder as fast as he could, ignoring the rungs.

At the bottom, Plato and Jericho were hiding in the shadows.

'What now?' Jericho asked.

'We get out of here.'

'But Colin's a wanted man, his face is plastered across the news,' Plato added, his voice higher and reedier than usual.

'Stay here, give me a minute.'

Tate moved away from the others and through the trees to the front of the building proper. The sounds of the city overwhelmed his every sense, but he had to try to filter out what should have been there from what shouldn't. He cocked his head and listened as he looked around. He was standing in the eternal Las Vegas twilight caused by the overabundance of neon. He was in a pool of purple created by a massive neon sign several floors above his head which proclaimed that the same building they had been held captive in, the Splendid Hotel & Casino would be opening soon. Tate made a mental note not to leave a good review on Trip Advisor. Ahead of him, he saw that whilst the looping in–out access road to the hotel was finished, there was a security pole on each end to prevent it being used.

Tate advanced on the path, but kept in the shadows at the side of the lower building, the building that would hold the hotel's reception. He neared the corner and glanced around. Marble columns adorned the front. He moved to the nearest one and again took a peek. He saw the glass-fronted reception area, and several men who were waiting for one of their number to open the padlock securing a thick chain to the double doors. The men, if they had not been holding handguns, would have looked like workers finishing their shift. Perhaps, Tate thought, that was the point? He fired a three-round burst into the glass panes next to the doors. The laminated glass held, but crazed and the workmen scattered. Tate ran past the front of the building and saw a sign for the underground car park, to be used by valets and those who liked to park for themselves. He bounded down the ramp, weapon up and out ready to react to any target. There was a barrier, which was up, and a glass and steel box to his immediate right which would house the valets and their clients' keys once the hotel was officially open. The box was empty, but on the wall behind, bathed in stark sodium lighting, were three keys on hooks. He stepped inside and grabbed all three. He ran deeper into the dimly lit car park. The roar of a powerful engine hit his ears, followed by headlights. Tate jinked sideways and opened fire at the car.

A metal door opened in the painted concrete wall and a line of figures hurried out. Tate froze, and then he changed target and fired. The two lead figures fell, dropping their own HKs. The next was unmistakable: Gu Joon. He didn't move a muscle, as though trying to comprehend what was happening. A third figure, his features obscured by a tactical cap, flashed forward from the shadows, firing his rifle single-handed at Tate whilst using his free hand to grab the old man's shoulder.

Tate flattened himself as more rounds rained down around him. When he looked up, all three had gone and he was left with a Rolls-Royce with steam rising from its round-riddled bonnet. Tate could go after Gu, but his primary concern was completing his mission, and that meant getting Jericho and Plato to safety. He moved further into the garage, knowing that at any minute a stream of men with guns could corner him. He now looked at the keys he'd taken – each conveniently on a branded fob. One was for a Chevy, another a Tesla and the third a Mazda. He wouldn't take the Tesla as he had no idea how far they needed to go and 'gas' was easier to source, so he threw the fob aside and continued on. The Mazda was an old 323, underpowered and too small. He sighed and opened the Chevy; he was going to be driving yet another Tahoe, but it did have a V8 engine, and could also double as a battering ram.

Tate made the tyres squeal as he lurched out of the parking space and slewed around the Rolls-Royce. There were men on the ramp, but he was moving too fast to stop and, besides, they were pointing guns at him, which he didn't find friendly. A round hit the SUV, Tate mentally crossed his fingers that it wasn't a lucky shot and carried on as the man who had fired it bounced sideways from the bonnet. There was another sickening thud of flesh on steel as Tate continued to accelerate up the ramp. He immediately hauled the wheel to the right, causing the heavy SUV to lurch as physics and gravity fought with modern American mechanical engineering. He rocketed past the hotel entrance and the car's nose came to a stop next to the large palm trees. He sounded the horn and opened the window.

'Get in! Move it!'

Jericho broke cover first, dragging a limping Plato behind him. Both men half climbed, half fell into the back and Tate floored the accelerator pedal to make the Tahoe shoot backwards. Pings of small arms rounds impacted against the coachwork, but it wasn't his car, so Tate didn't care.

Tate performed a 'J-turn', causing the Tahoe to buck and lurch before it faced the way he wanted it to go. Shifting the gearstick into Drive, Tate now aimed for the bollard blocking the way to the main road outside.

As they neared the bollard, Tate saw that it too had been lowered; in preparation for the Rolls-Royce, no doubt, but it worked for him too. They cleared the barrier and bumped up onto the road. Now parallel with the hotel, Tate looked back and saw a helicopter rising from the top floor. 'Elvis has left the building,' he muttered to himself.

Through his open window the screech of police sirens assaulted his ears. Then lights appeared from a junction ahead and came towards them. Tate slowed, to match the posted speed limit, and sat a little lower in his seat. A convoy of LVPD cruisers flashed past, followed by a dark-blue van with SWAT stencilled in white on the side.

Now that the initial escape part was over, Tate's mind started to focus on the evasion part of it. He saw a signpost for Phoenix, but decided to not take it; anyone looking for them would believe they'd taken the fastest route out of town. Instead, Tate turned north-east. Although Vegas was a friendly town, in a friendly country, he had to act as though he was behind enemy lines, and the fact that he was harbouring a wanted fugitive and had just killed an unknown number of men meant that he was neither going to ask the police for help nor book into a hotel and wait to be extracted.

'Are you both OK?' Tate asked.

'Yes.'

'Y … yes,' Plato stuttered.

'Look, we're going to make it. Gu is on that helo out of here, which means that he's given up on us.'

'Jack, what's the plan now?'

Tate did not like Jericho using his first name. In fact, Tate didn't like Jericho speaking at all. 'We follow this road out of here, grab a burner phone, some water and then call Box.'

'Box.' In the rear-view mirror, Tate saw Jericho smirk at his use of the nickname for the Secret Intelligence Service.

'Er, Jack,' Plato said, 'there's a phone by your right leg.'

Tate glanced down and saw an Iridium satellite handset lying on the passenger seat. 'Perhaps I should buy a lottery ticket too whilst my luck lasts?'

Tate started to laugh; he hadn't meant to, but it just happened. And then Plato did too, but his was more a whinny like a horse. Tate handed the phone back to Plato. 'Phone home and arrange an extraction, tell them we need a jet; anything, but we need it fast.'

Chapter 12

Las Vegas

Whilst Gu was furious at Tate's antics, Roe was impressed but not very surprised. Since taking off twenty minutes before, Gu had given order after order via a satellite phone whilst Roe thought through the tactical implications of their withdrawal. His uncle had the necessary resources to carry on the development of Project White Suit, but they no longer had Colin Jericho. Gu had let Roe watch a portion of the tape recordings in which Jericho explained, albeit due to narcotic inducement, about his work and breakthroughs. Roe was by no means an expert, but he had enough of a scientific mind to understand that what Jericho was explaining was possible. His process created the desired bonds in his material, which in turn provided it with its ultra-high tensile strength and ability to flex and absorb high impacts.

Roe understood the scientific and monetary implications of Jericho's research, but he had never been impressed by wealth nor power. What did impress him, though, was his uncle's vision. Jericho's breakthrough was a revolutionary material whose application would immediately change the fortunes of North Korea. It was a technology which would propel the DPRK's economy forward, making it a new industrial powerhouse; first militarily and then commercially. And, most important of all, it was a technology that could not be replicated without extreme skill and extreme luck. Jericho had estimated that it would take a dedicated laboratory a minimum of five years to chemically reverse engineer his product; whether this was true or not, Roe had no idea. What was important was that Pyongyang would have it first. A year, perhaps two, was more reasonable. In the meantime, he would become the right-hand man to the new ruler of North Korea. Yes, his uncle would take his rightful place as supreme leader as the feeble Hak dynasty, led by a bilious balloon of a man, were thrown into the labour camps they had themselves created. Roe felt his chest swell with pride, and it shocked him.

'It is a great pity our operation here has been compromised,' Gu Joon stated as his dark eyes fixed upon his. 'If we were not so far along with the operation I could perhaps intervene, grease the correct palms and continue to use the hotel. Now I will no longer take a risk nor make any decision that could jeopardise our success.'

'What about Jericho?' Roe asked.

'We have what we need, what we must ensure is that no other organisation or nation can claim that too.'

'You want me to eliminate him?'

'Yes. Kill them all. Leave their bodies where they fall. Jack Tate is nothing more than a terrorist, a white supremacist who targeted an Asian-owned and staffed hotel – which is what I have told the media. If the media believes it, the people and, of course, the authorities will follow, such are the sheep of this nation.'

'What if they do not?'

Gu smiled and his eyes narrowed. 'Roe, I am sure that eventually some clever computer system or some bright government employee operating said system will identity Tate, and then of course the US and UK governments will have a problem, but by then Tate will be long dead.'

Roe nodded. There was a tracker hidden in the vehicle Tate had taken, and a miniscule camera. He knew exactly where they were, and that Tate was driving.

Nevada

'Jack, you've stirred up one hell of a hornets' nest!' Pamela Newman's tone was terse. 'The local police have an image of you with a semi-automatic assault rifle blasting away at what they are calling contracted security guards!'

Tate let out a long breath as his eyes concentrated on the undulating road ahead. 'Yep. Busted.'

'Mr Jericho, your face is all over the news too, they are calling you – Cal Conners – Jack's accomplice. Neill, apparently you are a hostage.'

'At least I'm not a bad guy,' Plato stated.

'So, what are you telling us, Pamela?'

There was a sound on the line before she replied. Tate knew it was her sipping her tea. 'What I am telling you all is that it is impossible for me to get any type of aircraft into even the smallest commercial airport because the three of you will be immediately stopped.'

'So?' Tate knew they would not be hung out to dry, especially as they had Jericho and especially as Tate had Plato.

'So we have identified an out-of-the-way landing strip we think we can get in and out of and blame our landing on a technical malfunction. I'm going to send the coordinates to this phone.'

'That's great.'

'Now, until you're on that plane you stay dark, and that's an order.'

The call ended and then, a moment later, there was a ping alerting them that a message had been received.

'So?' Tate asked.

'It's the coordinates. Ah, I see.'

'See what?' Jericho said.

'It's another five hours from here.'

'Where the hell is this place?' Tate asked.

'Hm, it's immediately past a place called the Hite River Crossing.'

'As long as we're crossing in the car, I don't mind.' Tate stabbed the sat nav with his index finger. 'OK, give me the coordinates and then turn that handset off.'

They continued on in silence. It was full dark, and the black Tahoe moved in the lifeless landscape like a shimmering shadow. Staying on the I-15 was risky, but at night at least there were other vehicles around to hide among, unlike the smaller winding routes which branched off to places with ever-increasingly frontier-sounding names such as Valley of Fire, Arrowhead and Jackman. They uneventfully crossed the state line into Arizona at Mesquite and then entered Utah near a place Tate noted with a wry smile was named St George.

Tate looked again at the GPS and then the miles remaining on the Tahoe's information display. They had just enough fuel, which was good as stopping to get more wasn't an option for a pair of fugitives in a stolen car without a solitary dollar between them.

'I'm never going to see the light of day again, am I?' Jericho's tone was flat.

Tate made no reply.

'What do you mean?' Plato asked.

'For my part in the EMP and my association with Blackline. I could cure world hunger and it still wouldn't matter.'

Tate felt his anger starting to rise again. The EMP attack had affected the lives of untold millions and ended the lives of untold thousands. And, in his opinion, a single life lost in a terrorist attack was a life too many. His hands clenched and constricted on the leather-clad steering wheel. He was too angry to reply and too angry to do anything other than keep his eyes fixed on the dark tarmac ahead. He opened his window partway and fresh air blasted him in the face. It was cool and carried a scent of dust.

Two hours later and Jericho and Plato had fallen asleep in the back, their limp bodies held in place by seatbelts. He knew what stress the events of the last few hours of their escape and the last few days of captivity had put on them. He remembered back to his own 'escape and evasion' part of SAS selection. Tate had passed winter selection and it had been brutally cold in Wales. Dressed in an oversized army greatcoat missing its buttons he'd had to move from coordinate to coordinate on a map traversing the mountainous, wild countryside whilst being chased by a hunter force made up of green army volunteers, a dog unit and his directing staff. Everyone got caught sooner or later, and although there had been rumours of one recruit who managed to climb a tree and hide, he'd met no one who had met him or even knew him. Then, tired, cold, famished and wet, because winters in the Welsh mountains were always wet, came the fun part. Hours and hours of interrogation, and stress positions, whilst being bombarded by white noise or in his case Finnish Death Metal and sleep deprivation. But he had passed, come through the other side whilst many had failed. Yet, as he continued to drive, flashes of conversations and faces which he had no recollection of ever seeing, drifted in front of his eyes. They hung like apparitions in the beam of the Tahoe's powerful headlights. A cold fear started to take hold of Tate. Had he broken, had he spoken to the faces he now saw? Immediately he thought about the days lost, the time he and the others had been held captive, time that would have been customarily used to interrogate, to question. Gu Joon knew exactly who he was, and who Plato was too. Did this mean that either he or Plato or even Jericho had given him this information, or had it come from other sources?

Yes, Tate had passed the SAS's resistance to interrogation, but that had prepared him to face, and counter, traditional techniques … the bruising and puncture mark on his arm … had he been injected with something that had made him talk?

Tate had to imagine the worst; he had to plan for it, and in his case that meant that Gu's organisation knew the structure of E Squadron, and the names of the people who ran it. And what of the secrets that Plato knew? Tate shuddered. And if they had intel from both him and Plato then Jericho's secrets were out there too.

Tate rubbed his face, his stubble starting to itch, and blinked away his fatigue. It was going to be one hell of a debrief when they finally got back to the UK, and he knew this time he'd be questioned more intensely than ever.

It was three hours to sunrise, and out here among the rocky canyons that was going to be spectacular. Tate knew that staying on the I-15 was the fastest route; it was also the route that had the most traffic, yet that had lessened with each passing minute. Tate started to feel as exposed as the rocks that lined the road, but he had no choice, he couldn't cut across country even with the help of the sat nav for fear of running out of fuel or encountering local law enforcement on an otherwise deserted two-lane local road.

The miles ticked by and Tate's tiredness increased. He opened his window fully and let himself be battered by the cold night air until his eyes started to water. The two in the back were still out for the count and he doubted that anything apart from a cold bucket of water would now stir them from their slumber.

Tate followed the instructions of the over-complicated onboard sat nav and made the turn off the I-15, at Exit 132, and took the I-70 east. Although it was still pitch-black outside, Tate knew the terrain was changing from the flat desert plateau to foothills, and as if to illustrate this his headlights caught a sign warning that chains or snow tyres would be needed if the sign was illuminated.

The sky was lightening in the east. Streaks of pink had started to appear in what now was an almost navy-blue backdrop. If he hadn't been racing towards a rendezvous in enemy territory,

Tate would have pulled over, got out, waited for, and watched the sunrise explode around him. But he didn't. He made the decision he'd return; he was, after all, in canyon country, home to all the images of cowboy films he'd watched as a kid. Tate smirked. Some of those films he'd later found out hadn't been filmed in the US at all. He was now dog tired, and the promise of the rising sun should have given him a second wind, but it didn't. Without rest, without water, the bordering on a six-hour drive had wiped him out. Tate was on his last ounce of reserve, and he knew it. If he'd been walking, the physical effort of keeping upright, of planting one foot in front of the other would have been enough to have prevented him from falling into unconsciousness, but sitting on a US-sized padded-leather driver's seat gave him no such effort.

There was a rumbling and then vibration, a shaking and then a metallic grinding noise. Tate's eyes flickered open and then became wide, his whole body jerking as he grabbed the steering wheel and hauled it to the right, willing the Tahoe to get back on the road. But it wouldn't. It bounced along, two wheels on and two wheels off until finally the front tyre bit into the asphalt and the SUV was saved from slamming into the sheer rock face to his left. Tate started to pant like he'd just run an Olympic sprint race and his heart pounded in his chest. He opened all four of the SUV's windows and decided that it was time for everyone to wake up. If they were awake, then so would he be. He'd chat to Plato; he didn't have words to waste on Jericho.

'Christ, where are we?' Jericho said, as the wind whipped around his hair.

Tate said nothing.

'Was I asleep?' Plato asked, his voice thick.

'For about three hours,' Tate replied.

'Can you close the windows?' Jericho asked.

'No. We need it cold. We need to be alert.'

'What the hell for?'

Tate locked the rear window controls. His lights were still

on but outside the beams the undulating shape of Utah State Route 95, otherwise known as the Bicentennial Highway, started to take shape.

'Look at this place!' Jericho leaned forward in his seat.

'When Pamela said the extraction point was in the middle of nowhere, she meant it,' Plato added.

'I've not seen another set of lights for two hours; I'd say we're more likely to see the Road Runner and Wiley Coyote than we are another car.'

'Which one are we, Road Runner?'

'I hope so,' Plato replied. 'Wiley Coyote was always falling off cliffs.'

'We're Road Runner, he was never caught,' Tate said, with more certainty than he felt, as he noticed the low fuel warning light flick on.

The road lunged out of a canyon and into a valley that was bordered with iconic rising rock towers. The whole area now was bathed in a watery orange glow, the diffused light making the panorama look like an overexposed photograph. With full sunrise would come the searing desert sun, and with that the stark shadows and the contrast. Tate had never been a painter but often wished he could. He smirked. Who was he kidding? He could barely draw the curtains.

'Ten miles away.' Tate tapped the screen, making the map larger. 'There will be an airstrip on our right, just before we hit the river.'

'As long as we stop before we hit the river,' Plato said.

'I'll see what I can do.'

They continued along UT95, each mile more rugged than the mile before. On either side of them the red and ochre rocks rose like a film set, it could have been the backdrop to countless cowboy films, or it could have been *Star Wars*, if it hadn't been for the cracked and repaired tarmac beneath them. Each new twist and bend brought more rock, more cliffs. Sometimes close, hugging the road on either side and on others falling back twenty or thirty feet. And then the Tahoe rounded a bend and on the right the rock wall fell away to reveal their first glimpse of the Colorado River below. Even to Tate's tired eyes it looked magnificent, incredible, impossible, yet there it was: a wide ribbon of shimmering tungsten in the early morning light. They wound downhill now as the world opened up to them. Greenery appearing on the banks of the river, which would later run into Lake Powell.

'This road definitely wasn't built by the Romans,' Jericho stated.

Tate made no reply. The road had forced its way through, around and past impossible canyons and gullies for what had seemed like endless miles, and he was the one who, even though he was driving an SUV with every possible creature comfort, felt like he'd been fighting a gorilla. Tate was tired and ached, but he knew that one more push was all that was required; five more miles would take them to the airstrip and the airframe Newman had promised. It was too easy to start to relax already as they counted down the distance and the new day expanded around them.

Behind him Plato and Jericho were chattering about the landscape and the views, for Plato he knew it was the relief of finally knowing he was going home, yet for Jericho he imagined it was nervous talk to cover his fear, the fear of what was yet to come for him. However, Tate reasoned that whatever the UK government threw at him would be less than he deserved and less life-threatening than his EMP had been. Tate knew it wasn't his role or responsibility to judge, he was the protector and that was all he had to do.

The sat nav told him he was a mile away from the solitary airstrip named on the map as 'Hite Airport'. The rock walls on either side closed in again tight to the road and then, as they descended a hill, the view abruptly opened up again, giving way to a valley enclosed by distant rising, red peaks.

The sat nav continued to count down. Tate looked to his right.

And then he heard rotor blades.

Tate tensed as an all-too-familiar feeling engulfed him. They weren't expecting a helo, but one was here seemingly waiting for them in the early morning in the middle of nowhere.

Tate saw it rise into the sky from the right, from the still-hidden runway. Everything inside him hoped it was a coincidence, but everything else prepared him to act. His fuel gauge was just above empty, and he knew the Tahoe was all but running on fumes.

They carried on, nearing the entrance to the strip, and then the helo was directly above them.

'Jack, what's happening?' The panic was evident in Plato's voice.

'I don't know, and we can't stay to find out.'

'It's them, isn't it? It has to be,' Jericho said, his voice oddly devoid of any emotion. 'They've found us.'

Before Tate could reply, the helo swooped to a low hover, blocking the road ahead. Any doubt Tate may have had about the helo's intentions were blown away.

The sensible action was to slam on the brakes, put the heavy Tahoe into reverse and attempt a J-turn, but Tate knew they'd expect sensible. So, he acted stupid.

'Get down. Now!' he shouted as he floored the accelerator.

The Tahoe changed down a gear and its V8 engine roared. The pickup wasn't Porsche fast, but it would do, and it was unexpected. The helo had about ten seconds to move or both it and the Tahoe would collide, and he doubted the men inside the bird had signed on for a suicide mission.

Tate closed his eyes; there was nothing else he could do, the helo was too low and the highway wasn't wide enough for him to steer past it, especially at the speed he was doing in the cumbersome SUV.

Through the opened windows a sudden metallic whine reached Tate's ears and he felt the Tahoe shudder as though it had been hit a glancing blow, but then it carried on. Tate opened his eyes. He couldn't see the helo. Which meant it had to have moved.

Tate focused on the road, and the bridge less than a quarter of a mile ahead. If they could cross the bridge, it was, he estimated, less than a mile sprint to another gulley, which would engulf the road and prevent the helo from following them at anything less than a hundred feet. They could stop, hide and wait for help.

'They've got guns!' Plato shouted. 'There's someone hanging out of the door!'

Tate glanced back. Plato was right, but he was also wrong. There was a figure, attached to a line, sitting on the skids. And in his arms was the chilling yet familiar shape of an RPG.

Instinctively Tate jinked the Tahoe to the right. A second later there was an explosion on the bridge ahead as the first grenade slammed into the safety barriers. Tate knew the Tahoe wasn't armour-plated, and he now also knew whoever was shooting wasn't playing. He jinked now in the opposite direction, directly towards the last impact sight. He knew he shouldn't look, but something compelled him to do so. The helo was closer and the man on the skids had now swapped the one-shot RPG for what looked like an M4 carbine, but it was the grenade launcher attached to this that worried Tate. Tate saw the shooter's face and suddenly he knew who the man was. Memories of a mission long ago swam before Tate's eyes as an anger made the blood roar in his ears. But before he could process this revelation there was a flash of flames and an instantaneous explosion as the rear of the Tahoe was lifted into the air.

Tate felt himself hurled forwards into the steering wheel before the SUV crashed back down onto the bridge again. There was a third explosion to Tate's right, forcing him to steer left and then, seconds later, one more explosion causing a second impact which sent the Tahoe airborne again and out through the hole punched in the guard rail by the first rocket.

Tate felt a sense of weightlessness as he was lifted out of his seat, restrained only by his seatbelt while the Tahoe nosedived towards the silvery waters below. He was used to falling, used to jumping out of planes, but he'd always had a chute, and he'd always had time to deploy it. Tate knew it was an illusion, perhaps his brain trying to rationalise what was happening, but time felt as though it was slowing. The HK lying on the passenger seat glided past his head and struck the windscreen, as did the sat phone. All external sound became indistinct and blended into one, a wailing chorus of human screams, roaring engine and rushing air. It lasted no more than a couple of seconds, but, to Tate, time had warped, and then it sped up. The water rose to grab them, like a set of giant jaws and the interior of the cabin became momentarily a cloud of white as each and every airbag exploded. The seatbelt grabbed Tate's chest, his legs, arms and head continued forward, only to be jerked back. He felt the air being sucked out of his body by instant deceleration as the SUV's nose broke the surface of the concrete-hard Colorado River.

There was a moment of engulfing calm when all noise and motion seemed to stop. And then Tate knew he was injured. He knew he had whiplash at the least. A recognisable cold sensation flooded his every muscle, rising like a wave as his body tried to deal with the impact and then the all-too-real external waves of cold started to cover him. The Colorado River rushed in through the four open windows of the Tahoe and it was sucked further beneath the surface. Tate's lungs were empty, and he only managed half a gasp before the water enveloped him, rising above his head as the river tried to claim him. Trying to fight the urge to panic, Tate reached for his seatbelt and depressed the buckle. Once … nothing … two … still not working … three and the buckle popped open.

Tate kicked up and away from his chair and squeezed through the gap between the seats to the rear of the SUV. Both Plato and Jericho were still in their places, bubbles escaping from their mouths as, wild-eyed, they pulled and tugged at their seatbelts. Tate grabbed Plato's belt and pressed the button, it opened, and

Plato immediately started to float up to the back of the SUV, where the last remaining air inside the vehicle was trapped against the rear windscreen. Tate pushed Plato up and with burning lungs started to work on Jericho's belt but it was already undone and yet he was not moving. Jericho was flailing and bucking. Tate pushed away and followed Plato to the fast-diminishing air pocket. Tilting his head back he broke the surface. There was perhaps half a foot of space between the water level and the glass. Tate gasped and took a greedy glug of air. Plato was facing him, shaking. With no time or air to waste on words, Tate went back under to Jericho. The Yorkshire man was still thrashing, but less vigorously. Tate clamped his hand around Jericho's cheeks, pushed his mouth against his, and blew a lungful of air into him. Tate tugged at the passenger seat, the frame of which had twisted on impact and trapped Jericho's right foot. The man's hands grabbed at Tate, but he had no choice but to get more air. He pushed back towards Plato. The air pocket was now half the size and Plato's mouth and nose were barely above the waterline.

Tate filled his lungs again, pushed back down and blew more air into Jericho, who was manically twisting and pulling. He grabbed Tate and wouldn't let him go. Tate had no alternative but to push him away. At the same time, he grabbed Plato's legs and pulled him down from the air pocket. Tate swung Plato's feet out of the open passenger window and, using the last of his fading strength, shoved his flailing arms. The SUV struck the bottom of the river, and this jerked Plato up and out of the SUV. Tate's vison had started to grey out and his lungs now felt as though they were on fire. He moved to the rear of the Tahoe, to the air pocket, his mouth hungrily searching for air but only finding cold glass.

Using his hands now, Tate grabbed at the window frame and pulled himself out of the SUV as, from below, wild hands gripped his left ankle. Tate knew he shouldn't look back, but he did. Barely visible in the gloom, Jericho was shouting silently into the water, left leg kicking against the seat, right hand jabbing against the water whilst his left knuckles were white from the grip on Tate's ankle.

Tate broke away and kicked for the surface. Knowing that he had to go up before he could go back down. His eyes focused on the lightening water above him, each second taking him closer to the land of the living. He exploded upwards out of the darkness, gasping. The air was the sweetest thing he had ever tasted. Tate told himself to relax, but his body had other ideas as it attempted to drink in as much oxygen as it could.

He saw Plato, ten feet away and being carried by the current towards the middle of the river. On instinct, Tate struck out towards him, powerful strokes that had him next to his friend within seconds. Tate snaked his left arm around Plato's neck and dragged him back towards the shore. Tate's feet found the riverbed as it sharply shelved at the side and managed to stand.

'Neill, get ashore. Hide under the bridge.'

'Wh … where's C … Colin?'

Tate turned and took a deep breath of air, he had to rescue Jericho. The water around him suddenly fizzed and the sound of 9mm rounds zipped past his ears. He turned his head looking for the shooter and saw a man he knew standing on the opposite side of the bank with an M4.

'Go!' Tate shouted at Plato.

The shooter dropped to one knee to create a more stable firing platform and a second burst kicked up the water around Tate's chest. Another sound reached Tate's ears; the hum of an extremely low-flying jet engine. Tate took one last gulp of air, then threw himself forward to dive back into the depths of the river as a round slammed into him. Tate went underwater sideways, and then something else struck his head and his world went black.

Chapter 13

Undisclosed Medical Facility, California

Tate could hear voices. The words were indistinct, but he recognised the timbre and tone, although when he searched for the names of the owners, he came up blank. The world around him, he realised, was black. He tried to move his hands, but they didn't respond. Then streaks of an almost imperceptible dark grey, a dark shadow more than a colour appeared in his peripheral vision like waves, like a current of swirling water … and then he remembered the accident … the rear of the SUV exploding … the whole vehicle falling from the bridge … the impact as they hit the water and then the darkness. He remembered battling with the cold, black water and then being tugged and grabbed by both the water and hands. But, most of all, he remembered breaking the surface, hungrily gasping for air before diving back down and attempting to rescue the two passengers … no, he was rescuing one … but there had been two … what were their names … who were they … and why was he driving them?

There was a sudden rushing sound in his ears and the darkness that had enveloped him, perniciously smothered him, vanished as his eyes opened. 'Plato … Neill Plato!'

'I'm here, Jack,' Plato replied.

The room was dimly lit but even that hurt his head, and his eyes. Tate blinked. 'How long have I been …' Words failed him.

A second voice spoke; his brother, Simon Hunter. 'You were in a medically induced coma for two days. The good news is you're not dead.'

Plato held a glass of water with a straw to Tate's mouth. He drank thankfully, then spluttered, 'Jericho? What about Jericho?'

'He drowned.'

Tate met Plato's eyes as his words registered. 'Dead?'

Plato sighed. 'This time he really is. His body is already in the UK.'

'Why was I … out?'

'You were shot in the left shoulder,' Hunter said.

'My head?'

'You banged it against a rock.'

'Of course …'

'You were lucky, but then I've always known you were thick-skulled,' Hunter added.

'Thanks for … the sympathy.' Tate momentarily closed his eyes as he experienced an abrupt surge of pain and giddiness.

'I didn't bring any grapes either.'

Tate gingerly moved his right arm, it felt fine. His left was strapped to protect his shoulder.

'Ironically, the best rehab for your shoulder is swimming,' Hunter added.

The door opened and a red-haired man in medical whites entered. He nodded at the two others before addressing Tate. 'I'm Doctor Dattolo. How are you feeling, Mr Tate?'

'Like I've … been shot … and banged … my head.'

'Good.'

'Good?'

'What was the last thing you remember?' Dattolo produced a pen light and, bending down, shone it in Tate's eyes.

167

'Go ahead, Jack, tell him,' Hunter instructed.

'I was in the water … something slammed into me … a rifle round … then I was under the water … then … I woke up here.'

'Hm, that sounds like you've not forgotten anything but there is, as with all concussion, a risk of amnesia.' Datollo prodded Tate's shoulder.

'Oh.'

'That seems to be healing fine. The bullet went in, and it went out. There is no permanent damage and no sign of infection, but we need to let the antibiotics run their course. Do you have any questions?'

'How long … will I have the headaches?'

'Two or three days, perhaps. I'll prescribe some painkillers.'

'When can I go?'

'Now, Mr Tate, you need to rest for at least another day or so before we let you go, so that we can monitor you to be on the safe side. The most recent scan of your brain shows the swelling has gone. You are now conscious and making sense, which is encouraging. However, I don't suggest you fly anywhere for a week. I'd say you're almost normal.'

'But never quite,' Tate said.

'Thank you, doctor,' Hunter said.

'Of course. Now, if you'll excuse me?'

Datollo left and the room became silent.

Tate felt tired, and as though he was being pushed backwards into his pillow. 'So … we failed. It's over?'

'Yes.' Plato placed his hand on Tate's right arm. 'But it's my fault. If you hadn't saved me, Colin would still be alive, and so would his research.'

'Neill … No. I made the choice. We couldn't lose you.'

'Jack's right, Neill. We lost a traitor; he was brilliant, but a traitor nonetheless.'

'I know.' Plato's eyes were moist. 'The problem is that he was also my friend.'

'Your mum?' Tate said, abruptly remembering. 'Gu threatened your mum.'

'She's safe.'

'Good.' Tate frowned and turned his head. 'So ... where am I?'

'In bed,' Hunter said.

'Where?'

'A private medical facility in LA.'

'What?' Tate was confused.

'It was the nearest place we could get you into, under the radar. It's owned by someone who is, er, "owned" by MI6. Don't ask, I didn't. Anyway, now that you're awake we need to see about getting you back home as the doctor said, in a week or so.'

'No.' Tate's voice was louder than he had intended it to be. 'What about Gu?'

'The mission is over, Jack. This one we lost.'

'Wait, what about ... what about the shooter ... who blew us off the road?'

'What about him?' Hunter asked.

'He was the same man ... the same man who was in Germany ... at the farmhouse.'

'What?'

Tate saw the confusion and surprise on his brother's face. 'The same sod who ... slotted the triads and Fang ... then shot me. The same bastard who put us in the river ... the Colorado River.'

'Neill, did you see the face of your attacker?'

'No, Simon, I was too busy ducking his bullets.'

'Jack, are you sure about it being the same gunman? Perhaps your mind is a little foggy?'

'Simon ... I banged my head ... I'm not mental.'

Hunter took in a deep breath. 'In that case, there is something else going on here that we don't know about, if it was the same chap.'

Tate was adamant. 'It was. His name ... his name is ... I can't remember ... I can see his face ... but his name ...'

'Wait, you know him?'

'He was ... Delta.'

'Delta Force? You mean the guy who assassinated Fang and then showed up with Gu is American?'

'Yes ... but I can't ...' Tate closed his eyes as the pain in his head increased.

Hunter pursed his lips. 'Neill, have you got that photo-fit program on your laptop?'

'I'll get it.'

'Please do so.'

Plato stood and Tate waited for him to leave the room before he said, 'How did this ... go wrong?'

'Jericho is gone and with him goes our access to his "White Shirt" or whatever he called it,' Hunter said, bitterly.

'It was called ... White Suit.' Tate remembered that. 'How do you know ... it's gone?'

'If, as he claimed, he held all the data in his head, no one else has access to it.'

'You ... believe that?'

'In theory, sure. In practice, no. I don't believe he could possibly remember all that and would he trust himself to? Look, you were held for three days before you escaped. Plato's told me all about it but says that they must have pumped you all with something as he can't remember a thing. Do I believe that Jericho told them everything? Yes. I bet he told them as much as he could remember and the rest? Maybe he did hold out on them or forgot something? Perhaps there's a chance his research hasn't gone? I really don't know, Jack. I just don't think Jericho would let his data die with him. I think he's hidden it somewhere.'

Tate could think and follow the conversation, but speaking was harder, and he was feeling increasingly tired. 'Where?'

'Somewhere that only he, and perhaps a close friend, would think to look.'

'Close friend ... like Neill?'

'Who better? And who more trustworthy. The problem is that if that's the case, Gu's organisation is going to try to find it to make sure no one else has it.'

'Why didn't … they … ask … Jericho where it was hidden?'

'Perhaps they didn't know they needed to ask that? You don't know a ten-thousand-piece jigsaw puzzle has a bit missing until you count all the pieces. That's if a piece is missing.'

Tate's mind went back to their childhood. 'Do you remember … Dad's jigsaw puzzle?'

Hunter smiled. 'You mean the huge one of The Battle of Trafalgar?'

'Massive.'

'It was humongous.'

Tate managed a weak smile, but said nothing more as the throbbing pain in his head intensified. He squeezed his eyes shut and brought his hand to his temple. There was a bandage.

'Don't worry, there was one small cut, and all your hair is still there – I know you love it like life itself.'

'We must call Newman … tell her about the link … between the two operations,' Tate said with his eyes closed.

'I know, but let's just try to get a face for this mystery man first, OK?'

'OK.'

Fourteen years ago
Baghdad, Iraq

The car Tate rode shotgun in, looked unremarkable as it came to a halt to the east of their target address. Dirty, dented and dusty, the decade-old Toyota was so synonymous with this part of Baghdad that it was all but invisible. This particular vehicle, however, had been retrofitted with ballistic plates which whilst not defending against direct RPGs or 0.50 calibre strikes, would stop 'pray and spray' attacks from handguns and assault rifles.

The engine, too, had been fettled to provide more torque, needed to accelerate out of trouble. Now that the engine was off, sweat trickled down the back of Tate's neck, wetting his dust-covered civilian clothing. A cheap pair of knock-off Ray-Ban aviators, which were particularly popular with the locals, part obscured his face as did a dull-cream *shemagh*. At a glance, Tate's dark hair and suntan made him look like a local, and Page too had developed a tan while his tumbling Milky Bar Kid locks had been dyed a shade of Real Black.

Tate lounged languidly in the passenger seat, while his eyes constantly scanned for threats. In the airless afternoon a plume of smoke now drifted across from Page, who Tate thought was enjoying getting into character too much. Page took another drag on his cigarette before flicking it out through the open window.

'It's great training, this,' Page stated, quietly.

'For what?'

'Becoming a taxi driver when all this is over.'

'I don't think you're allowed to smoke anymore in the UK.'

'Sod it, school minibus driver it is then.'

Tate smirked. Page and he had passed SAS selection together and been in the same troop ever since. There was a crackle in Tate's earpiece and he frowned. 'Say again?'

'T … taaarg … mobile … ETA … fift … minu …' The voice was tinny and distorted.

Tate cursed under his breath. Something had been making the comms network play up all day; he didn't know if it was atmospheric pressure, interference from the surrounding buildings or a third party actively attempting to jam their signals. 'Repeat.'

This time the transmission was nothing more than static.

'Crappy comms,' Page spat.

'Repeat last.'

Now the transmission was clear, as was the West Coast accent of its speaker, Roe Kwang. 'Target mobile. ETA fifteen minutes.'

'Have that,' Tate confirmed and started to take deeper breaths

172

to keep himself calm. Even though he was no longer newly badged, Tate was still apprehensive, yet once it was time for action he flicked a mental switch and all fears were forgotten. An instructor had once told him that it was the ability to go from total calm to total controlled aggression in a second and back again that made the perfect SAS trooper, and Tate could identify with this. In fact, that made a lot of his own adolescent behaviour make sense.

Tate and Page were part of Task Force Knight, a group controlled by JSOC (the Joint Special Operations Command) and consisting of a SAS squadron with operators from other UKSF units and the US's Delta Force. Their objective in Baghdad had been 'find-fix-finish' – find the terrorist, fix a time and place to target them and then finish the operation by either eliminating or apprehending said terrorist. Some were followers of Al Qaeda, others Ba'athist party regime members still loyal to Saddam Hussein, and, still more – elements of the Iranian-backed insurgent group the Mahdi Army. It was a convoluted environment and Tate didn't care who his targets were; if they were responsible for prolonging the conflict and endangering the lives of the law-abiding locals, they were fair game and he'd happily find, fix and finish them.

Tate's missions had been targeted on putting an end to the prolific use of car bombs by Al Qaeda in and around Baghdad. The group had a network of garages which were used to store the donor vehicles and manufacture and fit the IEDs. One such address had been successfully targeted by a drone strike, but Tate's target today was not the garage itself, which was located in a densely populated residential area, it was the man who was believed to be running the entire car bomb network – a senior Al Qaeda figure by the name of Abu al-Attabi, nicknamed 'Cheeks' by Page due to the long, matching scars on each side of his face. Cheeks was a tall, powerfully built Jordanian in his late thirties who wasn't hard to miss. He lived in a heavily fortified and guarded compound in a formerly salubrious district and shared his street with the chief of police and a handful of Iraqi dignitaries, including a pair of pro-Western judges. There was no way, bar a drone strike or air assault, that al-Attabi could be taken in his own home, especially as he lived in his vast villa with a seemingly endless supply of wives and offspring. Hence, he had to be followed wherever and whenever he left his stronghold. Even now, with daily bombings and shootings, JSOC was hamstrung to some extent by rules of engagement and the law of the land. In short, they wanted to see him hand over an IED or finish him with one. Today was the 'fix' part of the mission, and it was Tate and the others' job to confirm that al-Attabi was indeed using the address which had been given to them by a local informer. Some operations had been an all-UK affair, but not this one.

'Target ETA in five, that's zero five minutes,' Roe said.

'Have that,' Tate replied.

At the far end of the street a cream-coloured Toyota Camry appeared and approached the target building. Tate and Page watched from their car, and a miniature camera mounted on the dashboard recorded the Camry as it drew ever nearer to the garage. A hundred yards behind the Camry an outwardly ancient-looking Ford Granada turned onto the street before parking next to an abandoned shop. This was the car which carried their counterparts from Delta Force, Roe and the driver Glen Thorn.

Their target's Camry straddled the kerb immediately outside the garage and the driver and a bodyguard clambered out. Both were dressed as locals. Tate didn't know if they were Iraqis or if they, like he, had been specially imported for the conflict. Tate's camera recorded the scene; the faces would be checked later against their Who's Who rogue gallery. The driver ambled towards the closed double doors of the garage and banged on them, whilst the bodyguard made a cursory scan up and down the road before opening the rear nearside passenger door. The tall figure of Abu al-Attabi quickly got out and surveyed the street. He looked directly at Tate before turning away.

'Have eyes on Cheeks,' Tate said, which made Page smile.

'Copy that,' Roe replied.

As Tate looked on, the garage doors opened. Now in the distance, Tate saw the Delta car start to move. They were making their run. Thorn would drive past whilst Roe ensured their onboard camera was turned to face the targets and recording the faces of the assembled group. Through the open garage doors another large man stepped out. He moved directly to al-Attabi, as he touched his hand to his chest in a formal greeting before he started an animated conversation. Al-Attabi nodded as the man shook his head and stabbed his right index finger into his chest.

'Who's this?' Tate said, aloud.

'Dunno,' replied Page.

Two figures dressed in burkas exited and stood behind the unknown man. Tate squinted; they were of a similar height to both the tall men. The unknown man pointed at the back seats of the Camry and the women started to get in.

Roe's car drew level with the group.

And then Roe opened fire.

Tate's eyes widened behind his shades. 'What the—'

'Shit ...' Page managed.

The unknown man dropped to the ground, his right hand instinctively grabbing at his chest. Meanwhile, the bodyguard had ducked behind the rear wheel well.

As Tate looked on, dumbstruck, Roe exited the car and, weapon up, shot the bodyguard at point-blank range. Al-Attabi was stock still, hands raised above his head. Roe gestured that he should get in the waiting Ford, but al-Attabi shook his head. Roe fired a round into the man's left arm, making him squeal and jerk. Roe manhandled the injured man into the Ford as Thorn stamped on the gas.

Tate pressed his transmit switch and tried to call up HQ, but all he got was static. He then tried Thorn, not knowing what to say but wanting to know what the hell was happening. He managed, 'Thorn, what—'

Gunmen now ran out of the garage and rounds from their rifles ripped into the Ford, tearing the tyres and making it fishtail.

And then the Camry exploded in a huge fireball which shattered and shredded the storefronts and hurled the retreating Ford up and into the entrance of an apartment building on the other side of the street.

'Drive!' Tate shouted to Page, and their own car leaped forwards towards the carnage. At the far end of the street, from the direction Roe's car had come, a white Landcruiser and a Toyota Hilux truck barrelled towards them. Small arms fire now raced their way. Page slammed on the brakes and the car slewed to a stop by the wreckage of the Ford as the first stray round hit the windscreen, which, unlike the door panels, wasn't upgraded, and it spiderwebbed. Tate grabbed his carbine from under his seat, opened his door and ran towards the Ford as Page started to return fire at the oncoming militants.

Roe was out of the Ford and dragging a bewildered al-Attabi with him. Tate started to put rounds down the road at the advancing vehicles.

'Thorn!' Tate shouted. 'Move it!'

'T … Tate!'

Tate turned and saw Thorn was trapped both by the rubble of the building and the car's twisted interior. Blood bubbled from his lips as he reached his right hand outwards. Tate yelled, 'Hang on, mate!'

Rounds started to strike the Ford and Tate ducked. Peering back up, he could now see a 0.50 cal gun, probably Russian, was mounted on the back of the flatbed of the truck. It hadn't been used yet, but when it was it would rip through every piece of metal in its path.

From behind, Roe bellowed, 'Tate, move it!'

Tate looked back. Page was back behind the steering wheel whilst Roe was by the open rear passenger door. Tate roared, 'I'm not leaving Thorn!'

Roe bounded away from the car, and skidded to a halt next to Tate.

'Roe, man – you've gotta help me here!' Thorn shouted.

There was a sudden and heavy retort and Tate knew exactly what it was – the 0.50 cal had opened up. Tate ducked as rounds hit the apartment block and then tore at the debris of the Ford above his head. He felt Roe fire a pair of quick rounds.

Roe grabbed Tate's shoulder. 'Move it, or I'll leave you too!'

Tate turned. 'We can't leave Thorn!'

'Thorn didn't make it!'

Tate's head jerked left, and his eyes focused on the second American. His head and torso were still upright, wedged against a piece of masonry, but there was an entrance wound in his forehead.

Tate blinked away the dust and confusion, momentarily not understanding what he was seeing.

But then he did.

Tate started to shake with fury; he knew what Roe had done, but he couldn't believe it.

Present Day
Undisclosed Medical Facility, California

Tate's eyes opened. The room was in semi-darkness. The only light came from under the closed door and a laptop to his right. There was a soft patter of keys. Tate managed to turn his head to see Plato leaned forward, typing at a small table that rested against the wall. There was another noise, snoring. Tate looked the other way and saw his brother Simon, slumped in a padded chair.

Tate spoke, his voice was croaky. 'Are you catching up on Tea Hub?'

'What?' Plato turned. 'You're awake again, then?'

'Yes.' Tate saw a jug of water on the over-bed tray table. He tried to reach for it, but Plato got there first and poured him a glass. Tate drank. 'Thanks.'

'You've been asleep for another ten hours.'

'Bugger,' Tate replied, his voice sounding more normal. 'But I bet I wasn't snoring like Wee Willie Winkie over there.'

'No, you weren't. How do you feel now?'

'Normal.' He remembered Plato's injured ankle. 'How's your leg?'

'Just sprained, it's strapped up.'

There was a yawn from the other chair. 'Whilst you've been asleep, Neill has been running a search on this Gu Joon chap. So far the results have been a bit strange.'

'Strange?' Tate replied and Plato placed the laptop on the tray table and swung it over the bed.

'I got three separate hits,' Plato said. 'One historical and the other two current.'

'Explain?'

'Well' – Plato shrugged – 'obviously we started by going with my memory of his face and then looking at local CCTV footage in an attempt to get a digital image of Gu Joon's face we could work with. I got lucky with a security camera at North Las Vegas Airport. Using this as my "baseline", I tried to find footage that showed a face that looks like that, in a geographical area that we would expect the face to be.'

'OK, so you accept a "ping" in Vegas, but the one from Bognor Regis on the same day you discount?'

'Yes.'

'Who'd want to visit Bognor?' Hunter pulled a face.

'And?'

'There was obviously the original one from the airport showing him arriving in Las Vegas. Then there was the one showing him leaving. Here.' Plato tapped the keyboard and showed Tate the image.

'That's him,' Tate confirmed. 'No doubt.'

'Yes. We think so too,' Hunter, now standing and peering at the laptop screen from the other side of the bed, said.

Plato continued, 'There is also one here, someone boarding a plane in Seoul. A passenger by the name of Po Bong.'

'Bong?'

'It's the Korean for "phoenix".'

'Do we discount Mr Bong in Seoul?'

'Remember,' Hunter chided, 'in Korean the surname comes first, so he's Mr Po.'

Plato continued, 'It's possible it was Gu Joon, there was enough time for him to reach Seoul.'

'So, where's Gu?'

'Ah. Gu Joon vanished after his private jet arrived in Mexico. And Mr Po is in Singapore.'

'Neill, show him the last hit.'

'There. It's a match from this photograph taken at a fruit farm in North Korea in 1979.' Plato touched the screen.

'Who is that, "The Man from Del Monte"?'

'No, Jack.' Hunter's tone became serious. 'Hak Il Sung, that one there – you know, the founder of North Korea. Officially, he had two wives and six children.'

'Officially?'

'Unofficially, we think there may be more. We believe the young man standing just behind Hak Il Sung is one of his children.'

Plato clarified, 'We think his name is Hak Kwang-Il and he is possibly a son of a secret wife or a mistress.'

'Wait.' Tate's head throbbed. 'Are you saying crazy Gu Joon could be the uncle of Hak Jong Un?'

'An uncle. Yes.' Plato nodded.

'So, if the assassin from Germany is the same guy who blasted us off the road?' Tate said.

'It would make sense,' Hunter added, 'that the two operations are linked. First their hacker Fang steals a few billion for the regime, and is then taken out, and then Gu attempts to get Jericho's technology for them too.'

'What are they planning?'

'Perhaps nothing, perhaps just nation-building.'

'Of course,' Plato said, 'the issue is that the man in the old photograph – Hak Kwang-Il – appeared in this and only two other images before he was reported as having died in a fatal agricultural accident.'

Tate tried to understand it all, but still felt peculiar. He closed his eyes.

Plato continued. 'Both matches are high. I'm inclined to believe that Gu is Hak Kwang-Il.'

'So, not Po?'

Hunter rolled his eyes. 'We don't know.'

'Who is Po?'

'He's an architect and also travels to deliver lectures on architecture.'

'Has he designed hotels?'

'Ah,' Plato said, 'that we should check.'

'So, what do we do?' Tate asked. 'How do we find Gu?'

'We don't, yet. Our operation is over.'

'But—'

'Listen, Jack.' Hunter gestured at the laptop. 'You get the face of our shooter into there and then we see what links he throws up. You said he's Delta, but you can't remember his name?'

'No, Simon, I remember his name all right,' Tate said, slowly. He still felt as though his head were full of cotton wool, and barbed wire. 'His name is Roe Kwang.'

'Roe? Roe Kwang?' Hunter frowned before recognition flashed across his face, 'As in *that* Roe? You're certain about this?'

'Yes, that Roe, the bastard from the Iraq mission.' Tate fell silent, closed his eyes, 'My brain must have worked it out whilst I was asleep.'

180

'OK, that's good. Neill managed to access the US military records database.'

'I compiled a long shortlist of ethnic Asian Delta Force operators, just a moment.' Plato's fingers swiped at his laptop. 'Got him.'

'He's ethnically Korean.'

'Christ, he is! I remember. I need to speak to Newman,' Hunter said. 'I've no idea where this is all leading and, to be honest, I don't know if we will be allowed to follow it.'

Tate nodded, and wished he hadn't as it made him wince. 'Right.'

'Hm,' Plato said. 'I took the footage of the assassin arriving at the farmhouse and played with it. I managed to enhance and clean up the image and then compared it to my long list. It threw up a couple of, well, frankly guestimates. One of which was Roe Kwang.'

Tate took the iPad. 'Because it was Roe Kwang. He had a nickname too. Hak Jong-Thin – that was what the other Delta guys called him because he was Korean, but wasn't fat like Hak Jong Un. Even before he shot me, I didn't like him.'

Fourteen years ago
Camden, London

Tate's squadron were rotating out and would arrive at Hereford within the week. Tate, however, was already at home in Camden. He was bitter and angry. He still had a room at his parents' house in Camden, even though he'd left some eight years before and joined the army. In Hereford he lived on base and hadn't considered getting his own place. Tate lolled on his parents' settee, they were both at work, and sipped from his third can of Kronenbourg. The TV was playing a taping of the latest WWE Royal Rumble event and his brother sat in an armchair munching on a piece of deep-pan Meat Feast pizza.

'Are you going to tell me the truth now?' Hunter asked, his mouth half-full.

Tate sat up and grabbed another slice of pizza from the take-away box on the coffee table. 'You do know I've signed the Official Secrets Act?'

Hunter rolled his eyes. 'And you know that I have too?'

Tate nodded. 'Secret squirrel.'

Hunter nodded back at Tate. 'Secret soldier.'

'Yeah.'

'So?'

Tate drank more beer.

Hunter sighed, 'Look, you may be able to fool Mum and Dad that everything's OK, but I know it's not. If you can't talk to me, who can you talk to? I'm MI6, but, more importantly, I'm your brother, remember?' Hunter munched a mouthful of pizza as he waited for a reply.

'Everything is not OK, and, before you ask, no I haven't been sacked or returned to my old unit. Something happened in Baghdad that shouldn't have.'

Hunter wiped his mouth with a paper serviette 'Tell me.'

Tate sighed and explained the mission, Roe's actions, what he thought he had done and what he couldn't prove. 'Roe was exonerated. The Americans recovered Thorn's body and examined the bullet wound that killed him. The slug they retrieved did not come from the carbine Roe was using or his sidearm. They were satisfied with Roe's account, his actions and the fact we got our target.'

Hunter sat back and crossed his arms. 'So let me get this right, Roe caused the firefight?'

Tate nodded. 'He recognised a second high-priority target, an Al Qaeda guy from Pakistan who was an expert in making suicide vests. Then he saw two men, dressed as women, getting into our target's car.'

'And they were wearing vests which went off and caused Roe's car, driven by Thorn, to crash into a storefront?'

'Yes.' Tate finished his can, crunched it up and dropped it in the Sainsbury's carrier bag by his feet. 'The thing is, I saw them too. I was about to say something when Roe opened fire.'

'So, he's as good as you?'

'He's nothing like me!' Tate snapped, then held up his hands. 'Sorry. Look, he took a chance – I understand that. It was an opportunity to stop those vests from going off in a crowded market or somewhere that would have killed innocent Iraqis or police or coalition soldiers, and it took the suicide vest maker out of the game. Looking back, I'd have done the same but then, shit, he shot Thorn in the head so he could escape the contact ...' Tate looked down as Thorn's bloodied face again appeared before his eyes.

'But you didn't see Roe shoot Thorn?'

'I told you I didn't.'

'And Paul Page didn't see it either?'

'Page was in our car; he couldn't see either Roe or Thorn from where he was.'

'OK.'

Tate rubbed his stubbly face. 'Look, there was no possible way that round could have hit Thorn from the direction it did if it had been fired by anyone else apart from Roe. It just wasn't possible.'

'Jack, it was a warzone, everything was possible.'

Tate reached into the bag of beer, tossed a can at Hunter, then opened another for himself. 'I'll tell you what's possible. It's possible the Americans have covered this up. I mean, it's not even a blue on blue, it's murder.'

'Come on, Jack, that's taking things too far. You didn't see Roe shoot Thorn, and the gun wasn't either of the ones he was issued with. Never leave a man behind, isn't that what the Americans say?'

'Not just the Americans.'

'It was your word against his, Jack, and the investigation has been completed.'

'Its findings are wrong,' Tate growled.

'Do you honestly believe Roe shot his own buddy in cold blood in the head, just so he could get away?'

'Yes, I bloody do!'

'Jack, you know I'll always take your side but you've got to let this go – for the sake of your career. You can't keep accusing Roe. Otherwise, well ...'

'I'll lose my job? I'm not stupid. I'm not going to bring it up.'

'Jack, there's nothing you can do.'

'There is. If I ever meet Roe again, I'll shoot him.'

Present day
Undisclosed location

From the overhead walkway, Roe was impressed by the set-up. The level of sophistication that had gone into designing and running the laboratory was staggering. The vast interior space had been sectioned off into different specific areas and each of them was a glass cube, which could only be entered or exited via airlocks. The technicians wore full white coveralls and masks. He counted at least thirty of them in the various enclosed labs. From this height above the floor, he could not see exactly what they were working on, but could imagine.

'Welcome to the future of the Korean peninsula!' Gu Joon's tone was buoyant, and his face was creased with a smile. 'I have head-hunted the best minds to work with me to turn my vision into a reality. Now that we have the complete puzzle, I am sure we will be able to proceed with the final part of the operation.'

'I'm sure we will, Uncle.'

Gu Joon continued to walk along the raised walkway over-looking the glass cubes as the sound of supressed gunfire reached their ears. Roe grabbed his uncle and attempted to block the path of any bullet.

Gu started to laugh. 'Your reactions are extremely quick, Kwang, but I assure you we are not under attack. Take a look for yourself.'

Roe followed his uncle's gaze. Below them a technician was

shouldering a HK416. Smoke drifted from the end of the screwed-on suppressor. Roe understood that he had been firing at a piece of suspended metal. The metal resembled a fuselage panel from a commercial airliner. 'White Suit?'

'Yes.'

They reached the end of the walkway and were now above the largest of the enclosed laboratories. In this one Roe was surprised to see four full-size drones with their wings folded.

'They are the Bayraktar TB3, manufactured in Turkey and specifically designed to be ship launched,' Gu explained. 'We have, of course, modified them with certain upgrades.'

Roe watched a technician affix a translucent sheet to the fuse-lage of the nearest drone.

Gu continued, 'We will be conducting test flights imminently. *Bayraktar* is the Turkish for "standard-bearer", and these drones shall be that for our operation.'

Roe noted the use of the word 'our' to describe the operation.

Gu studied him, as though reading his mind. 'If it were not for you, Roe, and what you achieved in bringing Jericho to me, my operation would not be feasible. Colin Jericho was indeed a genius; it is a great pity that we could not work together physically.'

'Yes.'

Gu led them through the door to the upper decks.

Chapter 14

Undisclosed Medical Facility, California

Two men entered the room, both athletic-looking. One was in his fifties with a full head of blond hair and the other was in his later thirties with a thick light-brown mane tied back in a ponytail. Tate immediately pinged them as operators.

Hunter rose to his feet and extended his hand to the older man. 'Vince, how good to see you. Pamela told me you were in the area.'

'I'm in the area?' The American shook Hunter's hand. 'It's you who's making a heck of a mess in my backyard.'

Tate noted the man's voice had a southern drawl. This and his appearance reminded Tate of a plantation owner, which he imagined wasn't a flattering comparison to vocalise.

'This is Neill Plato.' Hunter gestured at the technical wizard. 'And this is my brother Jack.'

The American nodded at Plato. 'Plato of The Republic?'

'Hello,' Plato replied. He'd learned to ignore comments about his surname.

'Jack Tate.' The American stepped forward, bent down and shook Tate's hand. 'Now you, I've heard of.'

'I'm flattered.'

'This,' the American said, gesturing over his shoulder, 'is Michael Parnell, and, as Simon knows, I'm Vince Casey. I think we all need to have a chinwag.'

'What would the Agency like to discuss?' Hunter asked.

'Hey, this is nothing for any of us to get worked up about really, it's just that I think you may have a lead on one of our own who's, how can I phrase it, "wandered off the reservation".'

'Oh, so I did trip your system then?' Plato sounded sheepish.

'Yeah, Plato, you did, but it's no biggie. Anyone else would have been lifted by now and taken away for "processing", but this is "Newman's Merry Men" so, hey, I want to hear you out.'

Tate noticed that Plato seemed crestfallen, whilst Hunter's face told him he was about to officially apologise. Which he did.

Casey nodded. 'Spooks gotta spook, right? Look, I understand you need intel and fast, but, please, I'm no stranger to Pamela Newman. It's kind of upsetting I was not notified of your operation. Now, Parnell, if you please.'

Parnell, who had been casually lounging against the wall, pushed himself off and nodded. His accent was Washington. 'A former Delta guy by the name of Roe. I've worked with him; he's quiet, a loner, and looks like he's always thinking. Solid as reinforced concrete in a firefight, amazing reflexes. He was part of the CIA team transporting Fang Bao to a new holding location.'

'Wait, are you telling me that the CIA had Fang Bao?' Hunter sounded outraged.

Casey sighed. 'Yes, we did. Hey, don't go giving me daggers, our deputy director has already informed Newman about it.'

Tate sat up straighter in his bed, now he understood. 'Roe helped him escape?'

Parnell fixed his eyes on Tate. 'That has yet to be determined. The convoy was attacked, Fang was taken and every single man on that mission was lost. It shouldn't have been possible. They were damn good operators.'

Casey now continued the narrative. 'The thing is, when Plato tripped our newest "intruder device" on our system – hey, it's nothing to be ashamed of, some ten-year-old kid just devised it – it was because he was trying to get a name for a face. Well, we have the name, and we also have the face and we've got the tombstone too. The face you were trying to get a name for was: first name Kwang, second name Roe. He is meant to be among those who died during Fang's escape.'

Hunter wet his lips. 'So Roe is involved in some type of rogue CIA operation?'

'Nope. I'm saying he may be involved in some type of rogue criminal operation. You see, the thing is that after Plato alerted us to your interest in Roe, we did a search of our own. It turns out that we got a match to his face, percentage wise not high enough for a court of law but high enough for us, on several pieces of surveillance footage. One puts him outside the office of a security company in Fresno and the other puts him next to a motel in Santa Monica.'

'What happened at those locations?'

'Death,' Parnell stated.

Casey continued, 'The owner of the security company, a guy by the name of Carter and an associate, were gunned down at Carter's place of residence. It looked like the work of professionals.'

'Somebody got Carter,' Parnell added.

'How's this for odd? The local PD found documents hidden in a cavity in the fireplace relating to a contract Carter had allegedly carried out for Eeshipil Consulting, a shell company owned by North Korea.'

'Unusual,' Tate said.

'What was the contract?' Hunter asked.

'It was to locate a Korean dissident.'

'And did they?' Tate asked.

'The guy disappeared, so I'd take that as a yes. Now we move on to the motel. The night shift guy was also shot the day after he reported to the local cops a sighting of a one Cal Conners. The same time he was taken out, a mother and a daughter – who was a serving member of the Santa Monica PD – were also slain. With the same firearm. They lived in a house directly behind the motel.'

'Why would Roe help in Fang's escape and then target these seemingly random individuals?' Parnell asked.

'We also got another hit for Roe, but this one we dismissed as a false positive. A Korean-American insurance broker, who was Roe's spitting image, travelled in and out of the US twice in the last month, first to Hamburg and then two days ago to Paris. He was pinged on the airport security footage, but his passport was in the name of one Dan Tae. Simple, right? It's either, as we believed, an error with the facial-recognition software or Roe has somehow risen from the dead and is working for someone else? So, we want to check this out. We look further back, and we get historical pings for Dan Tae all over the Hensley and Japantown areas of San Jose, at exactly the same time we know Roe was alive and actively working for the agency. All of this is very confusing, as we have two guys with the same face. So, it's that old chestnut, right, of everyone having a doppelgänger? Care to enlighten us, gents?'

Tate looked at Hunter, who nodded back at him before he addressed the two men from the CIA. 'We had credible intel Fang was heading for Germany. I was meant to see who he met, then snatch him and get him back to the UK. But I failed. Fang was executed by an assassin, whom at the time we believed to be in the employ of the Ah Kong triad.'

'Ah Kong? That's not a name I've heard in a while. Continue.'

'Jack encountered the same assassin here, on US soil four days ago,' Hunter added.

'I encountered his bullets,' Tate said.

'So, you were trying to tie this shooter in with two operations?'

'Yes.' Hunter nodded. 'And we also got the Tae hits.'

Casey pursed his lips and transferred his weight from one foot to another. It looked to Tate as though he was trying to process the ramifications of what he'd just learned. 'You do know just how closely I've worked with MI6 in the past, don't you? With both the Russian desk and your boss – Pamela.'

'I know,' Hunter replied tersely, although Tate thought the question was rhetorical.

'So please, chaps, lay it all out for me. What the hell is happening?'

Hunter sighed. Tate knew he'd been told to cooperate fully but only divulge as much as he was asked. 'North Korea was attempting to secure new technology. Our two operations were linked simply because North Korea carried out both.'

'The cyber robbery was the other mission?' Parnell said, knowingly.

'We believe that was for funds, pure and simple. A way around the UN sanctions. They're prevented from making money by trade, so they stole it from someone no one would care about.'

Casey's arms were folded, and he was shaking his head slowly. 'You couldn't share, could ya? If you'd come to us, come to me with this, we could have helped.'

'That wasn't my decision, Vince, and you know it wasn't Pamela's either.'

'Yeah, I know. That's the bitterest part of all this.'

'Besides,' added Tate, 'you stole Fang from us in the first place.'

'Not me.' Casey held up his palms. 'That was my predecessor. Tell me about this technology?'

'Our foreign secretary has, I believe, briefed your defence secretary.'

'Sheesh.' Casey folded his arms. 'Tell me, Simon.'

'It was defensive technology created in part by a British national and, in part, by Blackline.'

'Whoa, back up a block, Blackline? As in "fry the continental US with an EMP" Blackline?'

'Yeah,' Tate said.

'Who was the Brit? Gimme a name.'

'Colin Jericho. He'd been living in the US under the assumed name of Cal Conners.'

'The same Conners whose face was all over the news.' Casey nodded. 'The same Conners who the media said was Jack's accomplice?'

'The same.'

'Blackline wanted him so they can use his tech?'

'Not Blackline, a North Korean organisation. Hence the high-level briefing.'

'What?'

Hunter explained.

Tate watched the two CIA men as his brother set out all that they knew.

'Now,' Casey said, 'that's just world class. North Korea has the spec of this new defensive tech and no one else does.'

Hunter added, 'Vince, we only learned of Jericho's alleged breakthrough three days before he died. We have no proof it works.'

'Well, the horses have bolted and I'm in no mood to lock the stable doors. This presents a danger to the security of both our nations, but if North Korea already has it there's not a goddam thing we can do about it. As for our dead traitor walking, if it is Roe, well, I hope he enjoys the delights of Pyongyang.'

Tate felt he had to speak; it was a fact that Hunter had omitted, and its relevance niggled at him. 'There is one other thing. Gu Joon is probably Hak Jong Un's uncle.'

Pacific Ocean

Roe had used UAVs before, first with Delta and then the CIA. Drone technology was constantly evolving, making the electronics smaller, the engines more powerful and the lift capacity larger. Micro-drones were the future for both the battlefield, urban warfare and hostage rescue situations, and Roe himself had tested

191

the latest generations of these. What he was looking at now, however, was different. The Bayraktar TB3 was being operated from a ground control station that, with the exception of the various masts on top, looked like any other shipping container from the outside, but on the inside had seating for three men, screens and banks of controls. The UAV had been programmed to fly in a low and lazy pattern five hundred yards off the ship's port side. It was well below the level of any radars, and small enough to avoid satellite detection. As they were in the middle of the vast Pacific Ocean, the risk of compromise was minimal.

'The most distant point from land on earth is in this ocean, Roe. It is called The Pacific Pole of Inaccessibility, or, by yachtsmen, Point Nemo. It is much farther south than we are. However, one imagines it looks the same as our current vista. Out here even you and I are insignificant. This is the place where a man may become insane gazing at the endless horizon. Imagine, Roe, what it must have been like for the first men who traversed this place? Weeks with nothing but the sea and the sky? Water reserves dwindling and relying upon the whims of a pernicious and capricious wind. In truth, this is not a place for man. This is a place for all those who dwell below the waves; the sea monsters, demons and gods. I have often dreamed of this place, and I have often envisaged myself being cast adrift here to atone for my many sins.'

Roe made no reply, he didn't know what to say.

'Are you aware, Roe, of the British saying – "the proof of the pudding is in the eating"?'

'No, Uncle.'

'Well, we are about to sample the pudding.' Gu Joon pointed to a crew member who was standing alone some distance away, and next to a MPAD. 'That is an American FIM-92E Stinger, the model that was improved in order to detect smaller targets, such as drones.'

'I see.'

'Let us eat the pudding.'

Gu Joon raised his arm and then lowered it. The man with the Stinger took a moment to ready himself and the Stinger, then positioned it on his shoulder and fired. The missile streaked away from the ship and into the sky, leaving a trail of white smoke.

Roe watched, and, without the aid of binoculars, saw the missile seconds later slam into the belly of the drone. There was an explosion and then the debris plummeted into the sea. From what Roe could make out, it looked as though the drone had been split into two distinct pieces. 'It didn't work?'

'Didn't it? We shall recover what remains of our UAV and study it. This is the first time we have used the updated version of White Suit on sections of a drone, I am sure the results will be interesting.' Gu looked at his wristwatch, 'Time to eat.'

As his uncle turned, Roe watched a pair of Zodiac inflatables speed away from the ship towards the crash site. What they brought back to the ship would indeed be interesting.

MI6 Safe house, Santa Monica

The footage of Tate in action at Gu's hotel in Las Vegas was no longer playing on the news. In an agreed statement, the FBI had declared they had a suspect in custody and Cal Conners had been killed in a motor vehicle accident in Utah. At the proverbial 'pay grade higher than his' discussions, agreements had obviously taken place, but what mattered to Tate was that he was out of hospital.

Hunter and Plato had moved into a house rented by a MI6 shell company, to be debriefed. The team sent over by Newman to assess them had been courteous and thorough, but Tate got the impression they didn't believe him or Plato when they reiterated that they remembered nothing of their three-day incarceration. How had they been interrogated, what intelligence had they given up on the SAS, MI6, E Squadron, and themselves? All Tate knew was that once he'd woken up in his 'cell', he'd lost three days and Gu knew his name and exactly who he was.

Tate was drained, mentally and physically, as he leaned against the French window and looked out across the hills. From the next room he could hear Plato placating his mother on the phone. Assuring her he was fine and had merely hurt his leg when a taxi he'd been in had crashed. As far as a cover story went, it was the only one that he was allowed to spin.

Tate missed not having a family, or not knowing if he had one. His foster parents – Hunter's birth parents – were dead, and he felt adrift. He'd unconsciously made the decision years ago that family life wasn't for him, and that he didn't want to know who his birth parents were, but now that he didn't have anyone, except for Hunter, he'd started to long for something that, in reality, he had never known.

He took another swig from his glass of water as he watched some sort of bird of prey float on an eddy above the hills. They were still in California, and he still refused to believe the mission was over. Officially he was recuperating from his injuries whilst being debriefed, but unofficially he, Hunter and Plato were trying to work out what the hell was happening. And then there was Roe, the guy who'd got away with murder all those years ago.

In the hall, the toilet flushed, then the taps ran, and Hunter re-emerged into the lounge wiping his hands on his chinos.

'Did you fall in?' Tate asked.

'Yep, that joke hasn't grown old since Dad's time.' Hunter reached for the Coke he'd started earlier and sipped. 'You're still on the water?'

'I'm still on the painkillers.'

Hunter joined Tate at the window. 'Something big is happening, all of this must be going somewhere, surely?'

'No idea.'

'Look, I know they keep asking you this, Jack, but can't you remember anything at all?'

'Simon, I have no sodding clue what happened. And that was before I slammed into the river and lost even more days.' Tate knew he was becoming agitated and tried to relax, take a deep breath. 'I was in that tunnel, on the way to the airport, I was letting myself get taken and then "pop". They stick me with an autoinjector and I'm out, and I wake up three days later. What was in the middle? A few flashes of faces I don't know and darkness.'

'That's probably the most alarming part of all this.'

'You think?'

'Hey, I know.' Hunter placed his hand on Tate's shoulder, the one that he hadn't been shot in, and squeezed. 'Forget about supertechnology, or a new heir to the Hak dynasty, if Gu Joon's organisation has a drug that renders even the most stubborn of subjects, like you, unable to resist questioning. They can extract anything from anyone at any time.'

Tate shuddered. 'What about the toxicology report?'

'Inconclusive: there was nothing there that would not have been in a handful of known and well-used sedatives. In addition, you were pumped with a whole lot of new stuff for your injuries.'

'What about Neill?'

'No, nothing.'

'You know the Russians had something like this.'

'True, but theirs had severe noted side effects, which is why it wasn't a threat. But if your experience is anything to go by, this can be used on anyone, and they can just be left to go on their way.'

Tate shook his head, and was rewarded by a moment of dizziness. He blinked. 'How did Gu manage all of this? How's he been able to stay off the radar for so long and then reappear like this?'

Hunter didn't reply immediately, and Tate took the pause to mean he was considering the question. 'We don't know what intel he got from you, Neill or Jericho, but let's try to think what he was after.'

'Go on.'

'He wanted to get Jericho's formula; he wanted the know-how to create White Suit.'

'They had three days to ask him.'

'True, but did they finish asking him?'

Tate thought back to their escape. 'He didn't want to be rescued, I had to slap him and drag him out.'

'What if Gu didn't get everything?'

'That's possible.'

'But then again, they might have.'

'That's possible as well.'

Hunter finished his drink. 'How much can one person keep in their head?'

'Don't ask me that again, I'm thick-skulled.'

'I've been thinking—'

'Is it painful?'

'It's not just how much Jericho could remember; it's about how well he could explain and demonstrate too.'

'What do you mean?'

'Describe a painting, Jack.'

'Any painting?'

'Yes, but don't tell me the name of it.'

'OK, there's this long-haired, moody woman, sitting on her own.'

'What's she wearing?'

'Clothes.'

'What colour are they?'

'Dark, black or navy blue, I don't know exactly.'

'What's she doing?'

'Just staring at the artist, or rather looking at whoever is looking at her.'

'You said she was moody, what expression has she got on her face?'

'That's the hard part.'

'*Mona Lisa*,' Plato said, appearing next to them.

'Yes,' Tate replied.

'You see, we all knew you were describing the *Mona Lisa*, because we've seen the *Mona Lisa*, or at least a photo of the painting. But how do you describe something that someone else hasn't seen in enough detail for it to be replicated?'

'You don't need to with an algorithm,' Plato said.

'True, or a chemical equation, but what if it was important to know exactly what the physical product of a chemical equation looked like? Think about it, we know what snow looks like, but no two snowflakes are the same.'

'The Eskimos have forty different words for snow,' Tate stated.

'Inuit,' Plato clarified.

'Exactly. So my point is that perhaps Jericho couldn't give them everything because some things just cannot be described without photographs of the physical product. In this case, perhaps, I don't know the structure of his invention.'

'White Suit.'

'Precisely, the weave or whatever.'

'It sounds like you're clutching at straws,' Tate said.

'No, Jack.' Plato nodded. 'I think Simon may be on to something. Perhaps there is an element missing that is preventing Gu's organisation from carrying out Colin's process successfully?'

Tate and his brother shared a look. Hunter spoke first. 'Neill would you say Colin had many close friends?'

'At university he didn't, except for me.'

'No old girlfriends?'

'None at all. It wasn't that he couldn't talk to women, it was just that he didn't know what to say to them. Then, of course, the way he used to look, it put them off. He ate too much.'

'Would you say you were his best friend?' Hunter continued.

'Yes.' Plato's eyes darted to the floor. 'Why?'

'What I'm getting at is that if he were to tell anyone about his process or trust anyone with the location of anything, it would be you, Neill.'

Plato looked up, shock and surprise on his face. 'You don't think they'll come for me?'

Tate lied. 'No I don't. You're safe now.'

'You'll be back in the UK by the end of the week, and all this will be over,' Hunter added.

'Good.' Plato turned. 'I'm going to make a pot of tea, I won't raise my hopes we have any Earl Grey.'

When Plato was out of the room, Hunter asked, 'Why tell him he's in no danger?'

'Look at him, Simon, he can't take much more. Besides, it's a longshot, isn't it?'

'I suppose,' Hunter conceded, 'and if Neill doesn't know anything now, it's not as if Jericho can reach out to him from beyond the grave.'

'So, back in the UK by the weekend?'

'Yes. You two can return to the office and I'll go back to Washington.'

'Say hello to your hairdresser for me.'

Hunter rolled his eyes. 'Jack, she's just a colleague.'

'I know. I was trying to embarrass you. I mean, that's what brothers are for, right?'

'Right.'

The doorbell rang and Tate and Hunter exchanged glances. Hunter checked the app on his encrypted iPhone, linked to the security camera affixed overlooking the door. The doorbell rang again, and two figures waved at them; it was Casey and Parnell.

'No one's supposed to know we're here.'

'They are the CIA, Simon.'

Hunter left the room, opened the door, and let the pair in. Tate waited in the lounge, by the window.

'He lives, he walks,' Casey said, throwing a mock salute.

'Hello, Vince, Parnell.'

Parnell flashed a thumbs up.

Casey pointed to a heavily padded leather settee. 'That's got my name on it.'

'Go ahead,' Hunter said.

Casey sat and Parnell remained standing as if on guard.

'What can we do for the CIA today?'

'Simon, it's not what you can do for us, or what we can do for you, rather it's what we can tell you. We have new intel.'

Tate frowned. Casey liked to talk.

'On?' Hunter moved to the settee's twin, which faced the first and was separated by a heavy wood coffee table.

'It's regarding Gu Joon, or, as we now believe he is called, Hak Kwang-Il.'

'You've verified his identity?'

'As much as we could. I don't have to tell you what a precarious business it is being a member of the Hak family. I mean the Dear Leader had his older stepbrother poisoned.'

'Allegedly,' Parnell said.

'Before that he arrested his own uncle and had him sentenced to death by firing squad.'

'They used an anti-aircraft gun battery, allegedly,' Parnell added.

'So that brings us to the mysterious Hak Kwang-Il, a Hak who apparently vanished.'

'And now he's back.' Tate wished Casey would just tell them what he knew, rather than use theatrics.

'Yes, Jack, he is. You know there were two highly documented assassination attempts on the South Korean president carried out by the North? The first a commando raid in '68 and the second the Rangoon bombing of '83.'

'OK.' Hunter sat forward in his seat.

'There was a third direct attempt. It was highly embarrassing to the US. If it had become public knowledge, it could have led to military action against the North by the South. No one wanted that, especially as the Cold War looked like it may thaw. So, it was hushed up, and forgotten.'

'How?' Hunter asked.

'Guarantees, money, technology, etc. Look, I'm no Korean expert, my remit has always been Eastern Europe and Russia, but

I know a bit. Anyway, I spoke to a colleague, retired now, who knows a lot.' Casey paused and looked both Tate and Hunter in the eye in turn. 'In 1984 a four-man team was ordered to take out the South Korean president, Chun Doo-Hwan. They were ethnic Koreans, but were US citizens. They had no issues with getting into the country or with access because they were already in place. They were going to hit their target right here during the 1984 Summer Olympics.'

'I could see why that would have been an embarrassment,' Hunter said.

'That was the Olympics with the Rocket Man at the opening ceremony. Ironic, huh?' Parnell smirked.

'Anyway, the plan was to kill their target whilst he attended the opening ceremony, only we managed to find out before they managed to pull it off. I'm not going to go into details, gents, it's classified, but three of the four were killed when the rented warehouse they were using as a base was raided. The fourth guy was injured, but when he'd recovered enough to be questioned, he let slip that the operation had been run by a fifth man, who was a member of the Hak family. He claimed the guy was called Hak Kwang-Il.'

Tate was incredulous. 'And this wasn't followed up?'

'Hey, this was before my time. Yes, it was investigated, but never mind Reagan and his Star Wars initiative, you have to remember this was the analogue age. There was just nothing on this guy. Besides, Hak is one of the most popular names in Korea.'

'So,' Hunter said, and Tate could tell from his face that the cogs were turning, 'are we surmising that because of Hak Kwang-Il's recent activity he's now planning something new?'

Casey threw up his arms. 'Your guess is as good as mine, and that's all we have – guesses. Look, the world changed and nation states no longer target the heads of rival states. The buzzwords for the last two decades have been "regime change" and "soft power".'

'This is North Korea,' Tate said.

Casey nodded. 'I concede they are a little different.'

Neill Plato reappeared from the kitchen. 'Would you gentlemen care for a cup of tea?'

'Plato, what are you now, a butler? No thanks, we were just leaving. So should all of you.' Casey stood. 'It was good to chat, to see you all, but it's time you two returned to London and Simon toddled off back to Washington.'

'Are you throwing us out of the country, Vince?' Tate asked.

'I am. Your mission's over, Gu has gone and, as for Roe Kwang, he's our business.' Casey walked towards the door, Parnell followed, then turned and threw another thumbs up.

'That's that then,' Hunter said. 'I think our welcome has been officially worn out.'

Chapter 15

Brighton, United Kingdom

It was early morning and Plato couldn't sleep. He looked out of the lounge window of his mother's flat. She had the top half of a converted Victorian house. The benefit of this was the lounge and bedrooms had views of the sea. The house was the same place Plato had grown up in and, as such, it had many memories. Plato had always felt safe at his mum's place; that was, until Gu Joon had threatened her. Now he was uneasy, knowing that because of his job the one person he had left in the world to love was in danger. Newman had assured him she had liaised with Sussex Police and appraised them of the situation, but still he felt worried. He'd had a video doorbell installed before he'd flown back from the US, much to his mum's annoyance, and a CCTV system was being fitted within the next few days. Plato had not gone as far as to enquire about having ballistic glass to replace her windows, and besides he was home now, and he was who Gu Joon had wanted. The question, however, was had Gu Joon given up on him or did the man still want him or want to punish him?

The most annoying and, yes, he'd admit it, frightening part of the whole episode was that he had no clue whatsoever what he had or had not divulged to Gu Joon's interrogators whilst he'd been pumped full of whatever it was they'd given him. He felt despondent. He was a walking security breach. He'd made a list of every possible way he could think of his work being hacked or accessed by a malevolent exterior power and had gone through this with both his tech colleagues at MI6 and also his opposite number at MI5.

Plato felt as though he was at a crossroads. He'd been critically analysing his life, his work and his future. One moment he'd come to the decision that it would be noble of him to simply resign. To apologise for his failings and then to walk away, to lead a quiet life back in Brighton with his mother. But that would mean turning his back on his duty to his country, and the few friends he had within the service. Then, later, he'd decide he should stay on and prove that he was still the best MI6 had, and then he'd cringe for even thinking of himself in such a way. Plato hadn't had a crisis of conscience before, ever. Even though his actions may have broken a law here or there, he'd always been on the side of justice. Gu Joon had stripped that from him, and he'd not even understood it was happening.

He realised he'd been standing, motionless, at the window for over a quarter of an hour. The water in the kettle he'd boiled for his pot of tea would now be too cold to use. He turned away from the sea, the rooftops, the street below, and quietly padded into the kitchen, not wanting to wake his mother who was still snoring in her bed. He carefully shut the door, then emptied the kettle and refilled it with fresh water from the tap. He never boiled water twice it was just, well, it wasn't the right thing to do when making tea. He left the kettle to boil and meandered towards the biscuit tin. He'd filled it with Fig Rolls for himself and Bourbons for his mum, the night before. Plato opened the tin and reached for a biscuit. There was an electronic ping. His personal iPhone. He took a Fig Roll, then picked up the handset which was recharging by his side.

The tone was an alert. He had new email. He had new email in his private account, the one he didn't use, the one Colin Jericho had contacted him on. Plato opened the account, and his jaw went slack. The message was from Colin Jericho, from the same email account Colin had used to send his SOS message. Plato leaned against the kitchen worktop for support as the room seemed to wobble around him. He blinked and then he saw that the message had a video attachment. Was it a trick? Who had sent it? Was it some type of phishing tool sent by hackers or, worse still, instigated by Gu Joon?

He needed to interrogate the server, see where and when it had been sent, but Plato didn't have his work laptop, and his didn't have his work iPhone. Both were at the office whilst the rest of the tech team, without him, went through their systems to check for any security risks. The kettle boiled and the sudden 'click' prompted him to make a decision. He opened the attached video.

The image displayed Colin Jericho, with long hair and a carefully kempt 'hipster beard', looking directly into the camera lens, whilst behind was a messy bedroom.

Jericho started to speak. 'Hello, Neill! Long time, no see! I know this must be a huge surprise to you, but I'm not dead. Well, if you're watching this message, it means that I'm dead now, in my future and your past. Time travel, eh? Who says it's impossible?'

On screen, a door opened to the side of the room and a woman walked in wearing a bikini. 'Cal, are you coming or not?'

'Darcie, can you just give me a minute – I'm recording a message to an old friend from back home,' Jericho replied, his accent now American.

'Who?'

'The guy's name's Neill. It's for his birthday.'

Darcie walked towards the screen, placed her hands on Jericho's shoulders, leaned forward and said, 'Happy Birthday, Neill!'

'Okay, thanks. Look, can you give me, like, ten minutes?'

'Sure.' Darcie kissed him on the cheek. 'I'll see you at the beach.'

Jericho's head turned as he watched Darcie walk back out of the door. In the distance a dog could now be heard barking and then the sound of a door being shut. Jericho faced the camera again, using his own accent once more. 'Perhaps I should start again? No, you know what, I'll leave that in. That was Darcie. I think she likes me, but it's early days yet. Right, where was I? Oh yes, I'm not dead but I will be if you get this, simple? Right. Look, Neill, I'm not proud of what I've done. I only ever wanted my work to benefit humanity. God, that sounds lame, but it's the truth. I'm dead, but my work is not. Everything I was working on for the MoD, and for myself, I saved onto an SD card before I faked my death. Neill, I want you to have all of this, and I want you to know that White Suit works. In case this message is seen by the wrong people I'm not going to tell you where it is, but I'm going to give you some specific clues, which only you will understand …'

Plato shakily continued to watch the video as Jericho, from beyond the grave, set out where he had hidden his research. Alone, in his childhood home, tears started to roll down Plato's cheeks.

'What a waste … what a bloody waste …'

Plato put down the phone, wiped his eyes, blew his nose and made his tea. He'd watch the video once again, to make sure there was nothing he had missed before he called both Pamela Newman and Jack Tate.

Chapter 16

Lancing, West Sussex, United Kingdom

St Botolph's College chapel was a local landmark and clearly visible from the A27. Tate took the exit at the traffic lights, opposite the large fields of Shoreham airport, and then followed the access road onto the college's imposing grounds. They first passed brick cottages owned by the college, then carried on over a narrow bridge before meandering uphill past a stone-walled barn towards both the college chapel and the main college buildings behind. There was a sign reiterating that they were on public property, but also giving times the general public could visit the college chapel. They weren't within those times.

The road crested a hill and gave them two possible routes.

'Go right here,' Plato instructed, 'then head down and around the swimming pool.'

'You've been here before?'

'My mum dragged me around the chapel a couple of times as a kid.'

'This is like something out of *Harry Potter*,' Tate said.

'The board of governors were approached about filming here, but turned it down.'

206

Tate followed the road as it now followed the contour of the hill, back down to a plain which housed the indoor swimming complex and sports hall. They now saw the school miniature farm on the left and, immediately ahead, the vast playing fields on another larger, lower plain. Past this, high hills overlooked tall, ancient trees that screened the college from the Adur River, and real world outside. Tate brought the unobtrusive, dark-blue Ford Mondeo to a halt in a space directly facing the cricket pitch and next to the row of college minibuses emblazoned with the yellow and maroon St Botolph's College logos.

'Jericho went here?'

'He won a scholarship. Science, I think.'

Tate turned off the engine and even though the windows were closed, the car was filled with the cawing of the crows who guarded the trees overhead.

'I went to the local comprehensive in Camden, the only cricket the kids there saw was on their disposable lighters.'

'I went to a high school in Brighton.'

'At least you had the sea.'

'And the nudist beach.'

Tate cast Plato a sideways glance. 'Oh yeah? Who's a dark horse, then?'

Plato chuckled. 'There was a boy in my class – Justin Smith – who claimed he'd seen Ms Workman, our Home Economics teacher, there.'

Tate chuckled quietly. 'There's always one kid who talks crap.'

'The last I heard, he was the leader of the local council.'

'Come on.' Tate exited the car and Plato followed.

They could now hear the distant rumble of traffic on the A27, as it crossed the Shoreham flyover. On the pitch groups of teenagers trudged up from the lower playing field and took the steps up past the distant cricket pavilion to their right. Tate imagined them heading back to their dormitories to practise their wizardry. They looked lean and healthy, and despite moving with a gait that expressed fatigue, their voices – carried on the breeze – were tinged with enthusiasm. It was a world away from Camden, at least the Camden he'd known as a kid. He imagined he was looking at a few future world leaders, and probably a couple of foreign royals. The noise of an engine became audible overhead, causing Tate to look up. Past the playing fields, and over the river, a Cessna dropped out of the clouds and made a wobbly approach to the airport.

Tate glanced at Plato, who had a faraway look in his eyes. 'I know you miss him.'

'I've lost him twice, Jack.'

Every life lost on each and every mission affected Tate, but in this instance, he felt little grief for Jericho. The man had been a traitor; a brilliant but deluded traitor who had been neither tough nor noble enough to resist the lure of Blackline. How long before they launched the EMP had Jericho run away? Even a solitary day's warning would have saved tens of thousands of lives. Yet Tate knew he couldn't vocalise this again, and definitely not now. 'Neill, the friend you knew at university was not the same man you saw in the US.'

'I know.' Plato continued to watch the plane as it disappeared behind the treetops.

'So, where do you want to start?'

Plato looked up. 'Jack, you really don't know?'

Tate frowned. 'No.'

'I thought you knew? You watched the video.'

'You studied it.'

'OK. What are we looking for?'

'What's this, Neill? Twenty questions?'

'No, I don't think you'll need as many as that.'

'OK, I'll play.' Tate sighed. 'We're looking for whatever Jericho has hidden.'

'Which is?'

'Information on Project White Suit.'

'Yes.'

'What do you mean "yes"?'

'I mean, go on. Who would wear a white suit?'

'The Man from Del Monte.'

'And?'

'Don Johnson.'

'And?'

'Just tell me.'

Plato pointed at the grass in front of them, then at the thatched-roofed, white-washed dressing room and pavilion at the far-right side of the pitch. 'Cricket players wear white.'

'Finally. So, you think Jericho hid his files in the cricket pavilion?'

'Yes, I do.'

'OK then.'

They walked up the rise out of the car park and took the path towards the pavilion. The grounds were now empty with the exception of the odd passing car heading either to or from the main school building or the car park. They stayed on the wider path which would pass the pavilion, and then the tennis courts nestled next to a lower playing field below until the last moment when they veered to the left and darted between the pavilion and the dressing room.

The dressing rooms were two identical buildings side by side – one for each team – and the doors to both buildings were locked. The pavilion was a two-storey affair, with a balcony cum viewing gallery protruding from the thatched roof.

'It's in there.'

'How do you know?' Tate asked.

'He used to go on about a cup the team won when he was the Tailender.'

'Tailender?'

'The eleventh man in bat. According to Colin, he won the match for the team by hitting five sixes in two overs.'

'Jimmy Hill.' Tate rubbed his chin.

'So I think whatever he's hidden will be in or near that cup.'

'OK.' Tate shook his head; this was beginning to become a treasure hunt. 'Why couldn't he just have told you exactly where he'd put it?'

'Spy craft, Jack. I thought you of all people would understand that? It had to be in a code that only I could understand.'

Tate smiled. 'Yep, silly question – you've got me there.'

'Can I help you?' The voice was cultured, but loud, and carried across the grass.

Tate and Plato turned to see a figure approaching them. She was dressed in a yellow and maroon St Botolph's College tracksuit and a whistle hung on a lanyard around her neck. Neither man spoke until she had jogged up the incline from the pitch and came to a stop in front of them. She looked to be in her late twenties and had the ruddy, healthy complexion of someone who spent most of their day in the British outdoors.

Tate retrieved an ID card which bore his face but a false name. 'We're with the Security Service.'

The woman took the ID and her eyes widened as she studied it. 'MI5?'

'That's correct. Miss?'

'Ms Orchard. I'm one of the PE teachers.' She handed Tate back his ID.

'Ms Orchard, I'm going to need you to open the cricket pavilion.'

'Why?'

'We believe a former pupil, who later was in our employ, may have hidden sensitive material there. Material which could pose a risk to national security.' It was a lie. Jericho had never worked for MI5 and neither had Tate nor Plato, but it did carry with it the essential element of truth.

'Which former pupil?'

'I'm not permitted to divulge that information.'

Orchard took a step back, and folded her arms, 'How do I know any of this is genuine? Surely you should have phoned ahead and made an appointment with a member of the leadership team?'

Tate nodded and smiled. 'I'm aware this is highly unusual, but if you call the number on this card ...' Tate handed her a business card which carried the same details as his ID. 'You can speak to my department and confirm our identities.'

'I will. However, I still think you should go to the main building and wait for a member of senior management to grant you permission to be here.'

'Yes.' Tate nodded again. He'd forgotten how inflexible teachers could be. 'I could do that and complain I was hindered from doing my job, or I could ask you politely to let me in whilst you call my office. That would save time, and this is time sensitive.'

Orchard huffed. 'Fine, I shall do that.'

She moved past the pair and pushed down the door handle. Tate rolled his eyes; the door had been unlocked. She pulled the door to one side and with a sweeping gesture beckoned them inside.

The interior smelled of a heady mix of polish, paint and oil. Probably linseed oil, but Tate was no expert. Dappled light came in from the large wooden-framed windows that faced the pitch and the countryside beyond. Tate had never been a cricket fan; he'd preferred rugby, although he'd not played much of either sport as a kid. He could imagine though what the atmosphere must have been like in the pavilion at afternoon tea.

'Where are the cups?'

'Cups?'

'Trophies,' Plato clarified.

'There is a locked display cabinet on the first floor. Why? Is this where you tell me you have really come to steal the school silver?'

Tate allowed a smile to split his lips; his PE teacher had been a miserable sod with a Captain Pugwash beard. 'Like I said, Ms Orchard, please call the number on my card.'

Orchard put her hand into her pocket and retrieved a purple iPhone. 'I think I will.'

Tate said nothing as he waited for her to be connected to the dedicated number at Vauxhall Cross which Plato had set up to spoof that of their sister intelligence service.

Orchard frowned. 'That's odd. I've got no network coverage. I'll go outside and try.'

Tate asked. 'Can you give me the key to the cabinet? This really is time sensitive.'

'Fine. I'll open it for you.' Orchard strode deeper into the building and took the stairs, which were in the middle of the back wall and led to a single open-plan room. It had a pair of large French windows which led onto the terrace. Tate imagined innumerable adolescent sports captains holding aloft cups or shields or even each other whilst receiving the adulation of friends and their well-heeled families. On the far-left wall and taking up the entire width of the room, was a glass-fronted wooden cabinet. Tate and Plato watched on as Orchard retrieved a keychain with a bunch of keys on it. 'It's this long one. You have to jiggle it a bit, it's an old lock.'

'Thank you,' Tate said as the door swung open.

'I suppose I can leave the pair of you here whilst I go outside and make a call, after all you can hardly stuff any of those trophies in your trouser pockets.'

'Thank you, again,' Tate said, trying to keep as straight a face as the stern younger woman.

Orchard huffed and went back downstairs, swiping at her phone screen.

Tate nodded at Plato. 'Let's go.'

'What if the cup's not there?' Plato asked Tate, in a whisper.

'It has to be, a classy place like this had loads of trophies. They'll keep the academic ones in the school and the sports ones here.'

'Makes sense.'

'I'm just making it up, I could be completely wrong. Let's

have a look.'

Tate studied the cabinet and saw that there was an alarm pad on the glass, so there was more security than he had imagined, which was a positive sign. Through the glass a myriad of silver shields and trophies reflected the evening sunlight back at him. 'I don't suppose you know what type of cup we're after?'

'Colin left here in 2005, after his A levels. He said it happened in a match in his lower sixth so that's 2004.'

'So, we look for a cup for 2004?'

Tate opened the cabinet; thankfully the alarm was off. There were several trophies with the same date on them. Tate picked up one and passed it to Plato, 'Check this one for his name.'

Plato took a step back and started to inspect the cup whilst Tate worked on the second one. Neither had the name Colin Jericho engraved on it, so they moved on to the next two.

'This one has his name on it,' Plato stated, with excitement in his voice.

'See if there's anything hidden inside or taped underneath.'

'Will do.'

Tate was about to place his own trophy back in the cabinet when he noticed its base seemed slightly thicker than the others. He shook it and there was a slight rattle. He inspected the base again and saw that an extra piece, which wasn't made from the same pewter, had been moulded under it and sandwiched against the original base. Using the nail of his right thumb, he worked at the seam; the thin tin started to distort and bow.

'Well, this one doesn't appear to be hiding anything.' Plato shrugged.

Tate's trophy popped open. In between the original base and the new base was a sliver of plastic encased in a hard, clear plastic sleeve. Tate tapped it into his palm and presented it to Plato. 'If that's not it, this is the world's biggest wind-up.'

Plato inspected the SD card through the protective film. The initials 'SS' were written on it in a delicate hand. 'Sidney Stratton.'

Tate looked at the cup; the same fictional name was engraved on it.

'What are you doing?' It was Orchard again; this time she sounded outraged.

Tate turned. 'I think we've just about finished here.'

'You've damaged that trophy! I knew I shouldn't have just left you here!'

'But you did.' Tate put his hand into his pocket, retrieved his wallet and pulled out a pair of fifty-pound notes. 'Here, I'm sure that will cover any damage and, if not, the address to send a claim is on my card.'

Eyes narrowing, Orchard took the money. 'I couldn't call your office, the network appears to be down.'

Tate frowned then and checked his own encrypted iPhone, and saw that Plato was doing the same. 'Is yours working?'

'Full battery, no signal.'

Tate spoke evenly and quietly. 'Ms Orchard, I need you to stay inside and away from the windows until we've left the school grounds.'

'I'm sorry, why ever would I do that?'

'This may most likely be a coincidence, however we believe there is another party searching for the same materials we are. And they are far less friendly.'

'They? This is a school! Are you telling me your operation has endangered every single child at the college by luring, what, criminals or terrorists onto our grounds?'

It was true, but Tate couldn't admit to it. 'The item brought them here. Now please, just do as I've asked. If anyone is out there blocking the phone signals, they're after my associate and me. Not anyone else.'

Orchard looked angry rather than fearful. 'Get the hell out of here now, both of you! As soon as my damn phone starts working again, I'll call the police!'

Tate took the stairs back down, with Plato following. He

214

reached the door to the pavilion and paused. 'Neill, this may be nothing, but it may not. Stay here, I'm going to run back to the car. If we do have company and they see me sprinting like a loony, it'll draw them out. They should go after me. If that happens, hide. If not, I'll swing by and pick you up. Got it?'

'Got it,' Plato said but didn't sound convinced. 'But what about the SD card?'

'You keep it, put it in your shoe, under your foot.'

'What?'

'Just trust me. Don't let Ms Orchard leave before I get back.'

'Er, I'll try.'

Tate ducked out of the building and, rather than take the path, bounded in a straight line up the slope to the road. Reaching the top, he started to run towards the car park. He was exposed, and that was the point. It was movement that drew attention, that and anyone acting out of character, and he was sprinting, but not dressed in running gear. Tate scanned the area, both using his peripheral vision and by turning his head. If there was a team observing him, or if there was a shooter, he was definitely in their sights and with this much potential cover for the opposition he'd have no chance of spotting where the shot came from.

Tate reached the sloping exit road for the car park and slowed, his stride lengthening as he did so. The car park had fewer cars in it now and those that were left were mostly high-end German SUVs. There was even more cover here for watchers, a snatch team, or a shooter. Tate blipped the locks and scooted into his Mondeo. Making the tyres squeal, he accelerated back the way he had just come and took the road back to the cricket pavilion.

He brought the car to a sudden halt.

He waited.

Plato didn't appear.

That was when Tate knew he'd messed up.

Unarmed, and without a plan, Tate leaped out of the car and rushed back down to the pavilion. He reached the open door and, throwing any caution he had left aside, spun into the space. He immediately moved to one side of the door and waited and listened.

The building was quiet, but he saw something on the floor; something that created a trail from the steps down to the front door, a bloody footprint. Tate felt his stomach lurch as he advanced into the room. To one side of the space were a pile of folded metal chairs. He took one and held it up, like a WWE wrestler ready to bat away anyone in his path. Relying on speed now and not stealth, his feet hammered against the wooden boards as he bounded up the stairs. Wild-eyed he looked right and saw nothing, he looked left and saw that the display cabinet lay on the floor. Shattered glass cascaded away from it as did the dislodged trophies, cups, plates, and a whistle on a lanyard. There was a splatter of blood, and boot prints leading away from it. Ms Orchard and Plato had vanished. No, he corrected himself, not vanished. They had been abducted. He dropped the chair. Moving to the French windows, he delivered a well-placed boot to kick them open, and burst onto the balcony. Tate frantically searched the playing fields and trees beyond for any sign of Plato, Orchard and their abductors. There was nothing, which meant only one thing. They had left the college by the same route he had entered, the only exit route – the road that wound down and through the college grounds, past the private access road and the cottages to the A27.

In the distance Tate heard a sudden honking of horns and tyres screeching. Moving as fast as he could make himself go, Tate half ran, half jumped down the stairs and tore out of the building back to his car. He floored the accelerator, the rear of the Mondeo fishtailing as he took the right-hand bend and shot past the stone-walled barn and farmhouse. He bounced over the first sleeping policeman before braking to cross the narrow bridge over the brook. He bumped over two more speed-humps before being forced to slam on his brakes. On his right and half on the road, half in the hedgerow and front garden of one of the cottages, was a silver Mercedes M-Class. The driver was standing examining the damage.

Tate rolled forward and wound down his window. 'What happened?'

The man looked up. His face was white. Shock, Tate imagined. 'A bloody idiot in a black X5 forced me off the road!'

Tate nodded, said nothing, and powered on past. He followed the road as it wound left before he came to a junction. Fifty yards on the right it joined the A27. The traffic lights were red, and four cars were patiently waiting for them to turn green. Either the X5 had already passed them, or it had turned left.

Tate turned left.

The road was tarmacked, but rural. It wound past the bottom of the college grounds, with tall ancient trees bordering on the college side and shrubs and hedgerows bordering working fields and the river on the right.

Tate tapped the map function on the car's sat nav screen and details of the immediate area appeared. It told him he was travelling north on the Coombes Road. Tate sped on. There was a buzzing from his pocket; whatever had been blocking his signal had now either been fixed, turned off or he'd moved out of range. But he had no time to grab his phone. Was he heading in the right direction or had he made a mistake, a miscalculation, and had the vehicle actually made it to the A27 junction before the lights had turned red? But he was committed now, he couldn't second guess himself. Either he was going the right way, or he wasn't, but they had Plato, so he had to be right. And then he rounded a bend and had to slam on his brakes to avoid a pedestrian in the road. It was Ms Orchard, and she was holding her head.

'You OK?' There was a trickle of blood on her cheek.

She nodded. 'Yes.'

Tate couldn't stay, he couldn't help. 'Get to a landline, call the police.'

Tate accelerated away. He flashed past a large house on the right with a gated entrance, then around a bend and past a small car park for a picnic site and then the road narrowed to a single lane as it passed another secluded house, this one on his left, but Tate only had eyes for the road ahead. He knew the X5 was there, somewhere ahead. With less than a two-minute lead he figured on these roads, even it couldn't be more than a mile further on. Tate glanced at the sat nav. It told him that, apart from a farm half a mile ahead, and a few houses making up the villages of Coombes and Botolphs, there was no other turning until the road entered the larger village of Steyning. There the X5 could reach several faster, wider A roads.

Tate slowed for what he suddenly saw was an all but hairpin bend and then floored the accelerator again. And then he saw it. A black BMW X5, its brake lights taunting him as it disappeared around another bend. Urged on now, Tate increased his speed as the trees and hedgerows became nothing more than a blur on either side. He'd been trained in advanced driving, had gone out on rally stages in North Wales and now had to try to use those once-learned skills. A flash of red abruptly appeared, then a flash of yellow. A pair of cyclists, riding side by side, taking up as much space as a car and coming towards him.

Tate had no time to turn, no time to brake. He jinked left and the thick branches of the trees clawed at the paintwork of the Mondeo and then he saw a wall, part of an old boundary perhaps but either way it was something that wouldn't give like the trees had. The lead cyclist threw himself into a ditch on the other side of the road and the second, the one who was further towards the middle of the road, carried on towards Tate, mouth wide and probably screaming. Tate tugged the wheel. The whole nearside front wing screeched and scratched against the flints in the wall, the car cursed like cats thrown into a bath and then his wing mirror was ripped off and flew away and up behind the careering car. Tate didn't slow, he couldn't. He left the cyclists behind. They were alive, they were no longer his concern.

The road seemed to narrow even more now as Tate flashed past the walls of a barn, made from the same Sussex flints. The farm it belonged to straddled the road, with a wooden gate and a yard on the other side leading to a second barn. Tate sped on, passing several more houses and then again nothing but trees and hedgerows and fields for several minutes. Had the X5 turned off? Had it hidden in any one of the large drives or farm buildings he'd seen? It was then he saw a signpost stating he was entering Steyning, and then something else which gave him cheer. A set of temporary traffic lights. But they were red, and there was no one waiting for them to go green.

Tate ignored the lights. Swerving past them he saw the X5. It was in the middle of the road. It was stationary. It was facing some sort of industrial digger which was completely blocking its path. Just behind the BMW was the entrance to an access road and muddy tread marks indicated the route the digger had and now wanted to take again.

Tate could see figures in the X5, a trio in the back, and one in the front; a three-man team an odd number but not odd for a 'grab mission'; one to drive and two to do the grabbing. A workman wearing cut-off jeans, muddied tan-coloured boots, a hard hat and an orange hi-vis vest jogged out of the turning towards the target vehicle. At the same time the rear off-side passenger door opened, and a man clambered out.

He looked back.

He was holding a handgun.

All this Tate saw in the split-second it took him to decide upon his course of action.

Tate slammed the Ford into the off-side of the X5, shunting it sideways. His airbags exploded in a cloud of white powder, and he was flung forwards and then back, but his chin had been tucked into his chest and he'd been ready for it.

Still shaken, with adrenalin masking any new injuries, Tate tumbled out of the passenger door. The crumpled body of the gunman was pinned between the two cars. Tate grabbed the 9mm pistol from the man's broken hand and bounded to the front of the BMW. The driver was rubbing his neck. The man saw Tate and his hand quickly reached for something. Tate shot him in the head, then aimed the pistol at the last remaining member of the team. The man had his right hand covering his bloodied face and raised his left palm open in a sign of surrender. Next to him sat Neill Plato. His face was white, he had a gash on his forehead, and his gaze was far away.

Chapter 17

Private Medical Establishment, Haywards Heath

Tate was, by now, fed up with both hospitals and car chases. He felt as though he'd run into a brick wall but at least it was only bruises, although his recently repaired left shoulder ached. He sat in the private room as Neill Plato was checked over by a junior doctor. Plato seemed shaken, but, apart from the cut on his forehead, there wasn't a mark on him.

Pamela Newman entered. Tate rose from his seat, but she waved him back into it. She addressed the member of staff. 'How is he, doctor? Is he fine to leave?'

'Yes, he is.'

'Excellent. Can we have the room?'

'Of course.'

Newman waited until the other woman had exited and shut the door. 'The man who was brought in with you is claiming he has diplomatic immunity.'

'So what? It was diplomats who abducted Neill and the teacher?'

'That's what would have been the case, if his ID had not been an elaborate forgery.'

221

'So, who is he?'

'That we don't yet know.' Newman nodded at Plato. 'How are you, Neill?'

Plato shrugged, an action which made him wince. 'Bruised, but, if it hadn't been for Jack, it would have been worse.'

'If it hadn't been for me, you would never have been snatched in the first place, Neill,' Tate said.

'Yes, to you, and yes to you. Now listen, whilst both of you have been playing Miss Marple in West Sussex, we've had a new ping.'

'Who?'

'Gu Joon, Jack. It was from the port city of Manzanillo in Mexico.'

'So he didn't drop off the radar, he sailed under it?'

'Quite. It seems like Gu has used the same mode of transport that our Mr Fang did. From Manzanillo there are established cargo routes to Japan, China and South Korea.'

'What about Roe?'

'Nothing as yet. So, are we to presume that Mr Gu is heading home?'

'It's the only place we can't get to him, and, by us, I mean the Americans,' Tate stated.

'Which is why I've ordered the ship to be tracked, Jack. We still believe Gu Joon is on it because we don't have any hits of him leaving it.'

'So, what's our next move?'

'Officially we have no next move. Jericho is dead and you've recovered his work. We have what we wanted.'

Tate saw Plato was about to say something and quickly spoke before he could. 'We've exposed something here, something huge. Don't you think we should at least see it through?'

'What do you suggest?'

'We board the ship and search it, and if Gu and Roe are on board, we take them and throw them into somewhere dark and wet until they talk.'

'That's not very legal.'

'I doubt what Gu's organisation was planning was legal either.'

'Pamela,' Plato said, 'he wanted that technology for something. Who knows what he's got on that ship?'

Newman's phone pinged and she withdrew her reading glasses and phone from her bag. She read the screen. 'There's news from Seoul. A possible meeting between the leaders of The Democratic People's Republic of Korea and the South. Apparently, it's come out of the blue.'

'That can't be a coincidence, can it?'

'No, Jack, it cannot.' Newman tapped her screen and sent an email before she placed it and her glasses back in her bag. 'Right. To the office, all of us. Neill, I need you to be back and working your magic, and Jack you must draw up an assault plan for that ship.'

'So, it's a go?'

'It's a "let's have a think about it".'

'So, what's happening to the unknown abductor?' Tate asked.

'When his nose is finished being fixed, I'll have him taken somewhere.'

'She hit him, you know,' Plato said.

'Who?' Newman asked.

'Ms Orchard, the PE teacher. She punched him, hard in the face.'

Undisclosed location

Roe watched the man enter the room where he and his uncle sat. The man looked nervous. He bowed his head respectfully before he addressed Gu Joon.

'Uncle, I am afraid the UK mission has been unsuccessful.'

'How?' Gu Joon sat up straighter in his chair. 'Explain how this is possible?'

The man nodded. 'I sent the video message we intercepted

from Colin Jericho's account, as requested, and our team in the UK followed Neill Plato, but ...'

'But what?' Gu Joon steepled his hands on his desk.

'Plato was not on his own. He was with a man we identified as Jack Tate.'

'Tate.' Gu's eyes narrowed. 'Carry on.'

'Tate drove the pair to a large public school – St Botolph's College.'

'I know it. Continue.'

'The team watched Plato and Tate enter a building with a member of staff. Then, several minutes later, they observed Tate running out of the building, on his own, towards his car.'

'Why was he running?'

'They did not know, but did not give chase as he was not with Plato. They decided to enter the building. The team abducted both Plato and a teacher who was with them. Plato had the data hidden on himself.'

'Why abduct them both?'

'I don't know, Uncle.'

'So, the mission was a success?'

'No, Uncle. Tate chased them. He killed two of the team and the other man we believe is being held by MI6.'

'Pamela Newman?' Gu nodded knowingly, using information gleaned from Tate and Plato whilst they had been drugged up in Las Vegas.

'That I do not know.'

'We do not have the data, and that is that?' Gu asked, his eyebrows arching.

'Yes, Uncle, and we have lost the team.'

'The team is not important.' Gu flattened his palms on the desk. 'They were apparently disposable because they failed at their one, simple task.'

'Yes, Uncle.'

'Do not fail me.' Gu glowered at the man. 'Is there anything else you wanted to inform me about?'

'No, Uncle.'

'Go then.'

The man nodded and retreated through the cabin door.

'Can we proceed without the data on that device?' Roe asked as his uncle swivelled his chair to face him.

'I believe we can. My aim in retrieving that data was to prevent anyone else from using Jericho's work. This is a setback, a major one, but it does not impact what we can achieve; it merely speeds up our timeline. The drones are ready, we shall conduct more live tests today and if successful we can then continue to upscale White Suit.'

Secret Intelligence Service Headquarters, Vauxhall Cross, London

Jack Tate had never wanted to be 'a suit', a man who sat at a desk shuffling papers and sending emails but there he was, minus the actual suit. He sat at the hot-desk and started to shift through the pile of paperwork which seemed to have been generated merely to fill his time. His semi-permanent secondment from the SAS to MI6's E Squadron brought with it an increased chance to serve his country, and a greater probability of terminal paper cuts.

The door at the far end of the otherwise empty, glass-walled, open-plan office opened and he saw Plato enter. He beckoned at Tate, who threw him a mock salute and dropped the piece of paper he'd been pretending to read into the bin.

Tate rose from his desk, crossed the room, and the pair of them made for Newman's office. They entered and found Newman sitting back in her chair, twiddling her reading glasses.

'Do we know if Blackline ever had this technology?' Newman asked.

'No,' Plato stated, as he took a seat.

'Not that I'm aware of,' Tate added and sat in the last remaining chair.

Newman tapped the arm of her glasses against her bottom lip, 'If the North Koreans manage to get this White Suit technology working, they'll not be able to attack anything?'

'Not that I can see,' Plato clarified.

'So its applications are purely defensive?'

Tate frowned. 'Unless it made their men harder to kill and their tanks tougher to stop.'

'And their planes more difficult to shoot out of the sky,' Plato added.

'Interesting,' Newman said, seemingly to herself. 'So if White Suit works, they can create a vehicle or air frame that can survive a hit from a conventional missile, correct?'

Plato frowned. 'Yes.'

'Neill.' Newman placed her glasses on her desk. 'Is there anything at all Jericho has left that would indicate when or where any of this may be used?'

'Nothing, I'm afraid. He stashed his data before he died the first time. The message he sent me was recorded after he'd left Blackline, but before he'd had any contact with Gu Joon. He's left plans for White Suit but no plans as to how Gu Joon may use it.'

Newman nodded. 'I've made a decision. We have to go in. We have to grab Gu Joon. This is our mess, caused by the late Colin Jericho, which we need to clean up.'

'Let me at them,' Tate said.

'Jack, I know you think you're indestructible, but you can't be on the ground again so soon.' Tate opened his mouth to speak again, but Newman silenced him with a raise of the hand. 'You will continue to run this, from here. I'm agreeing your plan to hit that ship. We must board it if there is the remotest chance that Gu Joon is on board. Even if he has already passed on the technology, and it's working, I think it's better if he's not running around. Jack, choose a team and send them in.'

Pacific Ocean

The CIA bosses had not permitted him enough time to practise his art. Sure, they had fully equipped gyms and gun ranges, but Roe was a loner and needed time in isolation to work on his fighting form, speed and strength. Often, he lay awake at night silently moving on his bed, making sure his body remembered the traditional moves he had mastered, but it was not the same.

Sweat dripped into his eyes. He focused on his balance as the ship rose and fell in the swell of the open sea. Faster and faster he moved; fists and feet slicing through the salty ocean air, as with each passing minute he practised his shape and form. Roe had set up a training area at the stern of the vessel. In front of him, stacked three high, rust-flecked cargo containers watched over his workout whilst behind there was nothing but the gunwales and then the open sea.

Roe had no religion, no omniscient entity to seek guidance from; he had only himself, and now his uncle. For the majority of his adult life, he had felt as though he was a deniable prisoner of the Americans, as confined as those he ended up guarding. But no more. Now, however, he was free. His uncle, he realised, was a visionary. Roe understood what his operation would bring about. It was not seeking to create chaos, to be capitalised upon; it sought to create change for the greater good. His uncle was going to be the ruler of North Korea. He would be the first member of the Hak dynasty to acknowledge and seek justice for the actions of his family members who had ruled perniciously since the kingdom had been founded.

Roe continued his routine; it was a mixture of ancient Wing Chun Kuen and the contemporary Shadow Dragon. As a kid he'd been called Chinese at school so he'd decided to live up to their slurs and become Chinese when he fought. He sought out a local instructor who combined karate and kung fu. This gave Roe both a physical and mental edge. It taught him discipline, it showed him his own strength and, most of all, it trained him to clear his mind. And now, rolling with the waves in the middle of nowhere, his mind was exceptionally clear. For as long as he could remember he'd been killing time, waiting for something to happen. He'd felt it as a kid, as though he knew his uncle had something planned for him even before they'd met. He was who he was because of the old man. It was he who guided Roe to join the military, telling him he came from a long line of warriors and that he'd be good at soldiering – and he was right. Roe didn't think even his uncle believed he would go as far as he had, but Roe had. Yet he had felt empty. It felt as though what he was doing was not making a difference, as if the people he was fighting for were not his own. Roe knew he was Korean by birth and American by upbringing, but he'd never known he was North Korean, until his uncle told him. That was the day that everything suddenly made sense. It had been hard for Roe to explain, but he stopped being American. He understood who he should be fighting for.

Over the sound of the waves, he heard feet approaching. A crew member appeared from around the corner of the containers. He was small and sinewy. 'Uncle has asked for you to come to his cabin.'

Roe nodded and followed the smaller man back along the deck, in through a doorway, and down a corridor to the captain's cabin, which the actual captain had been demoted from. The crew member knocked, then stepped away.

'Come in.'

Roe entered. Inside, his uncle pointed to a plush chair and Roe sat.

'You two were training?'

'Yes.'

'It is a must that we train.'

Roe made no reply.

'The Singapore summit is confirmed,' Gu stated. 'Both sides will attend. Our plan will go ahead.'

'What about the British and the Americans?' Roe asked. 'What if they manage to track us?'

'Let them find us, for if they do, we shall be ready for them. We arrive in five days.' Gu Joon pointed to a crystal whisky decanter set. 'Pour us both a glass.'

Roe stood and splashed a generous measure into each glass before handing one glass to his uncle.

'To our success!' Gu Joon toasted the pair of them.

Roe held up his glass, then both men sipped. The whisky was unlike anything Roe had tasted before; it was rich, smoky, aromatic and there was real fire when it slipped down his throat.

'Some things, Roe, like this rare whisky, can only be enjoyed when the time is right. They are to be savoured. The same will be true of our victory. I have lived in the shadows for almost forty years, ever since I left our home country. Almost forty years, Roe, since our family blood was spilled. It is truly time for our revenge to be enacted, but you and I will both have to make some sacrifices.'

'I am ready, Uncle.'

'However, there is one last aspect of all this I must inform you of.'

Roe noticed his uncle had become misty-eyed, 'Please carry on, Uncle.'

Gu Joon opened his mouth to speak, but no words came. He took a gulp of whisky, closing his eyes as he swallowed. When he opened them again, his expression had altered and he took a deep breath before he spoke. 'Kwang, I am not your uncle.'

Kwang blinked. 'I don't understand.'

'Kwang, I am your father.'

Chapter 18

Pacific Ocean

Tate was a badged member of the SAS and whilst he was highly trained at conducting waterborne assaults, he knew that the men of the SBS were better. The need to keep the boarding of the vessel speedy and silent was paramount. No one wanted to have to explain away a panicked distress call in international waters. Or why a team of British Special Forces operatives had caused it. From his control room at Vauxhall Cross, Tate watched the four-man team who sat, dressed like ninja frogmen, in the cargo plane. The three SBS men – Salter, Silver and Adler he'd worked with before were now joined by another member of the service – Finn Cotton.

Whilst MI6 had no intel to say there would be armed opposition, they didn't have any stating that there would not be any either. The rules of engagement were simple; shoot if shot at, otherwise subdue with 'non-lethal means' and extract anyone on the target list.

Using a helicopter would have been a faster way to board the cargo vessel, but as the ship was in international waters this was a non-starter. So, the team would be dropped a mile off the vessel's stated course and then, using a high-powered Zodiac, would draw alongside the ship and board it by climbing up.

Tate noted that the team was five minutes out from their insertion point, where they would freefall then glide into the sea. Miles out from the nearest land, this was not an easy task. *In theory, the assault was simple, but theory always went out of the window in practice, or something like that*, Tate thought. A drone had been positioned over the vessel and was relaying real-time images back to Tate and Plato in London. So far there were no crew members on deck, and Tate hoped it stayed that way. The SBS men, forming the E Squadron operation, had trained for missions just like this and undertaken them successfully on numerous occasions. Yet out at sea, and at the capricious whim of the wind and the waves, it was not going to be relaxing.

Like a parent watching their child enter their first sporting competition, Tate felt his stomach lurch as Salter, who had been appointed team leader, rose to his feet and waddled to the back of the airframe. The interior lights went out and, just like the team members, the feed on Tate's camera became shades of an otherworldly green. The load master opened the rear of the cavernous C-17 Globemaster, and the four men and their equipment rapidly left the howling interior of the plane for the black abyss somewhere above the dark waters of the Sea of Japan.

Now came the gut-wrenching gap; the time between his men leaving the Globemaster, regrouping and inflating the Zodiac when they would be out of contact. Tate knew it would be no more than a few minutes, but as he and Plato waited, every minute became an hour. Each team member had an IR beacon affixed to the rear of their helmets which the man behind was to follow; this was to ensure that the team stayed together. The open sea was unforgiving, especially at night when a lapse of concentration, a sudden gust of wind or a rogue wave, was all that was needed to make a man lose his bearing, lose his team, and, ultimately, lose his life.

Plato nervously nibbled on a Fig Roll and offered one to Tate. He accepted and munched as he continued to wait. The feed from each of the four commandos' cameras appeared on their own designated screens in front of Tate and Plato. Each showed they were on the inflatable, with the throaty purr of the outboard as the background noise. The feed was jumping and jerky as the boat was buffeted by the wind and the waves. Tate could almost feel the humidity, even though he was half a world away. Plato tapped his key and on another monitor a map appeared showing the location and bearing of both vessels, the hulking container ship, and the miniscule Zodiac. Tate and Plato would only talk to the team if they needed to provide an intelligence or threat update and, likewise, the team would not break silence unless it was mission critical.

The overhead drone feed was displayed on yet another monitor. The IR camera seeking out heat sources and finding none on the open deck where containers had been piled four high. Switching his focus between screens and feeds, they saw the Zodiac – a dark shape in a darker sea – approach from the port side of the ship and then pull alongside. Lines affixed to magnetic clamps would tether the Zodiac to the ship and prevent it from being sucked back or, worse still, sucked under the hull of the gigantic vessel. The drone now picked up heat sources on the deck, one at first and then four in total as the team reached the deck and then moved in to cover behind a line of cargo containers.

'And that's the ship's CCTV system disabled,' Plato confirmed.

Tate nodded, said nothing. The technical abilities of their kit was forever improving; he was glad Plato was the one who handled it and not him.

The floor beneath the assault team's feet would be moving, almost undulating, as the ship rose and fell in the swell. Tate took in this information, but there was nothing that could be done about it. He focused on the feed from the headcams now, especially that of Salter; the man out front.

Salter advanced, then went into cover behind a row of containers. Within seconds the rest of the team joined him; a dark snake of men, coiled and ready to strike.

The team remained still and silent. They were listening for any hint they'd been heard. Together the team had studied real-time satellite images of the vessel, and they knew the fastest route around the containers to the bridge. They also knew how many crew were stated as being onboard. However, what they did not know was how many more men were hidden below, and, more importantly, if they were armed. It was the middle of the night, which in theory meant that most of the crew would be asleep, or if awake at least sluggish and they had counted on this. Coming face to face with an alert, prepared crew was not desirable. On the drone footage nothing moved.

Salter, weapon up, edged forward, around the container, out of cover. His movements were slow and measured as Tate knew his every sense would be focused on what he could see, and what he could hear as all the while the container ship gently rose and fell and rolled.

The drone now showed movement in the bridge. Tate made to relay this development to Salter, but the SBS man had already seen it and held up his left fist – the sign for the others behind him to stop. The team were ready to react. Salter's own headcam now picked up movement in the bridge. There was the flaring of a light which then faded to a glow.

'That's a screen of some sort,' Plato said to Tate as he analysed the footage, 'it's too stable to be a flame.'

The light went out. The team remained immobile. They watched, so did Plato, so did Tate. The light flared again, and this time a face was dimly illuminated. Salter edged forward, because as long as the face was illuminated by whatever light source it was gazing at, the SBS man knew it wasn't looking at him and the others; dressed in black on a black deck they would be virtually invisible. But not completely.

Keeping to the deeper-black shadows cast by the dim sodium lights positioned seemingly at random, high above the deck, the men moved. Their weak light would illuminate the very tops of the cargo containers, but not do an awful lot for the deck; in fact they made the shadows the team traversed darker and deeper.

They advanced again, narrowing the gap to the ladder leading down from the bridge. At the edge of rows of containers Salter paused, listened, and waited again. His headcam moved from side to side as he scanned the area ahead – there was an empty expanse of deck immediately around the bridge and it was completely devoid of cover.

'Movement. Bridge,' Plato said, calmly. 'The door is opening. I've got one x-ray.'

The team stayed still. Through the now-open door of the bridge a crew member wearing Crocs, shorts and a T-shirt came down the stairs. He had a mobile phone in his hands and was poking at the screen. Head down, he walked directly towards Salter before veering away towards the railings.

From the footage on the screens, Tate knew that if the crew member turned his head he'd see the rest of the team, and so did they. Without the need for any order to be given, the feed from the cameras of Adler and Cotton showed they were moving to intercept the crew member. If this was an assault on an enemy vessel the simplest, and the most brutal, course of action would be to simply break the man's neck, then throw him over the gunwale into the inky sea below. But this was a merchant vessel. Adler's headcam now showed Cotton carefully creep up behind the man, snake his left arm around the man's neck whilst his right stuck the sailor in the neck with an autoinjector. The man would be out in seconds and wake up in a few hours with a phantom hangover. The pair moved the body into the shadows between the rows of containers before re-joining the back of their snake.

Salter now burst forward to the bridge ladder. He bounded up the rungs, left hand grabbing the ladder whilst his right was clamped on his supressed HK. He pushed through the open door. The bridge was in darkness, but the headcam picked up a single crew member sitting in a low chair; he had been under the level of the windows. In his hand was some type of electronic device. He looked up and saw Salter at the same time as Salter's fist collided with his jaw. The man tumbled off the chair and his smartphone landed next to him. Salter jabbed him with an autoinjector, in the same way Cotton had.

Salter's voice came across the comms network. 'Bridge secure.'

The drone had been tasked to stay over the ship for another hour. After that it would return to base. Its job was done, but Tate had wanted it to stay, just in case. The remainder of the team now entered the bridge. Adler took over manning the space and checked the controls to make sure that the ship maintained its course and speed. The ship's CCTV system was also run from the bridge and now that the team controlled it, Plato turned it back on, but nothing happened.

'The CCTV system is inoperable,' Adler stated over the comms.

'Have that,' Tate replied. He glanced at Plato. 'Any ideas?'

Plato shrugged. 'If it's not working now, then it wasn't working in the first place.'

Their plan had been to use the surveillance system to aid the team in their search of the vessel. Adler was to remain on watch to monitor for any threats – possible contact and compromise – whilst captioning the vessel. Now he was underutilised as the helmsman, but there was nothing they could do; the hulking cargo ship had to always have someone on the bridge, even though it could in theory steer itself.

'Stay where you are, as planned,' Tate ordered.

'Will do,' Adler replied.

Plato and Tate concentrated on Salter's feed. He was taking a set of stairs down. Silver and Cotton followed; they moved in as near to silence as possible. They were highly trained and aware of their abilities and had memorised the ship's schematics. However, this was still home territory for the crew who had lived with the onboard layout for weeks.

At the bottom of the stairs, the team entered a narrow corridor. This deck housed the officers and senior crew. It was logical that if Gu Joon was onboard, he would be in the best accommodation the vessel had to offer, not sweating in the darker, airless lower levels.

'Movement,' Salter hissed over the comms as he pushed the door on his immediate left. It was unlocked and he spun inside. The room was small and consisted of one bed and a desk, chair and shelves. A flat-screen TV was on a bracket on the wall. The room was also empty. The two other men followed him inside as they listened to Adler relate the route taken by the two crew members. One had taken the stairs down, but the other was still heading their way.

Silver's feed became lopsided, as though he had cocked his head. Tate leaned forward, but, physically removed from the action, he heard nothing. The video footage showed the door handle turn. The door opened inwards, and a crew member stepped inside; in his left hand he was holding a magazine. In the confined space it was impossible to hide. Silver shoved a gloved hand over the man's mouth while Silver leaned forward and stabbed him with an autoinjector. The third pen to be used, the third man to be incapacitated. Whilst the two others dragged the crewman onto a bunk, Salter brought up a crew list on a mini-tablet and pointed to the man's face, then a photograph. It was the first officer.

Silver gestured for the tablet, tapped on the ship's schematics, and then pointed at the captain's cabin, which was further along the corridor.

Salter, Silver and Cotton exited the cabin and advanced along the corridor to the captain's quarters. Salter tried the door. It was locked. He felt around the edge of the door. There was no gap, no space to insert a 'snake-cam'. Cotton moved to one side of the door and Silver moved to the other. Salter knocked on the door and placed his hand over the spyhole.

Plato and Tate sat forward, watching the feed. They saw Salter knock again and then the door opened.

It wasn't Gu Joon.

A rotund man wearing a pair of boxer shorts and white vest stared at Salter, his face captured as though he was looking directly into the camera lens. He had a bottle of whisky in his right hand, Tate could see the label – it was an Indian brand – Officer's Choice. His mouth moved to start to question what was happening, but Salter pushed the end of his HK into the man's mouth and forced him back into the cabin. The two others followed and shut the door.

Salter's voice sounded over the comms. 'Confirmed ID as the captain.'

Tate's finger hovered over the 'talk' button, but he knew that Salter didn't need prompting. The headcams of the other two showed them searching the cabin whilst Salter's stayed on the captain, who had started to shake as Salter questioned him. The words were hushed, but the tone was curt. The captain claimed it was just a cargo vessel and that he did not have any extra passengers on board. Either the man was a great liar, or he believed he was telling the truth. Two minutes later, they could risk no more time, so Salter had Cotton stab the captain with an autoinjector. They left the man lolling on his bunk with his bottle of Indian whisky nestled by his side.

Salter, Silver and Cotton exited the captain's quarters and headed towards the end of the corridor. They turned the corner and immediately the feed from each of their cameras started to break up.

'We're losing visual,' Tate stated. 'Do you still have audio?'

The replies Tate and Plato received were garbled. Tate tried again and got nothing. The only feed now registering was that of Adler on the bridge.

'Bridge, we have lost both visual and audio with assault team.'

'Have that. Orders?'

'Stay on station.'

'Have that.'

'There shouldn't be anything on that level that would block our comms like that, but we did expect it to happen at some point.'

'I know.' The sheer amount of steel plating on and around the vessel, combined with the extra metal of the cargo containers and whatever it was inside them would, they knew, block the signals the deeper they ventured into the vessel. Like mission control for NASA's Apollo flights, the three SBS men were now in a complete blackout until they reappeared from the dark side of the moon or, in this case, came up out of the ship.

'Fig Roll?'

'Do they?' Tate smirked. 'Thanks.'

Both men chewed their biscuits.

'How long before HMS *Montrose* is on station?'

'Let me check.' Plato played with his keyboard. 'Her ETA is two hours.'

'Good.' Once the assault team had escorted their targets into the Zodiac, the Type 23 frigate, HMS *Montrose* was on standby to extract them. The ship was no stranger to these waters, having already operated in the area as part of the UK mission to the continued enforcement of UN sanctions against North Korea.

'Tate.' Salter's use of his name was unusual.

'Confirm. What is your status?'

'The targets are not on board. Repeat, the targets are not on board.'

Tate swore under his breath. 'Prepare to exfil.'

'We can't do that. The cargo is illegal.'

Tate frowned, 'Explain?'

Tate and Plato exchanged looks as Salter described what he

238

and the other SBS men had seen. A wide smile spread across Tate's face. The mission may not have met its objective in snagging their target, but what they had discovered was going to be a huge blow to Pyongyang. And, best of all, HMS *Montrose* was there to legally make the find.

Vauxhall Cross, London

The mood in the meeting was peculiar. E Squadron had not captured their target, but what they had seized was openly being hailed as a success in the battle against the North Korean regime. Global news cycles were playing footage, taken by a Royal Navy drone, which showed British sailors boarding the Togo-registered *Ibeji*, and then helmet-cam footage taken by the sailors as they investigated the hold, their lights illuminating a box of warheads. The news reports became hazy on the exact specification of the illegal items, but stated that it was believed to contain among other smaller pieces of ordnance, tactical drones and fourth generation surface to air missiles. In short, items which North Korea simply did not, as yet, possess.

As well as Tate, Plato and Newman, Casey and Parnell were in the meeting beamed in via an encrypted video link from CIA headquarters in Langley, Virginia.

'Hak has the world's largest *cojones*,' Casey stated.

'And how is that, Vince?' Newman asked, not fazed by Casey's visual language.

'C'mon, Pamela. Look, he's not allowed to trade so he steals. And then, thanks to your lot, the UN are meeting to discuss further sanctions because of that cargo ship bust, yet what does he do?'

'He doesn't apologise,' Newman stated.

'Damn right. He announces he's taking part in this regional summit in Singapore. The first ever China, Japan, South Korea and North Korea summit!'

'I see.'

'It's symbolic, Pamela, it means something.'

'A way to further reconcile past transgressions?'

Casey smiled. 'I like how you call state-sponsored terrorism a "transgression".'

'Thank you.'

'Look, we feel something is coming from Pyongyang. Some sort of an announcement.'

'So, what is it?' Tate asked.

In the US, Casey wagged his finger. 'What does he gain by being in Singapore? Last time it was to meet the US president and demonstrate to the North Korean people he is equal to the most powerful man on earth.'

'He's a god, he's more powerful than any man,' Tate said, not bothering to hide his sarcasm.

'You are exactly right, Jack. So, what is this powerful being wanting to gain out of meeting again in Singapore?'

'Recognition,' Newman said.

'Yep, recognition from a world that continues to shun him. I mean, he's a member of the nuclear club now. He thought that counted for something, right? But no. Apart from our former commander-in-chief and a flamboyant retired basketball player, no one likes or reveres him, and for a god that's a prerequisite. So he's after the three Rs.'

'Please enlighten us, Vince.' Newman flashed a smile, which Tate knew was as sarcastic as she ever became.

'Recognition. Respect. Revaluation.'

'Thank you.'

Casey carried on. 'You see, he needs to be part of the global community, but on his own terms. His country can't continue the way it has. How many real dictators are left in the world? One in each continent, perhaps? It's an elite club of failing, ageing men. But that's not Hak. He's not ageing, but his country certainly is failing, and with each day passing it's getting harder and harder to hide this from his own people. Sure, the peasants are revolting but they won't revolt – it's the intelligentsia that will. There are only so many executions, so many purges by the state security service that can be ordered before he's left with no one to carry out his work for him.'

'You told me you weren't an expert on Korea?' Tate stated.

'Ah, I'm a quick study, Jack. Besides, I know my dictators.'

A silence fell on the meeting, broken only by the grumbling of the air conditioning system in London. Newman drank from her teacup, then asked, 'How can he achieve his three Rs?'

'If he can negotiate an end to sanctions,' Casey said, 'he'll have a seat at the table; this new summit group is that table. A table for once that he hasn't bought or imported. Hey, and speaking of imports, you can bet he's bringing his own limos with him – limos that, according to the UN, he's not allowed to own or import into the DPRK.' Casey shook his head. 'But I digress. Hak cannot open up the North until he has the money to spend on the infrastructure to make the place at least not look like a failed state. The two billion he stole was a start, it showed him being tough on crime even though his father had been harbouring the very same triad for years, but even then, he still can't buy in all the materials and expertise he needs because of the sanctions. He needs a legitimate way to make money with what he has. He needs to be selling something the West wants and are willing to persuade the UN to relax sanctions over.'

Newman frowned. 'You're going to say that's White Suit?'

'It has to be White Suit. Think about it. Whichever way you look at it, it's a defensive product – both commercial and military. It's been designed to save lives. Who knows that Hak's Korea didn't create it? I mean, no one has seen the finished product; Jericho's invention may just have been a stepping stone. Look, you can bet the farm that if our experts say Hak didn't create it, the conspiracy theorist snowflakes will become apoplectic attempting to prove he did.'

Tate smirked. Once Casey was on a roll, he became less and less PC.

'But isn't it our technology?' Plato asked.

'Is it, Plato? Pamela, is there any record of HM Government ever working on this project?'

'I can't officially answer that question, Vince, but the answer is "no".'

'Yep.' Casey nodded. 'It's all Jericho, and he sold it – albeit unwittingly and unwillingly to North Korea.'

'As I see our mutual position,' Newman said, 'the technology, regardless of whether it is functioning or not, is gone. It is already in the hands of Pyongyang, and we can't change that. What we can do, however, is continue in our attempt to locate and apprehend Gu Joon.'

'And Roe,' Parnell added, speaking for the first time since the introductions had been made. 'He's on our wanted list.'

Newman nodded. 'Yes, of course.'

'Unless they're both already in North Korea,' Tate stated.

'Yep,' Casey said. 'Officially, and I can't believe I've been told to say this, the US are letting Pyongyang have White Suit. I know, it's not great, but Langley's thinking is that we want, long term, to bring the NKPD back into the fold and we want some say over their development.'

'They believe that letting North Korea have White Suit will achieve this, Vince, really?' Newman sounded sceptical.

'Hey, I don't buy it either, but the view is that if they can trade it with us, they will listen to us.'

'So, this is not regime change?'

'Yeah, it's regime development, and we all know how easy that is, right?' Casey said, with a shake of the head.

'Right.' Newman pushed her empty cup to one side. 'Moving on. Where is Gu Joon, Neill? Is he in North Korea?'

Plato sighed. 'Well, we've not picked up any chatter mentioning his name, which is not unexpected and, as yet, I've had no further hits on any global surveillance systems.'

'Ditto here, Plato,' Parnell stated.

'The ship we boarded was heading to the Chinese port of Dalian,' Tate said, 'is that relevant?'

Parnell nodded. 'It's one of the ports allegedly used in a North Korean smuggling route. Usually, goods just swap ships there without any real contact or interference from the local authorities.'

'Then where do the goods go?'

'It's Dalian to Nagoya, Japan. Nagoya to Busan, South Korea. Busan to Vladivostok, or one of the nearby coal ports. The vessels change each time, however, and then once in Russia chartered cargo planes fly into North Korea. This is how Hak got his two armoured Maybachs, except those also spent forty-one days on a cargo ship from Rotterdam.'

'OK.' Newman held up her hand. 'So we can't follow the ship, it's a real red herring.'

Tate frowned; something was nagging at him, but he wasn't sure what it was. And then he remembered – false positives and red herrings. And the way Gu operated. 'I don't think Gu Joon and Roe are in North Korea. I think they're in Singapore.'

'Excuse me?' Casey said. 'Where did that epiphany come from?'

'Oh, yes.' Plato smiled.

In the US, Parnell folded his arms. 'Say what, Tate?'

'When Neill was trying to find Gu Joon, we got two other hits, one a historical hit – a photograph of a young Hak Kwang-Il and the other the architect Mr Bong.'

'Mr Po, Jack. Po Bong.'

'Right, Mr Po was boarding a flight from Seoul to Singapore. How many times before all this have you encountered a doppel-gänger, Neill?'

'Never, and now we've got one for Roe Kwang and one for Gu Joon.'

'And where is Po Bong?' Casey asked.

'He's in Singapore.'

'Where's Roe's doppelgänger?' Parnell asked.

Plato shrugged. 'No idea.'

'Well, I for one am willing to take a chance. What about you, Vince,' Newman asked. 'Are you in?'

'For throwing the dice at Singapore? Sure. Parnell?'

'Rock & Roll.'

Chapter 19

Singapore

Singapore was humid and green, but it was also so clean it was antiseptic, and the architecture wasn't bad either. Tate liked it. He sipped from his signature Singapore Sling cocktail as he looked out from the viewing platform of the iconic Marina Bay Sands Hotel. It had been designed to resemble a ship held aloft on columns and was a huge tourist attraction. Tate was pretending to be one of the many who, whilst not staying at the hotel, had bought a ticket for the top. To his left, in a different section, hotel guests used the rooftop infinity pool whilst they ogled at the sights and were in turn themselves ogled at by the day-trippers.

'It's quite something, eh, Jack?'

'It is, Vince.'

'You know, I've been all around the goddamn world, and I've seen a few things, but this has to be the best "curated society" I've encountered. It's probably the safest place in the world, well, after the Gulf States, and I know where I'd rather be – cheers.' Casey necked the last of his cocktail. 'Let me get you another.'

Tate didn't say no. If the man from the CIA wanted to drink with him a while, he wasn't going to complain. Tate continued to enjoy the panoramic views whilst at the same time looking for any obvious places a shot could be taken from. Casey returned and thrust a second drink into his hand.

'Lots of windows but no viable vantage points.'

'Yep, that's our assessment too, Jack. You'd need to be either the world's best shot or a magician to take out a target up here, what with the distance, angle and fluctuating wind direction. No assassin's bullet is going to take him out here.'

'I wish whoever they are, the best of luck.'

'Ha ha.' Casey chuckled and slapped Tate on the back. 'Now, seriously, our man is a creature of habit.' Casey casually looked around, checking they weren't close enough to anyone to be over-heard. 'Which is why his itinerary is the same as before, officially. He'll visit the Gardens by The Bay, that's just over there' – Casey pointed – 'and then he'll come up here for a cocktail and the sunset. The hotel will be putting up notices tomorrow morning saying this part is closing early.'

Tate nodded. Since taking over leadership of North Korea from his father, the ruler had left his kingdom a mere four times, twice to China, once to the DMZ – the demilitarised zone with the South, and the last time for a meeting in Singapore with the then US president. This was to be a regional summit; the first time North Korea had been invited to the 'China–Japan–South Korea' annual summit, and as such a neutral yet convenient and highly accommodating location had been sought.

Both men fell silent as more tourists drifted towards them. Tate waited until they were alone again before he spoke. 'I can't explain it, but I've got this feeling that something is going to happen.'

'Intuition.' Casey paused as a waiter removed an empty glass left at a table next to them. 'But then I don't need to tell you that, Jack. Look, take the tech stuff out of the equation and this whole thing is simple. It's like a Greek tragedy; we got a disavowed uncle who wants to kill his nephew and take his place on the throne. It's all about revenge and pride and family.'

'And what a family.'

'Yep. Gu Joon is a ghost himself, we've no idea how he created his wealth; it's as though he materialised fully formed and fully funded six months ago when he bought that hotel in Vegas, although even that can only be traced to a series of shell companies. Then, on top of all this, he's not even Gu Joon at all but an unknown Hak?' Casey knocked back his cocktail.

'The Chinese won't be happy if Gu Joon gets into power.'

'That would be interesting. If he wants to work with the West? I can see Beijing doing a Kremlin and annexing the whole place, and who would or even could stop them? The US won't accept another Vietnam, Iraq or Afghanistan. You know, I bet if the Chinese – for all their faults – did take over, the people of the North would be a whole lot better for it. Yet we, the international community, cannot let China claim North Korea; it sets a precedent.'

'I think Russia's done that already.' Tate's mind wandered back to a past E Squadron mission in Eastern Ukraine.

'Anyway, tomorrow afternoon all four heads of state arrive, then the next day the fun starts. Hak gets his day in the sun.' Casey paused. A grin split his craggy face. 'He becomes a sun god.'

Lights started to flick on around them.

'Here comes the sunset,' Tate stated.

*

Half an hour later, Tate made his way back downstairs. Stepping out of the lift onto the main concourse, he was again struck by the immense size of the hotel complex. Between the hotel towers, it felt more like a huge, impersonal airport. Guests ate in restaurants in full view of bewildered passing tourists. It wasn't for him, which was why he was staying at the Intercontinental and he imagined the openness of the complex was also the reason why, again, the North Korean leader had booked the Presidential

247

Suite of the St Regis. As Tate walked out of the hotel complex, he knew there had to be eyes on him. Advanced teams of several national intelligence agencies were already in Singapore, scanning for threats and carrying out assessments. Tate knew that the UK had passed on its security concerns to South Korea and its other regional strategic partners, but they hadn't been able to mention White Suit, or Gu Joon's little gang. Concerns without verified intelligence were just words, and many believed now the UK talked too much.

Tate's encrypted iPhone vibrated in his chinos pocket. He retrieved it and answered as the cool, climate-controlled temperature of the hotel was replaced by the cloying, humid petrol-scented air of the street outside. 'Yo.'

'I think I've just got a hit for Gu.'

'Think, Neill?'

'Yes, it could be Po Bong.'

'He's still in Singapore?'

'There is no record he left.'

'Where?'

'Sentosa Island. He was filmed strolling across the Sentosa Boardwalk.'

'Boardwalk?'

'It's the name of the bridge.'

Tate paused and looked around; it was a ten-minute walk from where he was. 'That bridge is a mile long. He could have taken a taxi.'

'So he wanted to be seen?'

'Either that or he doesn't care about being sweaty. How long ago was this?'

'Just now.'

'Can you track him?'

'I'm on it now, but the light's fading and there's still a lot of people about.'

'Just keep me updated.' Tate popped his air pods in and

pocketed the phone. He saw a taxi and took it rather than waste time walking; it also prevented him from arriving on Sentosa as a wet mess.

The driver frowned at Tate's destination, but didn't say a word for the entire journey. They arrived at the island side of the bridge five minutes later, after negotiating slow traffic. Tate paid and exited. He tapped his air pod. 'Update?'

'He's in the queue, waiting to go into the S.E.A. Aquarium,' Plato replied.

'Have that. I'm keeping the line open.'

Tate turned right and headed towards the attraction. After another five minutes of walking past pristine bushes in concrete planters and numerous attraction kiosks, Tate reached the voluminous aquarium complex that had been designed to resemble the hull of a giant upturned ship. Barriers had been set up outside to funnel the queues of tourists who, at peak times, would wind one way and then the next in the humid air. Now, however, there were not more than thirty people waiting to go inside. The majority of them were Asian, with a family of white Europeans near the back and just in front of the man Tate was tracking. There was no way Tate could join the line without being seen, so he veered off to the right and the stretch of water separating the island from mainland Singapore. He leaned against the thick concrete safety walls and watched the swirling water below, angling his body just enough to see his target. The man would have to turn his head right around to see Tate diagonally behind him, which would be an odd thing to do unless he knew or expected he was being watched. Tate just hoped his target didn't have a sixth sense.

Singapore was a place Tate had been through but only fleetingly. Some said it felt almost too clean, too controlled, too eager. It was as though Disney had designed a country and the only dirt he saw was on the rusted containers being offloaded from the docks across the water. Yet, oddly, he had to admit it did appeal to him. He checked on his target. The man was nearer the entrance.

'I'm glad you're not dead,' a voice said to his left.

Tate turned, then stiffened as he found himself face to face with the man who had shot him. 'Roe.'

'Think of this place as no-man's-land, Jack. I won't target you, and by the same token I know that you will make no move against me, not here, not in public, not whilst we are on numerous security cameras and not with innocent families so close by.'

Tate was sick with fury as he continued to glare at the former CIA and Delta operative. 'This was a trap, wasn't it? You wanted to see if we had you under surveillance?'

'You got me, but that's not all.'

'What do you want, Roe?'

'I'm here to give you a message.'

'Which is?' Tate managed to say, his tone strained through his clenched jaw.

'Walk away, Jack. This is no longer about me, or Gu Joon. This is about something much larger and more important than either of us.'

Tate's brow furrowed. 'What the hell are you on about?'

'In the end you'll see, we're on the same side.'

'Like we were in Baghdad?'

'That's right.'

The events of fourteen years ago flashed before Tate's eyes. 'Shooting your teammates is just fine with you, isn't it?'

'I admit it. I shot Thorn. I killed him. We couldn't take him with us, and we couldn't leave him behind.' A smile appeared on Roe's face. 'Ah, it's true – confession does make one feel so much better.'

Tate was barely managing to control himself. 'Then you shot me, and you also shot Page.'

'Paul Page?'

'He was driving the bike in Germany. You hit him in the leg.'

'My bad.' Roe shrugged. 'I missed, I was aiming for his head.'

Tate's mouth clamped shut.

'Goodbye, Jack, I very much doubt we'll meet again.' Roe backed away, pivoted and joined the flow of pedestrians moving past the aquarium. He darted left and disappeared behind a support beam at the building's corner.

The line at the aquarium had moved forward and Tate caught a glimpse of the back of his target's head as he entered the building. Tate remained where he was as Roe's words niggled at him. The line to Plato was still open. He asked, 'Neill, did you get any of that?'

'Every word, and the confession. It was weird.'

'Tell me you know where Roe went?'

'He's not on any camera, it's as though he's vanished.'

'Blindspot?'

'Has to be.'

'Fantastic. Update Casey.'

'Will do.'

Tate remained where he was watching the water. He knew he'd been right about the events in Iraq, and Roe would pay for this and his other actions. Tate's instincts told him something was about to happen, and those instincts were being listened to by both his boss, Pamela Newman, and his new CIA friend Casey. The beauty of E Squadron was also its Achilles' heel. It was a small ad hoc group of serving military operatives who acted on specific orders and disbanded after each mission, apart from Tate, who was on a semi-permanent secondment from the SAS, and the support staff who were permanent MI6 employees. The unit was supposed to be the UK's secret line of defence against those overseas who would endanger the United Kingdom, but they had specific mission objectives. Yet now they were adrift, Newman had played fast and loose with their mandate and allowed Tate to operate in Singapore, a country with one of the world's lowest crime rates and the highest number of CCTV cameras per citizen. He couldn't mess up here because then he would be disavowed without a second thought by the Secret Intelligence Service. Tate shook his head. As well as him, Casey and Parnell knew that each of the countries participating in the summit as well as bringing in presidential security details had advance teams in place scanning for any and every threat. He imagined if he farted too loudly, he'd be taken in, never mind what would happen if he attempted to apprehend either Roe or Gu Joon.

'Are all the exits from the aquarium covered by cameras?'

'Yes, and I'm watching them.'

'Still nothing on Roe?'

'No.'

Tate was about to speak when he saw a white-haired man exit the aquarium; he had a phone to his ear.

'Jack …'

'Yep, I see him. He didn't stay long.'

Tate leaned against the railings and kept his eyes on the target. The man seemed relaxed and made no effort to hide his face or look for anyone who might be watching him as he spoke to whoever was on the other end of the line. In short, he was acting like every other tourist. Tate's gut told him that this wasn't Gu Joon, but then Gu Joon had also punched him in the gut, so he could be wrong.

The target took the same route that Tate had onto the island, stopped for an ice cream and then continued to head in the direction of the Boardwalk bridge.

'Neill, are you following us?'

'Yes.'

Tate hung back and tried to hide among the tourists, but given that he now seemed to be the only white European in sight, he was finding it trying. There was a beeping in his earpiece, Tate retrieved his encrypted iPhone from his pocket and checked the screen. He switched the line and answered it. 'Yeah?'

'Tate, Parnell. I'm five minutes out.'

'The suspect is foxtrot. I'm following on foot.'

'Roger. Will advise when I arrive.'

Up ahead, the suspect stopped and made for the railings. He watched the water and Singapore city beyond as he finished his ice cream. Then he turned to take in his surroundings. Tate had little choice but to step into the shadow of the nearest kiosk. 'Neill, I've lost visual.'

'I've got him. Do you think that's vanilla or lemon ice cream?'

'I'll be the lemon if we lose him.'

Tate waited and studied the window of the kiosk.

'He's moving again, he's walking faster and he's checking his watch. I think he's heading for the taxi rank.'

Tate stepped out of cover and continued to follow. The target reached the start of the boardwalk and, as Plato predicted, went to the taxi rank.

Tate made a phone call. 'Parnell, stay in your taxi, you're going to have to follow the target if he goes mobile.'

'Have that,' Parnell replied. 'We're on the bridge. My ETA is thirty seconds.'

Ahead now, Tate's target climbed into a taxi and, moments later, pulled away. Tate jogged towards the taxi rank. He heard a whistle and looked to see Parnell pull up on his left. He opened the door and got in.

'Where we go now?' the driver asked, a gold front tooth glinting in the evening light.

'We're on a treasure hunt and we've got to chase our friend in that taxi.' Tate pointed.

'What? You silly?'

'Very silly,' Tate replied.

The driver muttered something in Chinese into his radio and the taxi moved off.

'You OK?' Parnell asked.

'Sure, why?'

'Plato told me you met our mutual friend.'

'He's no friend of mine,' Tate said. 'He's not all there.'

'Yep, he was always a strange one.'

'There was something odd he said to me.'

'What?'

'He said we're on the same side.'

'Same side? No idea what he's on about.'

'Marina Bay Sands Hotel. Your friend go here for silly game,' the taxi driver said.

'Thank you.' Tate turned to Parnell. 'I was just here an hour ago with Casey. This feels like a wind-up.'

'Yeah, but the North Korean leader is visiting here tomorrow.'

'And that can't be a coincidence,' Tate said.

Both operatives became silent as they focused on the taxi ahead of them. It swung into the sweeping access road.

'Stop here,' Parnell ordered.

'Okay, but is not usual place.'

Parnell pushed a bundle of notes into the driver's hand and both men exited. Their target was also out of his taxi and walking towards the nearest entrance. Tate and Parnell followed, at a distance. Inside, the entrance concourse was just as busy and still reminded Tate of an airport. They saw their target walk directly towards a lift and press a button.

'We can't get in unless we have a room key.' Tate touched his ear pod. 'Neill, can you gain access to the security cameras at The Marina Bay Sands?'

'That shouldn't be too difficult.'

'And the booking system. Find out if Mr Po has a room.'

'Will do.'

'Look,' Parnell said, 'there's one way in and out of that tower. He's not going anywhere without being seen. If Plato can get into their systems, he'll be completely covered. I'll keep watch here; he doesn't know me.'

Tate knew it made sense, but he didn't like leaving. 'Fine.'

He exited the hotel and took the first taxi in the line back to his own hotel. It was just under twenty hours before the leaders of both Koreas arrived in the island state for their summit; if something was going to happen it would then, and not now. Now whatever was planned, if something was being planned, it would be in the final stages of preparation and Tate didn't have a clue what that could be. Ideas and theories floated through his mind but were just out of reach of his understanding. He decided to stop thinking or else it would drive him mad. He knew if he thought about something else entirely it would come to him, whatever it was that he was struggling to see.

A thought struck Tate. Plato, technical wizard that he was, was able to hack into the CCTV systems, completely illegally, the Singaporean authorities relied upon. He was running searches for their targets and watching Tate's back, but the question was what were the technical capabilities of Gu's organisation? Was Gu's organisation actually the North Korean government? If so, did they too have the ability to hack into the city-state's cameras? Were they tracking Tate? Were they tracking anyone else? But why was Roe and potentially Gu Joon here now? Why were they not safely hidden away in Pyongyang or some other Soviet-style North Korean city? It just didn't make sense.

'We're on the same side.' Roe's words rang in his ear. Were there sides? There was good, and there was evil, but what were the sides? Roe was evil, his actions had been evil, but what about Gu? Well, he'd ordered killings too, hadn't he? Tate tried again to reason it all out. What did Roe want? If Tate was on his side, and the thought of that made no sense, what did Gu Joon and Roe want?

InterContinental Singapore Robertson Quay,

Tate darted out of his hotel shower to grab his ringing phone.

'Jack, I think Gu Joon is trying to leave the country.'

'Explain?'

'The architect – Po Bong. He's just bought a ticket leaving in two hours to Seoul.'

'Neill, now you think it's Gu Joon?'

'It seems like too much of a coincidence not to be, especially after Roe told you to leave him alone. But then again, it could actually be Po Bong and that's the issue. I can conduct gait analysis on the footage we have of him when he enters the airport, but I don't have a set of Gu's gait to compare it against. All I would be able to do would be to see if it was the same man we saw outside the aquarium.'

Tate drummed his fingers on the windowsill of his hotel room and looked out at the flickering lights of the high-rise flats opposite. 'Is he still at his hotel?'

'Yes. He used the concierge service to book his ticket. I have him in the hotel lobby. He's just settled his bill.'

'He's hardly trying to slip away, is he?'

'No.'

'OK. Keep me updated.'

Tate ended the call, threw on a bathrobe, and phoned Casey. 'Gu Joon may be on the move.'

'Explain?'

Tate did.

'Look, there is no way we can let that lunatic get on a plane. I'm gonna have to pull a few strings and think of something, but the only place I can hold him is at the airport. And hey, if it's not him, well, no harm done. Look, you stay where you are and leave this to me and Parnell – if it goes wrong, you'll still be golden.'

The call ended and Tate knew he should try to get some sleep, but he was too hyped up and his body clock was still off kilter. He lay on his bed for half an hour and tapped out an update to Newman before he finally gave up on sleep, got dressed and took the lift downstairs. The architectural layout of the hotel meant that to exit it was a dog leg; he exited the first lift, padded along a corridor and passed the dark-grey reception desk, where the night porter politely smiled at him before he took the second lift for the last remaining two floors to the street level outside. The hotel was in the swanky residential area of Robertson Quay and next to the Singapore river, which, crossing Nanson Road, Tate now headed for. It was late, but not so late that the quayside was deserted, as although the restaurants had closed for the night, Tate saw a couple strolling across the bridge ahead and several other pedestrians meandering along the walkway. Tate walked to the water's edge and leaned over the railings. The air was slightly less humid than it had been during the day. The scene was one of inner-city serenity, and Tate tried to relax. He gazed one way and then the other at the river; a moving black mass highlighted with silver streaks courtesy of the moonlight, as it snaked past the apartment buildings and restaurants. The couple had paused in the middle of the bridge and Tate could see they were talking intimately. Tate sighed; here on the other side of the world he was still just a spectator of the real world. He'd never consciously chosen to be single, but the fact that he had a job he couldn't tell anyone about, together with the regularity with which he had suddenly to disappear overseas, which more often than not resulted in him killing people, meant that he would be an odd match for anyone. But Tate knew he was his job, and it was him.

As he looked on, the couple kissed and then carried on, now reaching the steps down to the walkway on his side. They turned in his direction and continued. Tate casually turned away and started to walk in the opposite direction. He had no idea how long the path was, or where it led, he just wanted to walk.

Twenty minutes later, Tate turned around and retraced his steps, feeling more relaxed and ready once again to try to get some sleep. Or perhaps not because he checked his watch and realised it was almost time to find out if it was Po Bong or Gu Joon who was attempting to board the plane to Seoul. Tate reached Nanson Road and waited for a taxi to pass before he crossed it.

He didn't reach the other side.

There were moving shapes in his peripheral vision and he started to turn as the couple he had seen earlier appeared behind him. The woman stabbed something into his upper arm. Tate jerked away, prepared to defend himself. He managed to take a step before his legs buckled and he fell backwards. A strong pair of arms caught him and dragged him into the taxi. 'Silly game,' he heard the familiar voice of the taxi driver say before everything went black.

Chapter 20

South China Sea

Tate couldn't move. He was bound to a chair with cable ties, but his mouth was not gagged; which said a lot to Tate. It told him he was somewhere where noise did not matter, which ultimately was not good because in a broader sense it implied that gunshots too would not be overheard. So where was he? And how long had he been out for this time?

Tate was angry, angry at his physical limitations, angry at the ability Gu's organisation had to take him in. Tasered and then drugged, again, and now here he was. He looked down, and, in the dim light, saw that he was wearing his own clothes, a good sign. He pushed his neck into his chest and rubbed it from side to side. His stubble was still short, so he'd not been out for more than what – twelve hours? How far could he have been taken in twelve hours? Halfway across the world in a plane, but something told him he was not in the air, and something told him he was not on dry land. Tate realised he was in a ship.

As his eyes became accustomed to the light, he saw that the bulkheads, floors and the ceiling were unpainted steel. There was a door set into the right bulkhead; it was lipped, the bottom not reaching the floor and it was closed. It was watertight. Tate wriggled on the chair; it didn't feel that solid. It was metal, strong, but the legs could be twisted and bent with the right pressure and angle of attack. The cable ties could also be defeated, easily enough, but then he would still be in what he had to guess was a locked storage room. Tate looked up. Past the light in the corner, he saw a camera, its red flight flickering. He smiled at it, there was nothing else he could do, and he waited.

Tate had counted in his head; he'd reached four hundred and ninety-eight by the time he heard footsteps outside and then the heavy-looking handle on the door turned with a creak. A man stepped in over the lip of the door and approached Tate. He stopped six feet away and glared. He looked like a wrestler; his white T-shirt looked as though it was close to ripping as he folded his arms. A second man entered; he looked like the first but was perhaps twenty per cent smaller, as though he'd been reproduced with a photocopier programmed on a reduction setting. He came towards Tate and the light struck his gold front tooth. Tate blinked. It was the taxi driver who had taken him and Plato to the Marina Bay Sands hotel; in his right hand he held a knife. Tate knew he couldn't show fear, he shouldn't show anything at all. If these people had wanted him dead, then he wouldn't have been sitting here for however many hours he had.

The Wrestler grunted, then said something in a language Tate didn't understand. The taxi driver took a step forward and cut the cable ties away from Tate's legs. The Wrestler unfolded his arms and let them swing slightly by his side, as though he was daring Tate to attack.

'Up,' the taxi driver ordered. 'Get up! Gold-Tooth say time for silly game.'

Tate slowly pushed himself to his feet, the effect of whatever tranquiliser he'd been given meant that, without being able to use his arms for support, he was unsteady. He decided to play on this, and let his captors believe that he had been more affected by the drug than he really had.

The taxi driver, who had referred to himself as Gold-Tooth, moved to the door. 'You follow me.'

The Wrestler grabbed Tate's right arm and dragged him forward towards the door. Tate stepped over the lip and found himself in a corridor. Gold-Tooth was several steps ahead, he then turned left as the corridor met another. The Wrestler pushed him, urging him to move faster, but Tate let his feet stumble and he took the time to look around, using his eyes only and not turning his head. On his left there was a part-open door and through this he saw someone eating at a long table. Tate was manhandled around the corner and saw that Gold-Tooth was waiting for him at the bottom of a set of steps. He started to climb them as Tate approached. The Wrestler had had enough of Tate's tardiness and physically pushed him up the steps. Tate let him, anything that tired out the extra-large man was fine by him. They reached the top and there was another corridor. Gold-Tooth was already at the end. He waited for Tate and then they exited.

The stuffy, sweat-scented air of the ship's interior gave way to sea-scented, cooler air as they appeared on the bridge. There was a man at the helm and next to him stood an older, but taller, man with a white mane of hair. He was dressed all in black, Mao suit. He turned and nodded at Tate.

'Hak Kwang-Il,' Tate said, using Gu Joon's real name.

'Quite so. I trust you are not in too much discomfort, Jack?'

'I'm peachy, thanks.'

'I imagine you would like me to explain why I brought you here?'

'If you must.'

Hak's eyes narrowed. 'I do enjoy your ever so British sensibilities. My tutors were English, you know, which accounts for my rather grand accent. A pure English accent, like your Home

261

Counties, is much preferable than the awful, drawling "voice of America" often picked up by youngsters in my region.'

'I'm from Camden.'

'Yes, your accent is a bit, shall we say, rough around the edges, but never mind. We have much more important matters to discuss than your slack diction.'

Tate said nothing; it was best to let the man say what he wanted to say.

'My country, The Democratic People's Republic of Korea, is neither democratic nor cares for its people. It is a failed state. I know it, the UN knows it and so does my nephew, their beloved leader. You notice that I do not refer to him as *our* beloved leader? That is because he is not my leader, he never has been, and he never will be.' Hak paused. Tate thought it was to gauge his reaction. When Tate continued to remain silent, the older man carried on. 'As you have managed to track me down and have discovered my true identity, you will have also uncovered the operation I undertook at the Los Angeles Olympic Games.'

'We learn from our mistakes.' Tate's tone was deadpan.

The older man continued as though Tate had not spoken. 'My half-brother, the current leader's father – we had different mothers – masterminded the Rangoon bombing a year before my mission. It failed to kill the South Korean president. I saw my chance to usurp him as my father's favourite. You see, Jack, my father's marriage to my mother was clandestine. It was a secret that only the immediate family knew of; as such I was tolerated. So, I planned an audacious attack, one that would embarrass both of my countries' sworn enemies. My half-brother was against it, yet Father gave me the go-ahead with my mission.'

Tate couldn't resist. 'And it failed.'

'Oh, much more than that. It was an utter failure, a catastrophe. My team's incompetence resulted in them becoming compromised. In the eyes of Pyongyang, I had but one option, and that was to not let myself get taken alive. I found myself sitting in a car, by the side of the Pacific Coast Highway, with a gun in my hand. I started to raise it to my temple, but the sun appeared from behind the clouds, Jack. At that moment I stopped thinking about my mission, my nation or my family. I realised that I wanted to live. I had no choice, I had to go into exile. I could not return to my home country because failure was simply not tolerated.' The older man's face took on a pained expression. 'This, of course, meant I was immediately labelled a traitor. As I could not be put on trial, the sentence was handed to my family. It was a death sentence, Jack. My wife and my eighteen-month-old son escaped north into China, but every member of her family was executed, and I was disavowed by my own father. My name and memory were scrubbed away, removed from history. I became someone else, and, luckily, that someone else became a success. My wife died before it was safe for me to see her again and be with them both. I paid to have my son placed with a fine South Korean family in the US. Like you, Jack, he was alone, but unlike you, Jack, his real father was alive. When I finally met him, I did so as his uncle. My son, Jack, is the eldest surviving grandson of Hak Il Sung.'

Now Tate understood; it had all been a deception. They had been made to look the other way. 'You don't want to attack South Korea; you want to attack the North.'

'No, you are wrong on both counts. I want to attack the current leaders of the North. But, as I am sure you personally are aware, the act of assassination is easy, regime change is harder.'

Tate started to shake his head, slowly. 'The two billion dollars you took from the triads and gave to the North, you did that as an apology for your actions in 1984.'

'You are extremely astute, Jack. I undertook negotiations and explained what I could offer. I expressed that I wanted nothing more than to return to my homeland and be a loyal servant.'

'Pyongyang doesn't know about your son.'

'My son's existence will not be shared with the people of North Korea until it is safe for him to enter his homeland as their leader.'

'What if they reject him? What if they choose democracy instead of living in a dictatorship?'

'I think you overestimate the ability of a nation who has been isolated and spoon-fed rhetoric for three generations to think for themselves. Yet I do understand your point, Jack. I have no wish to tear down one hereditary dictatorship merely to replace it with another. It shall be my son and I who will start the transformation. In time, others – duly elected – will continue it.'

Tate nodded as events started to make sense. 'You wanted to be seen on that cargo ship in Mexico so we would board it looking for you?'

'I think you now understand everything. It was a rather circuitous route; a gamble, but one that had no downside for me. I financed the highly illegal arms on that vessel, with other monies appropriated by the hacker you stole from me – Fang Bao. If my shipment had arrived, I would have been further in my nephew's good books, and, if it were to be stopped, that would aid my cause by giving the UN no choice but to implement further sanctions on North Korea. I have left other false yet incriminating breadcrumbs too, for fun. Everything I have undertaken, Jack, has been to bring about positive change for the course of my nation, by undermining my nephew; the man who is currently in total control of my country, Hak Jong Un.'

'So why am I here? Why have you told me all this?'

'This is not a Bond film, Mr Tate, where the super villain confesses to our hero just before he intends to have him killed in an ingenious manner. I have explained my position to you because I wish to make a deal with your bosses.'

'A deal?' Tate had no clue what he meant. 'I don't understand.'

'Then I shall explain. We are on the same side. We, and by 'we' I mean the G7 plus, of course, Australia, India, South Africa and South Korea, want a democratic, responsible and modern North Korea. This can only happen if my nephew is removed from power. My proposal to both your government and the Americans is this: if I am permitted to continue with my operation once in power, I shall hand over the full technical specifications for Mr Jericho's inventions. All of them. To both the US and the UK governments, and not the Chinese.'

'We have them.'

'You have old files, but what of the improvements Jericho worked on after he left Blackline? These he outlined to me, these are not on the memory device he hid in the cricket pavilion.'

Tate said, 'Why did you bring me here?'

'Because I could, to halt your meddling for a while, and it amuses me to have you acting as my messenger. It is indeed a great pity that you are not working for me; you and Roe would make for a formidable team.'

Tate made no reply.

'One day you will die, Jack, but it won't be today and not at my hands. You have my word on that.' The older man barked orders in Korean and pointed to the door. 'Now they are ready to drop you off. They will blindfold you, but this is nothing to become concerned with. Goodbye, Jack Tate.'

The Wrestler suddenly slapped his huge hands on Tate's shoulders and hauled him to his feet. Tate was tempted to fight, to slam his fist into the man's windpipe, then make a grab for Hak Kwang-Il, but he didn't. Not because of the other unseen men who must be lurking outside, but because Tate had a duty to report back on what Hak Kwang-Il had offered. So Tate let himself be blindfolded and have his hands tied behind his back. He was then pushed to the door and dragged along a corridor, up a flight of stairs, then out into the night. The fresh air did nothing to stop him from sweating, but it was a welcomed relief from the sourness of the ship's interior. Tate felt himself now be manoeuvred into a much-smaller boat. He half fell onto a wooden seat and stifled a groan as his healing shoulder took the torque.

He didn't know who else was on the boat, but from the tone of the outboard motor knew roughly its size. He felt the vessel be buffeted by waves he estimated were too high to be in a harbour. Tate tried to count off the seconds, but his fatigue had made this impossible; he estimated it was perhaps ten minutes before both the tone of the engine and the pounding of the waves reduced. The vessel continued on until the engine was throttled back and his blindfold was torn off. It was dark enough that Tate didn't blink, but there was still enough moonlight to make out the face of the man glowering at him, and the figure of another man. Tate realised it was the Wrestler and Gold-Tooth.

'Get up, silly,' the Gold-Tooth said.

Without warning, the Wrestler started to cackle, then lunged at Tate and pushed him into the sea.

Still bound, with his hands behind his back, Tate landed in the warm black water. He went under and almost immediately hit the bottom, making him realise that it was no more than five-feet deep. He pushed back up to his feet. As the boat moved off, the Wrestler was still laughing.

Tate waded, as best he could, towards the shore; the beach had been made spectral by the moonlight. The level of the sea dropped as Tate staggered forwards; the sand wanted to grip his boots like cement, but he pushed on until he was out of the water. Tate took another few steps before he dropped to his knees and then fell onto his side.

A torch abruptly flashed on and shone directly into his face, blinding him.

'Tate, is that you?'

'Yes.'

Casey and Parnell appeared. They pulled him to his feet.

'I got you, buddy,' Casey said.

Chapter 21

The Embassy of the United States of America in Singapore

Was he tired, or did he have a chemical hangover? Whatever. Tate felt groggy, and he ached all over. He also felt cheated. He'd been kept, in drugged unconsciousness, on the boat for twenty-four hours and in that time the presidents of the summit countries had arrived, met and concluded their business. All that was left now was the rehearsed, waved goodbyes at the airport. Tate was annoyed, hell, he was angry that Gu Joon had orchestrated all of this, and he'd just been a hapless, helpless passenger. The sole aspect Tate was thankful for was that nothing had happened to any of the visiting dignitaries or their entourage, yet. There had been no attack or attempted attack whatsoever.

The throbbing in his head increased. Tate popped a pair of painkillers into his mouth and washed them down with water before placing his empty glass back on the coffee table. He was in an office at the US embassy, which Casey and Parnell had requisitioned.

Tate picked up again the notes given to him by Casey on the summit. They started with the official post-summit press release:

The first ever China–Japan–South Korea–North Korea quad-lateral summit has concluded. The leaders of both North and South Korea pledged to continue their dialogue on the security of the Korean peninsula, whilst those of China and Japan pledged to offer their assistance and support. The Korean leaders promised to advance productive dialogue to further improve bilateral relations, and unilateral relations within the region. This summit marked a breakthrough in regional relationships with further economic and trade matters also discussed.

'Riveting,' Tate muttered to himself. He continued on now and read the political analysis of the summit, probably provided by someone paid big money to use big words, Tate presumed. This also really said nothing apart from that this sudden promotion of North Korea to an 'equal' indicated an erosion of Beijing's influence. All Tate understood from it was that North Korea had been accepted as a member of a 'new club' – the previous club being the annual trilateral summit between China, Japan and South Korea, that North Korea had not been chastised for its latest UN sanctions' infraction and that North Korea had not made any announcements regarding new military or any technology.

Tate threw the paper down; he'd grown out of politics. He'd also grown weary of trying to understand exactly how Gu Joon would strike, because there had been something in the man's eyes that told Tate extreme violence was always an option.

The door opened and Casey appeared. He had a phone to his ear. 'No, I don't in any way agree with that, but hell – who am I to have an opinion?' He sat heavily at a seat behind the desk, his face thunderous. He looked at Tate. 'This Gu Joon – and that's what I'm gonna keep calling the guy, is one sophisticated and sly operator. He grabs Fang, kills an entire agency team in doing so, so he can get at Jericho and then leaves a trail of what …?'

'Death?' Parnell suggested.

'Bodies in his wake before he wants to play nice and hand us a deal? Now I'm being told, from on high, that this is all over. "Hey, sorry about the guys that died." What about those people Roe killed? Oh, I'm told, "that's collateral damage". Not in my book!'

Tate blinked. 'What?'

'You better believe it! I've had the deputy director in my ear informing me Langley's position is that Gu Joon aka Hak Kwang-Il is potentially someone they can "work with" and what he's done to destabilise the current regime is right out of their playbook. Hell, they were never allowed to play, because, well, friggin' China.'

Tate was trying to fully understand the CIA stance. 'But isn't this summit an example of the current North Korean leader trying to come back into the fold? Isn't this what the US had been trying to make happen? It's a step towards him changing his ways.'

'Even dictators are allowed personal growth.' Parnell's tone was sarcastic.

Casey closed his eyes and shook his head. 'My orders are we forget about Gu Joon. So, he takes with him whatever he got from Jericho. Hell, the chances are he's already in North Korea, and that is the one place none of us can touch him.'

'We could track his ship?' Parnell noted. 'What's our window since you saw him, two hours?'

'About that.'

'So how far could a ship have gone in two hours?'

'International waters.' Casey stood and made for the water cooler. 'You're thinking we get a list of all the ships that left Singaporean waters within the last two hours?'

'No,' Tate said. 'That's exactly what Gu wants us to do.'

'OK, why?'

'Look, he's been using misdirection the entire time.' Tate explained his last conversation with Gu Joon. 'Then he had you focus on the airport whilst he grabbed me, and now when

I tell you he's on a ship he wants our attention focused on looking for it.'

'Whilst he leaves in the opposite direction?'

'Or,' Tate suggested, 'maybe he doesn't run, he just hides?'

'In Singapore? Tricky.'

Tate shrugged. 'He's managed so far.'

'Look, Jack, none of this sits well with me and I'm not gonna let it lie. I also spoke with Pamela. MI6, of course, will take the CIA's line on this, but she's not happy at all.'

'I'm getting the impression you want to do something?'

'FYI, I swept the room, so we can talk.' Parnell tapped his nose.

'Regardless of who they are, we can't let Gu Joon just ride off into the sunset after what he's done, and what he's potentially got.'

'Especially now that we know he was never actually working for North Korea,' Parnell noted.

'Correct. Then there's Roe, now that's a loose end or a loose cannon – hell, it's a loose something. Where is he? Sunning himself somewhere or is he with Gu Joon? We're not letting go, Jack, and we need all the help we can get. Look, me and Parnell here are one screw-up away from getting a "burn notice". If you wanna walk away, we'll completely understand because if this goes south, none of us are coming back.'

'I'm in,' Tate said. 'I'll always be in.'

Casey saluted Tate with his water cup. 'I kinda knew you would be, but thanks anyway.'

'We need tech support.'

Parnell said, 'There's a guy I know, works out of his basement in Bakersville, North Carolina. He's an "off the grid" type of guy.'

'He's good,' Casey commented. 'Perhaps not as good as Plato, but hey.'

'No. Plato will do it. He's invested in this, remember. It's about justice and not his career.'

Parnell nodded. 'Man has a point.'

Casey looked at his watch, and abruptly stood. 'We've wangled access to a vantage point overlooking the VIP terminal. Parnell and I are leaving now. Look, I know you feel like crap – you certainly look like crap—'

'Cheers.'

'But if you wanna come, follow us.'

VIP Terminal, Changi Airport, Singapore

It was just before sunset, still humid on the balcony, and Tate felt decidedly damp. From their vantage point he and the two CIA officers watched the North Korean president's security detail jog next to the Mercedes Maybach limousine of their Dear Leader.

'Rumour has it,' Casey said, 'Hak ordered his detail do that after seeing our president's detail.'

'I heard it was after he saw that Clint Eastwood movie – *In the Line of Duty,*' Parnell said.

'I'd just like to see him try to run,' Tate said.

They continued to watch the spectacle of the presidential procession, however without lines of manic spectators waving their arms like lunatics, Hak's 'running men' looked faintly ridiculous. Yet a risk still existed. Tate knew that all three of his targets were still in Singapore, and one of them was a skilled marksman. Taking out the Dear Leader with a 0.50 cal round was probably the easiest way to ensure a kill, but, getting into and out of position with a 0.50 cal rifle-shaped bag was a much harder proposition. Tate dismissed the idea again that something would happen on Singaporean soil, but, like a moth dancing around a flame, he could not take his eyes off the North Korean leaders' procession as it neared his loaned Air China 747.

But no, surely that couldn't happen, could it?

The Maybach slowed to a stop, perfectly, next to a red carpet which led towards the airstairs. The running men made a show of securing the area, which made Tate want to roll his eyes before,

271

with the nod of a head, and a whisper into a wrist mic, the door was opened.

The hereditary leader of The People's Democratic Republic of North Korea clambered clumsily out of the luxury limousine. He made no eye contact with his men but looked back at the viewing platform on the outside of the terminal building and waved.

A second figure emerged from the same door; it was his wife and she was dressed in an immaculate white suit.

Tate's left eye twitched; perhaps something was afoot here? Then another passenger exited, but this one used the opposite door. Tate took in the ash-white hair and the jet-black Mao-style suit. The figure turned, and any doubt as to the man's identity Tate may have had vanished. It was Gu Joon and he was finally appearing in public as Hak Kwang-Il.

'The slimy son of a shit,' Parnell said, the words spat into the humid Singaporean evening.

So, had that been his game, Tate wondered? The only way for a wanted man to escape was to make it impossible for anyone to prevent him from leaving. And who would dare stop the uncle of the North Korean president from leaving the country?

'That's it,' Casey sighed. 'Elvis has left the building.'

Tate felt despondent. They'd lost. The man who had caused all this was getting away, heading off literally into the sunset.

Parnell spoke, as though seeing Tate's thoughts as bubbles above his head, 'He'll get his – sooner or later – just you see. Justice always comes a knocking.'

'Roe is still out there,' Casey added.

Without another word said between them they waited and watched until the Air China 747 taxied onto the runway and took off into the setting sun.

Casey turned and extended his hand to Tate. 'We may have lost the battle, but this war is far from over.'

Tate shook his hand. 'Look, Jack, it's time to head home. We'll keep on looking for Roe. I just wanted to thank you for well, hell,

I don't know, exposing all of this. If it weren't for you, none of us would be any the wiser about Gu Joon or Hak whatever it is he calls himself, and, hey, even if we can't do shit to him – forewarned is forearmed.'

Tate nodded. 'The only thing my forearm wants to do is raise a cold pint.'

'I hear ya, brother,' Parnell said.

Chapter 22

One month later
Brighton, United Kingdom

Each time Tate had been to Brighton it had been blowing a gale, but at least the wind hadn't found its way into the narrow streets colloquially known as 'The Lanes'. Outside the tea shop a mixture of scruffy students in battered denim and oversized Dr. Martens, mixed with blue-rinsed pensioners and bemused Chinese and American tourists. Inside, Tate sat opposite Neill Plato and watched him carefully pour his 'first flush' jasmine tea into a porcelain cup.

Tate noisily sipped his coffee and then asked, 'Is this where you bring all your dates?'

Plato looked up as he breathed in the steam rising from his cup. He paused before he spoke. 'Oh no, no, this is my place. They have the best carrot cake in Brighton.'

Tate took in his friend's plate. 'I'll take your word for it.'

It was a weekday in early October; the place had just opened for the day and they were – at the moment –the only customers. Even the staff had hidden themselves in the kitchen.

'How's your mum?'

'Fine. Moaning at me as usual. I thought she'd be happy I

was home for a bit, but now she's telling me I make the place look untidy.'

Tate smiled. 'Must be all the crumbs.'

'And that's another thing. She vows and declares that she doesn't like Fig Rolls but as soon as my back is turned, she's eaten them all! Whoomph and the packet's gone!'

Tate smiled into his cup. Plato had been given extended time off to mentally recuperate from the Jericho affair. He had been assessed by an MI6-contracted psychiatrist who had diagnosed him as suffering from mild PTSD, although Plato himself had disagreed saying it was just the occasional bout of insomnia. Tate felt guilty; he blamed himself. It was, after all, his fault that Plato had been plunged into the sharp end of things, but without Plato the mission would have been an even larger failure.

'How are you, Neill?'

'Me?' Plato seemed surprised. 'I'm absolutely fine.'

Tate nodded. 'And now the truth, hey, it's me not a shrink.'

'I sometimes feel suddenly stressed for no reason, and I occasionally wake up at night.'

'That's your bladder – it's all that tea.'

'No, it is not. Look, I don't feel like I've fallen off the horse, it's more like I've been bucked off a bronco and trampled on. I want to get back in the saddle.'

Tate sighed. 'You know I never wanted any of this to happen, Neill.'

'Jack, shut up. For the umpteenth time, it is not your fault. I chose to go, I chose to leave my desk and, well, everything that happened, happened to me because of that. At least I got to see a bit more of the world. My mum won't go anywhere apart from Barbados or Portugal.'

'Strange mix.'

'She's fond of rum and port.'

Tate smiled. 'How much longer are you signed off for?'

'I shall be back on the first working day in November.'

'That's good.'

'How's George?'

Tate frowned. 'You've not spoken to her?'

Plato rolled his eyes. 'No, I meant how is she at doing my job?'

Tate shrugged. 'There's less tea drunk.'

'You know she prefers English Breakfast to Earl Grey?' Plato plunged his fork into his carrot cake.

'No, I never knew that.' Tate felt his leg vibrate; he pushed his hand into his jeans pocket and retrieved his work iPhone. 'Tate?'

The voice at the other end was American and instantly recognisable, 'We've got an update.'

'Hello, Vince, and how are you?'

'Yeah, good morning and all that jazz. Jack, listen,' Casey said at the other end of the line. 'Gu Joon is leaving North Korea. He's planned a surprise diplomatic mission to Myanmar.'

'Myanmar?'

'It's the new name for Burma, Jack.'

'Yeah, I know what it is, Vince.'

'He's going there with his nephew, the Dear Leader of North Korea. They will be there for the anniversary of the 1983 bombing. We think it's some sort of sign.'

'When's the anniversary?'

'This week. We also got a possible sighting of Roe Kwang, in Phuket. Likely he was heading for Myanmar too. Look, me and Parnell can be in the UK tomorrow morning. We need to meet. OK?'

'OK.'

'Great.' Casey gave Tate the name of a hotel at Heathrow airport. 'Be there in twenty-four hours.'

'Will do.' The call ended and Tate looked at his phone, perplexed.

'Casey's got a lead?' Plato asked, mouth full of cake.

'He's got something.'

'Good.' Plato nodded. 'I want to come back to work.'

276

Yangon River, Myanmar

Roe Kwang knew it was the future of warfare, but it wasn't his bag. Drone strikes had been a staple of the 'war on terror' for well over a decade, yet there was something about the option that made it unsatisfactory for him. He agreed, however, it was a fine weapon when attacking those without honour, such as the misguided fundamentalists who targeted civilian populations. In these situations, it was a message to others that the US respected them so little that they were not going to even endanger a solitary soldier to terminate them. It was like swatting a fly. It was done and then the drone pilot had a cup of coffee and moved on to their next target. He found himself now, however, working with drones, and whilst he had not been in favour of them, he did in fact agree with his father that their targets were men without honour. Politicians were men who gave orders without accepting any of their own, and who took lives without getting their own hands dirty. They were not real men, and, as such, Roe was for them being destroyed by drones.

Roe still thought of himself as Roe Kwang and not Hak Kwang-Chul, even though he now knew who he was and the obligations he had to his country. The country he would soon lead, the country which would hail him as their saviour. Roe smirked; the word 'saviour' had been highjacked by the Christian faith. True, with a capital 'S' it was a name for Jesus, but it came from the Latin word '*salvare*' which simply meant 'to save', so in his mind it had no religious connotation whatsoever. Yet if his people, because this is what he now called the population of North Korea, wanted to hail him as some mythical being, he wouldn't stop them. What he would not do, however, would be to act like one. There would be no huge statue of him adorning numerous public squares in Pyongyang, nor would he demand huge demonstrations of public adoration. He was just a man, and he wanted to lead his country as such.

Roe wiped away the sweat running into his eyes; there was a gentle breeze blowing into the wheelhouse of the ship as it bobbed on the turgid Yangon River, but, even so, the humidity was stifling. Roe was far enough away from his target not to raise suspicion – many such vessels were moored here, but close enough to watch the smoke and, hopefully, the flames it caused. Once the attack had been undertaken, he would quietly motor away from Myanmar's capital city.

Stacked with two other decoy containers, on the deck of the barge, the specifically designed control station his father's technicians had managed to miniaturise was completely concealed within a rusty orange shipping container. When it came time for the attack, each of the modified drones – which were currently concealed under tarpaulins on two neighbouring long vessels – would simply take off and fly the short distance to their target and deploy their ordnance. Roe could fly both drones relying on their 'triple-redundant' control system's autonomous taxi, take-off and cruise abilities. He didn't care if or where they landed. He didn't expect any resistance; they were not attacking a military or otherwise-fortified target.

He was going to miss the freedom to undertake operations himself like this and was ever grateful to his father for not preventing him from doing so on this occasion. This was to be the pinnacle of his father's plot and he was honoured that its sole success or failure fell upon him.

'Your grandfather was a military leader, Kwang,' his father had told him. 'You will be a great military leader.'

His father's words echoed in his head now as Kwang understood that his past, as well as his future, had always been entwined with that of his country. His grandfather had fought the Japanese invaders, but it had been the American atom bombs dropping on Japan that had created his victory. Handpicked by Stalin to become the ruler of the newly created state of North Korea, a country whose borders had been arbitrarily decided by an

American with a pen neatly ruling across the 38th Parallel on a map, his grandfather's status as an enemy of the United States had all but been written. Roe understood there should be one Korea. However, that was an issue for a much later date. First, he needed to usurp his fat cousin.

London

'... the sudden, eleventh-hour cancellation by the North Korean president will mean the diplomatic mission will be led by his uncle, Hak Kwang-Il. Hak Senior is somewhat of an enigma. The hitherto unknown son of the founder of North Korea is believed to be a successful businessman having spent many years in the West before deciding to return to the North to serve as his nephew ...' Tate continued to watch the BBC *Newsnight* report with ever increasing incredulity as it showed footage of the man he first met as Gu Joon descending from the Air China Boeing 747 used by North Korea for their international trip. A red carpet had been laid at the bottom of the airstairs and a smiling Hak Kwang-Il shook hands with those greeting him. 'A motorcade, including military and police escort motorcycles, whisked Mr Hak to the lavish hotel which will serve as his VIP residence for this the first leg of his Myanmar trip in the country's new capital city of Naypyidaw, before, in two days' time, Mr Hak will travel to the former capital of Yangon. There he will visit the iconic Shwedagon Pagoda before moving on to the Martyrs' Mausoleum where he will pay homage to the original martyrs who lost their lives in 1947. Sources say he will then make an official statement regarding the 1983 bombing of the same monument. A bombing North Korea has failed to officially take responsibility for. Mr Hak is accompanied on what has been dubbed The Reconciliation Mission by several high-ranking government aides, including the vice-chairman of the ruling Workers' Party of Korea, the foreign minister and the ruling party's vice-chairman of International Affairs.'

279

The footage abruptly paused on a close-up of Hak Kwang-Il's smiling face. Casey dropped the TV remote on the bed and said, 'So, Pamela, what d'ya think?'

'A sudden, eleventh-hour cancellation. Would you know anything about that?' Newman arched her eyebrows.

'Nope. He's a god, he doesn't get ill, so it has to be either very serious or planned. Either way the trip is going ahead for the outside world to see; you can bet that nothing either way is being shown inside North Korea.'

'I have to agree.' Newman pursed her lips. 'I think those "top aides" have been sent by his leader to keep an eye on him.'

'So do I, mam,' Parnell interjected. 'I mean, he's been AWOL for forty years and then bang he's suddenly appearing on behalf of their Dear Leader. Something's kooky.'

'It's very unlike Hak Junior to pull out of any meeting, especially to then agree for it to carry on without him. I mean, he is "the man".' Casey pointed at the screen. 'Those aides are three of his most fiercely loyal supporters.'

Sitting on the settee in Casey's hotel suite, Tate frowned as again the cogs turned in his head, 'And they would be fully against Hak Kwang-Il gaining any semblance of power.'

A wide grin spread across Casey's face. 'Go on, Jack, you're nearly there.'

'So, they would need to be taken care of.'

Parnell made a 'trigger pulling' action with his right hand. 'Purged.'

'That's our assessment. But the question remains, how can Hak Kwang-Il do this without implicating himself?' Casey shrugged. 'In fact, it would be best for him to implicate his nephew.'

An idea suddenly appeared in Tate's head, 'He wouldn't …'

Casey and Parnell exchanged glances, seemingly enjoying watching Tate's mental journey.

'We think he would. After the military coup, Myanmar is back now to being a pariah, a basket case, which means if the North

Koreans, or whoever, carry out an attack there – even take out the current military leader of Myanmar – the blowback will be minimal. The international community won't care. China and Russia have both armed the country, but, in reality, Myanmar doesn't have the capacity to start an international conflict or retaliate, and China won't let it attack North Korea. Then, and this is just beautiful, because North Korea cannot legally trade with anyone, they'll not be losing anything in trade.'

Tate rose from his seat and moved to the window. He gazed down at the River Thames, swirling below. 'What does Langley say?'

'That we're talking nonsense and seeing ghosts.'

'Boo!' Parnell said, dramatically.

'They're not going to do anything, are they?' Newman stated.

'The US is hardly best friends with the unrecognised military junta of Myanmar, then of course there is Hak Kwang-Il's assurance that he's going to give them all of Jericho's tech once he's in power.' Casey shrugged. 'Slimy old bastard.'

'We also have more news on Roe.' Parnell folded his arms. 'He could be a Hak.'

'A Hak?' Newman frowned. 'Please explain.'

Something clicked into place in Tate's mind. 'Roe is Gu Joon's son.'

'That is the wild-ass theory we have,' Parnell added. 'Er sorry, mam.'

'It's Pamela, and please carry on with your *wild-ass* theory.'

'Well, the dates and times just seem to fit.'

'His adoption?'

'No. There were no official adoption papers, the couple who raised him claimed they were his parents. We found out, of course, that they were not.'

Casey said, 'Where is the safest place to hide someone? In the military surrounded by men who will live and die for you. Anyway, I started to look at Roe's military career – which was outstanding, but then I dug down a bit and looked at his agency operations, specifically things that had gone wrong or were simply unexplained. It was like someone was passing on bits of intel.'

'Such as?' Newman asked.

'Pamela, I can't tell you. Let's just say that one of the operations was targeting a character involved with a shipping company. Now that shipping company was owned by a matryoshka of shell companies – you know, like a doll inside a doll inside a doll.'

'Yes, Vince, I know what a matryoshka is,' Newman said.

Casey continued. 'The real owner was a company called Eeshipil Trading. One of the registered owners of that company is a Gu Joon, who of course now no longer exists since he's become Hak Kwang-Il.'

Parnell spelled it out. 'Roe was passing on intelligence to Gu Joon aka Hak Kwang-Il. We found no financial trail to Roe; that means it was political or he felt obliged to do it or both.'

'Hence believing them to be related?' Newman asked.

'Here.' Casey handed her a sheet of paper on which was printed a photo of each man's face with various lines and percentages. 'It's a bit low tech for your Plato, which is probably why he didn't think of doing it. It's a photographic comparative analysis. In layman's terms, these two faces are 72 per cent similar. Without DNA from both subjects, that's as much as we can get.'

Tate sat down next to his boss and studied the document. 'I'm sold.'

Newman handed the paper back to Casey. 'What are we saying, Vince? Roe is heading to Yangon to help his dad?'

'Yep. Anyway, Langley ain't interested. Which means we're on our own.'

'Not quite. Gentlemen, we caused this problem, and we want to solve it.'

'We?'

'E Squadron, Vince.'

Casey laughed. 'Now that's what I was hoping to hear.'

'In my position, I do have some latitude.' Newman addressed Tate. 'Jack, how was Neill when you met?'

'He seemed fine, really, but I wouldn't take him on an operation.'

'Of course not, but you are going to need him to lend you tech support, yes?'

'Yes.'

'Do you think he's up for that?'

'Definitely.'

'Good. He'll work remotely from the UK, like he did when you were in Singapore. Now I think it would be prudent if we discussed how we are getting you all "in country" and how we are going to stop Hak Kwang-Il, or whoever, from creating a bloody awful mess.'

Chapter 23

Yangon, Myanmar

The captain had been an MI6 asset for decades. His ship was old, unremarkable-looking and as it had plied its trade, like its captain, up and down the waterways of Yangon River for years, was never given a second look. Below deck it was hot, humid and stank of fish and diesel. Tate, Casey and Parnell dared not go on deck until sundown, and even that could potentially compromise them. So, they rested as best they could among the cargo as the barge forged forwards towards their destination, the city of Yangon some forty-one kilometres north.

Getting this far had not been easy. With hours rather than days to plan the mission, their only available method of insertion was by air. In the middle of a moonless night, a C130 dropped the three men, and a high-powered Zodiac inflatable, into the Gulf of Martaban of the Andaman Sea, where they had then made the long run for the coast and the mouth of the marine estuary. Parnell and Tate had taken the method of insertion in their stride, but Casey was as Parnell had bluntly put it – 'Like Elvis – all shook up'.

Tate had pushed the Zodiac as fast as he dared go in the

choppy sea. They'd needed to be quick in order to outrun any naval patrol vessels who might spot them, believing the team to be either drug smugglers or gun runners from neighbouring Thailand, and to avoid any real smugglers who thought they were encroaching on their turf.

Myanmar's military rulers who had toppled the democratically elected government were continuously tightening their control over the country, but the uncertainty and chaos had caused incidences of crime and lawlessness to rise. The result being that Tate, Parnell and Casey were heading into a modern incarnation of the wild west. As Tate sweated below deck, he wondered if this was part of the appeal to the North Koreans. Perhaps they were there to give advice on how to crack down and control the nation?

Arriving just before dawn they had rendezvoused with the captain and then had to wait for several hours until he was able to enter the shipping channel up the busy river.

Already after midday and changed now out of their wet gear and into general civilian clothing – jeans and loose shirts – they looked like a trio of lost tourists as they hid below deck. Casey took a long pull of water from a plastic bottle, then blew out his cheeks. 'I gotta tell ya, boys, this ain't my idea of fun. Why jump out of a perfectly good plane?'

'OK, boomer,' Parnell stated, with a wink.

Tate put his eye to the grimy porthole, he could make out the riverbank, and on the road running alongside it, the passing traffic. 'Not far now.'

'Let's go over this again,' Casey said. 'The North Koreans arrive here tomorrow morning, accompanied by the guy who's pretending to run Myanmar.'

'The Commander-in-Chief of Defence Services,' Parnell said.

'They immediately go to the Shwedagon Pagoda and then the Martyrs' Mausoleum. There'll be a ceremony, photo opportunities and meetings. Then, later, a banquet is being held at The Strand

Hotel, before our North Korean friends are taken to their top-floor rooms at the Meliá Yangon.'

'One night in Yangon and the world's your oyster.' Parnell chuckled.

There had been a collective sigh of relief that nothing had happened during the first two days of the diplomatic trip when the North Koreans had been in Naypyidaw, because if it had they were on the other side of the world, and because the new Myanmar capital was locked up like a fortress. Yangon was a comparatively soft target. They had gone through the details in London, with what they then knew the North Korean delegation's movements to be. A single night at Meliá, then off to the airport the following afternoon. Hak Kwang-Il and the others would be in Yangon a little over thirty hours, and that was the window when if anything was going to happen, it would. Tate knew it was thin, yet that was all they had. He wished he knew who was going to be targeted and how.

The hatch above to the outside world opened and the barge captain peered in, his face unreadable in the gloom, and addressed Casey. 'We dock soon. Your man will meet us?'

'Yes, he will.'

'Good. All is OK?'

'All is OK,' Casey replied.

The captain retreated and closed the hatch. Casey had called in a favour with the CIA head of station. A contact with a car would be meeting the trio to take them to a safe house, on the condition of complete deniability. Meanwhile, Plato had hacked the relevant Myanmar government databases and inserted 'legends' – false identities for each of the three. Tate, Parnell and Casey were now Canadian geothermal power experts, in the region to explore the potential of the hydrothermal reservoirs which had been discovered close to Yangon. Something that the UN had agreed must carry on. The legends would stand up to general scrutiny, especially as the military government was still fractured. Tate just hoped it was enough to keep them out of hot water.

There was a chirping sound and Tate fiddled with his bag to retrieve his sat phone. He briefly glanced at the display before answering it. It was Plato, and he had some good news to share. Tate put the call on speaker: 'The CIA have tasked one of their satellites to be above Yangon.' Plato's voice was clear but slightly tinny.

'They've decided this may be worth a look at after all?' Casey looked up at the roof, as though imagining the satellite high above. 'Better late than never, boys.'

'How do you know this, Neill?'

'I hacked my way in.'

'That's impossible!' Casey's surprise was evident on his face.

'No, it's really not.'

'Excellent.' Tate smiled. One – nil Great Britain.

'Look, I've got full imaging of central Yangon.'

Casey cut to the chase. 'Is there anything that looks unusual near the pagoda or mausoleum?'

'No, Vince. It seems both have been sealed off and there is a heavy military presence outside. There was a crowd of people, perhaps protestors, but they were moved off.'

Parnell shook his head. 'So how the hell do we get in?'

'Perhaps we don't?'

'You don't think anything will happen there?'

Tate shook his head. 'Why target a "hard target"?'

Parnell said, 'Because they want to show they can?'

'What does that prove?'

'Nothing.' Casey nodded. 'Hm, so the hotel it is?'

'OK. There is also a visible military security presence at both hotels,' Plato said. 'The reports and feed I'm seeing from the CIA say there are snipers on the roof, and soldiers positioned in and around both buildings.'

'Keep us updated if you see anything, anything at all,' Casey ordered.

'Will do,' Plato acknowledged before ending the call.

There was a sudden jolt and the tone of the ship's engine changed as it came to a halt. Tate again peered through the porthole. 'I think we've arrived.'

*

The man sent by Casey's colleague didn't come until late afternoon, and his panel van was outdated and non-descript. Casey sat in the front next to the driver, a hoody topped with a baseball cap covering his bushy blond locks whilst Parnell and Tate bounced around in the cargo area. The driver didn't say a single word apart from the name of Casey's colleague as he drove them away from the dock and towards the safe house. The interior of the van smelled almost exactly the same as the ship had, which meant to Tate that either they both reeked of fish and diesel, or he did. Parnell, unlike Tate, had his eyes closed, but, like Tate, he had a Glock 19 within reach of his right hand. Full assault kits, including both fragmentation and phosphorous grenades and short-stock assault rifles, were awaiting them at the safe house.

Unable to see anything of their route outside, Tate felt tense, but the humidity also made him feel drowsy. He closed his eyes. He knew they were heading north and visualised the map he had memorised. The Strand Hotel was to their south and across the main road faced a park which screened it from the ferry terminal, whilst the Meliá hotel was to the north, overlooking Lake Inya. Tate's mind's eye followed the Yangon River as it became the Pun Hlaing River, curving to the west, the Hlaing River continuing north.

'Hey, don't go falling asleep on me, Tate.' Parnell kicked his boot with his own.

Tate's eyes snapped open. 'You can talk.'

'I was resting my eyes, *compadre*.'

'Sure, you were, *squire*.'

'We cross bridge, then five minutes,' the driver said, his accent heavy. 'We there in five minutes.'

Tate turned, got to his haunches, and pulled himself towards the seats, just as the metalled road decided to deteriorate and they hit a pothole. He slipped and fell sideways. Parnell laughed.

The five minutes, which in reality became fifteen, ended abruptly with the van coming to a stop outside a single-storey warehouse. Without saying a word, the driver jumped out and jogged to an 'up-and-over' door. He pressed a button and it started to slide up, before he reached up and gave it a hand. Once fully open, he returned to the van and steered them inside. The feeble headlights of the van were all that illuminated the empty space and a scattering of wooden-looking boxes that lay to one side.

'I go. You go out,' the driver said and looked back at Tate and Parnell with a grin.

Casey clambered out of his seat as Parnell opened the rear double van doors. Tate passed him the packs and they both got out. The van started to manoeuvre, and the reverse lights cast red dancing flames across the far wall. It exited through the large open entrance space.

'And he didn't even give us the Wi-Fi code,' Parnell grunted as he hefted his bag.

Tate started to smile, but then sudden movement and noise forced him to stop. Something sailed in through the still-open door. It was a familiar shape.

Tate yelled, 'Grenade!' and dived for the floor.

Seconds later, there was a violently loud explosion, and the interior darkness was turned to day for an eye-searing second. In that moment Tate knew it was a flash-bang and that they were in trouble. Ears ringing and eyesight ghosting, Tate scurried towards the far corner of the space, aware that he had only the Glock in his pocket for defence. Shots sounding distant because of the ringing in his ears pinged off the concrete floor and punched the metal walls. Tate went prone, blinking, trying to recover his vision, and continued to shuffle backwards. His feet hit the wall. To his immediate left he made out boxes, and in a final attempt to get into cover he rolled behind them.

The wooden shipping boxes were perhaps three feet by three feet, just enough to hide behind, but the most obvious cover in the barren warehouse interior. Tate worked his jaw as he took deep breaths and he blinked, anything to try to regain his senses. He'd been on the giving end of a flash-bang on many occasions, but it had not been since his regiment training that he'd been exposed to the receiving end, and then he'd been wearing ear defenders. At least, he mused, the size of the interior space had spread the soundwave somewhat. Powerful interior lights blinked on, and the interior shadows of night were banished. Tate realised that the place was not just a warehouse, it had once been a workshop and garage.

Tate pulled his Glock from his pocket, took a breath, and slowly rose above the boxes. Immediately he let his grip on the Glock go limp as he saw what had to be twenty armed men, members of the Tatmadaw –Myanmar's military. Ten or so had their assault rifles aimed in his direction, whilst the others pointed theirs at the prone figures of Casey and Parnell. One of the soldiers facing Tate shouted at him in what Tate assumed was Burmese and gestured for him to drop his weapon. Tate let the Glock fall from his grasp. His life now depended on the whim of whoever was in charge. Moments later, the man in charge appeared; he was shorter than most of the other soldiers and wider and looked a decade older. He sauntered towards Tate, as though he had all the time in the world and came to a stop facing him, but perhaps a metre away from him. He had a smile on his face, as though he found what he saw amusing. He raised his left hand and one of the soldiers advanced, collected Tate's Glock from the floor and handed it to him. The officer felt the weight in his right hand and nodded as though appraising it before he pointed it at Tate's face.

'Who are you?' the officer asked, his tone flat and his accent vaguely American.

Tate knew the rules, he knew what he should and should not say and he knew he should ration what he did. 'Don't shoot me … please!'

The officer's smile widened. 'Horseshit.'

'Please …' Tate repeated.

'You are three American spies. Maybe you are here to murder my senior general? Or to plot against him?'

'I'm Canadian,' Tate said, not willing to give up. 'I work for Kinross-Kirkland.'

'No. That is a lie. The driver told me he picked you up for the CIA.' The officer called over his back, again in a language that Tate couldn't understand.

Seconds later, Tate saw two soldiers drag a wet-looking figure into the warehouse. As they neared, Tate realised it was the old captain who had brought them up the river. The soldiers let go of him and, unable to support himself, the man collapsed to the floor by the side of the officer and Tate.

'Who are you?' the officer asked again.

'Please,' Tate said. 'There has been a mistake.'

The officer shook his head slowly. He looked down at the captain and spoke to him in their shared local tongue. The captain looked up, and Tate could now see the damage which had already been inflicted on his face. 'Who are you?'

'I'm Canadian—'

In a seemingly languid motion, the officer raised Tate's Glock and fired a round into the captain's face. His eyes then returned to Tate's. 'Two more men, two more chances.'

'Hey, pal, I'm the one in charge!' Casey shouted across the space. 'You wanna have someone answer questions then you speak to me.'

Without taking his gaze from Tate, the officer barked more orders.

Tate now saw both Parnell and Casey being lifted to their feet and hustled towards what looked like a pair of trenches. Tate realised they were vehicle inspection pits. The soldiers pushed them inside and stepped away.

More instructions were given, and four soldiers advanced towards Tate. Whilst two levelled their M16s at him, the other two grabbed his arms. The officer turned his back and strode away across the space towards an office that was positioned in the corner. Tate let his feet go heavy and made the soldiers drag him to the pits. He got to the edge; Parnell was in one and Casey was in the other. Hands pushed him forward and Tate dropped into Casey's pit. He landed on his feet, managing to miss the CIA officer. It was then that Tate realised the pits had been especially modified; this was not the first time they'd been used to house prisoners, they had been dug out to be two metres deep. Tate looked up. If he jumped up, he could grab the top but couldn't easily pull himself out without being seen or stopped.

Casey jutted his chin at Tate, as if to ask if he was OK. Tate nodded back. Both men knew that anything and everything they said could be overheard, and would, if understood, be reported back to the little officer.

There was a pattering of boots on the concrete floor above them and then they heard Parnell's voice.

'Take your goddamn hands off me!'

Tate looked up. He saw no one looking down at them, but had no idea how near or far away the soldiers were. Casey held up a finger to attract his attention and pointed to his own left ankle, then made his hand into a gun shape. Casey bent forward and in the narrow space pulled up the leg of his jeans. Tate saw the unmistakable bulge of a sub-compact Glock handgun just below Casey's thick calf muscle. There was more noise above and Casey quickly shook his leg.

A metal ladder was lowered into the pit and a soldier pointed at Casey. 'You.'

'Me?'

'You, you!'

With a wink at Tate, Casey climbed up the short distance to the top and was dragged away. Tate was alone. He tried to relax his body, and, placing his feet flat on the bottom of the pit on one side, he leaned forwards and placed his hands flat on the opposite side and performed a few standing presses. He needed to keep his muscles ready and relaxed. He closed his eyes and tried to inhale deeply, but the stench of oil rising from the floor of the pit made him stop. His throat felt dry, and he realised that he desperately wanted a drink. Dehydration was the salient enemy here, well, almost. He realised he still had his watch and checked the time. Night had fallen fast over Yangon; it was fully dark yet still a little before seven. Still sixteen or so hours before the North Koreans arrived. Tate cursed, silently to himself. They had to get out, and they had to get away otherwise they would have failed and, perhaps more importantly, they would be disavowed.

The sound of shouting reached Tate's ears. He could hear the officer and he could hear Casey and then he heard a gunshot. Next, he heard Parnell yell, and then there was another shot. And then the lights in the building switched off.

Tate desperately looked around, eyes scanning for any movement whatsoever, ears straining for any sounds. But in the pit, below the level of the floor in the garage, Tate's world was pitch black.

Chapter 24

Yangon, Myanmar

Roe had his hands in his pockets and was slouching as he walked. Even though it was dark on the streets, he kept to the even darker edges where both the sodium street lights and the passing lamps of the traffic failed to fully reach. He was heading for the target. He had studied the place from both military and open-source satellite photographs and, of course, the extremely helpful pages of Booking.com, but he wanted to see the hotel for himself. Carrying a large rattan-style shopping bag and with his dark hair, drab clothes and nowhere-to-be gait, he hoped he was passing for a local or, at the very least, a migrant worker and not an expat who would draw attention. At least he wasn't white, he snorted in the darkness. However, he was armed, both a knife and a handgun, but didn't want to use either, if he didn't have to. The curfew the military government had introduced to initially curb the volume of people on the streets, and hence the number of potential protestor,s had been repealed. Roe wondered if it was because the eyes of the world were now on Yangon, due to his father's unprecedented arrival, or because the senior soldiers wanted themselves to go out and have fun. Regardless, the streets again had people in them.

Roe paused to gaze at the Shwedagon Pagoda. Glowing in the otherwise dark sky, the golden stupa was over one hundred metres in height and covered in, he'd read, an estimated thirty tons of gold. It was far more impressive, he thought, than any US monument he had ever seen. He was glad that he wasn't going to destroy it, some things were just a 'no-go'. He continued to walk towards it until he saw the edge of the security cordon, the armoured vehicles, and the soldiers. He leaned against a tree and observed, unseen by all until he wasn't and one uniformed man who seemed keener than the rest pointed at him. Roe moved behind the tree and hustled away; he didn't feel like knifing the guy so hoped he hadn't followed him.

But he had.

Roe carried on back the way he had come, away from the pagoda, as he heard a shout from behind, first authoritarian, and then outraged that he hadn't stopped. An idea struck Roe; he turned to see the soldier waving angrily after him and slowed so that the man could lessen the distance between them. There was an alleyway on his right and Roe ducked into it, knowing that he had been seen and would be followed.

He waited, relaxed, in the darkness.

The soldier loudly entered the alley, his voice now angrier than ever. He walked directly past Roe without seeing him. Roe laughed out loud, with genuine amusement, as he stepped directly behind the man. The soldier's face was a vision of outrage as he rounded on Roe, who now noted from his insignia that he was a junior officer. He opened his mouth to say something, but Roe would never know what those words may have been as he deftly struck him in the throat with a knife-edge chop.

Larynx crushed and unable to breathe, the soldier stumbled backwards then fell flat on his back as he clawed at his throat.

Roe looked down at him. 'You know your problem? You talk too much.'

Roe watched as the soldier suffocated.

Roe looked at the man's feet and noted that they were smaller than his own, so he'd leave the boots, but the man's jacket and trousers were his general size. He removed the jacket first; he was surprised to see how clean it was, and then moved onto the trousers. His luck held and the guy had not emptied his bowels on making his exit, which suited Roe. He bundled the uniform up in his bag, along with the man's service-issue pistol and calmly walked away from the scene, just a guy strolling home.

Yangon

Tate could feel the rats running over his feet, but they didn't bother him; it was nothing compared to what he'd put up with in the jungle. A rat could nip him, perhaps pass on some type of disease, which could be treated with a course of antibiotics, but types of spiders, frogs, snakes and any number of other nasties – those could kill in minutes, seconds. He was being forced to stand up, or at least loll against the side of the pit and every few minutes or so a torch was shone down to check on him, both to make sure he wasn't sleeping and to curtail any ideas he may have of climbing out. What it also had done the first time was ruin his night vision, but Tate had got wise to that and now when he sensed movement, he closed his eyes and clamped his hands over them. Perhaps the soldiers thought he was doing it out of despair because it had brought unintelligible comments, tuts and sniggers. Tate had removed his watch and stuffed it into the pocket of his jeans, it wasn't that it was valuable – just a standard Casio G-Shock – but he didn't want to lose track of time if it was pinched. He fished it out of his pocket. The illuminated hands told him it was past midnight. Tate had heard nothing from Casey or Parnell, not since the gun shots, but wasn't naive enough to believe that was because they were dead. If they were, surely, he would have been told, or he would have joined them, or he would have been shown their corpses as an inducement to make him talk. All this went on the assumption that the man in charge both knew what he was doing and was rational. The truth was that Tate actually knew very little.

He heard a phone ring; it was the instantly recognisable tone of their sat phone. A voice answered; he couldn't hear the language, but the tone sounded angry. And then there was silence again. Tate's mind started to wander as he thought about their situation. What was the situation here? Their cover had been blown, but was this in any way related to the specifics of their mission or was it simply a low-level local asset wanting to make a few bucks? Tate didn't know and that annoyed him. He now started to time the length in between visits from the guards. Twelve minutes, for the first hour, then eighteen for the second before it lengthened to irregular intervals. By 3 a.m., fatigue was devouring his body. Tate knew that the soldiers too would be feeling it. They'd become tired or lazy or both. Tate knew he could wait no longer. He couldn't allow himself to still be in the pit when the sun came up and brought with it the heat, and the probable questioning and beatings. He lowered himself into a squatting position and felt his joints complain at him and muscles moan, before he pushed up and sprang skywards. His right hand slapped fully onto the concrete floor over the lip of the pit, whilst the tips of the fingers of his left hand clung on to the edge. His fingers started to slip but then there was enough grime and dust to create the friction and resistance needed to prevent him from sliding back any further. He could feel his shoulders starting to burn, but pulled himself up, like a pull-up in a gym but so much more important. His head rose above floor level. And then he froze. In the gloom a soldier was approaching him; incredulously, the man was lighting a cigarette. The flames illuminated his face, but they also burnt out his night vision. Tate squinted to preserve his own vision as his arms started to shake with the exertion of clamping the concrete. The soldier grew nearer until he flicked his match away and then looked down at Tate's pit.

Tate grabbed the man's right boot with both hands and jerked, letting gravity pull him and the soldier backwards. Taken completely by surprise the man lost his balance. Cigarette still between his lips he made no sound, at first smashing into the floor before quickly sliding into the blackness of the pit. Tate quickly snaked his arms around the man's head and broke his neck; he was in no mood to be polite.

Tate stayed stock still and listened. There was no sound of approaching feet or concerned shouts. Tate searched the soldier, who reeked of alcohol, and swore under his breath that he was completely unarmed. He stood on the man and once again hauled himself up to the lip of the pit. He paused; his fatigue gone as the adrenalin from killing a man surged through him. It was animal aggression and he had been forced to release it.

A chink of moonlight fell into the space from an exterior door that was part open, and a weak waft of smoke followed it. At the far end of the space there was a glow too from the office in the window, but this was far more diffused. They had to pass the door to get to the office.

Tate continued to rise and now swung his right leg up and rolled out of the pit. He stayed flat, prone on the concrete still warm from the day's heat, and, without moving his head, looked around. He sensed no movement and inside the building it was silent. Outside he could hear a distant diesel engine chugging, probably a barge he surmised, and voices low and conspiratorial. Tate rose to his haunches, and, as quietly as he could, padded towards the second pit. He paused a foot away from the edge and hissed, 'Parnell!'

'Tate?' a low voice replied.

'We're leaving.' Tate stepped to the edge as Parnell's hands appeared on the lip of the concrete. Tate grabbed the left arm and pulled as Parnell levered himself up.

'Thanks, bud. Where's Casey?'

'They took him.'

'Then let's take him back.'

Tate pointed at the part-open door and then the office. Parnell nodded.

In the shadows they reached the door. Tate peered out and saw several soldiers sitting around a campfire. They were cooking something on long sticks. Tate counted the men, he held up six fingers to indicate there were six of them. He couldn't see any vehicles but then this was the back of the building which gave onto the river.

They moved away from the door and edged along the inside perimeter of the space; he could make out the dim shape of the office in the corner. It was prefabricated, with two-metre-high walls which were glass for the second metre up on two sides. Nothing fancy, nothing flashy, utilitarian, and on the back wall was a shuttered window through which the pale moonlight attempted to encroach.

There were footsteps behind them. Both intelligence operatives flattened themselves against the wall. They could see a second soldier entering the building with a languid gait and the glow of a cigarette highlighting his face.

Parnell tapped Tate on the shoulder. 'Go.'

Tate carried on, hidden in the deep shadows, whilst Parnell turned to face the advancing smoker.

Now at a crouch, Tate passed the glass and felt for the door. He placed his ear on the panel next to it and listened. He heard breathing. He started to push the door with his left hand as he remained concealed behind the panel. The door half opened then stopped moving. It hit something soft, a body.

Tate moved through the half-open door, still on his haunches, and recognised the figure on the carpeted floor. It was Casey and he was still tied to a chair. But there was someone else there; a rhythmic breathing came from the back of the office, and there was the sour stench of spilled, cheap whisky. Tate moved further into the room, his eyes now seeing more of the space. Past Casey was another chair, this one empty, and then there was a desk but to the left of this was the source of the sound, a settee.

On it there was a body, and it was sleeping.

And then it wasn't.

The officer sat bolt upright; a whisky bottle rolled off his stomach, but Tate was more concerned with what was in his hand. It was a small pistol, and it was pointing at him.

Without any warning or hesitation, he fired.

Tate was already diving forward, and the round flew past him, tugging at his flailing shirt. Tate's bad shoulder hit the smaller man squarely in the chest, making both men grunt. The officer was fat, but fast and still holding the handgun slammed it down on the back of Tate's head. Tate roared with anger, and on instinct looped his arms tight around the man's chest, pushed up with his legs, jerked his hips and threw himself backwards. Arching his back, he let go just before he hit the floor. The diminutive Burmese officer had no idea what was happening until his back slammed into the desk. He dropped the handgun. Tate rolled over, panting, grabbed what he now saw had to be Casey's sub-compact Glock and shot the man in his face.

'Tate ... get me ...' Casey was alive and in the semi-gloom Tate could see that his face was misshapen.

'You're staying there until I've cleared this place. Play dead.'

'He found the gun ...' Casey said, his voice still slow.

The door suddenly swung open fully and a figure with wild eyes advanced at them. The moonlight glinted on something in its hand – a knife. Tate took a step back before he realised it was Parnell.

'Well, hello,' Parnell said, in a low voice.

Before Tate could reply, the overhead lights were switched on, bathing the entire place in blinding white light. Parnell and Tate instantly hit the floor.

Parnell said, 'The guy only had a knife.'

Shouts in Burmese now echoed through the interior space of the garage. They sounded wary.

'Shoot 'em …' Casey said, his voice thick.

Tate looked at the G26 in his hand. It had the standard ten-round magazine, and four of those rounds had been used – two by him and two earlier in the night. 'Five bad guys and six rounds.'

'You can miss a few then,' Parnell said.

'Perhaps I won't need to. Stay down.'

Tate commando crawled to the doorway, then rose to his haunches below the level of the window. He could hear feet now and the voices had become aggressive. He jerked sideways into the doorway, Glock up and seeking out targets. Two soldiers were standing hunched forward by the back door, weapons up and heads swivelling, a third man was midway between them and the vehicle inspection pits, and another was peering into one of them. Tate shot the man in middle, a round to his chest that hurled him back, before he quickly snapped another round off at the nearest man, who fell into a pit. One of the two soldiers at the door pulled the trigger on his M16, sending an uncontrolled burst in Tate's general direction. Tate hugged the floor again as the office glass smashed.

'Tate, we need to hustle!' Parnell yelled. 'Cover me!'

Tate looked up and fired a round back at the two soldiers remaining in the building as Parnell sprinted out of the office. He made it to the middle of the space and scooped up the dead soldier's M16 before releasing a burst of rounds at the doorway. Tate rose to his feet as the two soldiers retreated. To his surprise, Parnell ran after them.

'Jack, leave him. He loves it, just untie me.'

Tate turned and, using the knife Parnell had discarded, cut Casey from the chair.

'Shit,' Casey groaned, and he rolled onto his stomach.

Tate helped him to his feet. 'You OK?'

'Never felt better, after a one-sided fight.' Casey looked around. 'We need the sat phone.'

'He took it?'

Casey shook his head. 'It was on his desk, he couldn't get it to operate – I didn't know the code and he didn't believe me. It rang once, the guy spoke to Plato.'

'And?'

'Plato hung up. Then the phone locked itself again and that's when he really laid into me.'

'Sorry, Vince.'

'Ah, I've had worse. Wife number three especially could really throw a punch!'

Tate turned and inspected the space. Now in the blinding light he saw it contained a stash of items taken from whoever he had chosen to interrogate – mobile phones, several crates of spirits, a pile of hats and a pair of alligator boots. It didn't seem very military like and implied the officer had been primarily for himself. Tate's handset was part hidden on the floor behind the settee. He picked it up and crammed it into his back pocket. Then he saw something else on the floor, it was an envelope. Inside, Tate found their IDs and money. It went into his pocket.

'He kept saying we were CIA and that if we paid him, he'd let us go.'

'How much did he want?'

'One million American dollars. I was insulted he thought I was so goddamn cheap.'

'Clear!' Parnell yelled.

Tate left the office with Casey stumbling behind him.

'Jack, you were wrong, there were eight. Two more were asleep in the van around the side.' Parnell waited for them by the open back door. He held up the rifle. 'Sheesh, this isn't even an M16, it's a Chinese knock-off. A Norinco CQ.'

'You got the key?' Casey gestured with his chin.

Parnell shook his head. 'Course I do.'

They moved to the side of the building and Casey once more climbed into the passenger seat. This time Parnell drove.

'Do you know where we are?' Casey asked.

'Yangon,' Parnell replied.

Tate opened up the sat phone and called Plato.

'Jack, where are you? I called and got some guy on the line called Kenny.'

'Kenny's dead.'

'What? Oh, I get it, that's South Park?'

Tate sighed. He had no idea. 'So, any updates?'

'No. I wanted to check you reached the safe house.'

'We did, but Kenny was there. Look, call me if there is anything new, OK?'

'Yes, Jack.'

Tate ended the call.

'His goddamn name was Kenny?'

'Apparently, Vince.'

'We need to go south,' Parnell stated. 'We have to get near the hotels. Pretend to be guests, or expats.'

'What about Lake Inya?' Tate suggested. 'We can find somewhere there to dump this thing. And it's where their hotel is.'

'Oh, we'll go to the lake all right, but we're going to the embassy. There's a guy there whose got some explaining to do! Jack, give me the phone, there's a number I need to call,' Casey said.

Embassy of The United States of America, Myanmar

'What do you mean, I can't leave?'

'The British ambassador has asked we keep you here until he gets clarification from London,' the member of the American diplomatic corps informed Tate. 'Until that time, you will stay here.'

'So, I'm what, a prisoner?'

'No, you're a guest.'

Tate gestured to his sat phone, lying on a tray on the table. 'Then you can give me back my phone?'

The American frowned. 'I don't know, I'll have to clarify that.'

Tate lurched forward and snatched the handset. 'Cheers.'

The American nodded slowly, then rose from his chair and left the room. The door shut behind him, but Tate didn't hear it lock.

Tate yawned. He was exhausted. It was already 10 a.m. local time and he'd been held by the US embassy security people since they'd arrived in the small hours. First, he was in a room with Casey and Parnell and then by himself. The contents of his pockets had been brought in on a tray. This included the sat phone and he had then been asked questions about it. The American, who interviewed him and didn't give him his name, had not liked the fact that he refused to answer his questions. Each time he'd asked Tate a question and said that he must answer as a 'matter of national security', Tate replied that his 'national security' prevented him from doing so. It was a standoff and the American knew it.

The door opened and in walked Parnell. Tate could see some bruising had come up on his face. He had a sub sandwich and a can of Coke in his hand. He placed it on the table. 'Breakfast.'

'Cheers.' Tate opened the wrapper and greedily started to eat.

'And there's me thinking you Brits had the best table manners?'

Tate wiped his mouth on the back of his hand and popped open his pop. 'That is correct.'

Parnell rubbed his face. 'Vince is giving it to anyone who'll listen. He's ripped the station chief a new one, and the guy's an old friend of his.'

'What's the outcome?'

'He and I are "confined to base" until the North Korean delegation leaves.'

'And then?'

Parnell held up his hands. 'Not your problem, pal. Listen, this was a righteous mission and I still think it is. Maybe you can get me a job with E Squadron?'

Tate realised Parnell was only half joking. 'If it were up to me.'

The door opened again, and Casey appeared. His face now looked much worse than before. 'Yeah, don't say it. I know it'll get worse before it gets better.'

'You look like a Smurf.'

'Thanks, Parnell.' Casey sat. 'I see you got your phone back.'

'I did.'

'Listen, Langley put a bird overhead because it turns out they didn't completely want to ignore me. I can't name names, but a someone in a large office wants us to carry on. He agrees with our belief that Hak Kwang-Il AKA Gu Joon is a dangerous individual and is up to something.' Casey paused and shook his head. 'But, and this is a big but—'

'Big butt.'

'However, someone else in a larger office has stated our official line must be that we will work with Hak Kwang-Il. Why? Because the guy speaks English, hasn't hidden for most of his life in North Korea and isn't his nephew.'

Tate frowned. 'Well, I'm glad that's clear.'

'We' – Casey pointed at his own chest and then Parnell's – 'are not allowed on any level to interfere with or approach any member of the North Korean diplomatic delegation nor hinder its progress.'

'But I can?'

'Tate, you don't work for the CIA and you're not a US citizen. You're going to get a call, on that phone, from Pamela Newman telling you to stay put.'

Tate let out a long sigh. 'That's just peachy.'

Chapter 25

Yangon River

Roe watched the televised footage of his father as he stepped off the China Air 747. He felt an immense pride in knowing that soon his father, and then he, would be the true rulers of North Korea. It had been a long road they had travelled, and it had taken forty years but finally today the world would start to understand that Hak Kwang-Il, although much older than his nephew, was the only man who should be the North Korean president, until of course he ceded power to his son. Roe sipped his Coke and wished it was whisky. In less than a day it would be. He checked his sat phone was charged and ready; his father was going to call him later, giving him the final go-ahead, the final command. Roe looked around the crew mess. He'd miss being just one of the people, but he knew there was no way he could walk among them as a normal, everyday Joe Public once he took his rightful position.

On screen his father was waving at the various dignitaries, all military men with innumerable medals. He reached the bottom of the airstairs and a little girl, wearing traditional Burmese national dress, ran forward and handed him a bouquet of flowers.

A child was a good idea, he should have one. No, he'd have two – one of each – but first he needed a wife. Roe found himself smirking as he realised that as head of state, there would be no shortage of potential candidates. He would choose a nice North Korean girl, or perhaps one from the south would be a better pick, politically, as it would be the start of further acceptance and integration? Roe didn't know; he'd ask his father. How odd it was, he thought, that the US – the place he had spent forty years of his life living in and over twenty years of his life fighting for was now no longer his home. Roe instantly chastised himself; it had never been his home, it was just a place he had been whilst he prepared for the most important mission of all. And now that mission had started.

On screen his father had now entered a Maybach limousine and the news cameras followed him and his entourage as the convoy glided across the tarmac. Roe checked his watch. They were five minutes late. He hoped they would make this up because a five-minute delay now, at the start of the day, could result in a much longer one at the end, and it was going to be a long day.

A news helicopter, Roe had not considered the Burmese as having such a thing, now took over the coverage of the cars as they exited the airport and took a road south towards central Yangon and the Shwedagon Pagoda. His father had told him it would be viewed by the world as an act of strength for him to go immediately to the pagoda and then the Martyrs' Mausoleum rather than going to his hotel. Roe had to admit he was correct. If his father started acting like a man in his sixties then the world would view him as such, and men in their sixties rarely overthrew rulers in their thirties. Even though his father was fitter and thinner than the fat ruler.

The helicopter peeled away fifteen minutes later as the convoy entered the pagoda complex, out of respect for the most sacred place in the Buddhist religion in Myanmar. Camera crews on the ground now would take over. They had been preassigned their positions by the Myanmar military and knew to be impeccably well behaved. Roe sat forward and switched the channel to CNN. He wanted to hear what the Americans were saying about his father's historic visit. He watched the female anchor, with impossibly blonde hair, pose pointed questions about the visit thus far to a grizzled-looking political correspondent who, Roe now realised, was actually reporting 'live from Myanmar'.

He watched the broadcast, transfixed for the next two hours, until it was time for his father to make his big speech. Roe understood the eyes of the world would now be on his father and he knew the words he was about to deliver would be for ever remembered as would his father and exactly where he was when he voiced them.

His father had his head held high as he crossed the small stage and stood behind a lectern. He had a warm smile on his face. Then he started to address the world, in his perfect, British-accented English: 'There was once a time when my country was not divided. There was a North and a South, but there was also an East and a West. In those times we Koreans were a friendly, welcoming race. We shared with others what we had and expected nothing in return. Wars we did not start yet were forced to participate in, came to our lands. Even though we chose the noblest side, and through our great suffering and perseverance, we prevailed, we still were punished. Nations much larger than our own, but not greater – in any sense of the word – took our nation and with a line drawn on a paper map arbitrarily cut it in two. It was they who created the concepts of North and South, not us – the people of Korea. They conducted a huge-scale social engineering project by providing us with communism in the North and capitalism in the South, and they put my father in charge of his half. My father started out as a good man, a man with ideals and a vision. He wanted Korea to be a place where society enabled mankind to develop, to thrive, and at the time he believed truly that the communist utopia offered this. I am not too proud to admit that

I, for a while, agreed with my father but I have since come to accept the truth in the matter, which is that it was nothing more than my love, my adulation for my father I was expressing by adopting his political and ideological beliefs. My father was not perfect, and he made mistakes.'

Roe was all but open-mouthed as his listened to his father's oration. He was not a man of words; as a soldier and then as a CIA operative he was a man of physical action. He indeed had a lot to learn from his father before he could even contemplate calling himself a statesman.

'I am here today, in Yangon,' his father continued on screen, 'because this is the place that bore the brunt of possibly my father's worst mistake, after his ill-advised invasion of the South.'

Roe saw the camera wobble and a member of the North Korean delegation start to stand. Roe identified the man as the foreign minister. His father waved him back to his seat with several curt orders in Korean.

'I am here today to officially take responsibility on behalf of my late father for sanctioning, and my late brother for planning, the 1983 bombing of the Martyrs' Mausoleum. It was an evil act which took the lives of twenty-one innocent people and injured forty-six others. On behalf of my dead relatives, and the living, and the nation of The Peoples' Democratic Republic of North Korea, I accept responsibility and I apologise.'

His father bowed in the direction of the assembled dignitaries, then in the direction of the monument and then finally in the direction of the amassed national and international press corps.

*

'Bloody hell …' Tate couldn't believe what he had just witnessed.

'Well, that's made him internationally popular,' Parnell noted, 'with the liberals.'

Casey said, 'He's basically just called his father, brother and

309

nephew evil, and these are people who you can't even smile at funny! What he's done is signed his own death warrant.'

Tate sat back in his seat and looked at the ceiling as his mind found the necessary pieces of the puzzle and finally slotted them together. 'That has to be it! His entourage is going to be killed in an attempt on his life, and the North Korean leader will be blamed!'

'What now?' Parnell said.

'I see what you mean.' Casey rubbed his face. 'The only world leader, just crazy enough to kill his own uncle, and its believable because he's done it before, and his family are no stranger to letting off bombs here.'

Tate pointed at the window. 'The hotel Hak Kwang-Il has chosen to stay at is what, a five-minute walk away from here?'

'You think they'll hit them there?' Parnell asked.

'Yeah, I do. Think about it. Why did he choose that hotel? Because it's all but next to the US and the South Korean embassies. If North Korea is seen as hitting a target next door to a US facility, well, it kind of says they'll attack anyone, anywhere.'

'Right. I agree with you, Jack – one hundred per cent. After all, North Korea has form. I'm going to talk to Langley, and I'm not going to stop until they agree with us and take action.'

'Take action?'

'Warn the North Koreans and warn the government of Myanmar.'

'That'll be interesting,' Parnell said.

*

Tate took a call from Plato. 'I got into the hotel's central booking system and created a booking for you and Parnell, using your fake IDs. I managed to backdate it, so it looks like it was made months ago, and I played around with the system a bit so it can be explained away as a system error preventing the booking from appearing.'

'Cool,' Tate said, but had no idea how Plato could manage such a thing.

'Hak Kwang-Il will be staying in the Presidential Suite in a part of the hotel called The Level.'

'The Level?'

'It's the rooftop. His rack rate is £5,000 per night.'

'No wonder he's only staying the one night.'

'In fact, his party has the entire floor, all the rooms.'

'Where are we?'

'Three floors below in peasant class.'

'Nice.'

'He's currently at The Strand, there's increased security activity there too. Jack, are you sure the attack will happen at the Meliá?'

'No, but I think it will. And thanks for the concierge service.' Tate ended the call.

Parnell moved away from the window he'd been glued to for most of the past two hours since Casey had left the room, 'Update?'

'They've got the roof. The delegation is now at The Strand.'

'Where are we?'

'On a lower floor.'

Parnell started to pace the room. He'd been trying to persuade the embassy staff to give him access to the roof. Meanwhile, Tate had been on the phone to Newman. His controller had given him her unofficial 'go' to continue the mission.

'That was not easy, or fun,' Casey said as he re-entered the room, now a full two hours after he had left. He held his finger up to his lips in a 'stay silent' gesture, then motioned for Tate and Parnell to follow him out of the room.

They walked behind Casey along an empty corridor before taking a right and then a flight of steps down and into a room on the left. There was a table and it had two new sets of clothes on it and a pair of hand-luggage-type cases under it.

'Here.' Casey handed Parnell and Tate a burner phone each. 'Just in case you need another screen. They're unsecure.'

'Understood.'

'Plato got you in?'

'Yes.'

'In that case, get dressed, get out and get into that damn hotel.'

'You're not coming, boss?'

'Not with a face like this, Parnell.'

Tate saw Parnell open his mouth to make a wisecrack, but decided not to.

The two former Special Forces soldiers needed no encouragement to change into the clean clothes. Once he and Parnell were dressed, they left the room and turned another corner. There was a door to the outside, it was open.

Parnell quickly walked through it, followed by Tate.

Parnell pointed. 'This way.'

Tate followed as they took a path that wound past the rear of the embassy before it joined University Avenue Road which would take them to the target address, the Meliá Yangon hotel. It was late afternoon now and the diplomatic mission members were not expected to arrive back at their hotel much before midnight. Tate hoped they'd be able to check in without too many issues.

Chapter 26

Yangon River

Roe knew that he had to be on top of his game for what was to come. With the crew, who were loyal to his father's money, watching over him, Roe had retreated to his cabin and slept. He had no sooner got out of his bunk than his encrypted sat phone started to buzz. It was his father; he was the only person who had the number.

'Are you ready, my son?' Hak Kwang-Il's voice was low, and Roe could hear music in the background.

'Yes, Father.'

'That is good. I am at The Strand Hotel. I shall call you again when I am in my room at the Meliá.'

Roe felt like a proud child. 'I saw your speech.'

'What did you think?'

'Your words were those of a true leader. I have so much to learn from you.'

'I will be honoured to teach you, my son.'

'Father.' Roe realised his voice was unusually weak and he swallowed. 'What if the attack goes wrong? What if you are injured or worse?'

'Kwang, you are a highly experienced operative and I trust you to carry out the attack with perfection.'

'What happens if the technology fails?'

'White Suit will not fail, Kwang. Not in this form. Await my call, and my go signal. I estimate this will be within the next three hours. Understood?'

'Yes, Father.'

*

As they rounded the corner and neared the hotel, Tate and Parnell watched more soldiers arrive. A decision had been made somewhere to increase security and no one, apart from existing hotel guests, were being let in. The reinforcements eyed the pair of Westerners suspiciously as they walked up the short drive.

Each of the pair was guided through a full body scanner, which had seemingly only that morning been installed, then physically patted down and 'wanded' before being allowed to approach the hotel desk. The reception staff were friendly, but concerned that the booking had suddenly appeared. An email from Plato, explaining the situation and masquerading as the IT administrator from their regional head office and written helpfully in both English and Burmese, soon smoothed things over. Tate scanned the lobby before they entered the lift and noticed several eyes looking in his direction. A set belonged to a very obvious Russian and the others to two equally as obtrusive Chinese.

Their rooms were minimalist, next to each other, and had views of the Inya Lake. Parnell joined Tate in his room and together they ran through the standard operative procedure of searching for any listening devices. It was perhaps overkill, but had been ingrained into both men by their respective agencies. As expected, they found none.

Tate called up Plato, who was already in the hotel's CCTV system.

'OK, so I'm going to send my feed onto both of the phones Vince gave you. The Wi-Fi is not encrypted, but I can't do anything about that from here, but the program is.' Both Tate and Parnell's burner phones now had a grid of images on them. Each image was a hotel camera. Plato explained how to cycle through the cameras. 'It's a modified commercial program so it is limited, but foolproof.'

'That means we can use it,' Parnell said.

'I'm continuing to monitor the CIA satellite as well as the hotel cameras. The North Korean party is still at The Strand, but then it's still early.'

'The guy's knocking on seventy, I don't imagine he'll partying with the expats,' Parnell joked.

'Ah,' Plato replied, 'but the current leader of Myanmar is, from what I've managed to dig up, a party animal. He's at The Strand and may well come back to the Meliá.'

Tate frowned. It was a possibility he hadn't thought of and now it seemed to justify the extra military personnel stationed around the hotel. Securing a visiting foreign dignitary was one thing, but protecting your own leader was another.

'That'll be fun.' Tate ended the call.

Parnell sighed. 'I've gotta say, Jack, I've no idea how anyone can take out even the trash in this place. You've got Hak Senior accompanied by a phalanx of Hak Junior's bodyguards, and you can bet they'll take bullets for him and the others. Then you've got, what, thirty members of the Myanmar Army outside guarding the perimeter, plus however many more will appear if the Commander-in-Chief of Defence Services comes back here.'

'Yep.' Tate blew out his cheeks. 'We're powerless. We can't search the hotel, we can't sweep for IEDs, we can't search the staff or guests. All we can do is watch and react.'

Parnell had an amused expression on his face. 'Of course you do understand that if anything happens with us inside the hotel, we become the number one suspects. Being white.'

The thought had crossed Tate's mind. 'How would you attack this place?'

'If I couldn't get inside to hit my target, I'd do it from the outside.'

'So we're looking at, what, a long-range shot from across the lake?'

'Or on it, but that would be a much harder one to take.'

Tate shook his head. 'The angles are all wrong.'

'Not from another rooftop.'

'The nearest one is the South Korean Embassy.'

Parnell rubbed his face with his hand. 'No. That's just wrong. So, he's on the top floor, right?'

'Right.'

'So, I'd come from above. Fast rope down – in and out – in minutes.'

'Like Bin Laden?'

Parnell winked. 'I wasn't on that raid.'

'Yeah, that was the SEALs.'

'Yeah, but come on! North Korea is really going to steal an airframe, or pay someone to and then wait until they're somehow told that their targets are safely tucked up in bed? I mean this place is a military state. There's half an army outside and the other half is nearby. Whatever tries to get near will be shot out of the sky.'

'White Suit.' Tate got to his feet. 'They'll be using White Suit.'

'OK, but on what? That would mean some type of production facility, and then they'd have to get that White Suit-coated airframe into the country. There's no way any North Korean military jet is leaving North Korean airspace.'

'What about the China Air 747 they came in on?'

'Whoa, Jack, they're gonna crash a Chinese state-owned airliner into a hotel? I don't think so.'

Tate smiled thinly. 'No, that would be just mad.'

'Completely cray cray.'

'So, what does that leave us with?'

'Drop a bomb; he's on the top floor.' A thin smile spread across Parnell's face. 'It has to be a drone.'

In that instant, Tate knew Parnell was right. A drone could be smuggled into the country and assembled, or it could hover at a standoff distance before swooping in either hugging the ground below radar cover or attacking from on high and relying on its small size for cover. 'There were drones in the shipment we intercepted.'

'That was a diversion, Jack.'

'But that doesn't mean Hak Kwang-Il didn't have more. He wants the world to believe North Korea has been illegally importing drones, to make a drone attack credible.' Tate called Plato and put the call on speaker. The volume was low enough that no one outside of the room would be able to eavesdrop. 'Neill, we think they are going to use a drone. Can you start scanning for anything that could remotely look like one?'

'A drone? Sure. Erm, OK.' There was a short pause. 'Well, there's nothing I can see but I'll tell my algorithm to keep looking.'

Parnell held out his hand. 'I need to call Vince.'

Tate handed him his phone, then went back to looking at the footage on his burner phone whilst Parnell explained the conclusion they'd reached.

Several minutes later, Parnell handed him back his phone. 'Casey agrees. I mean, it's the only option that makes sense. He's trying to see if he can get something on the roof that would intercept a drone.'

'Like what, a surface to air missile?'

'Yeah.'

'I thought it was an urban myth that all US embassies have a couple of SAMs on their roofs for luck?'

'It is, mostly.' Parnell shrugged. 'But this place is kinda edgy, you know?'

'I can't see the government letting diplomats launch surface to air missiles.'

'Nor can I, but you know Casey.'

'There's one issue.'

'With a SAM?'

'No, with the drone strike idea.' Tate sighed.

'Which is?'

'Hak Kwang-Il can't be with his minders and "aides" when the attack happens? How is he going to get away?'

'That, Tate, I do not know.'

*

Roe was on deck. The daylight had gone, and the river had turned into a wide ribbon of black. Around him the twinkling lights of the city replaced the shabby lines of the decaying waterfront buildings. For a former capital city, he hadn't been impressed. He thought Yangon was a dump. Roe was moored with the two other ships just off Monkey Point, to the north and south the Yangon River flowed and to his west was the Bago River. A breeze was blowing, but it was nothing to be concerned about, certainly not violent enough for any recalibrations to be necessary. He heard laughter and chat from the crew of the two other ships as they crouched together, shared cigarettes and he imagined stories. Roe had never really felt any camaraderie when he'd been enlisted. He had always been the Korean kid, who was never quite one of the guys and who was routinely stared at and questioned by civilians as to his real nationality. He had been an outsider in what was allegedly the best country on earth. He knew it was a crock of shit. And now he no longer cared about the failings of his ex-brothers and their overinflated country. But despite all of this, he still felt alone, isolated, a man out of place. Ah, he was no good with words, he couldn't explain how he was and how he felt, but that didn't matter now.

Roe brushed down the sleeve of the uniform jacket he

now wore, the uniform he had stripped from the officer he had killed. He felt no remorse for such a fool who demanded respect when he'd earnt none. The dead man had been, he realised, just like his cousin – the current leader of North Korea. The man had done nothing to earn his respect, or his position. He had been schooled overseas in Switzerland yet was not even fluent in French or German, let alone English which when pushed, in private according to Hak Kwang-Il, he spoke hesitantly and with a whiny, nasal accent. Roe felt nothing for the man even though he was the closest thing on this earth he had to a brother.

Roe felt an unexpected chill, it wasn't the temperature, it was nerves, and it was unexpected, but Roe smiled in the twilight, willing those nerves to become energy, fuel to propel him forwards. He took a deep lungful of air and exhaled. He repeated this several times and he felt refreshed, revived. There was a vibrating in his pocket. Quizzically, Roe retrieved his phone and answered it.

'We are leaving The Strand now. This is earlier than anticipated due to both the vice-chairman of the Workers' Party, and our foreign minister informing me they are tired. They are younger than I, Kwang. I believe they are plotting something. Please be ready to initiate the operation immediately on my say-so. I shall call you once I am in place.'

'Yes, Father.'

The line went dead. Roe placed the sat phone back into his uniform trouser pocket and walked to the men inside the bridge. It was time to tell the captains to prepare their vessels, and this meant removing the covers from the drones and making final flight preparations.

The breeze abruptly dropped. It was perfect flying weather.

*

'Jack, the North Korean delegation has left The Strand. The roads are being closed to allow them to pass, but they are being led by the Myanmar commander-in-chief's armoured convoy!' There was a hint of panic in Plato's voice.

Tate shook his head. 'Why are they still coming here after our warning?'

'No idea, but I can see their lights. They are definitely heading your way.'

'I'm keeping this line open.'

'Understood,' Plato confirmed.

Tate turned to Parnell. 'Get Casey on the line. Tell him he has to do something!'

Parnell had his phone halfway to his ear. 'On it.'

Tate moved to the window and looked out. Past the reflection of their room, he could see nothing but an inky blackness and twinkling lights. The room had no balcony; none of the rooms did except those which had been nabbed by Hak Kwang-Il's party.

'I know, Vince, I know. But, man, I'm telling you their commander-in-chief is walking into a goddam trap!'

Tate looked at Parnell, who shook his head.

'Hell, no! Oh, an order, is it? Well, shit the bed, Vince.' Parnell held his phone up, as though he was going to throw it before he changed his mind.

'Tell me?'

'The CIA and MI6 have both reached out to representatives of the Myanmar government with their fears and have been told to stay out of it!'

Tate's eyes went wide. 'What about the North Koreans?'

'We can't get through to them.'

'Christ.'

'What?'

'He has to be in on it; the commander-in-chief of Myanmar has to be in on it!'

'What?'

'Why on earth would he ignore the threat? Why have himself driven to the exact same location where the attack is going to take place?'

'To look like a hero when he survives it?' Parnell said.

'That has to be it, it cements him as a true leader.'

'Jack, we need to get out, and we need to get out right now!'

Tate saw movement on the cameras. 'We've got company. Inbound Tatmadaw.'

'Now, Tate, we get the hell out now.' Parnell killed the lights.

As Tate watched, he saw the lift doors on their floor open, four armed men in military fatigues exited. They hustled past the camera and Tate knew they were coming for them.

'We need to take them out, no choice, Jack.'

'Agreed.' Tate flicked the light on in the large bathroom, then he and Parnell moved to the left of the door to the room and waited.

They heard feet approach, muffled by the thick carpet of the landing, but still sounding heavier than a guest. A fist banged on the door; an order was shouted in Burmese. It was repeated, the fist harder this time and the words louder. It happened for a third time and then the room key was used.

The door was flung open and two soldiers rushed in, rifles up, weapons that were too long to be used effectively in close-quarter battle. They immediately turned into the bathroom as the second two entered.

Tate and Parnell slammed the door on the last man, knocking him sideways and trapping him against the wall. He yelped and dropped his rifle. Tate turned and booted him in the groin as Parnell sprang at the man in front of him, the third man. Left hand grabbing the soldier's rifle whilst his right fist slammed into the man's face. The soldier went down. Neither of the two soldiers had sidearms, nor did the two who were in the bathroom, who were turning to face Tate and Parnell.

As one, Tate and Parnell charged them. Like a well-rehearsed tag team, they crashed into a man each. Both soldiers folded as they were hit and driven backwards. On Tate's right, Parnell slammed his soldier into the toilet, helmeted head smashing the white designer porcelain. Tate's own target toppled backwards into the deep marble bath. His rifle lay between the pair and Tate, using both his overwhelming strength and momentum, crushed the weapon into the soldier's throat. Tate was seeing red, there was no stopping him. The man had to die, and he had to die quickly, and that was all there was to it. His eyes saw a knife on the man's belt, his thin fingers pulling it out of the sheaf. Tate let go of the rifle and snatched the knife away, reversed the blade and stabbed it up into the man's throat and sawed left and right. He pushed away and let the man hold his neck in what Tate knew was a forlorn hope of living.

Parnell's hands were covered in blood and there was a puddle of pink water on the floor. His soldier was already dead. Tate turned and, without pausing, dropped his left knee onto the side of the next soldier's head, the one Parnell had punched, and drove the blade into the soft area behind his ear and into his brain. The final soldier was in the corner by the door, his knees up and hands splayed out in front of him, his head was shaking, and he was repeatedly saying something in Burmese. Tate kicked him in the head, slamming his head against the wall, and at the least knocking him out. He pulled the man away from the door and shut it.

Parnell picked up the nearest rifle. 'Chinese Norinco CQ, again.'

Tate didn't care, they'd just killed four more men who'd they never met. He moved to the table, picked up the burner phone and studied the screen. He saw no more movement inside, but then he saw vehicles arriving outside the hotel. 'They're here.'

Parnell was back in the bathroom, washing his hands and rinsing his face.

'Let's go.'

'Go where, Bro?'

'Up.'

Parnell shook his head. 'Who Dares Wins?'

'Yep.'

*

The small television in the wheelhouse was showing CNN and as Roe watched he saw Senior General Min Win Sein, the commander-in-chief of the Myanmar military, arrive at the hotel. A red carpet had now been laid and he took his time to walk up it towards the hotel entrance. He was followed by a crowd of other military men, all of whom looked younger. Then Roe saw his father's convoy arrive. First the security detail in their dark suits made a perimeter and then Hak Kwang-Il himself exited the armoured Maybach. He rose steadily and seemed to glide along the carpet. He turned and waved at the cameras. Roe knew his father was waving at the world, but he also knew he was waving at him. He watched until his father disappeared inside before he exited the wheelhouse and walked towards the container concealing the ground control station for the two drones. He shouted final commands at the men who had now removed the covers from the drones and prepared the area for take-off. Even though they were miniature planes, Roe had to admit that they were impressive. The dull-dark coating covering the once-white outer skin of the fuselage and wings made them look, in his opinion, like winged death. Hanging under the wings and glowing in the ambient light were the MAM-C and MAM-L laser-guided smart munitions which, whilst taking out their intended targets, would ensure that collateral damage was kept just this side of acceptable.

Roe nodded at the twin drones, as if to wish them luck, then opened the container door and took his seat at the controls. He had already powered the unit and the drones up, and all that he needed to do now was to press a button and they would race into the air and follow the pre-programmed course to the Meliá hotel. The flight time would be less than five minutes, and they would be impossible to stop.

*

With a Chinese rifle in one hand and a knife in the other, Tate and Parnell took the stairs up until they reached the top. The door was alarmed; Tate booted it with his foot and it flew open. They didn't hear any alarm, but that did not mean that there wasn't one ringing in a room somewhere. They moved through the door into the hot, humid night and found themselves on the roof, but the wrong one. Immediately to their right, the hotel carried on up for three more levels. And at the very top was the floor the North Koreans had.

'We'll climb.' Parnell moved to the wall and slung the rifle diagonally across his back. 'C'mon.'

Tate followed and pulled himself up onto the concrete ledge which was the start of the floor up. The pair hauled and grunted upwards, passing a window. Tate saw a guest wearing nothing but a red baseball cap watching a horse race on a large plasma screen. He almost fell as a laugh threatened to burst out of his chest but managed to carry on. There was a vibrating in Tate's pocket, but he didn't have a hand spare to retrieve his phone. They pulled themselves up the last floor and then paused just below the top of the ledge. Tate was wet with sweat; it was running into his eyes, but he couldn't move his hands to wipe it away. They were twenty-two floors up, had only climbed three, but three floors was still too far to fall.

With a grunt, Parnell pulled himself up and fell over the ledge. After several seemingly endless seconds his hands reached down, and Tate gladly took them. They were on a balcony and immediately in front of them was a private infinity pool, past this and to the left was a table and dining chairs for eight people and past this was the glass-fronted entrance to the Presidential Suite.

324

It was in darkness, so they advanced. They reached the wall, the only part that was concrete and used to separate the two glass-fronted areas, and what they could see was a large dining area on one side and a lounge area on the other.

'Phone,' Parnell said and slipped his hand into his pocket. He pulled out his burner. 'What?'

Tate remembered the sat phone had vibrated and looked at the screen. He moved a pace away from Parnell and returned the call. 'Yes?'

'Jack, we've found the drones!'

Tate felt queasy. 'Where, how many?'

'Two, on two ships on the river. Jack, this is happening!'

'Tell Pamela!'

'I have!'

The lights flicked on in the room in front of them. Parnell and Tate retreated behind the concrete partition, pocketing their phones. Tate went low and chanced a glance around the edge. The entire North Korean diplomatic delegation was in the dining room. Two of the three aides looked angry, and the other just looked drunk. Hak Kwang-Il was standing at the head of the table, gesticulating with his arms. His voice was carrying through the glass, his tone controlled but firm. As Tate watched, four of the North Korean security detail came in and stood behind Hak Kwang-Il, blocking the entrance to the room. Tate now heard another voice, and this was angry, then a second joined in. The two aides were berating him, probably passing on a message from their president that his behaviour was unacceptable. Hak Kwang-Il shook his head and pointed into the other part of the suite. The men continued to shout, now he pointed at his groin and started to walk past them.

'He's in the lounge area.' Parnell, who Tate saw had been peering around the other side of the wall, stated. 'Looks like he's gone into the bathroom.'

Tate remembered the bath in his own room. It had been large, and it had been sturdy and made of impossibly thick marble. If his own had been that impressive then the one in the Presidential Suite must be a monster.

*

Roe wiped the sweat from his brow; this was taking much longer than he had expected. He checked his watch; his father had been in the hotel for almost twenty minutes.

His finger hovered over the Call button, but then it rang.

Roe put it to his ear.

It was his father. 'Go!'

'Yes, Father!' Roe pressed the 'Go' button.

'Hak Kwang-Chul, please remember, I have always loved you, my son.'

Roe blinked; his eyes were moist. Was his father saying goodbye? Impossible. Roe had to focus on the drones now. There was a roaring, not much louder than that of a finely tuned motorbike and first one then the second modified drone took off from their improvised runways.

Via the onboard cameras in their noses, Roe could see their progress. He adjusted the speed so the drones would be even quieter as they skimmed north, at tree height, keeping to the contour of the Yangon River.

*

'Jack! Jack!' Plato's voice was hysterical. 'The drones are in the air! They're in the air!'

'What's their ETA?'

'Less than five … no, four minutes!'

Tate stuffed the phone away and stood up. There was no time for words, no time for explanations. He looked at Parnell and simply said, 'Follow me!'

Assault rifle up, Tate kicked the outside door to the Presidential Suite. It buckled. He kicked it again and it opened. Tate barrelled into the dining room, firing a burst of rounds into the ceiling above the startled diplomats. 'Bomb! Bomb! Bomb!'

'Go!' Parnell joined him and fired a second burst. 'Out! Out! Out!'

The three diplomats threw up their hands, as did two of the security detail, but the other two reached for their sidearms. Tate drilled a line of rounds into the flooring at their feet. Their hands stopped moving. Tate shouted again, this was not working, 'Get out now! Bomb! Get out!'

One of the security detail spoke in English. 'What is happening?'

Tate thought of the first words to come into his head, words that would explain everything the quickest. 'Drone strike!'

The man translated this into Korean and the others got the message.

Parnell moved past, grabbing one of the diplomats. He opened the front door and shoved him through it. Tate fired another burst at their feet as encouragement. He didn't care if the security detail kept their guns, he didn't care who they were, all he knew was that in three minutes they'd all be vapourised if they didn't get off that floor.

Tate herded them forwards and Parnell shoved them out of the room. The first diplomat was already at the stairs leading down. Tate yelled, 'Go!'

He knew he perhaps had less than two minutes left but something inside him compelled him not to leave. Tate turned, dropped his rifle, and ran back across the room; he had to find Hak Kwang-Il. His feet skidded across the white marble tiles as he turned into the lounge and then sprinted for the bedroom. The door was ajar, and he barged his way in. Desperately, he looked around like a wild thing, searching for the man who had masterminded this entire attack. He was nowhere to be seen, then Tate saw a shadow move under a door, the door to the bathroom. He shouldered the door. It moved an inch then stopped.

'Gu! We need to move it!'

'No!' a voice shouted back.

Tate backed up several paces, then barged the door with all his might. It gave way and he crashed into the bathroom. It was a dazzling study of white marble and gold fittings. Directly in front of him, across the space and covering the bottom of the side wall was something that Tate didn't understand. It looked like a thick, industrial tarpaulin but it was white, and the vivid vanity lighting of the bathroom made it sparkle, as though it was constructed of crystals.

'Time's up!' Hak Kwang-Il shouted from below the cover, his voice muffled.

And then Tate instantly knew what the cover was although he could not explain it.

The timer in his head was counting down. It was on seconds now, perhaps the last ten. Like a NASA rocket launch. However, this would herald a missile falling and not a rocket thundering skywards.

Tate darted towards the white cover and, pulling it back, saw what beneath the lining of a second cover had to be the world's largest marble bath.

'TATE!'

A fist flailed up at him, slamming into his cheek. It took him by surprise and he rocked back, almost losing his balance. Tate grabbed at the bath and pulled himself in, landing on top of the son of the founder of North Korea, the uncle of the current president, Hak Kwang-Il. Tate grabbed the thick white cover, dragged it down and closed the gap, sealing them inside.

And then the world seemed to end.

There was a thunderous rumble, the lights went off and he felt himself being violently pushed towards the wall as though the entire world had suddenly tilted. The air was forced out of his lungs before he was suddenly righted again. He gasped and managed to take a breath. There were more impacts now, seemingly further away – presumably munitions falling on the other rooms on the floor.

Tate lay on his back, looking up at the cover above him; it was bowing inwards.

By his side Hak Kwang-Il said excitedly, 'It works, Tate, it works!'

Tate sat up and pushed the covers away. Immediately, clouds of pungent, cloying smoke and dust attacked his eyes, his nose and, worst of all, his lungs. He pulled himself out of the bath as the side of it broke away. Tate dropped to his hands and knees on the shattered, blackened tiles and started to cough.

Moonlight, coming in through a hole in the wall that wasn't meant to be there, illuminated the scene. Tate clambered to his feet and grabbed the arms of the older Korean. 'Get up, Gu! We have to move it!'

Hak Kwang-Il didn't struggle, but let Tate pull him upright. He started to cough, but seemed otherwise unharmed. He pointed with his left hand. 'There's another stairwell … a private one … my escape route …'

They left the bathroom to see that it was the only part of the Presidential Suite that still had any of its roof remaining. There was a fire to his right where the dining room had been, and it was being whipped into an inferno by the billowing air rushing in through the gaps left by the glass walls that were no longer there.

'Left … left!' Gu urged.

Tate let the Korean take the lead as he hobbled over broken chunks of concrete, reinforced glass and shattered furniture towards a door which was hanging by a sole hinge. They entered the stairwell; these were not the concrete steps of an emergency escape route but the opulent marble of private access. Hak slipped forward, his hand reaching for the railings, Tate grabbed him and prevented him from falling. They continued down, turning a corner and losing the light from the moonlight from the open door above and having to feel their way. They came to a door. Gu calmly pressed down on the long, square security handle and it opened. Fresh air flooded in, as did the noise of sirens. Tate realised he was on the same level that he and Parnell had climbed from mere minutes before. He bent forwards and spat out a gob of grey phlegm before he drank in the wonderfully, fresh, yet humid Yangon night air.

There were voices now on the flat roof around them as a group of Myanmar soldiers, members of the Tatmadaw, appeared from a door on the far side. Weapons up, they advanced, aiming at Tate. He shook his head and raised his hands above his head. Two soldiers took Hak Kwang-Il under the arms and hustled him away across the roof to the exit, whilst the others kept him in their sights. The uniformed men gradually backed away then double-timed it after the rest of their party. Tate fell to his haunches and let his back rest against the wall. He knew it was unsafe, but he just had to rest and take stock. He took a minute, then pushed back up to his feet. Moments later, a piece of falling masonry landed where he had been sitting.

Coughing and spitting out the last of the dust and smoke, Tate found the exit the soldiers had spirited Gu through and continued to descend. It was dark, but his feet found their way and, minutes later, he burst into the hotel's main foyer.

Shocked and hysterical guests were pouring past. He joined them and let himself be pushed out of the hotel by the swell of the exiting humanity and carried out onto the street. He searched the faces and saw the North Korean diplomats to the side of the main entrance. One was on his feet and another was being helped up off the ground by the English-speaking member of the security detail, his once-black suit now a cloudy grey. The third diplomat was sitting, leaning against the wall and holding his head.

'Tate!' a voice shouted. Parnell.

Tate turned, seeing the American was already across the road.

'Lake,' Parnell said. 'Get to the lake path.'

Shakily, Tate jogged across the road, past the emergency vehicles that were blocking it.

Parnell's hair was grey with dust, as was his face, but he was smiling. 'What are you, man, indestructible?'

'Hak Kwang-Il is alive ... White Suit worked ... using it as a shield!'

'What?'

The pair now slipped down the bank, towards the path. At the bottom, Tate felt in his pocket for his sat phone. It was there, he pulled it out, but saw that the screen was smashed.

'Same here.' Parnell held up his burner.

'Embassy,' Tate said, between coughs. 'Your embassy!'

They hurried at a fast stumble along the lake path as best they could, each step taking them further away from the hotel and the scene of the attack. Tate felt his lungs continuing to clear and his senses returning. By the time they had rounded the corner, they had broken into a jog.

A pair of military vehicles flashed past them on the road, then a third stopped. Two soldiers got out and shouted at them.

Tate pointed back at the hotel. 'Bomb go bang!'

Parnell pointed in the direction of the US Embassy. 'American Embassy!'

The soldiers didn't move for a moment, then got back in their Chinese knock-off Willys Jeep and drove off. The pair of intelligence operatives had no choice now but to run by the side of the road as the path ended. The passing vehicles paid them no attention until one flashed its lights and slammed to a halt in front of them.

The battered face of Casey appeared from the front passenger window of the white Land Cruiser. 'Get in!'

Tate followed Parnell into the back. Tate saw their driver was the embassy staffer who had questioned him earlier. He looked sheepish. The Toyota surged forward with tyres squealing.

'There's some water and electrolytes in my seat pocket. Get them inside you.' Casey turned. 'Now, tell me what the hell happened?'

'Tate saved the Koreans.'

'We saved the Koreans, Parnell herded them out of their room.'

'What about Hak Kwang-Il – Gu Joon?'

'He's alive.'

'He got out?'

'I got him out, but he was grabbed by the Tatmadaw.'

'Crap! Now listen to this, the drones were launched from two ships on the river to the south of the city. They are moving with a third ship. We think the third barge housed the ground control station.'

Parnell asked: 'What does Langley say?'

'Pure bullcrap. They say they're tracking the ships and that we should let them do it. We have no assets in the area, so they want to pick them up when they make dock.'

'No.'

'Exactly, Parnell. Are you two up for hitting it and taking in whoever was manning it?'

Tate coughed, then said, 'The hotel bar's closed, so why not.'

Chapter 27

Yangon River, Myanmar

The water had become choppier as the ship moved further south. Roe had no illusions; he had seen the devastation the two drones had wrought before he had ordered them to fly out to sea, where at a pre-set time they would self-destruct. He did not understand how his father could have survived the attack, but he was also aware of the faith that the old man had put into the technology of White Suit. His father's convictions were strong enough that he had taken years to plan and plot his revenge and this added to the sense Roe had that he must still be alive, he had to be.

Roe checked his watch and his heading. He had decided to captain the ship himself and the Tatmadaw officer uniform he now wore meant that he was far less likely to be approached or questioned by the authorities and, if he was, a single phone call would sort it out.

It was, in nautical terms, a short run to the sea, and from there they would make for international waters and continue south to Malaysia and, finally, Singapore. Roe really cared not if the men around him were eventually caught. Very little weight would be put on the word of a deckhand or a sailor when he was pitted against a world leader. Roe still could not get his head around the idea that he eventually was to become exactly that, a world leader. He had once seen a documentary about a guy from Idaho who'd met a woman in a club and, after a whirlwind romance, he'd married her to find that he was now the sultan or king or something of some place he didn't remember, but this was his birthright and, unlike the lucky schmuck from Idaho, he'd earnt it.

*

'Jack, you're alive!' Plato sounded relieved.

'If I'm not, you'd better record this call for Channel 4's *Most Haunted*.'

'But how?'

'White Suit.'

'It works?'

'Listen, this is Casey's phone, it's on speaker. I'm with him and Parnell, heading south. What can you tell me about the vessels?'

'There are three in total. Two launched drones. The feed from the satellite is showing that we have potentially five crew members on each of the vessels which housed the drones and a further six on the other.'

'That's sixteen bad hombres,' Parnell chuckled. 'Piece of cake.'

'Yeah, but how many are shooters and how many are just sailors?' Tate added.

Casey said, 'Let me know if there are any changes, or updates on Hak Kwang-Il.'

'Will do.'

Tate handed the phone back to Casey, who addressed their driver, 'We need to speed up, son. The quicker we can get to that boat, the quicker we can chase 'em down.'

'What type of boat is it, Vince?' Tate asked.

'It's a fast one.'

Ten minutes later, the Land Cruiser came to stop at the Botahtaung Harbour. Casey wasted no time in jumping out. 'There's two full tactical packs plus extra body armour in the trunk. And a pair of Plumett AL-52 compressed air launchers. See, I got the toys for the boys.'

As the Land Cruiser pulled away, Parnell and Tate carried the equipment down to the water. There were an assortment of dilapidated-looking boats bobbing on the fast-flowing river. Casey pointed at a battered red powerboat. 'Don't let looks deceive you. I've been promised she's a mover.'

They boarded the boat. Casey pulled a key from his shirt pocket, pressed it into the ignition and at the first try the boat came to life.

Tate ignored the body armour; it wouldn't help him float if he fell in the drink. He attached a Glock in a leg holster to his right thigh.

'Here.' Parnell handed him a short-stock HK 416.

'Thanks.'

'No, that's fine, don't you boys worry about me,' Casey called back. 'I'm just the river-boat captain.'

'I was going to say, Don Johnson,' Parnell quipped and placed another HK 416 by his side.

They powered along the increasingly choppy river for another twenty minutes, without seeing much water traffic but ever wary that if the military stopped them, they'd be taken in.

Casey tapped the screen of his phone and said, over his shoulder, 'We're closing the gap. They've now got about five kilometres on us.'

'So, what's the plan?'

'We get near them, you two take them out.'

'Oh, it's as easy as that?'

'For you and Parnell, Jack, I hope it bloody is.'

As the water pounded the hull of the boat even harder, Tate started to think about the events of that evening. It was blatantly clear that their assumption had been correct, Hak Kwang-Il had planned the drone attack to assassinate the men who had been with him and put the blame on a failed plot against himself. But then what? How did he take over North Korea? Had he expected the world to rally around him? For that he would surely need Chinese intervention. Tate pushed this all from his mind. He had to focus on the here and now.

'I can see 'em!' Casey shouted. 'There, all three, just chugging along in the moonlight, all romantic like.'

Tate rose to his feet.

Casey pointed. 'See the middle one? Its deck's not flat.'

'That's the control ship. That's where our man will be.'

Casey turned to Tate. 'You thinking that's Roe Kwang?'

'Who else would Gu trust?'

'I hope you're right; I mean, it would make life simpler for us.'

*

Roe sipped from his can of Coke. It was warm and tasted foul, but it was better than the coffee the real captain had offered him earlier, and he needed the caffeine. He checked his bearings. If they continued on their current course and speed, they would be out of the river and back into the Gulf of Martaban within the next two hours, and by the time the sun came up they would be in the Andaman Sea. His father's agreement with Min Win Sein, the commander-in-chief of Myanmar, guaranteed that they would not be stopped by any Burmese naval vessels, and he doubted the Malays would pay them any attention.

Roe blinked away the tiredness. It had been agreed with his father that neither one should attempt to contact the other until a set time had passed, and this set time was just enough for Roe to make his way to the safety of Singapore, where he would meet the last man who shared his face and then take his identity.

Roe heard voices from behind, agitated voices, and then the

all-too-familiar retort of gunfire. The captain opened the door to the wheelhouse. 'Sir, we are being pursued by a speedboat!'

'Take over,' Roe said.

Roe spun around, instantly his fatigue forgotten. He drew his sidearm from a holster and walked onto the deck. His command vessel was in the middle of the three-ship flotilla and was slightly ahead of the other two ships. Logically, if he was being chased it would be by the authorities, but the agreement was in place. His father had both paid the military government a hefty fee and also apologised for a historical attack on their country. No, this could not be the Navy, nor the police and, besides, there had been no warning, either in the form of being hailed or shots across the bow. This had to be someone else, but who? Pirates, no, they were all in Africa. Logic also dictated that whoever was coming after them would want to approach the wheelhouse and take control of the vessel.

So, he would wait. If whoever it was managed to board his boat and shoot his men, he didn't care. If his men were pathetic enough to let themselves get shot, then they were no good to him. His men had been trained, however, and knew how to repel any attack.

*

The speedboat gradually gained on the three ships, which were barely visible as black blocks on a grey sea until they weren't. Two night-sun floodlights abruptly switched on, illuminating the speedboat as though it was daylight. Casey squinted and tried to jink to port to escape the light, but they just followed him.

'This is not good,' Casey observed.

'There ain't no point in trying to hide,' Parnell said. He trained his HK on the light nearest to them and opened fire. Without tracer, and accounting for the hammering of the waves on the speedboat's hull, it was difficult even for him to get a direct hit, but his second burst did and the night-sun popped into darkness.

Tate raised his rifle at the second lamp when a plume of flames flared from the other barge. There was only one explanation for it: 'RPG!'

The grenade rocketed across their bow and splashed harmlessly into the water on their port side, but Tate knew that the next shot may not miss.

'Hang on!' Casey shouted needlessly as he pushed the speedboat's power to maximum. The nose of the boat raised, and all three men took an involuntary step backwards. The speedboat now powered alongside the stern of the barge.

Tate swung his HK back over his shoulder and picked up one of the Plumett AL-52s. It looked like an M16, but had a compressed cannister in place of a barrel which launched a grappling hook. Parnell now held the second one. Tate knew they each had only one shot at this. He aimed the hook high above the gunwales of the barge and fired. The launcher pushed back into his shoulder and then became light as the hook was propelled skywards.

But Tate was too late; a second flare heralded a second incoming grenade. Casey swung the boat to starboard and directly at the back of the nearest barge, but the RPG struck the stern of the speedboat. Tate, still holding on to the launcher, was jerked out of the vessel as his Kevlar line became taut. He slammed into the dark water and the air was forced out of his lungs. A voice inside his head told him to 'relax and let go'. If he did that he would live, but he would also lose Roe. Tate held on and, some seconds later, his head broke the surface of the water. He spat the salty water from his mouth and blinked his vision back into focus. The barge was moving much slower than the speedboat had been, but it was still dragging him through the rough water with enough force to make his muscles complain. Tate let himself be dragged for what seemed like minutes whilst he recovered his breath and his bearings. He couldn't see the speedboat, couldn't see anything apart from the dark hull of the barge that was pulling him, a few faint lights of the distant shore and now the dazzling stars above him which had seemingly, suddenly stepped out from behind the clouds. His ears picked up voices shouting from the barge in a language he didn't understand. Tate knew the mini-armada was heading out to sea, and he knew that he had to get out of the water before that happened if he had any chance of surviving, or stopping Roe from making good his escape.

Tensing his arms, Tate started to pull himself along the Kevlar line. He felt it dig into his hands, yet he had no choice but to ignore the scraping of his skin and continue on. The pressure on his hands and shoulders increased as he started to rise out of the water. He was very close to the hull of the barge now and if it changed course, he was in danger of being slammed against its unforgiving steel construction or being sucked under into its props. He was now less than a metre from the hull, the most critical time of all. Using his core strength, and grimacing, Tate managed to swing his legs up so that his feet were now flat against the sturdy steel. The water tugged at him as he rose completely out of it and the strap of his HK dug into his neck and right armpit. He felt his legs and arms start to shake, and the voice inside his head again told him to let go and give up and live, but Tate was stubborn and continued to pull himself, one step at a time, higher up the side of the barge. His hands were numb with pain, shoulders red-hot with exertion but still he climbed, trying to take some of his weight with his legs and looking for any foothold, however small it may be – an exposed rivet or a dent in the hull. Finally he was within reach of the gunwale. He should wait, he should listen, but he had no choice, it was either grab the gunwale or plummet back into the sea. Tate grabbed the curved, cold metal with his right hand, then repeated the same with his left and, using the last of his strength, hauled himself up and over. He fell into the deep shadows, exhausted, and unable to move.

*

'Sir!' The sailor ran at him.

Roe held up his right hand in a 'stop' motion. 'What?'

'It was a speedboat, with three Westerners on board. We struck it with a RPG.'

'Westerners?'

'They were large and white-skinned.'

Roe nodded, it had to be the CIA, he could think of no one else, but if there was a boat after him that would mean there also had to be a satellite or, his heart started to race, a drone. 'What about the men?'

'They didn't make it off the boat.'

'Tell the captain of each vessel to remain vigilant.'

'Yes, sir.' The sailor scurried away.

Roe looked skyward, as if trying to spot the glinting of the moonlight on the skin of the drone he suspected was somewhere above him. His escape was falling apart around him. The three ships were large and cumbersome vessels, and couldn't outrun anything except fishing boats. He cared nothing for the ships or the men or the remaining technology on board. The only person who had to survive was himself, because he had a nation to lead. The land behind them was starting to drop away and they were about to enter the Gulf of Martaban, and once through this they would be in the Andaman Sea and international waters. It was time for Roe to leave. At the stern of his command vessel, covered with a dark tarpaulin, was a small RIB. It had a powerful outboard and could be in the water and racing away in under a minute. Roe knew it was his only way out of the situation he found himself in, and he hoped that if he could move quickly enough, the combined wake of the three vessels may mask him from being tracked from either a satellite or drone. Without another thought, Roe made for the RIB.

*

340

Tate was feeling ready to continue. His body was aching and his lungs didn't feel right, which he guessed had to be due to smoke inhalation, but he had no choice. He had moved behind a tarpaulin, which he found had been strung across a Zodiac RIB. From his hiding place, Tate had watched several gun-wielding members of the crew search the sea, presumably for himself, Casey and Parnell. He didn't know where either man was but, providing they could swim, he expected them to turn up on shore somewhere. No more shots had been fired and the crew, by their tone of voice, seemed to be becoming more relaxed. One nil to the bad guys. Tate assessed his situation. He was alone and on the wrong ship. If Roe was anywhere, he would be on the command vessel, so that was where Tate had to be. But how was he going to get there?

He slowly rose to his feet, HK up and ready to engage anyone who stood in his way. A new sound reached his ears. Tate cocked his head; it was a high-powered outboard motor. He moved back to the gunwale and looked over, searching for the source of the sound and hoping, praying to see Casey's boat. The sound also drew the attention of the crew of the ship. Figures emerged from the other end of ship and advanced towards him. Tate became immobile, knowing it was movement and not shape which attracted attention in low light conditions. He could now make out the eyes of the nearest two men, then there was a crackle of static and the man on the left raised a radio to his lips and spoke in his mother tongue. Tate saw the man start to relax as he listened to the reply before he spoke to his colleague, who said something and shrugged. Both men lowered their rifles and walked back towards midships.

Tate frowned. Why were they no longer interested in the speed-boat? Why were they not trying to spot it or stop it? Was it out of range, or was it a friendly? Tate's eyes darted to the RIB he'd been hiding behind and the penny dropped. Someone had launched one from one of the other ships. Who would be leaving any of the ships with impunity? It had to be Roe. Knowing he really only had one decision to make, Tate pulled the tarpaulin from the RIB, found the winch mechanism and pressed the button to start the launch process. There was an electronic whine, which sounded like the screams of a thousand gulls in the dark night as the RIB started to move. Tate hunkered down in the shadows, ready to engage any of the crew who came to see who was launching their RIB. The boat rose up, then it was over the gunwale and then it started to descend. Tate got to his feet as a pair of wild rounds roared passed his head. He fired blindly back and jumped into the boat. He was now below the level of the gunwale and slowly dropping towards sea level. A head appeared above, and an outraged voice shouted at him. Tate fired upwards and the figure dropped away. The RIB continued to lower and then it abruptly stopped, jerking Tate to one side. Two more heads appeared above him, but this time they were firing down at him. Tate cursed, found the emergency release lever and pulled it.

Tate and the RIB dropped into the sea. The impact of the hull against the water again knocked the air out of his lungs as he found himself lying on his back. He gasped for air and sat up, now praying that he hadn't broken anything. The hulking hull of the ship he had been on mere moments before was slipping away, heading ever nearer to the sea. Tate searched frantically for any sign of the other boat. He caught the whine of a distant engine and then, illuminated by the moonlight, he saw a speeding hull heading for shore. Tate managed to start his engine on the second attempt and steered towards the fleeing RIB.

*

Roe had ordered his men to carry on with their voyage without him. The captain he had spoken to knew better than to question him and had accepted his commands without a word. Now, as the starry night enveloped him, Roe started to relax a little. The

342

further he got away from the three ships the harder it would be for him to be tracked and he was in such a small, manoeuvrable RIB, that he doubted even the best drone pilot would be able to engage him. And then, of course, there was the legal and geopolitical implications of the United States launching a drone strike in Myanmar just hours after someone else already had. But anything was possible with the Americans. A cold fear suddenly gripped him; what if they did try to strike at him, and what if the world then believed that it was the US who had targeted the hotel and, by extension, his father? No, no, no. That would not be good at all, it would completely ruin his father's plan.

Roe felt worry, for the first time in years, not for his own life but for his father's legacy and vision. He slapped himself on the cheek and cut away from his spiralling, pernicious thoughts. He had learned long ago to stop worrying about events he could not control, and the US launching a drone strike against him was something he really had no control over.

The wind had picked up now and was blowing from the land out across the water, carrying with it sounds and scents. Roe would go ashore and then lose himself in the Myanmar interior before he made his way overland to Thailand. He had money, and he had weapons and he had his own battle-tested skill set. There was no way anyone could stop him, especially not the pasty-faced frat-boys of the CIA. He pushed the RIB harder, faster and then felt it ground out on the sand. Wasting no time, Roe was out of the boat and onto the sand, moving as fast as he could inland.

*

Tate cut the engine, as although the wind was blowing out to sea he still did not want to advertise his arrival. The other RIB was directly ahead of him, and he thought he saw something moving on the beach beyond that. He rolled out of the RIB and landed in the thigh-high water. He remained still until he was sure that no one had targeted him before he waded ashore. In the moonlight he could make out what he imagined was mud flats or sand ahead, which gave way to what he could only imagine was fields. He advanced towards the other boat, found the trail leading from it up the beach, and followed it. He was relieved to discover it was sand he was having to negotiate and not sticky, sucking estuary mud as found in UK river mouths. The footprints were distinctive in the fresh, flat sand and he had no trouble following them, yet Tate realised he could be running into a trap.

He made it off the exposed sand without seeing another soul and the trail abruptly vanished as the sand gave way to soil and grass. In the dim distance Tate could make out a shape moving, a figure pushing forward through the grassland and, unlike the swaying crops of Germany, there was no cover to be had here. Highly aware of his own exposed position, Tate held the HK tactically and poised to snap off rounds at the figure if it turned. He still could not be sure it was Roe, but by the way it moved he would have bet anything it was. As Tate continued to follow, the figure paused, and then it started to turn. Rather than open fire, Tate immediately went prone, and hoped he was concealed by the shadows of the night. The only sound in his ears was the slight sea breeze rustling the grass around him and the thumping of his own heartbeat. Tate lay still for almost a minute before daring to raise his head and, when he did, he saw that the figure had vanished. Tate cursed, not because he thought his quarry had got away, because Roe may well have also hugged the ground and was setting him up. HK held out in front as he remained flat on his stomach, Tate now searched for any indication that Roe was lying in wait for him. But the longer Tate remained where he was, the further away Roe could be slipping. Abruptly and with speed, Tate rolled to his right and sprang up to his haunches. If anyone was targeting him that should have caused some type of reaction. Nothing happened. There was no flash of incoming rounds, no supersonic snaps; the land around him remained flat, silent and unmoving. Tate stood and hurried north, hoping Roe had disappeared only because he had reached the edge of the field.

Several minutes later, Tate's feet were on the compacted dirt of a rural road running parallel to the shoreline. East he knew would take him eventually back to what in the area passed for civilisation and eventually Yangon, whilst west would take him towards Thailand. Tate understood Roe had to be heading for the border. Without thinking, Tate started to jog as the colour of the sky above him started to change colour; he'd taken a battering and his chest felt tight, but, wheezing, he continued. Dawn would be arriving soon, heralding a return of the heat and the locals. Tate was into a rhythm, and, although he was more than tired, he refused to stop even if his body demanded he do so. The flat fields on either side of him provided no cover whatsoever, which meant that Roe must still be ahead somewhere. The sky continued to lighten, and that meant Tate could now see further. He noted the fields on the right were paddy fields, whilst those on the left seemed featureless and dry. The road made a sharp turn to the north as it split into two, and on rounding that bend Tate saw buildings on the new spur. He slowed now, ever cautious that this was the first cover he had encountered for several miles, wary that Roe must be not too far ahead.

And then it hit him. Fatigue. A total burnout, a shut-down. Tate fell to his knees. His head was spinning, his hands reached forward, and his palms prevented his face from slamming into the pre-dawn, dusty earth. He vomited a mixture of salty seawater and whatever detritus he'd sucked in from the attack on the hotel. He continued to retch until nothing came. He was shaking.

And then he heard a scream.

A sudden surge of adrenalin made him stand, made him move.

Tate moved off the path and advanced towards the first house sideways on, through the flat field. As the building loomed into view he saw it was a farmhouse, but its walls were constructed from cheap, poured concrete. Moving as quietly as he could, Tate reached the nearest wall and pressed his back against it. He cocked his ear and listened. There were distant voices. He cautiously moved along the wall until he spun around the corner and was greeted with a gaping, open space where the front door and wall should have been. The building was a shell and completely empty.

Now the voices were nearer as they drifted towards his ears. Tate peered further up the road and saw a dim light escaping from the open front door of another building. Approaching in the pre-dawn light, he could see it was the twin of the farmhouse he had just left, but importantly this building had walls and it also had a garage. In front of the garage stood a boxy-looking saloon car. That was Roe's way out, and Tate couldn't let him get away.

Tate stalked across the dead ground, in an arc, weapon trained on the open door, but staying beyond its pool of light. He was in the shadows; he was just a shadow himself.

A figure moved inside. Tate froze, took aim. He heard two hushed voices, and a third louder one. Two different languages being spoken but then one harsh word that he did understand – 'no'.

There was a gunshot, roaring like thunder in the still morning air. Tate dropped to his haunches, his heart pounding in his chest. The louder voice spoke again, and Tate knew it was Roe. There was a shrill scream, a woman in pain. Tate knew he had to act. He ran at the wall, took a moment's pause with his back pressed firmly against the cold concrete then spun around the corner and in through the open door. Directly in front of him was a woman. She was kneeling over a body, and she was shaking.

And Roe was standing over both of them with a pistol in his hand. It was aimed at her head, and he was about to execute her.

Without thinking, Tate squeezed the trigger of his HK. There was a click and nothing happened. He squeezed again. Still nothing.

Roe's eyes met Tate's. A grin split his face in two. He fired his sidearm.

Tate dived to his right, behind a piece of furniture, as a round sliced the air where, less than a second before, his head had been. He slipped out of the HK's strap as he drew his Glock from its thigh holster. Tate sprang to his feet, Glock now held in two hands, and extended forward.

'Stop!' Roe ordered.

Tate's eyes narrowed. Roe had his left arm snaked around the grey-haired woman's neck and his own Glock was millimetres from her right temple.

'Drop it, Jack, and I'll let her live.'

A headshot would end this now. Tate thought back to Iraq, back to Baghdad when Roe had slain Glen Thorn, his own Delta Force blood with a single round to the head. Tate knew he could take the shot, knew he could finish this now, but Roe had to answer for what he'd done. Tate squeezed the trigger and sent a 9mm round into Roe's right thigh.

Shock flashed across Roe's face and he fell sideways, but not before he jerked his arm and returned Tate's fire.

The round clipped Tate's left shoulder and spun him around.

Both men were on the floor, both men were bleeding.

'Go!' Tate yelled at the old woman.

Eyes wide, she didn't move, either not understanding the word shouted in a strange language, or rendered immobile with fear, or both.

Roe rolled into a sitting position and fired off a single round. It hit the woman in the head, propelling her backwards and onto the man, already lying dead on the floor.

Tate roared, the outrage and revulsion exploding from him like a primeval force. He sprang to his feet. His Glock dropped from his hand as his fists sought out Roe. He didn't care anymore, he was going to rip him to pieces. Roe swung the Glock at Tate, but Tate's left arm forced it out of the way. Tate clamped his forearm across Roe's throat and slammed his fist into the man's face. There was the sound of cartilage cracking as Roe's nose was instantly flattened. Tate's hand became slick with blood as he delivered two more sickening strikes.

Roe jerked, bucked and as blood gushed from his nose he thrust his fingers into Tate's injured shoulder. Tate's arm dropped away from Roe's throat, and Roe managed to now lock his arm around Tate's neck in a chokehold. Tate felt his throat being crushed as he arched his back, pushed up to his hands and knees and moved towards the wall. Roe's head was tucked in behind his own, so there was no way he could slam Roe's head and not his own. Using the wall as leverage, Tate rose to his full height. Roe was still clamped to his neck and Tate could feel himself starting to become dizzy.

Vision greying out, Tate saw a large wooden table on the other side of the room. Using his last ounce of consciousness, Tate drove himself backwards towards it and let himself fall, gauging that his own head would strike the thick, wooden edge. It did, but was cushioned by Roe's own head making contact first. The grip on Tate's neck instantly went slack. Both men dropped to the floor, Tate gasping for air and Roe groaning incoherently.

*

Roe didn't know how the MI6 man had found him, but that wasn't important now. What was, was the fact this man was between him and his destiny. His head was numb as his body was, trying to block out the pain, and he knew he was losing blood from the bullet wound to his leg, but he refused to accept that Tate had beaten him. He tried to get up, but his legs wouldn't take his weight. He looked down and his right leg was a bloody mess. Roe realised he was bleeding out.

'Tate! Tate! Are you in there?' It was an American voice, shouting.

'I'm here.' Tate's reply was weak, Roe noted.

A figure appeared in the doorway. Roe recognised the man,

and then he realised he was in serious trouble, there was no way out. 'Parnell?'

'Affirmative, compadre.'

'Where's Casey?' Tate asked.

'He's a way back. He was never a runner.'

'What … happens … now?' Roe asked, feeling groggy.

Tate was back on his feet, Glock back in his hand – pointed at him. Roe studied the men in front of him, two former operatives who until a couple of months ago would have regarded him as a member of the Special Forces brotherhood. *Well, perhaps not Tate*, he mused. Roe swallowed and tried to control the pain. 'You won't shoot me dead, Tate … neither will you, Parnell … you both know why.'

'Yeah, I know who you are, Hak Kwang-Chul, and the CIA knows too,' Parnell said.

'The North Koreans don't know yet. Imagine if they did?' Tate added.

Roe felt a tightness in his chest. 'What do you suggest I do?'

'Kill yourself, I won't stop you.'

'No … I think I'll … throw my hands up … surrender … I'm the true heir to the Hak dynasty. I'm sure good ole Uncle Sam will want to protect me.'

Parnell shrugged. 'Perhaps I'll just shoot you, Kwang?'

'Do it.'

Parnell raised his weapon.

'Don't, he'd be better off dead.'

'You're a good man, Jack Tate,' Hak Kwang-Chul said.

'And you,' Tate said, bitterly, 'are not.'

Epilogue

Washington, D.C., United States

'Senior General Min Win Sein, the commander-in-chief of Myanmar, who some in the media have dubbed 'The Hero of Yangon', arrived in the US yesterday. In a meeting in New York he addressed the UN, stating he intended to make broad, wide-sweeping changes to the structure of the current government of Myanmar which would develop democracy and end the state of emergency he himself imposed. Sein led the first responders, who, one month ago, after a terrorist rocket attack, entered the still-burning Meliá hotel in Yangon to search for survivors. Sein is said to have personally located and dug Hak Kwang-Il, the uncle of the North Korean president, out of the rubble and saved his life. Subsequently, Mr Hak has been granted political asylum in the United States after the attack which many have viewed as an attempt on his life. The attack has been blamed on a Burmese anti-government group and a full investigation has been launched.'

'Granted political asylum.' Tate shook his head. 'The Americans bought him from the Burmese.'

'Either way, he's yesterday's news.' Hunter muted the TV. 'He lost and the fat man's still in power.'

351

'Hey, it's not over until the fat man sings.'

Hunter chuckled. 'I can't believe you hid in a bath.'

'It wasn't any bath,' Tate replied. 'It was the world's biggest marble bath.'

Hunter frowned. 'Why would you wash a marble?'

Both brothers started to snigger.

Tate had arrived in Washington late the night before. He'd decided to spend his two weeks' leave with his brother Simon Hunter, the only family he had. The past few years had been difficult for the brothers, and at times he'd doubted either of them would survive, but they had. Tate felt as though he could now finally relax as Hak Kwang-Il and his son had been stopped. In his first debrief with US officials, Hak had claimed he had not shared Jericho's White Suit Technology with the North Koreans. Tate imagined the US and the UK would 'work' on any future version of White Suit together but now that the UK government had Jericho's data it was no longer MI6's responsibility, nor his. Tate was free for a while; he now had the time to do nothing at all. Perhaps he was getting older, or just getting tired, but he was enjoying simply sitting and being. Although he was hungry. 'So, where's my breakfast?'

'It's just gone five in the sodding morning!'

'For you, maybe, for me it's almost lunchtime.'

'OK.' Hunter stood. 'Come on then, let's go grab some breakfast. There's a diner I know that should be open.'

'Fine, but I don't want any gravy on my Hobnobs.'

Hunter sighed and shook his head. 'Jack, you do know that's a different kind of biscuits and gravy?'

'Whatever do you mean?' Tate winked at his brother.

Acknowledgements

In bringing *Total Control*, the latest instalment of the Jack Tate saga, to life I've continued to be extremely fortunate to have the support of my family, colleagues and friends.

Firstly, I need to thank my wife Galia, and my sons. Without their support, I would not have been able to carry on writing.

I'd like to thank my editors at HQ, Abi Fenton and Finn Cotton, and my agents, Justin Nash and Kate Nash, for continuing to believe in my work and wanting to publish it.

I'd like to thank my friends both inside and outside of the book business for putting up with me whilst I worked on *Total Control*, and for being such vocal supporters. This list includes, but is not limited to: Neill J Furr, Liam Saville, Steph Edger, Paul Grzegorek, Alan McDermott, Paul Page, Jamie Mason, Jacky Gramosi Collins, Louise Mangos, Rachel Amphlett, Claire Kenmuir and Karen Campbell.

Dear Reader,

We hope you enjoyed reading this book. If you did, we'd be so appreciative if you left a review. It really helps us and the author to bring more books like this to you.

Here at HQ Digital we are dedicated to publishing fiction that will keep you turning the pages into the early hours. Don't want to miss a thing? To find out more about our books, promotions, discover exclusive content and enter competitions you can keep in touch in the following ways:

JOIN OUR COMMUNITY:

Sign up to our new email newsletter:
http://smarturl.it/SignUpHQ

Read our new blog www.hqstories.co.uk

🐦 https://twitter.com/HQStories

📘 www.facebook.com/HQStories

BUDDING WRITER?

We're also looking for authors to join the HQ Digital family!
Find out more here:

https://www.hqstories.co.uk/want-to-write-for-us/

Thanks for reading, from the HQ Digital team

If you enjoyed *Total Control*, then why not try another gripping thriller from HQ Digital?

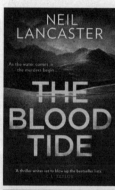

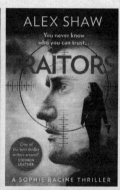